THE
SOVIET
SISTERS

ANIKA SCOTT

DUCKWORTH

*To my husband, Jürgen, who keeps my feet on
the ground when my head is in the sky*

First published in the United Kingdom by Duckworth,
an imprint of Duckworth Books Ltd, in 2022

Duckworth, an imprint of Duckworth Books Ltd
1 Golden Court, Richmond, TW9 1EU, United Kingdom
www.duckworthbooks.co.uk

For bulk and special sales please contact
info@duckworthbooks.com

A CIP catalogue record for this book is available from the British Library

1 3 5 7 9 10 8 4 6 2

Trade paperback ISBN: 9780715654668
eISBN: 9780715654675

Printed and bound in Great Britain by Clays Ltd, Elcograf S.p.A.

Anika Scott grew up in Detroit and was a journalist at the *Philadelphia Inquirer* and *Chicago Tribune* before moving to Germany, where she now lives in Essen with her husband and two daughters. She has worked in radio, taught journalism, and written for European and American publications. Her first novel, *The German Heiress*, was an international bestseller. *The Soviet Sisters* is her second novel.

Praise for The Soviet Sisters
'Electrifying, meticulously researched and expertly plotted, *The Soviet Sisters* is at once a Cold War thriller, a gripping spy story, a page-turning mystery and a familial drama'   Lara Prescott,
author of *The Secrets We Kept*

'A fascinating tale of secrets, surveillance, and sisterhood set against the burgeoning Cold War. But who is the real traitor, and who is hiding the biggest secret of all? *The Soviet Sisters* will suck you in to the very last page!' Kate Quinn, *New York Times*-bestselling
author of *The Alice Network*

'A masterful novel, brilliantly plotted. I was gripped from the first pages, never knowing whom to trust, or what would happen next. Cleverly playing on concepts of truth, ideology, and loyalty, the characters are put to ultimate tests'   Louise Fein,
author of *People Like Us*

'What a page-turner! East and West, love and hate – *The Soviet Sisters* gives beautiful insight into the opposites that can make or break a sisters' bond. Compelling'   Mandy Robotham,
d the Wall

'One sister faces West, with an open mind and an open heart. The other faces East, armed with ambition, ideology, and an agenda. One sister is ruthlessly trapped and manipulated by the other. It's a compelling read, and a terrific portrayal of the edginess of post-war Berlin as the Iron Curtain lowered'

Mara Timon, author
of *City of Spies*

'Beautifully atmospheric − at once an intricate portrayal of the ties that bind, and a tense and timely exploration of truth'

Freya Berry, author of *The Dictator's Wife*

'Tantalising and moving... Epic in scope, forensic in detail, this is a beguiling and riveting story'   Georgia Kaufmann, author of *The Dressmaker of Paris*

'A thrilling spy novel with many twists and surprises, and a beautifully nuanced portrait of sibling love and rivalry'

Zoë Somerville, author of *The Night of the Flood*

The past is so long ago, it never happened.
—POPULAR SAYING OF PRISONERS IN THE GULAG

Marya

Siberia, 1956

Shoulder to shoulder, we're marching down the packed snow road. There are five of us in the row, me on one end, the coldest place in the line, my arm dragging against the snowbank. We're like marionettes joined by the sleeves, women made of wood. We lurch forward at the same pace, careful where we put our shabby boots. If one of us falls, the guard might get angry. When I move, the ice cracks in the fibers of my coat. I want to march faster to stay warm, but I can't.

"Halt!" the guard calls behind us.

We don't turn our heads to see how far away we are from the rest of the work brigade. Out the corner of my eye is the snowbank and behind that, the white trees all around. In front of us, the road goes on and on, long and empty, vanishing in the fog at the foot of the mountains. That's the edge of the world. There's nothing on the other side of the mountains, nothing at the end of the road. Not for me. Not yet. I have six more years here. I've lost track of how long a year is, so I concentrate on today. *Now.* If I get through enough days, enough *nows*, I'll be free.

Behind us, the guard is pacing. I hear his gusting breaths and the crunch of his boots. We're far enough away from the work brigade that I can't hear their shovels as they clear the road of hard snow. The guard has us to himself, and I'm glad the five of us prisoners are here together. We all are. Instinctively, we press closer, arm to arm, mitten to mitten, like a wall.

"Anyone have to go behind a tree?" the guard asks.

We don't move.

"You haven't had a break all morning. Go on. If you need to relieve yourselves, go ahead." Something in his tone reminds me of my sister. Even when Vera was nice, she was always *something else* underneath, something I couldn't trust.

Down the line, I feel a shift. One of the women really does have to go, but she can't; she can't break the line. I've been in the Gulag more than a quarter of my life; I know all the games the guards play. He might let her relieve herself in peace and rejoin the line, or he might shoot her for trying to escape. He gets 50 rubles for that, I think. That's what our lives are worth. Fifty little rubles.

None of us break the line. The guard paces behind us, his tone suddenly different. "What are you anyway? Traitors. Spies and traitors. You think you can afford to be ungrateful?"

We're standing with our backs to him, but I know, we all know, that he's raised his rifle. It's pointing at her, and then her, her, her. Me. We might be spies and traitors, but we aren't stupid. We don't move. Don't say a word.

"Let's warm you up, then. Sit," he cries.

We drop to the snow. My bones feel like they'll snap in the cold like twigs.

"Stand."

We're slower on the way up. I press my mittens on the knees of my trousers, straightening my back.

"Sit."

Down we go. The minute I'm down, I hardly know how I'll get up.
"Stand."

I don't know how much longer I can do this. As I struggle to stand, I dream of being rescued, Henry appearing in the road, pointing his Browning at the guard, a car idling behind him, ready to take me away.

"Sit."

Nine years. For almost nine years, I've been a prisoner in this or that camp. Nobody is going to save me. Nobody is going to take away the pain and the cold place on my spine where I feel the guard's rifle pointing at me.

"Stand."

Get through today. That's all I have to do. Get through my now. One day nobody will shout at me anymore. I won't hear the guards in my head. That's when I'll know I'm free.

We're standing shoulder to shoulder, five women, the wall unbroken, but the guard is determined. "You!" The woman beside me stiffens. The guard is right behind us, his rifle at her back, touching her coat. I can feel it too. I might be next. "Walk."

I'm dreaming again, but instead of Henry in the road, it's Felix beside me where the snowbank is. He's enduring this too. His arm presses into mine, holding me up. He understands the lesson this place teaches me every day: I'm never going home, not as the woman I used to be. I'm worth nothing now. I'm not even human.

But I am.

I turn to the snowbank and the white trees. Deep in the thickening forest, I see Vera as a wraith peering at me from the shadows.

I am.

MILITARY COLLEGIUM OF THE
SUPREME COURT OF THE USSR
25 JUNE 1956
MOSCOW

To Comrade Rudenko

Enclosed are a series of recordings made by your former colleague, Vera Ilyanovna Koshkina, regarding the case of her sister, who was convicted of treason in 1947. These recordings are remarkable for their vivid detail and confessional tone.

However, there appear to be some inconsistencies with the known facts of the case. The contradictions in her account may only be a fault of her memory, since the events took place nine years ago. Regardless, I believe an external review of these recordings is in order before we make a decision about her sister's case.

Chairman, Military Collegium
Cheptsov

1

Vera

Testimony for Chairman A. Cheptsov
Military Collegium of the Supreme Court of the USSR
Moscow, 28 February–3 June 1956

[BEGIN RECORDING]

Comrade, we live in a new age. Stalin is dead, three years dead, and with him the fear of speaking the truth. At last we can speak free from the threat of a bullet or of men knocking on the door at night. This is what I believe, and why I'm trusting you with this account of my investigation into the case of my sister, Marya.

The preliminaries for the record: My name is Vera Ilyanovna Koshkina. I'm a lawyer by training and serve as an aide to our highest government officials in the Presidium, my specialty in legal and security matters and topics related to Germany. Years ago,

I served as an officer of state security, assisting the prosecution in the war crimes trials at the International Military Tribunal in Nuremberg.

My work at the Kremlin focuses on government policy, but at heart, I'm a lawyer concerned with justice above all else. The guilty should be punished, the innocent freed. It goes without saying that this work should never be done at the expense of the truth. But there are the more difficult cases, where innocence and guilt, truth and lies, are harder to untangle.

On 13 August 1947, the court found my younger sister, Marya Ilyanovna Nikonova, guilty of espionage, counterrevolutionary activities, and treason to the Fatherland under Paragraph 58. There were many unanswered questions about her true activities in Berlin, where she was arrested, but after a quick investigation, she was sentenced to fifteen years in the Gulag. At the time I wasn't permitted access to her case, for reasons I'll be laying out for you here in these recordings.

The taint of having a traitor in the family has weighed on me, our mother, and my youngest sister for nearly nine years. While Stalin lived, the smallest suspicion of disloyalty could lead to imprisonment, exile, or death. To protect ourselves, we did what it seemed right to do at the time: cut off contact with Marya, removed her photograph from our homes, and relied on the support of the friends and colleagues who knew us to be good and loyal comrades. My husband, Nikolai Koshkin, the deputy foreign minister, has been crucial to my family's survival. Without him, I believe we would have shared Marya's fate, and I would not be here in a position to seek the truth of her case.

Making the decision to do this has not been easy. By the time Stalin died, the silence about my sister had become a habit. I admit to being too frightened to break it. Too many years had passed. I needed courage, a sign that it was time to overcome the fear that had kept me from looking truthfully at what my sister had done.

Several days ago, I finally heard the call for change that I needed to bring me to this moment.

It happened at the Great Kremlin Palace. Without warning, all of us Soviet delegates and functionaries were called to attend a secret, unscheduled session of the Twentieth Party Congress. I sat with my husband in the second row, my notebook open on my lap, ready to take notes as I'd been doing throughout the congress, even though I, like everyone else, thought the congress had already ended.

When First Party Secretary Khrushchev took the podium, he began to speak about what I assumed was an afterthought the party leadership wanted the rest of us to learn, something about the "cult of the individual" and its harmful consequences. But Khrushchev's tone hardened the moment he mentioned Stalin. He quoted Lenin, saying that Stalin "is capricious and abuses his power." From there, we knew, all of us in the room knew, what was happening. We should've guessed it the moment we arrived at the hall to see a statue of Lenin and nothing, not even a portrait, of Stalin. Behind his row of microphones, Khrushchev delivered blow after blow against Stalin. He spoke of repression, torture, terror, purges, the long list of injustices committed in our country since as long as many of us could remember. For hours, we listened in shock as he raged and shook, dismantling the shining image of Stalin that had dominated our lives. "Comrades," Khrushchev said, "don't repeat the errors of the past." This phrase resonated so deeply inside me, I hardly heard what came after until he declared, "Long live the victorious banner of our party—Leninism!" I was swept up in the applause that exploded throughout the hall and rose to my feet in a standing ovation.

After the speech, my husband and I filed out of the hall in silence, the delegates around us looking numb with shock. Side by side, Nikolai and I walked home across Red Square and past the mausoleum where Stalin and Lenin are laid to rest, and then through the city to the river, following the water to the skyscraper that is our home on the Kotelnicheskaya Embankment. In the living room, Nikolai drifted to the drinks cabinet, I to the cigarettes on the table. We still hadn't said a word to each other since the speech. The shock sat too deep. Khrushchev had called the last thirty years, Stalin's entire rule, into question.

The KGB inhabits a part of our building, and it is no secret our apartment is bugged. If I want to discuss anything of real importance with Nikolai, we must turn on the radio, and so I did, a broadcast about industrial quotas, at full volume.

"It's time, Kolya," I said to my husband. "I'm reopening Marya's case."

Nikolai was at the window. The rooftops of Moscow spread out below us, a soothing view that always gave us a moment of rest, the belief that we were high above the squabbles and intrigues at the Kremlin and the Foreign Ministry. He was as shaken by the speech as I was but didn't show it. Always the diplomat, his tie was precisely pinned and knotted, his face thoughtful. When he answered me, he used the tone he reserved for when he had to state uncomfortable facts.

"Nothing has changed, Vera. I'm afraid your sister is still a traitor and a spy."

It stung me to hear it said, especially from him, no matter how he tried to soften it.

"You heard Khrushchev today," I said. "We don't have to be afraid to talk about the past anymore. He already has. In front of everybody. He talked about things we all knew and were too scared to admit. People executed on the word of an informant, or sent to the Gulag without evidence of a crime. We know—I knew all along—innocent people were sent to Siberia. What if Marya—?"

"Marya wasn't innocent. You know what she did. You were there."

He meant in Berlin, the place where everything had happened, my sister's downfall. "I have to find out the truth of her case," I said. "I owe it to her."

"You don't owe her anything. You barely survived after what she did in Berlin."

"We don't know precisely what she did. They rushed the investigation. She was convicted within weeks of her arrest."

"Because everybody could see how guilty she was."

"Because no one wanted to look any closer. I was in the security services back then, Kolya. I know how much they cared about the truth."

Nikolai took me by the shoulders in the way of an equal, a comrade in arms.

"Leave it alone, Vera. We'll have enough to do shielding Khrushchev from the fallout from his speech. Stalin may be dead, but his friends aren't. They're going to fight back. This is no time for us to get distracted. I'm sorry about Marya, I truly am, but your duty is to the nation and people. Is your sister more important than your country?"

It's a legitimate question, and one I still contemplate as I begin this investigation into my sister's case. I'm recording my progress for the court to capture the evolution of my thinking about Marya in a form that is much harder to edit or redact than written testimony. To preserve the authenticity of events, and to aid my memory for detail, I will narrate my actions as if they are unfolding in the moment. To be safe, these recordings must remain classified. Marya's case may force me to divulge sensitive information related to my work as an officer of state security in Berlin from May to July 1947.

As this case develops, I pledge to keep an open mind about my sister. She may very well be guilty of spying for a Western intelligence agency. Then again, maybe she isn't the traitor we took her for all these years; and if she isn't, what does that mean? What would it say about all of us, the country that condemned her, the family that kept silent for so long? If she's innocent, what does that say about me?

2

Marya

Berlin, 1 June 1947

An hour after I should've left, we were still on Henry's balcony, me in my lounge chair, fanning myself with the cover of his favorite record, Henry dozing, hat over his face, shirt hanging open. Through the French doors, Billie Holiday's voice melted in the heat, singing about the love she'd lost. The balcony was just large enough for our chairs and the few potted flowers Henry hadn't watered to death. His chair faced mine, our bare legs a warm tangle between us.

I shaded my eyes and looked out at the blue sky over the Schloßstrasse, the wide boulevard where he lived. All around us, the rooftops of the villas baked in the sun, and the smell of hot asphalt mingled with the wisteria climbing the wall of Henry's house. This was our first summer together, and I was grateful for how the days seemed to go on and on. I wanted to stay another hour, the night, wake up with him in the morning for the first time. But I couldn't. I had to be heading home before someone missed me.

"Wake up, Henry." I ran my big toe ever so slowly down his bare chest and over his stomach to the edge of his shorts. He twitched; he was dreadfully ticklish but he could practice heroic self-control even while napping. "Say goodbye to me, sleepyhead. I have to go soon."

"Already?" Henry lifted his hat from his face. He was all damp, poor thing, his reddish hair blazing in the sun. If he were standing on one side of the world and me on the other, I'd see him clearly if he only took off his hat.

"It's past seven."

"Plenty of time." He crowded me on my chair, kissing my neck where *I'm* the most ticklish. I howled and nearly fell off the chair trying to writhe away from him.

"Stop!" I gasped. "Really, it's too hot for this. And I do have to go."

"Why?"

He was being stubborn. I'd told him the MGB looked for patterns. If the secret police noticed that every Sunday an interpreter from the Soviet military government—that is, *me*—left the Soviet Sector of Berlin, traveled west to a certain address on the Schloßstrasse in the British Sector, staying until six—in this case, seven—and then circling home, arriving back in Karlshorst by the curfew at nine . . . Well, it would interest them a lot more than I wanted it to. Really, it was no one's business what I did on my day off. Unfortunately, in my sector, everything was everyone's business, romances included. The secret police suspected anyone in a private relationship with a foreigner, since every foreigner was a potential spy to them. People were arrested for less than what I was doing now. Meeting someone privately in a Western sector of Berlin was considered politically unreliable. If I were caught, I'd be hauled home to Moscow, forced to answer questions, and if state security didn't like my answers, I could end up in prison. I'd known it since I met him, but I still came every Sunday. He was worth the risk.

I reached between the flowerpots and picked up Henry's binoculars. After a good polish with my hem, I passed them over, and with a sigh, Henry peeled himself off of me and went to the balcony railing. "You've been coming here for eight months and nobody's caught you yet, Mouse. This is starting to feel a bit mad."

"We're all mad where I'm from. Go on. Take a look for me." I set his hat on his head and then carried the record cover into the sitting room. "What do you see?" I called as I lifted the needle on the gramophone.

"Usual. People out for a walk. Chap on the second floor opposite has rigged up a hammock on his balcony. We need one of those. The Carters on the third floor right must be on their tenth pink gin of the day. Carter looks like he's about to fall over the railing."

Soothing to hear how very boring his neighborhood was, the reason he'd picked it and this lovely villa of flats confiscated by his army, now a home for bachelor officers. Women were to be out of the house by midnight, or else. The German landlady, Frau Koch, who lived in the attic, kept a moral household. She and our MGB would get along well.

After I put the record away, I soaped a washcloth in the bathroom and returned to the sitting room wiping my neck. "What else do you see?"

"Pucky is out walking Nelson. Or maybe Nelson is walking him. Old Pucky looks on his last legs." Ah yes, I remembered him. Old Colonel Puckton, his mustache as flared as his trousers. A few weeks ago, we ran into him walking Nelson, his Scottish terrier, on the boulevard. Pucky ogled me from head to foot and called me Fräulein as if it were a dirty word. I didn't know what he would've called me if he'd known I was Russian.

"Wait . . . Marya, come look at this."

My breath stopped. "What is it?"

"Jerry's just streaked down a lamppost, slid under Nelson's belly, and they're off!"

If Henry had been nearer, I would've thrown an ashtray at him for scaring me like that. Jerry was one of the neighborhood squirrels. Henry had named them all, insisting they were each different when they all looked alike to me. He pitched his voice to a sportscaster's on the radio: "Nelson has broken away from Pucky. Jerry's ahead at four lengths. But Nelson is having none of it. He's coming up at speed. Will Jerry live to see another day?"

"Go Jerry," I called from the bathroom as I peeled off my damp negligée and reached for my dress.

"Nelson is making a final desperate play. He's lunging at Jerry . . . who is scurrying over the tram tracks. No, he's taken a mighty leap onto a street sign! That's stumped Nelson. He's spinning around his own tail. And there's Jerry taunting him from above. Well done, lad."

We sent up three cheers for Jerry the squirrel. As I pulled my dress over my head, I heard shouting from the street and Nelson's yiping bark. Colonel Pucky was dressing down Henry for cheering, half-clothed, against the dog of a superior officer.

Laughing, I found my belt between the sofa cushions and slipped it through the loops at my waist. I fetched the hairbrush Henry kept for me near the sink and attacked my hair.

"What else do you see, Henry?" I asked after Pucky had moved on.

"There's a woman alone on a bench. Probably nothing."

"What does she look like?"

"Bench faces the other way, love. And she's wearing a hat."

"What kind of hat?"

"You do have eyes, you know. Come and look for yourself."

It was probably nothing, but I crossed the room aware of every knot in the carpet. The soles of my feet tingled. On the balcony, I took the binoculars and focused on the street, the strip of land in the center of the boulevard, the path where people were strolling by. Then I spotted the woman sitting on what looked like a scorched and rotting bench, her back to me. I could just make out her bright yellow hat. If she was observing Henry's balcony, she'd have to have eyes in the back of her head.

"You're right. It's nothing."

Henry kissed my hair. "Tea before you go?"

"Black as tar, please. None of that weak English stuff. And I'll get you a fresh shirt." I sniffed at him. "That one needs to be washed."

In the bedroom, I tossed his shirt into the hamper and then made the bed since I was partly responsible for messing it up. Next to his alarm clock on the nightstand was the portrait of me he'd taken the day we met last November. Back then, I sat on the steps of our Soviet memorial in the Tiergarten, the wreaths and flowers for the Red Army dead arranged behind me. I looked straight at the camera, at Henry, a man I'd met only ten minutes before. Without me asking, he'd helped me tidy the wreaths, looking somber, very respectful. When we were through, he took off his cap and transformed from the typical British officer in his drab coat into a man full of color I hadn't noticed before—not just his red hair, but the blue of his eyes, and the pink tint to his cheeks and the tip of his nose where the cold had gotten to him. He lifted the camera around his neck and asked if he could snap a photograph of me. "Why?" I asked, and he said, a little embarrassed, "Because I'd like to remember you. If it's all right."

We started up something that was unheard-of back home—a casual affair. Every Sunday we met for the pleasure, for the fun of it, and nothing else. We had no future; one day I would go back to Russia, he would go to England, and that was that. And since we knew this, we shared our countries with each other the only way we could. The smallest and dullest things interested us because they came from each other's worlds: I brought him a packet of Russian cigarettes to smoke; he gave me a bottle of a sweet, lemony English soft drink; I showed him how to write his name in Cyrillic letters; he taught me to pepper my English with the Lancashire accent of his home. Everyone in his house thought I was German, even his roommate, Johnson, a funny man whom I only saw coming or going. Henry bribed him to clear out on Sundays so the flat was all ours.

After fluffing his pillow and planting a kiss in the middle of it, I went to his dresser and opened the top drawer. His undershirts were folded with military precision. I lifted out an undershirt, and beneath it was a small, framed photograph.

Curious, I carried it into the light of the sitting room. In the photo was a little girl, perhaps three years old, with cropped hair and a puzzled frown. She was holding a stuffed rabbit. "Henry?" I called.

He moved the teapot to the table. "Toss it over, Mouse." He meant the shirt in my hand. I gave it to him, and after he'd pulled it over his head, his gaze dropped to the portrait I was holding.

"It was in the drawer," I said. "Maybe I shouldn't have—"

"It's all right." But it wasn't. Something was squeezing his voice. "That's Fern."

I knew this to be the word for a type of plant. "Fern?"

He took the photograph out of my hand, gazed at it for a moment, and then set it on the table. "My daughter."

"You have a child? Why didn't you tell me?"

"She died." He turned quickly to the cupboard. "Blast, I forgot the biscuits." At the shelf, he searched for the packet when it was right there next to his hand.

"Oh Henry, I'm so sorry. When did this happen?"

"In the war—" He cleared his throat, began again. "I was posted to Egypt, and Fern was in London. She had polio. In the lungs."

"A terrible thing. Terrible." I stroked his arm.

"I didn't get the news until it was too late. My wife told me to come home, but I was in Cairo. By the time I'd get back to London, the funeral would be over. I didn't see the point of going back."

I let go of him. "Your wife?" Louder, "Your *wife*?"

"I should've been there for her. For the both of them. She called me a selfish, cowardly bastard, and that was damned accurate."

"You're married?"

He turned from the cupboard, his eyes inflamed. "She divorced me. Only what I deserved. I should've gone home. I should've tried."

He set the biscuits on the table. He'd done wrong to his family, that was clear. The rest was tangled up in my head. That he'd been married. That he was the father of this child looking up at me from a framed photograph. That she was gone. He carried all of it alone in his heart, and I'd never noticed.

"She was a beautiful girl, Henry. She had your eyes."

Nodding, he poured the tea. He'd given something of himself to me, the burden of his grief, and the shame too. I understood how risky that was. I wanted to give him something of me in return, but I didn't know what. The oldest and deepest things. My family, the war. For the tiniest moment, I thought of telling him about Felix. But no, I couldn't. The shame sat too deep now that we all knew the extent of the atrocities the Germans had done in the war. Maybe . . . Vera. I could tell him what she was. I wasn't sure how to do it, if he would understand.

I went to the clock he kept on the sill and turned it facing away from us. "I think it's time for me to tell you about my sister."

I didn't know where to begin and surprised myself by starting on the day when Vera was eleven and went missing. Everyone in our apartment house on Arbat Street in Moscow looked for her, in every flat on every floor, in the yard, in the alley, in the square. I was six and wasn't supposed to help; our mother took me to bed, tears in her eyes behind her thick glasses. My brother, Yuri, was eight, and as we lay together in our bed listening to our neighbors call "Vera! Vera!" he patted my hair and told me not to worry. If somebody tried to snatch Vera away, she'd kick and bite them, and they'd regret picking on *her*.

I wasn't so sure; Vera was a big girl to me but I knew she was a small girl to the rest of the world, with serious brown eyes and thick hair the color of honey that she wore in two long braids. She was the cleverest girl in her school, and I was proud that she taught me calligraphy and numbers and other things the big children knew. She was always patient and kind when I was listening and applying myself to her lessons. When I made a stupid mistake, or babbled about something other than the lesson, she was severe. She never hit or pinched me—that was Yuri's way when I annoyed him—she would just . . . shut me out. Pretend I didn't exist. She could do it for days, floating around me in our little apartment as if I were a ghost, not speaking to me, not looking at me. She kept it up until I cried and begged her to stop. Then she would hug and kiss me, and I knew her punishing me hurt her almost as much as it hurt me.

And so, when she went missing, I lay in bed sure that I was the reason she'd run away. I'd done something wrong, though I didn't know what, and she'd run away and maybe she'd fallen into the river or gotten hit by a bus, and it was my fault. I had to help her. I told Yuri I had to go to the toilet, slid out of bed, and joined the search.

Most of the adults were outside the building now, and I took it upon myself to slink into the neighboring flats, which wasn't hard since all doors were generally open and we children ran in and out of one another's homes all the time. "Vera," I called in the rooms upstairs. "Vera, come out." I tried to think of it as a game of hide-and-seek. Where would she hide?

I looked in places the adults hadn't, behind doors, under the washing, in the small spaces under the stairs. I dared to do what I was normally not allowed, opening other people's closets and cupboards. In the flat of the downstairs neighbors, in a wooden cupboard, I found her—Vera, in her Young Pioneers uniform, hunched into a small circle like a snail. I gasped, and she shushed me. "Is anybody around, Masha?" she asked. "Check the hallways." I did, and returned shaking my head. She unfolded herself from the cupboard, grasped my hand, and crept with me to the door. I imitated her careful footsteps, and when she began dashing up the stairway to our flat, I stumbled to keep up. We flew into the bedroom and leapt onto the bed. Yuri looked unimpressed.

"I knew you weren't really missing," he said.

"What were you doing in the neighbor's cupboard?" I asked, relieved, but also confused.

"Being vigilant." Vera unknotted the scarlet scarf around her neck, the symbol of the Pioneers, and carefully folded it. Ever since she'd joined the communist youth league, she'd hinted at the important work she did for the party and the Motherland. It all seemed mysterious and exciting to me. But what did it have to do with Vera disappearing for a whole day? "You learn a lot about people," Vera said thoughtfully, "when you hide in their cupboards."

When Mama came in and found her with me and Yuri, Vera said, "You didn't have to worry about me, Mamochka. I was just up the street playing at Svetlana's."

Even Mama doubted that. Vera didn't really have friends and was the only girl I knew who didn't seem to care. But Mama chose not to argue, and after she hugged and scolded Vera and then left us alone in the dark, I rolled over and asked in a whisper, "Why did you lie to Mama?"

"She'd just worry if I told the truth. She'd think I was strange and tell Papa."

"But you shouldn't lie, Vera." I was genuinely upset. Our parents raised us to be honest and moral children. Our papa was a veteran of the Revolution, a skilled tradesman at the Red October factory, and when his long weekly shifts allowed, he would crowd on the couch with us and tell us stories of the glorious days when the people broke their chains and rose up against the czars. In his gentle voice, he told us how important *we* were, the children of today, "not just you, Yura," he said affectionately, taking a warm swipe at Yuri's head, "but you girls too. Do you know what you have to do?"

Vera opened her mouth, while Yuri and I shook our heads, and baby Nina babbled sleepily in Papa's lap. Vera said, "We must carry on the work of the Revolution." She'd learned that in the Pioneers.

"We're building a new society," Papa said, holding me close with one arm, since I was the third of four children just like him, and as he used to say, we third children were often ignored in families. He smelled wonderfully of tobacco and the sweets made in the factory. "You work with your hands?" He held up his strong, wiry fist. "Then you should own your workshop or factory or farm along with everybody else who's working it with you. Girl or boy, you should go to school and learn to do the job best suited to your talents. Like words," he said, smiling at me, "or engineering," he said to Yuri, who was always fixing things and taking them apart. "And even political philosophy," Papa said to Vera, who puffed up with pride.

"What will Nina do?" I asked, speaking up for the baby who lay slack in Papa's lap, her mouth hanging open, sleeping through the conversation.

"Maybe she'll be a doctor," he said. "Or a scientist. Who knows? All of you have a good future because of the Revolution and the party. To me, you're the generation of hope. You'll work and live for the greater good, not selfish greed and profit. You're going to show the world a new way to live as Soviet people." He exchanged a look with Mama, who was pulling a needle and thread through a rip in Yuri's trousers. I was sensitive to people's moods and didn't understand why Papa's look seemed to be a warning to Mama, something that unsettled me even back then. Only much later in the war, when we soldiers of the Red Army began to talk real truths about our country, did I remember those cautious looks of Papa and guess what they meant. His lectures had been a way to protect us children. We would be happier and safer if we grew up to be Soviet people in harmony with our society.

If Papa had believed everything he told us, he should've been happy too. But as a girl, I saw him gradually fall apart. More and more, he came home smelling of drink, and sometimes he wouldn't come home at all. He might disappear for days. Our mother stopped sleeping. She was an oboist who worked at the Moscow Conservatory, a palace compared to the modest houses we were used to on Arbat Street. When Papa didn't come home, she would sit up at night moistening the reed of her oboe, letting out tiny squeaks like a distressed mouse. She began to do strange things, quietly inserting papers into the stove, examining the books we had, looking under the mattresses or behind the furniture. She wouldn't say what she was looking for.

Once, after Papa had been gone five days, a neighbor came with his cap in his hand and whispered something to Mother. She covered her mouth and stared at us. Yuri was screwing together two bits of wood, little Nina trying to grab a piece with her chubby hand. Vera was watching Mother, who came back to us and sat at the table with a special silence that made even Yuri stop his work.

"Papa has drowned in the river," Mama said, and then she stared down at the table.

"Isn't he coming back?" I asked, confused. I was eight at the time and knew what drowning was, of course, but Papa could swim.

Yuri caught on faster than me. "He drank too much vodka and fell in."

"Shut up," Vera said.

Yuri set aside his wooden pieces. "I'm the man now."

"Nobody cares, Yuri. I'm the oldest. Do you want me to leave school and go to work, Mama?"

I said, "You're only thirteen, Vera," and began to cry. Nina, who was always watching me, burst into tears.

"I should go to work," Yuri said, crying now too. "I'm the man."

Vera slammed her fist onto the table. "Stop blubbering! All of you!"

Mama took up her oboe and blew into it violently, a terrible sound like a dying goose. "We'll be all right. None of you are leaving school. That's what Papa wanted. For all of you." She pointed to each of us in turn: Vera, who would go on to study law at Moscow University; Yuri, who would go to technical school before volunteering for the army, never to return. Nina would study chemistry. I wanted to learn languages and translate great literature, but my plans were cut short by the war.

But that was far in the future. For now, we had to learn to survive alone without Papa to guide and support us. We never went hungry, but it got harder to find enough food to fill us up, or clothes to replace what we'd grown out of. I never had anything new, only Vera's old things. If she could, she would've lived and slept in the uniform of the Komsomol, the *real* youth league, she boasted when she joined at fourteen. "I'm going to be a political activist," she announced to the family. "I'm going to meetings every day."

"Oh no, you're not," Mama said. Our apartment was small, but there was housework to be done, lines to be stood in at the grocer's, clothes to be washed, food to be cooked. We girls shared the work, while Yuri didn't have to lift a finger. After school, Vera and I had to go home and do our chores and look after Nina. Yuri could streak off on his bicycle, free as could be. Nobody seemed to care where he went after school.

Vera and I explained to Mama the unfairness of this situation. Vera argued how it violated the 1918 Bolshevik Code of Marriage, the Family and Guardianship, which gave women and men equal rights. "Yuri should do an equal share of the chores," she declared like the lawyer she would later become, "based on a weekly plan drawn up by us"—she gestured at herself; me, who was in awe; Yuri, who was staring at her like she had a turnip on her head;

and Nina, who was playing with her doll—"in the spirit of a true soviet. If every member of the proletarian family works together, each of us will be free to—"

"I'm not washing clothes," Yuri said, "that's girls' work."

"Shut up, Yuri. Each of us will be free to attend meetings." Vera gave me a hard look, a reminder that it was my duty to join the Komsomol too one day.

Vera's argument failed to convince our mama, so she began to avoid chores, coming home late and lying about where she'd been. Over the years, I'd caught her lying again and again, about where she'd been or who she was with. I grew wary of her, and ashamed of myself for feeling that way about my own sister. Vera, the oldest and best of us children, the child we all thought Papa would've loved the most for becoming exactly what we thought he wanted. She was the first of us to go to university, the first to go to war. By then, I loved her as I always had, but it was a careful love, full of caution.

"Vera led the way," I said to Henry, "in all things. School and the war and . . . She's the strong one. The clever one. Brave. She always knows best. Even if she isn't easy to live with. Or understand."

"Marya," Henry said in such an odd tone, I blinked and realized I was here, in Berlin, speaking to him. I held his hand on the tabletop.

"Yes?"

"If you squeeze my hand any tighter, they'll have to amputate it."

I let go of him and said in a rush, "Vera is in the MGB, an officer of state security. I'm not sure what she does exactly. Investigations. Counterintelligence . . ." I stopped.

The silence lasted long enough for the clock on the sill to click over louder than usual, sign of the minute hand on the twelve, a new hour. Henry said, "Say that again?"

"Vera, my sister. She's—"

"All this time, you've been scared of the secret police finding out about us, and your own sister is one of them?"

"I should've told you earlier. But she doesn't know about us. I haven't seen her since the war. She's not even in Berlin."

He shook his head and looked at the portrait of his daughter. It was easier for him to look at her than me. I didn't know what his people would do to him if they knew he was not only seeing a Russian in secret but a Russian whose sister was an officer of Soviet state security. I imagined the worst, Henry arrested by his own people and taken in for questioning. They would assume I had ensnared him for my own and my country's ends. He wouldn't be trusted to work for the military government anymore and would lose his rank and his job. He might be court-martialed, sent back to England in disgrace.

"I understand if you're angry. Henry? Henry, are you going to throw me out?"

He wrapped his hands around his teacup and raised it to his lips. He still wouldn't look at me.

I went into the living room for my purse and shoes, everything awash in the thin wall of tears I could not, would not, let fall from my eyes. Because of Vera, this affair—casual or not—was over. I should've never said anything about her. She wasn't an immediate danger to us. *Why* did I have to tell him?

I thought about the things of mine I should take with me, things he wouldn't want to see anymore, my hairbrush, my negligée, the soaps and perfumes he'd bought and kept for me here. I didn't have the heart to pack any of it. He could throw them out himself if he wanted. What did people say at the end of a casual affair? It was fun while it lasted? So long?

I was never coming back. Eight months of Sundays, of whatever I'd had with Henry . . . gone. Well, if he was the type to condemn me because of my sister, I didn't want him anyway.

Henry came up behind me, his bare feet hushing over the carpet. "You can't just leave, Mouse. I haven't thrown you out properly yet."

Ah yes, the English. He'd make a joke of it. I should've known. I marched out of his flat and into the hallway. A swing orchestra played on a radio behind one of the other doors, and men laughed suddenly from a flat down the hall.

At the top of the stairway, my legs suddenly went out from under me. Henry was lifting me up, hefting me with a grunt into his arms.

"Put me down." I could barely get the words out; I was laughing too hard, my anxiety and relief flooding out. Our center of gravity shifted, his foot on the first step. "Henry, put me down right now!"

"Do you want me to throw you out or not? Make up your mind, love."

Doors were opening behind us, his comrades, young officers like him crowding the stairway, cheering him on. We were several lurching steps down when I realized I was clutching his bare arm. He was in his undershirt and shorts and nothing else. I was scandalized, but Henry seemed oblivious to everything but working his way downstairs huffing and blowing as if I were a bag of bricks. The door to the cellar opened and Frau Koch, holding a bucket and mop, gasped in shock. "Captain Barrow!"

The officers along the stairway sent up a chorus in falsetto— *Captain Barrow!*

He carried me past Frau Koch, who darted around him to open

the street door, and he stepped over the threshold, into the little patch of front garden.

There, he planted me back on my feet. To the cheers of his comrades, he kissed me long enough for me to know that he'd swept Vera out of his mind, and the risk of the secret police, and the fear that had salted this affair all along. None of it mattered now. We wouldn't let it.

3

Vera

Testimony for Chairman A. Cheptsov
Military Collegium of the Supreme Court of the USSR
Moscow, 28 February–3 June 1956

[RECORDING]

If I may paraphrase our late filmmaker Dziga Vertov: The eye is for spying, the ear for eavesdropping. He meant the eye of the camera, but as I stand on Dzerzhinsky Square across from KGB headquarters, it is human eyes that I see in the windows, brightly lit even now, at night.

Bent against the wind, I pick my way across the icy pavement to the yellow façade of the Lubyanka. I haven't worked here in years and need permission to enter. To the guard, I state my name and the intention to see Leonid Ivanov of the KGB's North American Department. It is after nine and I'm still in evening clothes, smelling, I'm aware, of wine and smoke and salmon. I slipped out of a reception at the Ministry of Culture. Nikolai won't notice or care where I am now. He is at the Kremlin monitoring the unrest that has broken out in places since Khrushchev's speech. The anniversary of Stalin's death has turned into days of protests against the speech in his native Georgia, where crowds have been chanting, "Glory to the Great Stalin!" To restore order, we've had to send in tanks, and I'm afraid that people have died. Even from his mausoleum, Stalin is still deadly.

In the cold entrance of the Lubyanka, I follow the guard across the red carpet to his telephone, which he murmurs into while staring at me, then replaces the receiver on the base with a soft click. As I wait for him, I sense the layers of this building under my feet, the cellars where the prisoners are kept. After her arrest and transport from Berlin, Marya was brought here too. I've known this from the beginning, but now that I'm here on her behalf, I seem to hear the echoing clang of a door, my little sister, our Masha, forced into the dark cells below me.

My old friend Leonid Ivanov meets me in the fourth-floor hallway. His mild face is fatigued; his wife has just had their fifth child. I ask about the vagaries of fatherhood while we shake hands warmly, then pass together into a small unused office. I hang my coat on the hook and set my cigarette case on the desk. Ivanov has already turned on the lamp, the yellow light pooling on a file. It is a strictly secret file, and Marya's name is on it.

"You've looked at it?" I ask Ivanov. Years ago, as university students, we were both recruited by the security organs because our thirst for knowledge, public or secret, was insatiable.

Instead of answering me, he says, "As a general observation, not every political prisoner in Siberia is innocent."

"I suppose we did catch a few actual spies, Leo."

"If I recall, your sister's case was clear."

"You're saying she's guilty?"

Ivanov spreads his hands and says, "I'm only wondering what you're after."

"The truth."

"Even if it confirms your sister really is a traitor?"

"If that's the truth, I'll have to live with it. I've been trying to do that for years."

Ivanov stubs out his cigarette and takes his leave, insisting I should come to him if I have any more needs. After he's gone, I sit for some time smoking and looking down at the file. My husband's reach does not normally extend into the Lubyanka, but something about Ivanov's argument has a whisper of Nikolai, a warning to leave the past alone.

After I stub out my cigarette, I open Marya's file. The smell of years, of aging paper, hangs in the air. I browse the contents first, sifting my fingers through the fragments: brief and conflicting reports about her activities, a faded love letter in English, a newspaper clipping she had translated in Berlin as part of her work, and other ephemera of her life. As is often the case, there is no strict organization to the file, but I soon find the general parts: the thin surveillance section and the more substantial investigation report. As noted on the documents, the chief investigator was a man named Valentin Gusev. I write his name in my notebook. I'll get Ivanov to find him for me. With any luck, he's in Moscow.

Sometimes a case file reflects the investigator nearly as much as it does the suspect. A brief glimpse at the materials shows me that this Valentin Gusev was trained in the old ways of state security. He believed once a suspect falls into the hands of the police, it is not the investigator's prime task to uncover what the suspect did, it is to discover who that person is. If we operate under the assumption that only guilty people are arrested, there is nothing left to do but discover the weaknesses and flaws in the suspect's character to understand why this particular person has become a criminal.

And so it was with Marya. I prepare myself for this redefinition of my sister's life by skipping the surveillance materials and turning to the start of the investigation section. And there she is. Marya, photographed after her arrest in Berlin. The mugshots send a blaze of offense through me—how dare my sister be photographed like this, her hair disheveled and her eyes glazed with shock and fear? I note the tender smoothness of her face. She was young back then, in Berlin, so very young.

For comfort, I rub my fingers on the lid of my cigarette case, the only artifact I kept from my time in Berlin after the war. It's a small wooden box, its lid decorated with four pieces of tin that represent the division of Berlin into four allied sectors. In the days of our occupation of the city, this cheap trinket was sold everywhere. I've held on to it because it reminds me of the consequences of defeat.

The broken map also shows the reality of the fascist capitol at the time of Marya's alleged crimes. Of course, we Soviets had won the Battle of Berlin, taking the city with our blood. But at Yalta, we had agreed to share power over Germany and its capital with the Americans, British, and eventually the French. These were the conditions that led to my sister's arrest and conviction, and my own posting to Berlin in mid-May 1947.

Back then, the city's heart was in ruins, full of half-blasted buildings, mountains of rubble, and mangled bridges over waterways still clogged with debris. For the Germans, there was a shortage of everything, from nails to glass to bread, and by the time I arrived in Berlin, they had settled into an existence marked by scarcity, a constant awareness of just how low they'd fallen.

My first impression of the city was one of corruption, streets and squares crawling with vice and foreigners and the most dangerous creatures in the world: bored young soldiers. What fertile soil for my work! I was eager to begin, to inhale the dust of the ruined houses, the dirt on the streets, the aroma of soot on long-burnt monuments. In Berlin, more than in any other place in Germany, I felt our victory in the war had been total. The enemy was truly vanquished, never to rise again.

Though I was posted to the military courts as an investigator, I took days walking the city when I first arrived to get the feel of its streets and landscapes and taste the grit between my teeth. At that time, there was no East and West Berlin as there is now. One could move easily between the four international sectors. It was a matter of crossing a street, passing a sign, or stepping over a white line painted on the pavement. We discouraged our personnel from spending time in the Western sectors, but I made a point to visit them all. Berlin may have been a divided city on our maps, but in our heads, it was one—and it belonged to us by right of conquest.

Marya had already been in the city for quite some time. As a military interpreter, she had witnessed the Battle of Berlin in 1945. The last time we had seen each other was when she visited me two years earlier in a field hospital, where I was recovering from a leg wound. After our victory, she didn't come home during the demobilization of the Red Army but signed on to stay with the military government in Berlin. By the time she got home leave to see our family in Moscow, I was already working with Chief Prosecutor Rudenko at the trial of Nazi war criminals in Nuremberg. Our duties kept us apart and our letters to each other were short and rare. I arrived in Berlin during her last summer of freedom unaware of any dangers to either of us. I was looking forward to our reunion.

But I didn't contact her at first. I'm an observant woman by nature and wanted to form an impression of her life and who she'd become since the war. What was my little sister doing in that city of ruins and black markets, beggars and prostitutes, soldiers with roving eyes and hands?

Purely out of curiosity, I consulted the file kept on her by the local MGB in Berlin. I knew our security organs would keep an eye on her; her language skills meant she often worked with foreigners, a cause for concern when foreign agents were so eager to recruit Soviet personnel.

That old file from nine years ago now forms the bulk of the surveillance section of the KGB file now open on my desk. It is thin, maybe only a dozen pages, and as is usually the case with these things, the information is fragmented and contradictory. The Berlin MGB spoke to her colleagues and housemates, and came to the conclusion Marya was a quiet girl, a fun-loving lively one, that she stayed home a lot, went out a lot, and so on. The usual muddle.

The surveillance eased off in the fall of 1946. She no longer interested the MGB. But she interested me, and by the end of my first week in Berlin, I thought it prudent to pick up the thread to be sure my sister was still behaving. We had ways to keep track of our personnel quietly, and I enlisted an informant, a local German woman on the MGB payroll, to report directly to me about my sister's activities. I was very clear with this woman that Marya was under no particular suspicion; I only wished to know about her habits.

A week later, I went to Treptower Park in the Soviet Sector to get the first report from the informant. The park was full of people in uniforms of every description, from many nations, and civilians as well. It wasn't unusual for me, an officer in uniform, to be strolling the pathway with a German woman. I remember her gaudy yellow hat. I thought it was too conspicuous for an informant, though it was also the way I spotted her that day in the crowd.

"I have disturbing news," she said to me in German. Her manner was stiff and awkward, and I guessed why. Like many Germans, she struggled with the fact that I was both a woman and an officer with the power and authority to reward her for truth and punish her for lies at my discretion. Such equality of the sexes was foreign to Hitler's people.

I also understood that the informant was nervous about bringing bad news, and I controlled my eagerness to hear it. I told her that an honest and complete report, no matter its content, would satisfy me. I was not the type who expected to be told only what I wished to hear.

The previous Sunday, the informant said, she had observed Marya leaving her cottage in Karlshorst dressed in civilian clothes. She traveled on foot and with the S-bahn, the elevated train of the city, into the British Sector.

I was displeased by this news, but not unsettled. It was a fact that our personnel sometimes traveled to the British Sector to shop in their stores. We strongly discouraged this. I would have to speak to Marya before the MGB got wind of her activities and pulled her in for a very unpleasant talk.

But the informant wasn't finished. Marya's destination, she said, was a house on the Schloßstrasse near the Charlottenburg Palace. Marya remained in the house, she said, for five hours before emerging onto the first-floor balcony with a man.

"A man," I repeated. So this was not merely a matter of my sister indulging in a desire to shop in a Western sector.

At my request, the informant described the man. Tall, her estimate was one meter ninety, perhaps more. Reddish-brown hair she called coppery. She couldn't say what color his eyes were, but she was more or less sure he had hair on his chest.

"How in the world do you know that?"

A flush crept up the informant's face, but she looked quite pleased with herself when she said, "He was practically naked." Then she laughed into her fist.

"And my sister?"

"She was wearing a negligée of some sort. Silky. The color of eggshells."

I thanked her. Good, reliable informants were valuable indeed. And I reminded her that if she reported what she'd seen to anyone else, anyone at all, and I heard about it, she should leave the city for her own good. I tolerated no gossip about my family.

Until I observed the situation with my own eyes, I wouldn't act. So on the following Sunday, in a civilian summer dress, I traced the same route the informant had taken into the British Sector to the house on Schloßstrasse, and took up position on a rickety bench nearby, a pile of knitting on my lap.

Within the hour, I spotted her. I would know her anywhere, her buoyant walk, the brightness of her face. She wore a white dress with a pale-blue flower print. My first impression was that she was plumper than I remembered her, and more feminine. I hadn't seen her in anything but her uniform since she was eighteen.

She was coming up the path in the middle of the boulevard, heading right toward me. At the last moment, she veered into the street just as a tall man with copper hair bounded out of the iron gate that led to the doorway of a white villa. He picked her up and swung her round and they kissed—kissed in the open air, for all to see!

Clearly, this man wasn't one of us. The cut of his suit was too good, the summer linen too fine. His foreignness glowed in the way he walked, how he talked loudly and freely. He moved through the world in a carefree manner, as if no one was watching. He was, without a doubt, a Westerner.

"Hello, love," he said, his arm around her. "Fancy coming in for a drink?"

Based on his accent, the man was obviously a British national. For a moment, I considered rushing across the street, taking Marya by the ear and dragging her all the way back to the Soviet Sector. But I confess, I was too stunned and missed my chance.

The man held open the gate for her, and for the briefest moment, he turned a searching gaze to the street as she passed. A car rolled by, and when I looked up from my knitting, Marya and the man had disappeared into the house.

It was true, then. My sister was conducting a personal relationship with a Western man. It was far more than a foolish mistake. At that time, the British were like the Americans, who were quickly forgetting our wartime alliance in favor of a crude anti-communism. Their former prime minister Churchill had said as much when he accused us of imperialist motives behind what he called "an iron curtain." High hypocrisy from an Englishman. As a result, Stalin had warned us to prepare for the next great conflict, which would be with the West.

Back then, we thought it necessary to protect our personnel on foreign soil from Western plots. We were severing personal ties between our people and foreigners of all kinds. Men with German girlfriends were ordered to abandon them, or were sent home. Depending on the severity of the violation, the courts sentenced these men to some years in prison. In Berlin, it was my job to investigate these and other political crimes.

I had never personally come across the case of one of our women fraternizing with a Western man. If it had not been my sister, I would have come down on her severely.

But I handled Marya's situation differently. How could I not? She was my sister, a good woman, a good officer. I resolved to save her from her own folly.

4

Marya

Berlin, 19 June 1947

At the end of the day, I locked up the translations in the office cabinet, put out the lights, and ventured into the sticky heat outside. The Soviet military government took up many buildings in Karlshorst, the heart of our sector, but I'd worked that day in the walled-off compound that used to be training grounds, offices, and barracks for the German Army. We thought nothing of working in the same places the Germans had; it was a fact of the occupation, and no matter what some Germans thought, we were treating their buildings and land much better than they'd treated ours.

The compound felt claustrophobic and not a part of the real Berlin, and I was glad to skirt the wall and walk toward home along the tidy houses on Zwieseler Straße. I was desperate to get out of my uniform. The summer issue didn't have the high collar of the winter tunic, but it was still a uniform, itchy, heavy, hot. I was close to violating regulations, taking off my shoes and stockings and walking home barefoot. It was Thursday night and I wasn't scheduled to attend any political meetings or dreary educational lectures. I could go to a film with one of my housemates. Or a party. Find a lake to swim in? There were plenty of those in our sector. Maybe I could borrow a bicycle and take it to the parks that bordered the River Spree. That sounded refreshing, and it just might keep my mind off Henry and what he was doing right now over in his sector—having drinks at an officers' club, maybe, or swimming in a pool built for the Olympics years ago. Things I wasn't allowed to do with him.

Behind me, a man called, "Comrade Lieutenant! Wait!"

I pretended not to hear, almost plausible since I was on the opposite side of the street. I'd been on duty since seven that morning, mostly meetings, committees, and translations. My hand ached, not to mention my bottom. SMAD, as Henry called the Soviet Military Administration, could get through the rest of the day without me.

"Lieutenant Nikonova!" A sub-lieutenant in baggy battle dress trotted up to me. "The colonel needs you." He pointed across the intersection toward several officers gathered outside a low wall. The only one in Soviet uniform was gesturing past the gate to the stone building behind them. The other two officers wore the funny flat caps of the French Army.

"They need an interpreter? My French isn't very good."

"It's probably better than the colonel's. He saw you walking by and asked for you."

Since I conversed with the French so rarely and loved the rhythm of their language, I crossed the street, glad for the chance to improve my skills and hear the musical way they spoke. Meeting people of different backgrounds was a perk of my job, and I loved how I built bridges between people and nations through speech. Only by talking to one another and listening could we maintain the peace and prevent the next war that seemed to be rumbling beneath the surface of Berlin. But it wasn't inevitable. We had to remember all that we'd achieved as allies and keep that spirit of friendship alive. That's why I'd stayed in Berlin instead of going home to take up my life again in Moscow like other young women, studying, working, meeting a boy, marrying, children. There was time enough for that. For now, I was needed in Berlin.

It was part of my training to recognize the rank and insignia of our old allies, and I greeted the French colonel and commandant, saluting smartly. The Soviet colonel said, "They want to see where the Fritz signed the final surrender. Let's give them a tour."

"My pleasure. This way, please."

We filed through the gate and onto the grounds of the squat stone building the Germans had constructed as an officers' casino and mess hall, I explained to the French as well as I could. Now it contained the office of the Soviet city commander and head of the Soviet Zone of Germany, Marshal Sokolovsky. It was the center of SMAD, our HQ.

The colonel led the Frenchmen through the echoing anteroom and into the hall of victory itself, where the war officially ended. The curtains were open on the tall windows, but the colonel still ordered me to switch on the lights. Under the sparkling glow of the chandeliers, the Frenchmen murmured in admiration at the ambiance, the feeling seeping from the walls and the high ceiling that history had been made right here.

"There," the colonel said, me translating, "is where the tables were, long tables where the Allies sat." He crossed to the space now filled by surplus desks and chairs. "Over there is where the

Germans signed the surrender. They were slow and finished after midnight on 9 May. This is why we celebrate Victory Day on that date, not the eighth as others do."

"Ah," the French said, nodding. One asked, "Were you here that night?"

He addressed the colonel, but only I understood the question. "Yes, I was here."

"You, Lieutenant? You must tell us. Tell us what it was like."

This pushed my French skills to the limit. After gaining the colonel's permission to speak, I said, "I was here on that historic night of 8 May 1945. I had the privilege to help with translations and to serve as interpreter wherever I was needed." I felt a head taller whenever I remembered that. "At first we did not know the French were coming to the ceremony." I tried to say this as diplomatically as I could. The day before our ceremony, the Germans had signed a surrender on French soil. Our side refused to acknowledge this solely Western event. We wanted a total surrender of the Nazi government and all German forces in Europe made to the Allies as a whole, which, of course, included us first and foremost. When we learned the French were coming to Karlshorst, the whole Soviet staff frantically made arrangements to accommodate them.

"We did not have a French flag. Where to find one?" I shrugged and held out my hands like a mime. "But one appeared, and then, where to put it? Over there." I pointed at the long wall at the back of the room. "There were only three places to hold flags. Soviet, American, and British. What did we do? We took up the Tricolore"—I brandished my hands as if holding the flag at that moment—"and put it in the same place as the Soviet flag. They shared a home that night. And that is why France and the Soviet Union will be friends for all time."

The Frenchmen enjoyed this interpretation immensely. I translated what I'd said for the colonel, and when I was halfway through, my gaze wandered to the double doors of the hall. I stopped speaking midsentence.

There, standing tall and straight-backed, was Vera. My sister.

Vera in a high-collared tunic with epaulettes on her shoulders and medals on her chest. She puffed at her cigarette and smiled at me through the smoke.

Irritated at my pause, the colonel said, "Something the matter?" He followed my gaze and fell silent. I knew his anxiety came from the trim of Vera's uniform, the cornflower blue of the MGB. He outranked her, but the MGB had power over everyone.

Vera took a piece of paper out of her pocket, tapped her cigarette ash into it, folded the paper, and tucked it away. I hadn't seen her in four years, and I couldn't believe she was there. She hadn't written or warned me at all she was coming.

But she was really there.

Then my mind jumped to Henry.

The colonel rushed the French through the rest of the tour then out of the building.

"Masha, so glad they're gone. Let me get a look at you." Vera grasped me by the cheeks and gently shook them. Our mother had done this when I was home on leave last year. She'd held me and pressed her face closer and closer, trying to make out the shape of me. Vera did much the same, but unlike Mama's, her eyes were sharp. It made me nervous. If she looked close enough, she might see Henry deep in my pupils.

I extricated myself from her hands. "It's so good to see you, Vera. When did you arrive in Berlin? How long will you be here? Maybe I can show you around."

"Oh, Masha," she said, laughing, "I've been here a month already."

WHEN WE STEPPED into the humid street, she walked with an odd rhythm. Not exactly a limp, but each step she took seemed slightly smaller than it should considering her height. I supposed she walked strangely because of the bullet she'd taken in the leg in 1943. I'd visited her briefly in a field hospital where she'd sat up in bed chain-smoking and swearing at the nurses because the wound was nothing, she insisted. She had things to do, places to go, but they wouldn't let her out. She even whispered in my ear, "Help me break out of here, will you?" Her eyes were glazed from the pain, or maybe morphine. Of course, I didn't help her, though I assumed her leg couldn't have been too bad if she was still her old, uncompromising self. I never considered the wound would affect her gait so permanently.

Her odd walk was such a tiny flaw, but it reminded me of her pain and sacrifice. She'd been a soldier and had fought like I had. I linked my arm in hers. We'd survived the war, my sister and I. Survived and prospered. "I missed you, Vera."

"You should've written me more."

"I didn't know where you were after you left Nuremberg. Mama said you were in Dresden."

"And Magdeburg." She didn't say what she'd been doing there. I didn't ask for details. There was a more important question to be asked, and my stomach clenched as I asked it.

"So you've been posted to Berlin?"

"Yes, finally. There's much to do with the military courts. Discipline must be restored."

I loosened my hold on her arm. Her being here changed everything. I wanted to turn back the clock to last Sunday. Yesterday, even. But then I remembered she'd been in Berlin yesterday, and last Sunday. And the Sunday before.

Outside the formal perimeter of SMAD, we crossed to Rheinsteinstraße and continued down the long and quiet street that was part of my daily commute. "Discipline?" I asked to keep up the conversation. And to feel her out. I dreaded what she knew about my discipline. Or lack thereof. I did all sorts of things that weren't allowed, tuned the radio at home to the BBC or Voice of America when I was alone, read Western newspapers or magazines Henry gave me, saw Western films in German cinemas. As for the rest of our troops, they were behaving a lot better than they used to because the front soldiers had been largely demobilized and sent home. I didn't like to think about what had happened at the end of the war when their fury was unleashed on the German populace. Our victory had been degraded by their violence, and I was grateful for the more peaceful days we lived in now. "There are still problems here and there, especially when the men are drunk," I said, "but things are much better now."

"Are they? We're seeing an alarming increase in political crimes."

I let Vera talk as we reached the wide intersection at the Treskowallee and passed the Karlshorst station. We'd be at my cottage in ten minutes. I hadn't planned to take her there, but somehow she seemed to steer me to my home over and above my better judgment. I'd offer her a drink and at all costs keep her from seeing my bedroom. My heart rattled at the thought of all the evidence of Henry lying around. Just that morning, I'd been reading one of the love letters he'd insisted on sending me now and then. He always found a street urchin to deliver it for food or cigarettes. I'd left the latest one on my bed. Having a personal letter from a Westerner was a political crime. So many things were. The littlest things. I'd gotten sloppy.

Vera was talking about the case she was investigating, a soldier who'd returned to Berlin from his leave spreading what she called rumors comparing life in the USSR unfavorably with the conditions in Germany. Many of the officers in our army and government lived in spacious houses and flats not available to us at home, if they existed at all. We had access to foods and clothing that our families at home didn't, the reason I sent packets back to Mama and Nina whenever I could. Because of all this, before I'd gone home on leave last year, I'd had to sign a paper swearing I wouldn't say a word in Russia about how I lived in Berlin.

"The fool will have to be sent home for good," Vera said. "He's obviously grown unaccustomed to our Soviet way of life. Too much time in Germany."

She'd soon see how my way of life was far different from how we grew up in our little apartment on Arbat Street.

"Maybe we could go out for a drink, Vera. There's a nice pub—"

"And the violations of our fraternization laws," she went on. "Ask me how many cases I have on my desk of our men enamored by some local Fräulein. If he doesn't break it off with her, he'll get two to five years' forced labor. Is any romance worth that?"

I thought it was a rhetorical question until I noticed her staring at me. "People do fall in love," I said.

"Anyone who thinks love is worth going to prison deserves whatever he gets. It's moral corruption disguised as sentiment. We need to come down harder on all that. I've even heard our female personnel have grown free with their affections. Have you observed that?"

I flushed and hoped she didn't notice. "Some. There are so many men and so few of us. They pester us. It's terrible. If you hadn't showed up, that colonel would've probably badgered me into going out with him."

"We must maintain discipline. Is restraint so hard when we're in the service? We were all comrades in the war. You don't have a new boyfriend every week now, do you?"

"Of course not!"

"It was a joke, Masha. You have too much self-respect to allow yourself to be courted by every soldier who comes your way. We must meet corruption wherever it may lurk, you know that. We can't be afraid to speak of it. As Lenin says, 'But we shall not perish, for we do not fear to speak of our weaknesses and will learn to overcome them.'"

The station behind us, we followed the rail tracks that edged my neighborhood. On our left, we passed villas as grand as any in Henry's sector. One in particular was blocked from the street by a wall being constructed by soldiers, their uniforms smeared with mortar. The ground and first-floor windows were already invisible. Those of us in the neighborhood had theories about who worked there. I looked at Vera as we passed. She barely gave the building a glance, but it had to be a facility of the MGB. What other building would guard itself from prying eyes, antenna on the roof? That big house on the edge of our quiet neighborhood meant: We're watching you.

We curved around to Lehndorffstraße, a quiet cobbled street of modern apartment buildings and wooden cottages that reminded me a little of the dachas of Russia. In all my life, I'd never lived anywhere so spacious, orderly, and peaceful. I ached at the thought of having to leave it one day. At some point, I'd have to go home to Moscow and start my life again. Thinking about it made my chest hurt. Leaving this city, Henry, my work . . . I couldn't imagine it. Not yet.

"I want you to know," Vera said, "if you want to speak to me about anything, you may. Anything at all."

I looked at her serious face. I didn't know what she meant, was scared of what she meant.

"If you come to me to confess a weakness," she said, "I'll help you overcome it."

"Weakness?" I struggled to keep my voice level. "I'm not sure what you mean, but thank you, Vera."

"You remember what keeps us strong, don't you? What allowed us to win the war?"

I groped in my mind for something Lenin would say about such things, or Stalin, but there were blanks after their names. I couldn't match Vera's knowledge and convictions. "What?"

At the little path in front of my cottage, she stopped. "Unity," she said. "Never forget, our strength is in unity."

MY COTTAGE HAD plank walls of dark red with blue shutters and windowpanes all around, letting in the light. We confiscated the building at the end of the war, and to us, it was a palace. After the water and electricity were restored, it didn't go out again. At first, the other girls assigned to the cottage and I would gather at the kitchen sink, turning the tap off, turning it on again. The water flowed, and it was some time before we trusted that this luxury wouldn't suddenly end. When the Red Army first crossed into Germany, we'd seen their spacious and tidy houses like this and wondered why? Why had they invaded our land when they had it so comfortable at home?

I opened the gate and held it for Vera before dashing ahead of her up the steps to the cottage's front door. It was unlocked. I heard someone rummaging in the sitting room and found my housemate Natalia, a secretary at SMAD and in the cottage about half a year, prying a painting off the wall. It embarrassed me, with Vera coming in. "What are you doing?" I asked.

Natalia's face was stained with tears. She was about to say something, but then Vera was in the doorway behind me, and Natalia acted as if she were straightening the painting. I was glad to leave her for the kitchen, but there, another interpreter named Olga, who had lived here about a year, was stuffing cutlery into a pillowcase. She jumped when we came in, then slipped out, pounding up the stairway. I apologized to Vera for the strangeness of my housemates. They were usually so friendly.

"I don't take things like that personally." Vera opened the cupboards and took down two glasses. I noticed many were missing compared to this morning. I frowned as I poured the vodka.

Vera raised her glass. "To Comrade Stalin, our great leader!"

It was hard to conjure up the proper enthusiasm, the glow Vera expected from me. Something was wrong in my beloved cottage. I could hear Olga stomping over my head. Natalia was moving the furniture next door.

"To Comrade Stalin." We clinked glasses and drank. Vera said, "Do I get a tour of the house?"

We went out the back door to the garden, where I tried to act neutral about my lovely cherry trees and my magnolia shading the lawn. Then I showed her the sitting room again. Natalia was gone, along with the painting. The doors of the sideboard hung open, its shelves bare. We'd kept linens there.

"Spacious," Vera said. "A family could live in this room alone."

Our family had, in a room of similar size in an apartment building that was hardly better than a barracks. It was no way to live.

"Where do you sleep?" she asked.

"Oh . . . upstairs."

She began up the stairway before I could think of how to stop her. I slipped ahead and pushed open the door to my room, only seconds to tidy it before she came. I dove for Henry's letter on my crumpled bed and shoved it into my tunic. With horror, I noticed the little portrait of him gummed to the vanity mirror. I snatched it down just as Vera entered the room.

"Isn't this nice," she said, heading directly to the bookshelf. My heart sank. I'd forgotten about the English books Henry had bought me. I didn't know which were forbidden, but I could argue they were for my work, to improve my vocabulary, which was true. But she took down my book of fairy tales and her face lit up. She remembered it, our parents' gift to me as a girl. She browsed the illustrations with an absent smile.

Then she put it back and frowned at my mussed bed; as girls, she'd always made ours first thing in the morning. My dressing table interested her next, and her face went neutral. I'd forgotten the lipsticks and the two small bottles of perfume, Henry's gifts. She fingered them, and then selected a palm-sized red box. I could barely breathe as she opened it and without a change of expression saw the gold bracelet Henry had given me. Sighing, she snapped the box shut and put it back in the precise place it had been. Yanking open the drawer, she immediately plucked out a small tin cross that had belonged to our grandmother. I didn't know if Vera recognized it. She merely scowled and replaced it, then opened the wardrobe closet.

"Marya, I'm getting the feeling you've been in Germany too long," she said, shutting the closet doors.

My muscles wound tight as screws. I'd been waiting for this.

"Living with foreigners in a foreign land corrupts, we all know that," she said. "When you don't live with your own people, in your own culture, you begin to lose your way. You forget who you are."

"I haven't forgotten."

"Look at this place. We're in a German house. You sleep in a German bed on German sheets."

"It's just a bed."

"Alone in this room," she withdrew to the door as if the room offended her. "It's not normal to live alone."

"In the war, and at home, there was no privacy. You know that—"

"Privacy is unsoviet. This luxurious lifestyle isn't natural to us, Masha. It breeds a spoiled and lazy people. We don't want to end up like the Americans, do we? You have to get out before it's too late."

"Too late for what?"

She took my army bag out of the wardrobe. "Come. It's time to bring you back to the light."

"What? Vera, what are you doing?"

She took down my tunic and skirt, two civilian outfits, a pair of sandals, and shoved them into the bag. I tried to yank it away but she held it fast. "It's for your own good."

"I'm not going anywhere. This is my home."

"There are new regulations. We've decided to consolidate personnel in appropriate facilities. This is not an appropriate facility."

Natalia's tears, Olga's anger and plundering. "You're forcing us to leave this house?"

"It has nothing to do with me. Moscow and the military government have ordered a total separation of living space between our personnel and the Germans. I remind you that we're in this country to plant the seeds of an anti-fascist government. The Germans are finding this political goal hard to accept because our rule has become heavy-handed in places. It's best that we draw clear lines between us so the Germans feel less oppressed and our personnel have less opportunity to make them feel that way. Only then can we make strides in growing socialism on this ragged soil. The isolation order is a necessary step in the country's renewal. We all have to play our part. The good news is I've found you more suitable lodgings."

"I'm an officer of military government. We're allowed to choose our own billets."

"That mistake is being corrected. It's not a punishment, Masha."

"It looks that way to me."

"We're enforcing more strict territorial boundaries. It'll be good for everyone. You'll be around your own culture and language and symbols all the time. It'll be almost like home."

"I'm not going. This is my home now."

"You're not in Germany to enjoy yourself. As you said, you're an officer of military government and you will go where the government commands you."

She had me. "Vera, you can stop this. You can talk to someone."

"About what? Him?" She was glaring at my hand, the one holding Henry's portrait. I hadn't noticed I'd been waving it about as I followed her. I stumbled backward and landed hard on the vanity stool. "It's . . . he's no one."

"I know all about him. Do you think I wouldn't notice my own sister spending her days off in a Western sector?"

"The MGB knows?"

"It's enough that I know. I'm trying to save you, you idiot, so listen to me. You'll come with me and quietly. You have ten minutes to destroy everything necessary." She snatched the portrait out of my hand and tossed it onto the vanity. "Leave nothing that could incriminate you. Should I stay and be sure?"

I looked around the room and didn't know where to begin to liquidate my life. "No. No, I'll do it."

Vera waited in the hallway, closing me into my bedroom for the last time. I rushed to put on Henry's bracelet, hiding it under the cuff of my tunic, then slipped my grandmother's cross into my pocket. From the shelf, I took down my fairy-tales book and added it to the bag Vera had started packing. Then I dropped to my knees and reached under the bed, pulling up the rug. Groping in the dust, my fingers closed around a small coin, Felix's lucky pfennig, as he called it, a long piece of string looped through a small hole in the center. He'd given it to me the day we parted, and I'd kept it throughout the war in my boot or in the hem of my beret, a secret I could show to no one. What Felix predicted when he gave it to me came to pass: I got through the war without a scratch—at least, none that anyone could see.

I shoved the coin into my pocket. Back on my knees, I pulled out Henry's letters. I sniffled as I tore them into little pieces, along with the portrait, and put a match to them in the bathroom sink. I had to get a message to him in the British Sector. I had to tell him how things had changed. With Vera watching, I didn't know how. Turning the tap, I rinsed away his loving words to me, a part of my freedom and happiness—gone.

When I opened the door, Vera frowned at my wet face. "Pull yourself together. You're an officer in the greatest country in the world. Act like one."

I followed her down the stairway for the last time. In the street, I turned back. My home, my beloved cottage. Vera yanked my arm and got me walking again. I didn't know where we were going, but I knew it was somewhere I didn't want to be.

5
Vera

Testimony for Chairman A. Cheptsov
Military Collegium of the Supreme Court of the USSR
Moscow, 28 February–3 June 1956

[RECORDING]

From Marya's KGB file, I take out the letter in English. It lays flat on my desk after years of being nestled in her file, but when I lean in closely, I see the faint memory of folds, the slightest curl of the paper. Investigator Gusev noted that it was found rolled up in the handle of Marya's hairbrush. I have no doubt this secret letter helped seal her fate.

Dearest Mouse,

I've been thinking a lot about what we talked about last, and I want you to know I'll stand by you no matter what happens.

If you get into trouble, I'll help you even if it means singlehand-edly invading your sector. That might sound like a joke but it's not. I'm here for you. Don't forget that. I've also stocked up on those lemon biscuits you love so I can keep bribing you to come see me again. Come earlier if you can. Missing you,

H.

Investigator Gusev found this letter interesting for several reasons, particularly the reference to invading what was obviously the Soviet Sector. I see nothing in that, mere hyperbole, a statement of emotional intensity, not an actual plan of action. I turn my attention to the fine line Gusev had drawn underneath the word *bribing*. If I had been prosecuting Marya's case, I would've armed myself with this word and taken it with me into my examination of the suspect. What was the writer of this letter bribing you with? Biscuits? Really? Love? Certainly. And what did he ask of you in return?

I hold the letter under the lamp, examine it in the usual ways, turning it front to back, changing the angle of my observation, looking for some missed clue hidden in the paper, some secret code perhaps. There is equipment that might reveal more, but instead of calling for Ivanov to send it to the laboratory, I tuck the letter back into the file. My dress shoes are pinching my feet, and so I kick them off and pace the office in my stockings, aware of every cold step. My thoughts have snagged on the letter's first line.

. . . thinking a lot about what we talked about . . .

"H" was obviously Henry Barrow; even the MGB had managed to guess that after he tried to hinder Marya's arrest in Berlin. At some point in their affair, a conversation had occurred between the lovers that left Barrow so uneasy, he sent Marya this assurance of his support in case of danger. His words seem genuine; he was serious about wanting to help her. What he doesn't mention is that the danger she was in came directly from him.

When I first saw him with Marya in Berlin, I sensed something off about him. I believe it was in that brief moment outside his house; when he glanced away from her, the warmth vanished from his face leaving something wary and calculating. I had to find out who he was. Quietly, I tapped certain friendly sources working in the British military government to gather basic information about him.

He was born in 1917 in a place called Blackburn, the son of a policeman and a dressmaker. He was divorced, one child deceased. As a young man, he moved to London and joined the Metropolitan Police, where he stood out as an intelligent, hardworking officer who could be tough when required. He advanced into investigations, and when the war broke out, he joined the investigative arm of the military police.

In the war, he made a name for himself investigating smuggling and black-market operations at his army's depots. Eventually, he became a specialist in logistics. With the help of patrons, he rose in the army until the war ended, when he became an officer in the military government. He was considered an up-and-coming man with a reputation for hard work and clear, quick thinking. In the summer of 1947, he was thirty-one and a captain on the edge of promotion to major.

Gusev had gathered much of the same information into Marya's file, but like me, he couldn't find when or how Marya met the Englishman. But through informants in Berlin, we both knew Barrow had been seeing a German woman until early November 1946, when he abruptly broke it off. It was safe to assume Marya met him in the fall of 1946. Their secret relationship had been running about eight months when I discovered it.

Armed with my suspicions and my basic knowledge of Barrow, I couldn't resist intervening in my sister's foolish romance. Shortly before my reunion with Marya, I arranged a meeting with Barrow through the German informant who had first reported their relationship to me. I named the place and time, open about what I wanted. Barrow should know that as Marya's older sister, it was my duty to meet him and discover his intentions.

Half an hour early, I arrived at our meeting place, a dance hall called Clärchens. It was in the Soviet Sector, but at that time, anyone of any nationality could go there to drink and eat and dance. At the coat check, a waiter in black gave me a little bow and, without a word, led me up a dark and curving stairway to the first floor. Through the double doors, we entered what they called the mirror room. Staff were moving tables, spreading cloths, unstacking chairs in preparation for the evening's amusements. Several musicians tuned their instruments at a niche in the dark-paneled wall.

The waiter showed me to a narrow stairway, and from there I went up alone and through a door, turning immediately into the small loggia. It overlooked the entire mirror room, giving me a view of everyone coming or going, and all of the tables. The large mirrors on the walls were mostly blind or marred by bullet holes. They reflected what little light penetrated the room, augmented by the massive chandelier on the ceiling, and smaller lights all around. I sat on the loggia's bench to smoke and wait for Barrow to come.

I saw him from high over his head before he saw me. He arrived in civilian clothes, entering the room through the doors beneath the loggia. He took off his hat, and his copper hair gave him away. I watched as he slowly walked between the tables, looking over the few patrons, the walls, the mirrors, as well as the exits. I was nearly certain: Henry Barrow was no simple government officer.

He examined a new environment with the care and precision of an intelligence agent.

When he finally looked up and spotted me, his eyes widened, struck, I assumed, by my resemblance to my sister. This vulnerability, the openness in his face as he stared up at me, didn't fit my idea of a British agent. I remembered: Barrow had been a policeman in civilian life. Maybe that was the root of his close observation of the room.

He climbed the narrow stairway to the loggia, and I retreated to the bench, unsure of his role again, what I was seeing in him. Policeman or agent? This uncertainty made him fascinating.

He sat beside me but as far away as possible, his hat between us. He was a man who took up space, and I saw the attraction for Marya, his physical magnetism. He was very still as I stated the facts in my imperfect English: I knew my sister was seeing him in secret, which was forbidden. I was concerned about the consequences of their rendezvous and wished to know if he was aware of them, of the danger he was putting Marya in.

"What exactly do you want from me?" he asked.

Ah, I thought at the time, an agent after all. A maker of bargains.

"I want nothing from you," I assured him. "I want to protect my sister and our family from consequences of a romance with a Westerner. I need to know your intentions. If you see my sister as a plaything, you must break if off and get yourself a German girl. Many would eagerly oblige your physical needs."

"Thank you for the suggestion," Barrow replied. "I would've never come on it myself."

He put on his hat and stood up, but I wouldn't let him slip away that easily. I decided to gamble.

"Before you go," I said, "I will tell you I assume you are British intelligence."

"Bollocks. Rotting, flaming bollocks."

"We are colleagues, are we not? There is no need for drama between us. I admire British intelligence service; we have much to learn from you. But I cannot allow you to use my sister and corrupt her. She is innocent. I believe she is in love. If she learns you are using her, it will destroy her. Do not do this. Walk away from this operation."

Throughout this, Barrow had stood over me, his anger bubbling beneath the surface. It was amusing to watch it rise with the color in his face.

"Be decent," I told him. "I do not doubt this operation is a most pleasant job for you, but—"

This was his tipping point. He slung his words at me in a thickening accent that became harder for me to follow.

"How dare you speak of Marya, your own sister, as if she's a common strumpet? A stupid girl to be used? I'd never do anything to hurt her. Never. My intentions? They're none of your damned business. Leave her alone, or you'll be dealing with me."

It was either a masterful performance, or Henry Barrow was truly a man defending his woman and his honor. I was uncertain again. What was he at bottom: agent or policeman? If he wasn't an agent, if he was merely a man in love with my sister, why was I so sure there was hidden depth in their relationship, something I couldn't find or see?

Nine years later, my questions haven't changed. Who was Barrow really? What was the true nature of their relationship? Was Marya a foolish girl in love, willing to risk her freedom for a man she couldn't have? Or did she have other motives? Did he?

There's a knock on the door, and Ivanov comes in, closing it behind him. I'm perched on the desk, the information about Barrow in my hand. At the tiny shift in Ivanov's face, I gather the papers back into the file and close it.

"Your husband called looking for you," he says.

My dear Nikolai, checking up on me as if I'm a wayward youth straying from home.

"You told him I'm not here, didn't you?"

"Of course I told him you aren't here. I don't think he believed me."

I slap the folder against the desk, then hold it out to Ivanov.

"Lock it up safe for me, will you? And send me a message when you find Gusev."

I'm very interested to talk to the man who investigated my sister after her arrest in Berlin. He may have insights that aren't in the file, details that I've missed. I am missing something. I can feel it lurking like a shadow behind the romance of Marya and Barrow, and I'm determined to find it.

6

Marya

Berlin, 19 June 1947

We circled back the way we'd come, Vera leading me past the Karlshorst station, up Rheinstein, and back to the secured perimeter of SMAD on Zwieseler Straße. We were farther north than I was used to, closer to the sports field. The streets curved around into dead ends and short branches that led nowhere. In the distance, I could see a tall barracks the Germans had left behind, and an old concrete bunker, an ugly reminder of the air bombardments the Western Allies had flown in the war. Vera stopped at an empty guard post. "Here we are. Welcome to the Hirschfeld Barracks, your new billet." She pushed open the gate.

I didn't want to go one step closer to the gray, three-story block that was supposed to be my new home. There was something faceless and forlorn about it and the bare grounds it stood on, and I was already longing for my friendly little cottage. Men were strewn along the perimeter of the grounds, sinking wooden slats into the dry soil and unfurling barbed wire or chicken fencing. They weren't in uniform, so they were Germans, gaunt and grim-faced. A few stopped working to glance at us, but when the guards shouted, they went back to their tasks. Vague shapes were watching them from behind the bare glass windows of the building. Soldiers, I assumed, taunting the men when they should've been worried about that fence. Inside the perimeter, I felt the world grow smaller. Henry was farther away than ever before. I touched his bracelet on my wrist beneath my cuff.

"Come on, then." Vera pulled my arm, and I stumbled after her through the doors of the barracks. Instantly, the smell hit me, a stink I remembered from the war. Cabbage, garlic, body odor, motor oil. I used to think only our men smelled that way, but no, I'd smelled like that too. I would again if I lived here long enough.

We passed a kind of reception area, empty, and then entered a long white corridor with scuffed floors and notices on the walls. I paused to glance at one. It looked like a rotation for kitchen duties. All of the names were female. "Is this a women's barracks?"

"Yes, and all ranks, though our facilities are slightly different."

Several girls my age came toward us, chattering. At the sight of Vera, they pressed themselves against the wall, stiffly saluting as she passed. I noticed their uniforms, the trim of cornflower blue like Vera's. When we were well past them, I said, "This isn't an MGB barracks, is it?"

"It's a mixture of personnel."

"Are there other interpreters?"

"There will be. We're some of the first to move in. The consolidation will take time."

"Isolation."

She paused outside a dark wooden door. "This isn't a prison, Masha."

"They're fencing us in, and there's a guard post."

"Necessary security measures."

"To keep people from coming in? Or is someone afraid of us leaving?"

She pushed open the door. The room was the size of my bedroom in the cottage, but much simpler with white walls and a single window at the far end. Each wall had a single bed made up with identical blankets and pillows. Under the window was a small table with one chair. To the left of the door was a closet, open, with shelving and two long compartments for hanging clothes. The right side was full. On a shelf, I recognized *The History of the Communist Party* (short course). We all had a copy. It was turgid reading.

Vera clasped her hands in the middle of the room. "Well, what do you think? It's a quiet room, and we don't get noise at night even with the window open unless there's a big event at the field. I made the bed for you," she said, gesturing to the bed on the right.

I hugged my bag to my chest. "We're sharing the room?"

"Of course. We're sisters."

I set down my bag then sat on the mattress. It was stiff and unforgiving compared to the one in my cottage. The room smelled of cheap soap. I'd grown accustomed to the fragrant bar Henry had imported from his homeland. Lavender. I'd forgotten to bring it.

"The washroom is at the end of the hallway. I was issued a towel for you."

Something else I'd forgotten to pack.

"I'll show you the canteen. There's a study circle tonight too. It's the first thing we organized. We'll be examining the German communist party."

I didn't give a damn about the German communist party, but I wasn't allowed to say it. As I hung up my clothes, I thought of the Germans building the fence outside, if there was a way to get a note to one of them. Maybe a man would cross Berlin to the British Sector and deliver it to Henry. I had no idea what it would cost me. Food was the obvious payment, and cigarettes, I thought, as Vera opened her cigarette case.

"Isn't it a relief to share a room again? It's like when we were girls. We can share each other's secrets."

"I think you're one big secret, Vera." I wasn't being funny, but she laughed as she lowered herself stiffly onto her bed, her leg seeming to bother her. "I always wondered how exactly you got shot. Even when I visited you in the hospital, you never told me and the doctors didn't seem to know either."

"How much do you know about what I was doing in the war up to that point?"

Vera was wounded in the summer of 1943, and before that, I had only a general idea about what she was doing. Technically, we were both in military intelligence. I was attached to the regular army while Vera was in a special arm of military counterintelligence. By the time she was wounded, it was called SMERSH, Stalin's little word game that meant Death to Spies. "In our battalion, there was always a SMERSH officer around being sure no one deserted or shot themselves to be sent home," I said. "I can't imagine you doing that kind of work." In the war, almost a million women served in the Red Army, and if there'd been a single court-martial of a female soldier, I hadn't heard about it. We were famous for being more disciplined than the men.

"Actually, I was an operative on a mission to liaison with partisan groups in Belarus. It was a bit of a messy political situation; I won't go into it here. We were ambushed by the Germans and . . ." She patted her leg. "It was fantastic, Masha. A gun in my hand, pointed at the enemy. Everything was so clear. It was us or them." Her smile faded. "If only the world was so easy to navigate in peacetime."

"I'd always take peace over the war."

"I spent the rest of it in Moscow. You saw more of the war than I did." Vera left it unsaid, the question of whether I had seen the Nazi concentration camps. I hadn't, though I had seen some of the people who survived.

"I was garrisoned in Posen for a while. People were streaming through, refugees, liberated POWs, many in terrible condition. And then, the people from those horrible camps. That was something else completely." I remembered a group of Jewish women staggering into our garrison, skeletons in rags, their eyes sunk into their skulls. A group of tattered French POWs escorted them, carrying the little bundles belonging to the women, their homemade Tricolore flying on a long stick. We'd gone out to greet them with tears in our eyes. There was such joy, and yet I couldn't take my eyes off those women, and what captivity had done to them. They seemed hollowed out, and when they looked at us, they seemed to either not see us, or they did, but from a place deep inside of them, dark and far away. As an interpreter for the garrison, I spoke to them as I did to the POWs, getting information from them, where they'd been, where their homes were. From me, the women got the comfort of my words, of being spoken to with respect and gentleness, one of the few gifts I could give them.

Vera was watching me. "It must've been hard for you."

"Hard for them." I went to the window and touched Felix's lucky pfennig in my pocket. His people had done those horrible things, and I didn't want to talk about it anymore. I was glad when Vera suggested we go eat.

Dinner was in the canteen of the barracks, a hall as white-washed as the rest of the building except for a mural of color-ful fruits and vegetables someone hadn't finished painting on one wall. The tables were of different sizes, and Vera led me to a small one next to the canteen doors. She watched everyone who came in and out.

All through dinner, as she chatted next to me, I carefully spir-ited bread into a handkerchief in my lap. It was one of Henry's I'd forgotten I had. He would see it and recognize it. By the end of the meal, I'd wanted to write a quick note to him in ink directly on the cloth, but Vera was always there beside me. Only after dinner when she went to the washroom did I find a pen and write: *Dear Henry, I'm in a barracks now and can't come so easily. Wait for me Sunday. I will try. Love, M.* I remembered to add, *Give cigarettes to the man who delivers this message.* I heard Vera in the hallway and tied the bundle just as she opened our bedroom door.

"The study circle is in half an hour."

"I want to get some air first, or is that not allowed?"

"Of course. I'll come with you."

I couldn't protest, and I couldn't let her see the bundled hand-kerchief. I found a bag large enough for my own copy of *The His-tory of the Communist Party.* "I never go to a study circle without it," I said with a straight face.

"Oh really?" Smiling a little, Vera took hers off the shelf and packed it in a satchel.

While she did that, I quietly slipped the bundle into my bag. The small deception got my heart pumping. Through the window, I saw the Germans still working on the perimeter fence. Summer nights in Berlin were one long, lingering twilight, and the men would be forced to work until they couldn't see the ground they were digging.

In the main hallway, I broke away from my sister. I lost my orientation, not sure anymore where the canteen was. I followed the cabbage smell until I found it, several gray-faced German women cleaning countertops and tables. A pitcher of water still stood on the table at the mural wall. I picked it up and carried it back into the hallway, where Vera was lighting a cigarette.

"If you're thirsty, it's usual to drink out of a glass."

"It's not for me."

In the heat, the German workers were stripped to their trousers and suspenders, sweat on their bare backs and chests. A man my age with closely shaved hair rested his shovel for a moment and wiped his brow with the shirt he'd draped into his trousers. Instantly, the guard shouted at him, and the man hurriedly took up his shovel again. He reminded me so painfully of Felix, a wave of pity rose up in me, smothered quickly by the shame of feeling that way. It seemed a betrayal of all the men and women who had died fighting for our freedom in the war.

"It's good to see Germans working," Vera said. "Keeps them out of trouble."

I ignored her and crossed the dried grass to the men, holding the pitcher carefully. The man who had rested a moment before looked up from his work in surprise. At the sight of my uniform, he straightened.

"You're thirsty," I said in German, offering the pitcher. "Drink."

The guard was on me instantly, but I wasn't in the mood. I shouted at him, "Is this any way to treat men? Let them drink."

The guard backed off. I was a woman but I also outranked him. He looked around for help, saw Vera observing from close by, and he approached her, complaining about me, but in respectful tones.

The young German took the pitcher from me and drank, a small swallow before passing it to his neighbor. The men sipped and kept the pitcher moving down the line. The first man nodded at me. "Thank you, Fräulein Lieutenant." The words echoed in my memory; Felix had sounded just the same, at first. The thank-yous were taken up by the other men all down the row. It went a long way to soothing the storm in my heart.

The guard was still complaining to Vera. My back to them, I showed the handkerchief bundle to the young German, explaining quickly what I wanted. I repeated Henry's address twice so he wouldn't forget. "Please," I said. "Help me."

His eyes were still wary. After a moment, he shook his head, spat on the ground at my feet, and went back to his shovel. I couldn't believe it. I'd done him a kindness, I'd asked a favor, and he—

"Fräulein Lieutenant?" The next man in line spoke in a whisper. He was older, losing his hair. Then I realized he was actually young, but something—war? Captivity?—had aged him terribly. "Cigarettes?" he asked.

He'd heard everything. He was interested. "You'll get them if you deliver this. I promise."

He quickly tucked the bundle into the band of his trousers, took up his shovel, and got back to work. I gave the empty pitcher to the guard. "Fill it up and give it to the men who haven't had any water yet." His face flushed, but after a glance at Vera, he obeyed.

As we returned to the barracks, I breathed more easily, though I still tingled with what I'd just done under Vera's nose. The German might eat the bread and discard the handkerchief in the ruins, but I hoped he'd help me, if not for the cigarettes Henry would give him, then out of human decency, the urge to help another person even if he still saw me, a Russian, as the enemy.

THE STUDY CIRCLE was held in the barracks library. There was only one bookcase, not very well stocked. On the walls were notices and posters. One showed a proud and sturdy woman wielding a shovel, a bombed house and a building crane behind her. Another showed Stalin in a dark room, writing by the light of a lamp, a little red star in the window. The caption was: *Stalin works for each and every one of us.* I was glad he was looking down at his paper and not at me.

Vera and I seated ourselves, and as the long table filled with women, she said into my ear, "In future, if you're going to smuggle messages out of here, don't be so obvious."

I blustered, "I didn't—"

She touched her finger to her lips and pointed at the lecturer, a political instructor taking her place at the head of the table.

7
Vera

Testimony for Chairman A. Cheptsov
Military Collegium of the Supreme Court of the USSR
Moscow, 28 February–3 June 1956

[RECORDING]

leave the Lubyanka and walk home through the dark and empty streets. Inside me is a core of angry heat that keeps the cold from nipping at my toes. My husband has called me home as if I'm a child, and what's worse—I'm actually going. I'm thinking up excuses and lies to soothe him, but why should I? Marya is my sister. I have the right to find out the truth about her. Nikolai doesn't know her like I do, what she's always been to me, even if it was sometimes hard for me to show it.

I haven't talked much about her to anyone over the years. It hurts too much to remember what we were like before Berlin and the war. When I first saw her, a newborn, in the crook of Mother's arm, I knew she was mine. My sister. That was something special. I peered into Marya's cradle all the time, and when she wasn't sleeping, she gazed up at me with a wrinkle in her forehead. It made her look funny and curious as if she didn't know what manner of creature I was but found me fascinating anyway.

That was her power over me, for years, following me around, asking me questions, demanding I explain this or that, or teach her my school lessons. Everything I did seemed good to her. I was wonderful—*me*, no matter how I treated her. No one else was like that. If I hit Yuri, he hit me back. If I dared yell at Mother, she had some choice words for me, or a wooden spoon. Father could stop me with a look from his sad eyes. If I screamed at Marya, she might scream back, but she'd dissolve into tears afterward and ask, "Why are you being mean to me?" She was so soft. I wished she'd retaliate strongly, prove to me that she had some steel inside her.

Over the years, I tested her in what I'm afraid were petty and spiteful ways. I wanted to see what it took to break that worshipful look on her face. When she was fifteen, she joined the youth league. She didn't have her heart in it, but she wanted to go to university one day so join she did. When someone became a new member of a Komsomol cell, it was common back then for the existing members to pull practical jokes on the newcomer. I was the first-ever female leader of our local cell, so I had assured her that, as my sister, she'd be welcomed with respect. The cell was two-thirds boys, and I had a talk with them before Marya arrived. They were to toughen her up, test her resolve.

As was usual with the boys, they did their mischief with gusto. My deputy offered her a chair at the table and then pulled it away so that she tumbled to the floor. The room erupted into laughter. Marya picked herself up, swatting the dust from her skirt, and looked at me. She was confused and annoyed, I could tell, but she'd always been an easy-going girl and didn't take what happened to heart. "I'll stand, then," she said sweetly, and that got the boys laughing even more.

They rushed to their chairs, and I started the meeting. Marya stood the entire time, stared at by the other members. Every time she wanted to speak, one boy or another would tell her to be quiet, teasing her that no one cared what she had to say, a scrawny little girl like her. They didn't call her comrade as they called each other and the other girls in the cell, but Baba, a term of disrespect in our circles. In a dozen other small ways, she was humiliated in front of her peers, and I acted as if I noticed nothing. I was waiting for her to explode, defend herself. Walk out, even though that would've been a sign of defeat. But she stayed until the end of the meeting, and when we walked home afterward, she frustrated me by asking, "Why did you let them do that to me?"

"Why did *you* let them?" I demanded. "Don't you have any self-respect? You have to stand up for yourself in this world, Masha. I won't always be there to do it for you."

I was nearly twenty at the time, and I confess I thought highly of myself and my notions about human nature as taught by the party. I let my Komsomol cell humiliate her for a full month, and she held out. Meeting after meeting, she took the jibes and insults, and I began to see something I hadn't seen in her before, a quiet strength. She let the insults slide right off of her. The boys grew tired of abusing her and were even starting to admire her resilience. That's what it was. Resilience. It was a strength I never knew she had.

She must've got this resilience from our mother, since I wouldn't consider our father an example of how to weather life's difficulties. He was an old revolutionary and was proud he had joined the battle against the czarist White Army. Sometimes he would regale us with stories of the battles, gruesome tales that made us children clutch each other. Marya had nightmares after he told us about finding a row of bodies, good simple comrades like him, slaughtered by the Whites, their bellies slit open so that blood and entrails colored their skin. Carved nearby was the message: *They are red now!* Our father would say we must remember these things. We must never forget how the People are hated when they throw off their chains and rise up.

But he had a troubled soul. I believe it was the ghosts of those comrades slaughtered in the road. He died when I was thirteen, and it was like losing a star I'd always thought was fixed in the sky. Papa was gone, and our mother needed my help. I was the oldest, and I was strong so I would shrink my grief to the tiniest jot of darkness inside of me and take my new place as the support of my family. The only times I nearly slipped and let the grief out was when I read his old books and pamphlets, many works of Lenin, where Papa had written little notes in the margins. I could stomach looking at the chair he'd sat in, or even his portrait. But those fading words he'd written on the page, his thoughts and questions, nearly cracked me open.

Some years after Papa's death, the secret police came to our flat demanding to see him. It was evening, and all of us, Mother and all three girls and Yuri, were home in our kitchen. I was eighteen and preparing a speech for a Komsomol meeting. Marya was thirteen and writing poetry in German, what she called her secret language, since she didn't want me to read it. A half-German neighbor named Rosa had been teaching her for years, and Marya's skill would be a deciding factor in the war and the events later in Berlin. Yuri was fifteen and building a miniature engine out of scrap metal. Nina, eight, was helping our mother with her sewing. It was quiet, all of us busy with our projects, when suddenly, there was a commotion in the hallway, the pounding of boots, then harsh knocks on the door. The policemen of the People's Commissariat of Internal Affairs burst in, and we abandoned our things and stood up in surprise. Up to then, we weren't the type of people who expected the NKVD to knock on our door. It happened to other people, not us.

"Where is Ilya Mikhailovich Nikonov?" the leader demanded.

Mother calmly told him that Ilya Nikonov had died five years before. The NKVD man was livid. He had an order for our father's arrest. Mother pointed out that it was difficult to arrest a dead man.

She was stating the absurdity of the situation, but the NKVD, as we know, had very little humor at the best of times. They ordered her to produce the death certificate while they tossed things out of our cabinets and ripped up our beds. This behavior appalled me, this violation of our home. When they'd seen the certificate and found not a trace of a man living in our room, the NKVD left us with the warning they would be back.

Throughout this ordeal, Marya had been silent with terror, holding the hands of Yuri and Nina, and in the following days and weeks, she brooded as I'd never seen her do. She began to take an even closer interest in our political education and read material far above her age, though I didn't let her read Papa's books. Those were mine. Marya never spoke of it, but I believe she thought that if she was a good girl, a good little comrade, patriotic and zealous, the men would never come for our mother. They never did come.

As for me, the incident with the NKVD had a profound effect on my life. At that moment I decided I would join the security services myself one day. They needed good and moral comrades to step up and ensure that the police were a shield of the people, not a weapon to inspire fear. After those men left our rooms, I decided then and there I would never be frightened again.

Which was, of course, absurd. Living in the times we did, especially under Stalin, life was one long corridor of fear that is hard to escape, even today.

A few lights still burn in the windows of the massive tower that is my apartment building; it strikes me as a strangely Western monolith, one of Stalin's gothic cathedrals piercing the black sky. I approach the building from the embankment just as Nikolai stalks out of the front doors looking grim and distracted. I don't know if it has to do with me being at the Lubyanka or is related to the unrest brewing in the country because of Khrushchev's condemnation of Stalin.

"What's happened?" I ask softly as I examine the street for moving shadows, listening ears. As far as I can see, we're alone. It's safer to speak outside than in our apartment, but it never hurts to be cautious.

"Politics has happened," he whispers. "What else?"

It's one of his favorite phrases. As he paces in the frost, he quietly complains about the Kremlin and the Foreign Ministry and the intrigues swirling in the halls. Since Khrushchev's speech, the factions have been growing in the center of the government, men like Malenkov and Bulganin favoring a critique of Stalin and his crimes, while Molotov, Voroshilov, and others see no point in stirring up the past. As usual, Nikolai can see the sense in both sides.

This political talk is soothing; it has always been a way for us to communicate on a topic that interests us both yet doesn't dig too deeply. These days, Nikolai rarely asks about Marya. I rarely ask him about his first wife who died in the Urals before the war, or his adult son, an engineer in Magnitogorsk, whom I've met only twice in the years we've been married.

"Where were you tonight?" Nikolai asks.

I don't want to lie to him. I'm too tired. "Kolya, you're my husband, and I love and respect you, but I should remind you that I don't like to be followed, asked about, or checked up on by the person I trust the most in this world."

"Then why are you acting behind my back?"

"My sister's case has nothing to do with you."

"You know it does."

It's true that Nikolai was in Berlin as well. Neither of us likes to remember those difficult days, though they led us to where we are now.

He tosses the butt of his cigarette into the river and grasps my arms. "Vera, I'll say it again. Leave your sister's case alone. I'm this close to being appointed foreign minister, you know that. We've worked for years to get here. If the wrong people find out what you're investigating, they'll twist it against me. Everything we've been working for is in danger. The life we've built."

"We can weather this, Kolya. We're strong enough. And maybe she's innocent. Consider that. What she's endured unjustly while we live like this." I gesture at the glittering tower of our apartment building, the privileges we've struggled to attain.

He shakes his head as if I'm a lost cause. "The only way you'll convince the court Marya is innocent is if you deny the facts about what she did. Is that what you plan to do? Manufacture the truth you want?"

I draw away from him, offended. "You believe I'd lie to the court to free my sister?"

"Show me a court that isn't in the business of being lied to."

Sometimes my husband infuriates me to no end. "You're letting your cynicism rule you. I'm gathering facts about my sister and looking at the evidence from a new perspective. If I dig deep enough, and analyze the case with a clear head, I'll discover the truth. I don't need to lie. I'm not scared of the truth anymore."

"Are you so sure?"

He has the nerve to ask that when he's the one who is scared of what my investigation could do to his career. I'm concerned about that too—of course I am—but I won't let fear stop me. "There's more to my sister's case than we were willing to see in Berlin, and I'm going to find out what it is. We'll continue to have a harmonious homelife if you accept this, my dearest."

"Is that a threat, Verochka?"

"Only a fact, Kolya."

"Then we know where we stand."

He says it in the tone he would take in a diplomatic negotiation at the moment the two sides see that there is nothing left to say.

8

Marya

Berlin, 19 June 1947

When we got back to our room after the lecture, it was dark. Vera turned on the overhead light; there were no reading lamps by the beds or other individual comforts. I put the notes I'd taken on the desk. Part of me had listened while the rest thought of the German I hoped was crossing Berlin with my message for Henry.

Vera changed out of her uniform with her back to me, smoothing her tunic on the hanger and folding the skirt on the shelf. In her plain white nightgown, she cleaned her shoes before setting them under her bed. Her self-assurance and contentment irritated me. This was her world, and she fit it well. She couldn't let me be different; she never could. She could never mind her own business. When we were girls and I came across her reading my private diary, she justified herself with "We are Soviet children. We have no private thoughts." I had to find a place to hide my most private things—Henry's last letter, Babushka's cross, Felix's lucky pfennig—though I had no idea where in this bare room. For now, I had them all under my pillow.

I turned to the wall and readied for bed, then lay down, hugging my thin blanket. Vera switched off the light, and for the first time I noticed the glow at our window. A floodlight was nearby for security, no doubt. A woman's barracks was a temptation for male troops who weren't allowed German girlfriends.

"Don't bother being angry at me," Vera said in the dark. "It's a waste of your energy."

I pretended to sleep. Deep, even breaths.

"You know," she said, "I have cause to be angry at you."

"*What?*"

"I don't want to count how many of our regulations you've been violating. Fraternization with a Westerner isn't even the worst of it. I'm more concerned about your convictions, how they've . . . shifted. I'm beginning to question your loyalties."

This was the first day she'd talked to me in years. She didn't know who I was anymore. Even if she'd been spying on me and Henry, she couldn't have found anything else about me to make her question my loyalties. "I served in the war and I'm serving now. Of course I'm loyal."

"If I thought you were a lost cause, I would've sent you home weeks ago. I'm not angry about your relationship with the Englishman. You always acted from your heart, not your mind. It's your nature. I'm much more concerned about what your actions mean in a practical sense. If I were to draw a line on the floor with our homeland on one side and England on the other, which side would you choose?"

"Ours, of course," I replied instantly.

"I'm relieved your infatuation hasn't led you so far astray you've become enamored with all things foreign. You've always had a disturbing interest in German things."

"The language."

"And with language comes the danger of becoming too familiar with the people who speak it."

I wasn't about to let her lecture me about my profession. "Being friendly with foreigners and learning their language doesn't mean I'm turning my back on my own country. If we understand what people are saying, we can work with them. Look what we achieved in the war. We needed our allies. We might not have won if they—"

"Masha, you'd do well to think about what you're saying."

"In this room. Alone with you. Are you going to denounce me for telling the truth? That we might've lost if the Allies hadn't sent us supplies and machinery? I was there when we liberated Western POWs on the way to Berlin. The British cheered us. We sang the Marseillaise with the French. We won together."

"Masha! This is precisely what I'm talking about. The leadership of Comrade Stalin and the Communist Party was the deciding factor in our victory. If you deny this very basic truth, then your loyalties are questionable indeed."

"I didn't deny it. But there were other factors too. I was there. I saw it with my own eyes."

"Any idiot can see things. Deciding what they mean is another matter. What conclusions you reach are based on what you already know from the teachings of the party."

I grumbled and tossed on my mattress and then lay as still as I could. Deep, even breaths.

"Masha," Vera said, "you're not going to get out of this discussion by pretending to be asleep."

I rolled onto my back and stared at the glow on the ceiling

made from the floodlights outside. "I thought I made my point, Vera. I can be interested in foreigners and loyal to my country. I can be with Henry and be an officer of the government at the same time. How I feel about him doesn't change how I do my duty."

"Maybe. Maybe not. We can put it to the test."

I pulled myself up onto my elbow. "How?"

"You can keep seeing him. Under one condition."

Our window wasn't quite sealed from drafts; the blinds tapped gently against the sill. After a few moments, she said, "Does the Englishman ever talk to you about his work?"

The draft chilled my arms. I tried to rub the goose bumps away. "No. We don't do that." He didn't, but I did. I loved talking about my work. How could I not tell him what language meant to me? How learning one felt like opening a new and complex lock?

"He's drawing up contingency plans in case we close off transportation routes to or from Berlin," Vera said. "If we can find out what they're planning, we would have a strategic advantage."

She'd been looking into Henry. Investigating him. Carefully, I said, "That has nothing to do with Henry and me."

"You say that, and call yourself loyal?"

"I don't care what he does."

I heard her move, saw the shape of her sitting on the edge of her bed. "You need to understand what he's really doing, and what it means. He and the other Westerners are plotting against the peace. They've already fused the Western zones economically, a first step to dividing Germany for good. They're plotting to cement this division by printing new German money. We know this is in the works. They're plotting to ensure Germany stays divided. It suits them to use this country as a buffer, a potential battleground in an open war with us." She was breathing fast. "Those are the realities. Their plans. But our zone surrounds Berlin. We will take the city, all of it, if we're provoked. With intelligence from your Englishman, we could plan our response when they retaliate."

"Get it some other way."

"It's not for you to say how we get it. You serve the people and state. You take orders and execute them."

"Not from you. I won't do this, Vera. Not this."

"Maybe you're under the mistaken impression the British aren't quite as against us as the Americans. But right after the war, we were able to confirm reports that the British left a number of captured Wehrmacht units intact. Uniforms, weapons, armor, everything. Germans reported to us afterward that they could have started another war if they'd wanted. There was talk that was exactly what the British intended."

It was a lie. Our propaganda. It had to be. "The British were going to use the Germans to go to war against us?"

"The idea was considered in some circles in London. Level heads prevailed and the plan was abandoned. But it shows you the truth. Times are changing and they won't stand still for anything. The lines are drawn, Masha. Choose your side."

"Not like this. I'll do anything else—"

"You don't get to decide how you serve. The opportunity is there in that flat on the Schloßstrasse. Does the Englishman keep any work documents at home?"

"I won't go rummaging in his papers for you."

"You're not doing it for me. You're doing it for the Motherland."

"Oh for God's sake!"

"The last time your country was in danger, you answered the call to action. Without hesitation."

"We're not in danger. We're at peace now."

"The next war may look different than the last one, but it's already here."

"Not for me." I flopped onto my side and pulled my blanket over my shoulder. "Good night, Vera."

I felt the blanket yanked away from me, the whip of it on my skin.

"Have you forgotten what you did in the war?" Vera was looming over me in the dark. "You were an intelligence officer."

"I was an interpreter serving in an intelligence section group. That's different."

"I know your record, Marya, believe me. You did splendid work. Your prisoners told you everything. You know how to get a man to shift his loyalties—"

"I'm not doing it!" I climbed off the bed and went to the window. In the glow of the floodlights, I saw the half-built perimeter fence in the distance, the dark wooden slats like a palisade that closed off my horizon. Behind me, Vera struck a match.

"I'm offering you the only way to see Barrow. If you don't cooperate, I'll send you home to Mother. She'll be glad to have you."

Vera could do it. She could have me sent home for a hundred reasons that had nothing to do with Henry. Listening to Western radio, reading Western papers, having a drink in a Western sector, it all added up to a political unreliability that my country couldn't stomach. I'd heard rumors that personnel who'd lived outside the USSR, even as soldiers, were considered suspect. Even at home, I'd be watched.

And Henry . . . He'd only know that I'd vanished. I'd taken most of the risk in our relationship, and he'd blame himself. I couldn't let that happen. I'd be lying to myself if I thought he and I were still in a casual affair. Once we started talking about our families, our losses, something changed in us. I didn't want to lose what we were building together. Whatever it was. I wasn't ready to let him go, and I knew I'd do whatever it took to stay in Berlin.

My chest was too tight to breathe. Vera's cigarette burned the air. "Why are you doing this to me?"

"You read *Anna Karenina*, didn't you? It's a terrible book. A woman's duty is not to her selfish desires but to her people. You knew it in the war. Be that woman again, Masha. I know you can do it."

"Or you'll destroy my life."

Her silence lasted a long time. I could hear the quick puffs on her cigarette, the smoke pooling inside her. "Be with your Henry Barrow. And do your duty as an officer. You said yourself, the one doesn't affect the other. Well, then. Think of all this as an addition to your regular duties. Nothing more."

9

Vera

Testimony for Chairman A. Cheptsov
Military Collegium of the Supreme Court of the USSR
Moscow, 28 February–3 June 1956

[RECORDING]

At the Lubyanka, Ivanov meets me on the fourth floor, the rings around his eyes even deeper than they were the last time I was here. His newborn has the colic and his household never sleeps. He comes to work to rest, he says with a tired smile as he opens the door to the same little office I used before.

"Is Gusev teaching tonight?" I ask, taking out a cigarette. Ivanov has already informed me that the officer who investigated my sister after her arrest in Berlin is now serving as an instructor at the KGB Advanced School here in Moscow.

"If you shout, he'll hear you," Ivanov says. "He's just over at the Metropol, then a seat at the Bolshoi." Ivanov flicks his thumb toward the window and its view of Dzerzhinsky Square and the lights of the buildings beyond. "We can invite him whenever you like. He'll come."

"How do you know?"

"Gusev's new girlfriend is a KGB operative in training, but he doesn't know that. He thinks she's a librarian and follows her around like a little boy telling her everything. If he's wary about coming when we call, she'll convince him not to worry."

I make a noise of disgust. Not only do I dislike such spineless men, but I don't wholly approve of the KGB's use of women agents as mattresses with ears. I see their usefulness; I simply don't like the method, as effective as it is.

Once Ivanov leaves, I open Marya's file, turning the pages until I find the interrogations conducted directly after her arrest in Berlin. I place my hand on the top page and feel a heat the paper can't possibly have. This will be my first glimpse into what the security services—my own colleagues—did to my sister once she was in their custody, since I had been barred from attending her interrogations or taking any part in the investigation. I smoke another cigarette, fingering the page before I begin to read.

As an officer of state security and a prosecutor, I conducted many interrogations in my career. There is an art to getting suspects to speak the truth, and in cases where I had the time to work as I liked, I guided them like a friend to what I believed—or tried to believe—was an honest, cleansing confession. I have never condoned the more robust methods of interrogation. A forced confession has the aftertaste of the pain it was acquired with. Even if the suspect finally speaks the truth, it is, at bottom, dishonest.

In the file, I scan the transcripts for the phrase "physical methods" or similar words that signal Marya's treatment while in custody. Gusev was careful; he shrouded his actions in words like "pressure" or "compel." I flip back to the first page of the transcripts. Gusev begins with the usual question:

G: Why do you think you were arrested?
N: It's a mistake. A misunderstanding, I was only—
G: We never make mistakes!

I shake my head at this exchange. I've heard or read it hundreds of times. I'd done it myself. This is the legacy of Stalin, how we all knew the theater we were to play and spoke our lines perfectly when required. For pages, Gusev and his colleagues began chipping away at Marya, breaking her down, breaking her very self, in order to reassemble her for their own purposes. This was common in those days, but it hurts to read it knowing my sister is behind the transcript letter N.

Some time into the interrogation, Gusev asked her about me:

G: What is your relationship with Vera Ilyanovna Nikonova?
N: I have no relationship with her.
G: None with your older sister, who you share a room with?
N: None.
G: Did she know what you were planning to do?
N: I never tell her anything. We hate each other.

I stop reading. This isn't the sister I cuddled as a child, the woman I lived with in Berlin. I would agree our relationship had always been complex. But hate? I stare at the paper, wondering where hate had begun in her heart. It was never in mine.

I can't read on yet. I seek out Ivanov in his office and find him with his head down at his desk. Rousing him, we go to find tea in the cafeteria and chat of inconsequential things. With time, the sting of Marya's words fades somewhat. I begin to think I can face the rest of it.

"Call in Gusev, will you, Leo?"

Ivanov leaves me at my office and goes to make the necessary calls that will bring Marya's interrogator to me. Still hesitant to go back to the file, I smoke at the windowsill until the door opens and a secretary announces Valentin Gusev.

He presents himself crisply, a man of about forty in evening dress, smelling of the wine he must have spilled when he was called to the Lubyanka. The stain is still dark on his sleeve. There is another stain, a red smear on his jaw, a gift from his KGB girlfriend. I don't bother to alert him to it. Covering the photograph of my sister with my hand, I turn the file on the desk and he glances over the first page.

"That girl in Berlin, yes, I remember the case," he says. "What of it? Who are you? And what is all this?"

"Be at ease, comrade. I'm working on behalf of Comrade Khrushchev's special commission examining old cases of party members incorrectly sentenced for counterrevolutionary activities. You were the chief investigative officer in the case of Marya Ilyanovna Nikonova?"

Gusev shifts uncomfortably on his feet. "Her case shouldn't have anything to do with the commission," he says. "She wasn't a party member. And she wasn't incorrectly sentenced, I can tell you that. We caught her with—"

"Please sit, Comrade Gusev."

There is only one chair in the room and I'm sitting in it. Gusev looks around twice as if another chair will materialize, and then he turns back to me warily.

"I assure you," I say, "this won't take long. I only have a few questions related to the interrogation protocol. First, I would like to know: Were physical methods used to get the suspect to talk?"

"We caught her red-handed and she still wouldn't confess, so we had to apply the usual methods. Standard procedure," he says hastily. "She got no special treatment just because her sister was a somebody."

"Her sister?" I ask, browsing the pages of the file. My hand is clammy and my fingers are sticking a little to the pages.

"Her sister was MGB, and if you ask me, she was deeply involved in the whole thing. But we couldn't get anything out of the girl, and the sister was off-limits in the investigation. She was into some big things, all very hush-hush. Protection from Moscow. I couldn't get near her."

I make a show of turning back to the part of the transcript that mentioned me.

"Vera Ilyanovna Nikonova. That was the sister?"

He blinks at me, and I can see the suspicion take root in him as he searches his memory for Marya's face, compared to mine. But then he blinks again and says, "That's correct. She was in Berlin in 1947. I didn't believe the suspect when she said her sister didn't know anything. Either Comrade Nikonova was a blind fool or she was a liar pretending she didn't know what the girl was doing."

I nod as if his opinion interests me, though I'm disgusted at this man. He is reverting to the lowest of impulses to accuse someone else of irregularities so that no one looks too closely at his.

I turn back to the file, and the words seem to blaze on the page. Early in the interrogation, my sister endured one of the more petty punishments. She asked to use a toilet, and it was refused again and again. One can't underestimate the pressure the bladder puts on the body, and the humiliation at the thought of wetting oneself in front of men. I have seen full confessions made by prisoners who would rather talk than endure the shame. This was just one of several signs in the transcript of Gusev stripping Marya of her dignity, and her self.

Gusev's shoes squeal as he shifts his weight again, and swallows loudly. "She was a tough one," he says.

"Tough how?"

"She was stubborn as a goat and called us all sorts of names. When she wasn't lying to save her life."

"Lying?"

"For a while, she tried to convince us she was spying on that Englishman she was carrying on with."

I look up sharply from the file and try to keep my voice level. "Marya Nikonova was convicted of spying for a foreign intelligence agency, presumably the British because of the Englishman."

Gusev shakes his head. "She claimed she spied *on* him. Not *for* him."

He comes closer and delicately turns the pages of Marya's file, going over some of them twice. Finally, he taps a certain line deep in the transcript.

G: How long had your romantic relationship been going on
    with the Englishman?

N: It wasn't.

G: Wasn't what?

N: Romantic.

G: Were you sleeping with Barrow?

N: Yes.

G: Well, then. Answer the question.

[Prisoner answers angrily.]

N: I did it so he'd trust me.

G: Why did you want him to trust you?

N: So I could get information out of him. He would tell me things. Secrets. A man will tell everything to a woman in bed with him. Everybody knows it. He made it so easy. He was . . . He pressed me. He wanted me. Well? Why not? I could use that, couldn't I?

G: You claim you conducted a personal relationship with a British officer solely in order to spy on him?

[Prisoner pauses for several seconds.]

N: Yes.

I hold up the page of the interrogation and shake it at Gusev. "She really said this? These very words?"

There is something in my voice that makes Gusev pale and quake. "Yes, comrade, but as I said, we took it as a lie. We didn't believe a word of it. We'd been working on her all day and half the night. She wanted it to stop and she threw any old nonsense out there. It was insulting."

I return to the transcript. After the revelation from Marya, she deflected every further question about her self-styled intelligence operation against Henry Barrow. As time went on, the interrogation became more robust. The more she was punished, the less she spoke until the interrogation was terminated without—as was usually the case—a confession. On the following days, no attempts to get her to speak succeeded. After that, she was transported to Moscow, where she was convicted within a week, the trial record barely half a page long.

"Why," I ask Gusev, "were you so sure the suspect's claim to spy on Barrow was nonsense?"

"She was arrested with fake papers that made her out to be a German working for British HQ. But it was her photo all right. She got a new identity from British intelligence. What more evidence did we need?"

"Fake papers?" I begin to flip through the file, front to back, quickly, then every page. "There is no British paper here. Where is it?"

Gusev shrugs. I make a note to ask Ivanov if he's seen such a thing. Its absence from the file makes me very uneasy indeed. Maybe Gusev is lying, but I can't think of why he would do so now.

"British document aside," I say, "did anyone check her story? You could have looked for evidence someone authorized her to conduct an operation against Barrow. Or better yet, located intelligence that she'd passed on to us."

"There was no point. After we worked on her some, she didn't bother to lie anymore."

In Gusev, I see the spirit of the old security services under Stalin. Always right. Never wrong. Never questioning their own assumptions. Abusing the suspect was easier and safer than doing the work to uncover the truth of what she was saying.

Gusev is a scoundrel, but with the missing British card, he's given me a crucial line of inquiry in Marya's case. I get up from the desk and gesture toward the door.

Ivanov must have been waiting for us. He leaves his office down the hall, looking official, a file under his arm, just as we enter the hallway.

"All through, Vera Ilyanovna?"

"Comrade Gusev was a great help, yes."

Gusev, eager to go, is already halfway down the hallway. Then he stops, and I feel him thinking, remembering the name of the suspect's older sister, the blind fool, the liar with protection from Moscow. Out the corner of my eye, I see him turn slightly, think better of it, and move quickly to the stairs.

"That man," I say to Ivanov on our way back into my office, "is wasted in Moscow. A comrade with his talents and judgment deserves a responsible post in a place like . . . Kazakhstan."

"That kind of good fortune is easy to arrange."

"I'm so glad. Leo, did you see a British employment document with Marya's picture in her file? Apparently, there was one, but it's missing."

Ivanov shrugs as Gusev had. I begin to doubt the paper exists. To hurry along an investigation, our security organs have been known to manufacture evidence in order to gain a confession. Though this seems elaborate in Marya's case, and in the end, she didn't confess.

"One last thing. Try to find out if we ever authorized Marya to work as an operative."

Ivanov adds her file to the one under his arm. "When this is done, you're going to owe me, Vera."

I nod, grateful as ever for his help. My head is abuzz as I leave the Lubyanka, pausing in the square to light a cigarette. Back then, in Berlin, no one said anything to me about Marya claiming to spy on Barrow. At her arrest, the assumption was that Barrow had been grooming her for his country's intelligence service. I'd had the same suspicion in Berlin, the reason I'd gone to see Barrow myself. I never found evidence he was a British agent, but the court had no doubts. Marya was convicted of spying against the Soviet Union. I never thought she'd done any actual spying; she'd compromised herself by meeting a Westerner in secret, which was more than enough for a conviction.

But what if she told the truth in her interrogation? What if she was a spy, not for the British, but for us?

Maybe Marya was capable of more than any of us imagined. Maybe even I overlooked something fundamental inside her, an ability to deceive everyone. Even her lover. Even me.

10
Marya

After I moved in with Vera, SMAD assigned me to translate confidential economic reports from our zone of Germany into Russian. That Sunday, after breakfast, when Vera had left me with a smile and a warning to "be good while I'm gone," I changed into civilian and headed to Henry's. He was waiting for me on Schloßstrasse, pacing outside the gate to his house. When he saw me, he flailed his half-smoked cigarette into a rain puddle and came at me with open arms. Seeing his anxiety eased mine, at least a little.

"You got my note? From the German?"

"Days ago. I didn't know how safe it was to contact you. What's happened?"

"Vera, my sister. She's here. In Berlin." I hadn't known I was going to tell him that. But it slipped out. Under his breath, he said a curse that I would never repeat, and then steered me through the gate to the door. I couldn't wait to get up to his flat, I had so much to tell him. In the foyer, I shoved my umbrella into the stand, and then it all tumbled out of me. "She made me leave my cottage, my lovely cottage! She said it was too German, too luxurious. Can you believe that? My bedroom, my garden, my privacy, all gone."

Henry gestured for me to be quieter. I kept to a whisper, a very loud one, as we climbed the stairs. "She made me destroy everything. Your letters, your photograph. Remember the one you had taken in Treptower Park? Where you pretended to look so serious? It's gone. I burned it. I don't have a picture of you anymore."

"You don't need one. I'm here."

In the flat, I threw myself onto his sofa and kicked off my shoes. The sitting room was just like I'd left it last week, the same Persian carpet, the sheers on the windows, the utility chair, Henry's favorite; it was arm's length from the bottles on the sideboard. My muscles unwound for the first time since Vera bludgeoned her way into my life. Henry stooped at his record collection, walking his fingers through the covers. He selected one and slid the record out of its sleeve, handling it so carefully, I smiled for the first time in days. He put on the record and waited, his hands on the console until the music started. A trumpet, drums, a gentle piano, and then the smooth, warm tones of Billie Holiday.

"I Gotta Right to Sing the Blues," Henry said, fetching the brandy bottle and two glasses and sitting down on the floor beside the sofa. "I've listened to it over and over since I got your note. Billie has kept me from invading the Soviet Sector with a jeep and my Browning."

I reached for him. "I'm so glad to see you, Henry."

After a long kiss, he poured the brandy. "You're in a barracks now?"

"There's a guard post and a perimeter fence and floodlights. I didn't sleep at all last night. I didn't know if I should come."

"Was it hard to get out today?"

"The guard doesn't like me. I humiliated him in front of the German workers, including the man who delivered the message to you. The same guard was on duty this morning at the gate. He saw I'm dressed in civilian and said, 'Off to see your man, are you?' He'll note it in his book, that I saw a man today. Did I tell you I'm sharing a room with Vera?"

He drained his glass and sat on the floor in front of the sofa. "What do you need from me, Mouse? How can I help you?"

"I don't know. I don't think you can. Vera is . . ." I groped for the English word. ". . . untouchable."

"Nobody is untouchable."

"She's MGB. The MGB is always right. She's a party member. The party is always right."

"You believe that?"

"No. I . . . Maybe I used to. Before the war." I slid off the sofa onto the carpet beside him. We'd never talked about this kind of thing, what we believed, the values we lived by. These things never seemed to matter as long as we never let the world into the apartment.

But it was here now. The anxiety I'd felt for days was still brewing in my stomach. Vera wanted me to get information from him and deliver it to a drop-off point on the French–British Sector border. I was to do this by ten that evening at the latest and be back at the barracks by midnight. Vera would be at the gate to explain why I was out after curfew, though she'd taken the precaution to give me a pass and the evening's watchword for the checkpoints tightening around Karlshorst.

On the other side of the sitting room, near the French doors, was Henry's rolltop desk, open as usual, and full of papers, envelopes, a ruler, a cup of pencils. I was sure he'd worked that morning before I came. His favorite tea mug sat on a stack of files, and the ashtray overflowed with cigarette butts. He never talked about his work—I told Vera the truth about that—but he did work at home a lot more than he needed to. Now that I knew about Fern, I thought maybe he did it for the distraction. In the evenings, he didn't have time to think of me far away in my sector, or his ex-wife in England, or his poor lost daughter, or what he was ashamed of in himself.

He topped off my glass though I'd only had a sip so far. "What's your sister's next move?"

It was a strange question. "What do you mean?"

"She pulled you out of your cottage and made you destroy everything related to me. So she knows about us. She put you in the barracks with an informant at the gate but you still got out today. Does she know you're here?"

"I told her I wasn't going to stop seeing you." That was true, at least.

"We're violating your bloody fraternization laws. Why did she let you come?"

I took a big, burning swallow of brandy. Vera's talk of loyalty and duty and the new war was one thing, but her motives always went deeper. "When I was eight, a bit after my father died, our mother got us a cat. Nastya. She was gray and mangy and spat up a lot but I loved her. I was the one who took care of her, and she wouldn't listen to anyone but me. One day I was in our room in Moscow, and Vera came home. She told me, cool as can be, 'Masha, the cat's been run over by a cart.'"

Henry looked incensed, the same way he did when Nelson once caught a mouse on the boulevard.

"I ran outside and looked for her in the street. Nastya wasn't anywhere. There wasn't any blood on the pavement. So I went home and told Mama what happened. Just then, Vera walked in. With Nastya in her arms. 'Found her behind the bins,' she said. 'Sorry I was mistaken, Masha.' She kissed Nastya on the nose, handed her to me, and then gave me this *look*. Disappointed, like she was thinking: *Don't be such a gullible idiot, Masha, believing every word I say.* She started being like that after Papa died. Always testing me to see how tough I am, or how quick I can catch her out. I don't know."

The look on Henry's face hadn't changed. He was as disgusted as I still was about what Vera had done to me. "You see, Henry, that's how she is. Never what she seems. She let me come today to prove a point. She can take away what I love and then give it back so I know she can take it away again whenever she wants."

"There's no talking to someone like that."

"That's what I said. There's nothing we can do about her."

"Right. There's only one solution. Don't go back. Seek asylum in the British Sector."

I upset my glass onto my skirt and cried out.

"I could take you to Lancaster House right now and we'd have you out of Berlin and safe within a day," he said. "I'd flog half the government until you got a visa to Britain. You'd have to stay in Germany until then, in our zone, far away from here, in the West."

The West. I fetched a tea towel from the kitchen and went back to him, dabbing at the wet spot on my skirt. "Do you know what you're asking me?"

"I do. Marya." He cupped my face in his hands. "When you get to England, we'll live in the country. I'll find you a new cottage. You'll be safe."

"Henry, it's not possible. Your men would send me back. People caught fleeing to the West are punished. Punished terribly."

"We don't refuse anyone asking for asylum. Nobody would send you back, and if they tried, they'd have to get through me first."

"If it did work, I would be an exile. My people would call me a traitor."

"Let them. You'll be gone."

"What about my family? My mother and little sister could be questioned or arrested because of me. They could lose their home and jobs because they have a traitor in the family. I won't put them in that situation."

"What choice do you have? Are you going to do nothing? Let Vera play with your life?"

"I don't know." I threw the towel hard at the floor. "I never know what to do with her."

"Come with me and problem solved. You have the chance. Right now."

"I can't!"

Henry gave me an angry look, then stalked to the French doors, threw them open, and went onto the balcony. I couldn't leave things like that. He needed to understand. I stepped around our lounge chairs and the flowerpots and joined him at the railing. The balconies were still dripping on the boulevard, the paths empty and spotted with puddles.

"You're offering me a wonderful thing, Henry. A wonderful, generous thing, and I thank you. But I can't accept it. The consequences are too severe for too many people. Please try to understand."

"If you disappear . . . if she makes you vanish, I'll come for you."

I didn't know how that was possible. But I put my hand on his and said, "Yes, I know you will."

I WOKE UP beside him, tangled in his thin summer blanket. White daylight still showed through the bedroom curtains. I went up on my elbow to see his alarm clock; just before nine. Gently, I kissed Henry's hair and then slid out of bed.

As long as possible, I delayed what I was about to do to him. I tidied the sofa cushions. I put away the record on the console. I rinsed out our glasses in the sink and added water to the violets on the windowsill. The quiet soothed me and made me anxious at the same time. If the neighbors played the radio or Nelson barked in the boulevard, I wouldn't have to worry about the crackle of paper removed from a file, the click of a shutter on the small camera in my purse.

Henry's rolltop desk was still open. I felt sick looking at it. But I had to be stronger than that. My loyalty was clear and it wasn't to Henry first and foremost. I closed my eyes. It wasn't. It wasn't.

Quickly, silently, I looked through his papers, picking through the files, opening and closing drawers. Vera had told me to find "anything with numbers," but most of Henry's papers had statistics I was too anxious to understand. Finally I settled on a ten-page report at the bottom of the last file. It was dated nine months ago and listed the personnel requirements for a twenty-four-hour supplying of the British Sector via air drop. I dug into my purse and fetched the camera Vera had given me the night before. She'd showed me the basics of how it worked. My hands were shaking, and I snapped photographs of several pages before I gave up. The images would never come out. They'd look like I'd taken them in a cart rumbling down a cobbled road.

I'd have to take the originals. I folded the report and tucked it into an envelope with the camera, then slipped the envelope into my purse. I couldn't bear to stay in the flat any longer, or even look at Henry. I tiptoed out and fled down the stairs.

The air still smelled of rain. The boulevard was empty, and I walked it in the twilight to the Charlottenburg Palace, scorched, riddled with shrapnel holes, but there was scaffolding, repairs to be done. I hoped it was true that almost any damage could be fixed.

Vera had told me it would take about an hour to get to the drop-off on the north side of the Berlin-Spandau Canal, but I was late and double-marched as much as I could, following the directions she'd given me. My muscles were heavy and liquid at the same time, fighting me as I crossed the Spree, carefully balancing on a temporary bridge over the murky water. In Moabit, I pressed on northeast and followed the tracks until the air changed, smelling of coal and fumes. I crossed the canal on the patched-up Föhrer Bridge and, as Vera instructed me, turned onto the Nordufer.

She had told me this was the French Sector, though if there was a sign saying so, I'd missed it. I left the street and slid down the grassy slope to the edge of the canal. Just as Vera had said, a foot-path stretched along the bank. I followed it thirty steps and found a fat stone where Vera said it would be. It was a romantic, secluded spot. This must've been where lovers watched the sun reflected off the surface of the canal or gazed at the dark brick of the port warehouses on the other side of the water. Vera was mocking me.

As agreed, I carefully pinned the envelope containing the camera—and the originals now—under the stone. Whenever Vera got them, I hoped Henry's papers would be illegible from the damp. Not my fault. My instructions were to go directly back to Karlshorst, but I wanted to know who was doing the pickup. I didn't think Vera would do it herself. She said she'd be waiting for me in Karlshorst. I also doubted she'd leave the envelope there for long. She'd said ten o'clock at the latest; my watch read five after.

I scrambled up the slope and tucked myself between two bushes on the roadside. From here I had a good view of the drop-off spot while staying hidden.

Five minutes passed. Ten more. At half past, my skirt was soaked from kneeling in the bushes and I was beginning to think the courier had come and gone empty-handed before I got there.

When the last daylight was only a glow on the horizon, I saw a little girl in a rain cape picking weed flowers along the edge of the water. She was maybe seven, her hair in two brown braids under a spotted rain cap. She stopped at the stone and plucked the envelope as if it was a flower like the others.

"Hey!" I called.

She turned to me, and something about her face, her eyes . . . I'd seen her before. I was sure of it. "Please, little one, put that down. It's not yours."

The girl dashed off. My shock vanished and I took off after her. Up the slope to the road, a long gentle curve with the canal on one side, and houses on the other. I almost had her. I reached out for the end of her cape, tripped on the pavement, and slowed. She darted across a small intersection to the building on the corner.

Men and women were mingling outside, smoking and talking in German. There was the faint sound of music. I supposed it was a bar, the patrons out for fresh air and space. People parted for the girl. One called, "Hey there, Greta, slow down!"

That voice.

It couldn't be.

The girl Greta flew into the arms of a man who'd been smoking near the wall. He picked her up and swung her around and then hugged her on his hip. She gave him my envelope, twisted in his arms, and pointed at me. He stepped away from the crowd for a better look, and the glow from the nearby window illuminated his face.

Felix.

It was like we weren't in Berlin at all. The two of us were back in the war, on the front outside Moscow on a road packed with frozen snow. The air crackled when I breathed. It hurt my chest.

Felix looked older, tired. His face—I'd never forget it, that brittle, intense look as he stared at me, as surprised as I was. It shocked me to see him in a civilian suit and hat, not his filthy Wehrmacht uniform. It seemed all wrong, like I was seeing his twin.

His face changed, a spark of something I remembered from the war, his fingers touching his forehead in a salute. Greta spoke in his ear, and he turned back to her, softening instantly. I realized who the girl was—his daughter—and where I'd seen her, in a photograph I'd confiscated from him five years ago.

My envelope under his arm, Felix carried Greta through the crowd and into the bar. I stood rooted in the street, ignoring the people who stared at me in passing or stopped to ask if I needed help. I shook my head and dug his pfennig out of my purse. Felix was alive. He was as real as this coin. Over the years, I'd wondered where he was, if he'd survived the war, but I didn't really believe he had. At times, I'd hoped he hadn't. It would've been easier for me if he was gone and stayed a ghost who couldn't come into the world again to remind me that once, early in the war, while his countrymen brutalized my land and people, I had nearly forgotten what he was and who he fought for.

I started walking east toward the Soviet Sector, and the street seemed to turn into the snow-trampled track of a road west of Moscow. I could smell the cold again, feel it creeping through my clothes and under my skin. I was the girl I was in the war, barely eighteen, my lieutenant's pips fresh on my uniform. I was wandering village to village searching for my first posting, an intelligence unit somewhere in our line of defense against the fascist horde that had invaded my country. We were on the offensive now, pushing the enemy back, liberating land in hard fighting along a front that stretched from Finland to the Black Sea. What I saw on the way to my unit, as I passed through lands abandoned by the retreating German Army . . . It wasn't war. What was the strategic value of the bodies I saw piled in a windowless room? The weeping girls running to us in the snow? The poster that said *The Russians must die so we may live* that I tore from a wall and threw into the bonfire in the square? I moved on, another village, rubble, men hanging from a makeshift gallows. I didn't know where Yuri was fighting and I forced myself to examine every face. My brother wasn't there, but these were someone's brothers, someone's sons or sweethearts or fathers. When I found the village where my unit was stationed on the old road to Smolensk, I was wounded to the soul by the barbarity and viciousness of the same people who had given the world Goethe and the Ninth Symphony.

The village had been wiped out by the Germans, the log cabins that survived scorched and without rooves. Villagers were straggling in from the fields and forests, the ones who'd survived, old people, children. Everywhere our soldiers took them in tenderly and cared for them as best they could, sharing their rations and fires. I found a soldier gleefully ripping down a German sign that said "Moscow" with an arrow. "They won't be needing this anymore," he said, grinning, and I felt a little better. We had the enemy on the run. This was a righteous war, and we would win it. I asked him about my unit, and he pointed to the edge of the village, where a plywood hut on wheels sat on the side of the road. A major was leaning against the wall smoking a cigar, and a young man I later learned was the cryptographer sat in the open doorway with a book on his lap. That was my unit.

Worn and frozen from my trek to the front, I presented my orders to the major. He lifted the flaps of my fur hat and said, "My God, they're sending us little girls."

I showed him my certificate that proved I'd completed my training course as a military interpreter. It had been a three-month course completed in two, but the major didn't have to know that. "I'm eighteen and I speak fluent German."

The major looked skeptical. "Well, then. Welcome to the family, little sister." The soldiers called us this sometimes, the girls of the army, and I beamed with pride.

My primary work involved translations, including the interrogations of German prisoners of war. The new prisoner's personal effects would land with me: his letters home, his private diary scrawled in a damp notebook, his photographs with the fading pink edges. It was my job to examine each thing for clues as to what the enemy would be up to next.

My first prisoner came a day after I found my unit. I opened the door of the hut and stepped back in the blast of frozen air. The guard said, "A squealer for you, little sister. Caught him up the road giving cover while those bastards retreated." He hauled the German over the threshold and passed me his personal effects. We called the men we captured squealers, for obvious reasons. I hated the term. It made me wonder what they called us.

The German stayed half-hunched, staring at nothing, his eyes painfully wide. I examined his Soldbuch, learned he was Felix Markow, a simple soldier, age twenty-three. In his photograph, he was young and handsome, a spark of mischief in his eyes. This man cringing in front of me had aged ten years. His milky skin stretched over the bones of his face. Slowly, he unwound the scrap of wool he'd been wearing over his cap and under his chin. His hair was dark with grime.

We were alone in the hut. This German soldier was my prisoner, mine alone, and in my heart and mind I saw the ruins of our towns and villages, the people who suffered though they'd done the Germans no wrong. I shouted at him in his language, "Did you do those things? Those terrible crimes? Did you?"

The shock in Felix's eyes cleared. He looked at me, terror rushing in, and I was delighted to see it.

"Did you burn down a church with the people sheltering inside? Did you hang boys? Did you violate girls? Did you drive grandmothers into the forest to starve? Did you?"

Felix gasped, tears rolling down his face. That made me angrier than I already was. What right did he have to cry?

"You're weeping because you're caught, because you can't commit your filthy crimes anymore. Ha! This is how an Übermensch acts when he's captured? Some superman you are. You have no dignity. No decency. *Barbarian*."

Head bowed, he gritted his teeth, tears cutting rivulets through the dirt on his face. Only he knew deep in his heart what unspeakable acts he had committed in the name of his army and country. I was accusing him in his language and he couldn't escape. He couldn't pretend he didn't understand.

Remembering I was a Red Army officer now, I pulled myself together. "I am Lieutenant Nikonova." I gestured at the crate next to my footlocker. "Sit down. I'll get you a tea."

I didn't know what else to do with him. The major and the cryptographer weren't back yet. I had to do something to bridge the time until an officer from the communications point came to begin the interrogation. I wasn't authorized to interrogate prisoners myself.

I gave him the tea. His eyes were tightly shut and his hands shook so hard, the liquid spilled onto his torn mittens. His struggle to control himself cracked something in my heart. "Drink," I said more harshly than I felt.

Felix drained the cup on command, and I took it from his hands as if he were a child. My army training had been a complete failure. I could speak the language, but no one had prepared me for the violence of the front, or for this, the deep waves of pity that were rolling through me. Pity for the enemy. How could that be? I gnashed my teeth, I wrestled with my own heart, wanting this feeling to be gone. This was war and he was the enemy; I'd seen what they'd done. They—this man—didn't deserve the tiniest jot of sympathy from me. But as much as I tried to push it down inside of me, it rose back up. No one had told me what to do when a man stood in front of me with no defenses left. For him, the war was over and maybe his life. Everything he'd known, everything he'd hoped and wished for, lay in ruins at his feet. It was my duty to harden my heart to this, but how?

I sat beside Felix and made a decision that would change how I looked at the war and the enemy as a whole. I would not forget that he was a human being even if he was a German. The men and boys of his army shivered in the cold like we did. They were hungry like we were. They wanted to go home too. It was easy to hate a whole country and its army, but I couldn't find it in my heart to hate one man sitting beside me. I would be better than their hate, better than our anger. I would try.

NO ONE CAME to process the prisoner Felix Markow, and since the major jokingly blamed me for Felix being there, he declared him my responsibility. As I stood in the snow with a pistol I couldn't use while wearing my thick mittens, Felix constructed a kind of dugout near our hut. The ground was frozen and could be moved only by blasting, so he had to form his shelter out of snow he rubbed into smooth blocks. The result was his igloo, as he called it, and he tried to insulate it with rubbish from the village, boards scavenged from the cabins his army, or maybe he himself, had destroyed.

As his guard, I followed him around with the gun pointing in his general direction and didn't interfere when one of our soldiers cursed him, or a grandmother, with tears in her eyes, asked him, "Why? Why did you do this?" while crossing herself and casting her eyes to heaven. The children threw icy snowballs at him, which thumped his coat and exploded. He let out a theatrical gasp, spinning around, clutching his heart, the children screeching with laughter. He staggered between the ruins of the cabins, under attack by the children, and finally sank to his knees, keeling into the snow as if he were in a comic opera. By the end, even I was laughing. As he climbed to his feet brushing his coat, he caught my eye. His face bloomed with happiness, and I quickly turned away.

After that, the village put him to work. We had much to do rebuilding the cabins and mending the walls. The worst jobs, those involving dead bodies or cleaning latrines, were left to Felix. By the third day, I didn't follow him around anymore; the whole village knew who he was. They referred to him as Masha's German. "Masha's German, come dig out this hole," or "Masha's German, go secure that roof." He scurried to obey, his face concentrating on the instructions shouted or spat at him in a language he didn't understand. I began to call him "my German," and when he wasn't working for others, he became something of a valet who would get my tea or clean my boots. I shared my ration with him, and we sat on my footlocker in the hut, eating in silence.

The third night, I kept watch by his igloo. He curled himself into a ball in the ice, and I noticed the cruel reality that if he got any closer to the little fire I'd built, his shelter would melt. He lay, his cheek on his hands, the firelight reflected in his eyes until I said, "You can sit by the fire for a while if you want."

He crawled out of his igloo, stretching his mittens toward the fire, and his leather boots, sprouting with the newspaper he stuffed in them for insulation. "Thank you, Fräulein Lieutenant." I didn't see his smile behind the scarf, but his eyes changed shape, and I grew warm. To fight it, I looked past the fire at the dark shapes of the ruined village, the destruction I had seen since I'd come to the front. "Why do you want to destroy us like this? Why do you think we're less human than you when we've created the greatest art, literature, and music of all time?"

Felix looked confused in the firelight. "I don't think you're less human than me. But we did have Beethoven and Bach."

"Yes, but we have Tchaikovsky and Prokofiev. And Shostakovich."

"Do we get to claim Mozart?" He shook his head. "How about literature—"

"Ah, literature." I gestured. "You have no chance against us."

"Try me. Goethe, Schiller, Brecht, Lessing, Heine." Quieter, "Rilke."

"Tolstoy, Dostoevsky, Pushkin, Gorky, Akhmatova—"

"Marx. Engels."

That was a low blow. I scooted around the fire closer to him. "Lenin. Krupskaya. Stalin."

"Kant, Heidegger, Schrödinger."

"Herzen."

"Sounds German to me."

I was about to burst. "Art, then: Vasnetsov, Serov, Kandinsky, Chagall."

"I'm pretty sure some of them lived in Germany. Dürer, Dix, Klee—"

"Ach!" I was angry, or trying to be, but we were both shaking with laughter. I didn't expect a conversation with my German prisoner to be fun. "Beethoven's Ninth is magnificent," I said. "I heard a recording once. My mother dreamed of playing it. She plays the oboe."

"My mother played the violin."

"Really?" This excited me, as if Felix and I were related. "Mama tried to teach me to play but I'm a butterfingers. Did your mother teach you?"

"She died when I was little. I mostly remember her singing. Do you know any German songs?"

"When I was small, Old Rosa—she was the neighbor who first taught me German—she sang lullabies. *Alle meine Entchen . . .*" Felix joined in, and we sang the simple little song about ducklings on a lake. By the end, we were laughing again.

"Did she teach you 'Thoughts Are Free'?" Felix asked. "It's a hundred years old almost, from our revolution."

Ah, I remembered something about that, a German revolution in 1848—failed, of course—but I couldn't fault a people for trying. I had learned about it briefly in school in relation to Marx's *Communist Manifesto*, published shortly before people across Europe erupted against tyranny a century ago. Felix spoke with such longing of this revolution that I felt akin to him.

"You're a revolutionary," I said with pleasure. "Are you a communist?"

"Are communists free?"

The question troubled me; it made me think of the NKVD coming to arrest my dead father, and I shot back, "Are you a Nazi?"

"Of course not, I'm from Wedding!" He sounded genuinely offended. He had to explain that his district of Berlin had been a socialist stronghold, and for years, the Nazis didn't trust themselves to go there without getting a beating from the workingmen who organized against them and the police, fighting bloody battles when he was a boy.

"But you serve in their army," I said, trying to understand. "Why?"

"I was drafted. Nobody asked me if I wanted to be here."

"Why didn't you say no?"

"You think the swine running my country take no for an answer? I decided to take my chances in the army, but that doesn't make me a Nazi. It makes me a damn fool and maybe a coward, but not a Nazi."

His argument wasn't quite convincing. "Then you are a socialist?"

"Look, don't try to label me this or that. I don't want people shoving their beliefs on me anymore. I can think for myself."

"You must believe in something. You're not alone on a desert island. If you want to live, you must dedicate yourself to your society and work for it with your whole heart." This was a basic discussion among us at school, the loneliness of the person who belongs to no society, who is an outcast from her own people. It made me desolate to even think about living that way. Maybe because he was a prisoner, Felix was rejecting his society and clung to what was eternal—his culture, its art, music, and literature—what would live long after we crushed Nazi Germany with our righteous fury.

"The song," he said gruffly. Pulling his scarf under his chin, he cleared his throat and began to sing: *Our thoughts are free, though men imprison us. Though they stop our mouths and take our voices, our thoughts are free.*

11

Vera

Testimony for Chairman A. Cheptsov
Military Collegium of the Supreme Court of the USSR
Moscow, 28 February–3 June 1956

[RECORDING]

Since learning of Marya's claim that she spied on the British national Henry Barrow, I've set myself the task to find out if she was telling Gusev the truth in her interrogation. So far, Ivanov has failed to find any evidence she was authorized by our security organs to act as an operative in Berlin. If she did, it was deeply secret. To test her claims, I need intel that links her to Barrow and to us, and for that, I need access to the secret holdings of the Central State Archives.

I'd hoped this task would be easier in the slightly more open environment in Moscow since Khrushchev's speech encouraged us to talk about the wrongs of the past. However, every request I've made to access files in the secret archives has been rejected. Ivanov is doing what he can with the KGB archivists, but we both sense resistance growing around us, the old wall of silence we were accustomed to under Stalin. I need to tap an ally with more influence than we have. I may work at the Kremlin, but only as a functionary; I have very little power outside of my sphere. After careful consideration, I decide to send an invitation for tea to Yekaterina Furtseva, first secretary of the Moscow Party, secretary in the Central Committee, candidate member of the Presidium, and the most powerful woman in the country. Because of the KGB listening devices, my apartment in the Kotelnicheskaya Embankment is out of the question. I propose to have the tea at my mother's apartment in Arbat Street. I'm delighted when Furtseva accepts, and that afternoon, I rush to my mother's to help prepare.

We grew up in Arbat Street, Marya and I, and as I climb the shabby staircase in our building, I feel her all around me. I remember her chubby hand on the railing when she was a toddler learning to take each stair one by one. I still see her proudly showing me how she could reach the doorknob and open the door of our apartment all by herself.

From the hallway, I hear the high, lilting tones of Mother's oboe. From the dreamy melody, I know she is alone and not practicing any particular piece but is playing whatever music comes into her head. As she grows older, this music has become more tense and brooding. It's a long way from her glorious days at the Moscow Conservatory, and something in the music makes it clear that she knows it.

Carrying a parcel of delicacies for Furtseva, I enter the living room quietly. Mother is in her chair at the wall, back straight, eyes closed. I set the parcel in the kitchen and return stomping and scraping my shoes on the floor. Her music cuts off, and she smiles.

"Sneaking around, Vera?"

Mother can't be fooled. She knows us by our footfalls now. I hug her and kiss her on the cheek.

"That sounded like Shostakovich."

"No, no, it was nothing. A ghost in my head. Is it already time? Is our guest here yet? I'll make the tea."

Mother rises slowly, moves directly to the stand at the wall where she stows her oboe, then crosses into the kitchen. She never quite recovered from the war and the loss of two of her four children: Yuri's death, and Marya's arrest. She's become a shriveled woman, the bones of her wrists jutting out of her sleeves as she fills the kettle. I should make the tea myself, but I allow her to do what she can for me. There isn't much anymore, and I know it pains her.

As she takes down the dishes, I lay out the food and then go back into the living room to look at the photographs on the wall. An old hazy image of my father as a fit young man in a welder's leather overalls, a clear image of Yuri in his Red Army uniform looking dashing and afraid to die. Here at home, I can still feel him too. He'd be busy repairing the splintered wood of the windowsill or the wiring of the ceiling lamp. I believe Mother doesn't allow these repairs because they remind her of the Yuri we knew, not the soldier who died at Kharkov, his tank in flames.

I skip the photographs of me and find Nina as a girl grinning as she forks summer hay. My youngest sister is very much like Marya in the sense that she can find her happiness anywhere. She is a technician in a hospital laboratory and is getting married later in the year. Her fiancé is an engineer and a quiet man who seems devoted to her. After the wedding, they'll live with Mother in this apartment, and I'm grateful for that. Life with me and Nikolai wouldn't suit Mother at all, no matter how well appointed our apartment is.

Missing from the photos on the wall is Marya. It was a long, old, and shameful tradition to destroy the photographs of people arrested and convicted of treason. In my time with the courts, families had begged us for photographs from the files because they had forgotten what their loved ones looked like.

"You're quiet," Mother calls from the kitchen as she sets the glasses on the table. "Do you have news of Marya?"

Mother's intuition has always surprised me. I go to the table and help set out the spoons. "I was wondering if you have a photograph of her somewhere."

"What good is a photograph to me?" She's holding on to the back of a chair, her face turned toward the sound of the water boiling. She doesn't bother to wear her glasses anymore. They don't help, and none of the eye specialists I've sent her to have done any good. "You told me to destroy her pictures."

"Yes, it was safest, but—"

"You told me to do it, Vera. I did what you said."

"I thought maybe you kept one. Just one."

Mother twists toward my voice, her face furious, and then she stomps out of the kitchen. I take the kettle off the burner and find Mother in the living room again, sitting in her chair, her head tilted down to the photograph in her lap. Her doctors told me it's impossible for her to see anything but shifts in light and darkness. But she sees my sister in that photograph, Marya in her Red Army uniform about to be sent to war. She's eighteen, a proud little thing beaming at the camera, ready for adventure.

"My lost girl," Mother says, stroking the photo. "My poor Masha. When she was little, she would lean her ear to my back as I played so she would hear the music in my chest. Remember? Later she told me this was why she learned languages so well. Language is music, and she first heard it here"—Mother taps her blouse at her chest—"with me."

I kneel by her chair and tell her what I never intended to say, but I can't keep silent when I see how much she has been suffering in secret. "I'm going to get her back, Mamochka. I'm going to try, though Nikolai is against it. Don't tell anyone. Not even Nina. I don't want her to get her hopes up."

"You have that much power now? You're going to make Masha not a traitor? Not a foreign spy? All these years, you said she was. Now she isn't?"

"That's what I'm trying to find out. The truth."

"I don't need the truth. I need my daughter back. How will you bring her back? What will she be like when she comes home?"

"Please don't cry, Mama." I stroke her hair and face but the tears flow silently down her cheeks. I shouldn't have told her. I should have kept this hope to myself. I must remember: maybe my sister is guilty and there's nothing I can do.

When Yekaterina Furtseva arrives, my mother welcomes her dry-eyed and smiling, hospitality taking precedence over her sorrow.

"So this is where you grew up, Vera Ilyanovna," Furtseva says, appreciating my proletarian origins for the first time. She has brought a plate wrapped in a towel, pastries, I see as I add her offering to the food on the kitchen table.

My mother serves the tea and our conversation is light, about the weather and food and fashion. When we've had our fill of tea and chitchat, Mother turns her unfocused gaze on Furtseva. "I'm tired. Am I very rude if I leave you two alone so I can rest?"

I get up to help her. "I'll take you to your room, Mother."

"I'm blind, not infirm, Vera, I know the way." She says her goodbyes to Furtseva and leaves us alone.

I drop into my chair and let out a long sigh. "I need vodka. Care to join me, Yekaterina Alexeyevna?"

"I'd never refuse your hospitality."

I take down the bottle and two glasses. Furtseva is nearly a decade older than me, from a humble family, and has risen from being a weaver at a factory to the very center of our government. To me, she's the model of the Soviet woman with intelligence, drive, and ambition, and I admire her greatly. After a quick toast and a first drink, I tell her about my sister's case and what I've been doing to gather facts about her past that have been forgotten or hidden. "I was hoping you could help me."

Furtseva looks puzzled. "I don't know what I can do about any of this. It's an issue for the court and state security, nothing to do with me."

"I think there might be evidence in the secret archives to prove what my sister was really doing in Berlin. I've made several requests for access, and they've been ignored. It's like banging on a door that never opens. An archive can be as impenetrable as a fortress. But I doubt they'd deny a request from you. You're a candidate to the Presidium," I say, reminding her of the power Khrushchev has recently given her. "The archivists won't say no if you demand full access to all records on my behalf."

Furtseva toys with her glass. "Have you asked your husband to try helping you with this?"

"He thinks I shouldn't be doing any of it. He doesn't want me poking around in the past."

"He might be right, you know. It might be better if you wait to see how the political situation develops. If things go the way Khrushchev hopes, there might be a general amnesty for political prisoners at some point."

"I've been waiting to see how the political situation develops for nine years. Now is my chance to help Marya if I can. In his speech, Khrushchev challenged us to look honestly at the past no matter how painful it is. He's opened a door."

"He opened a door and then tossed a grenade through it. Do you know what's been happening out there? Across the country, and in Poland?"

Of course I know, but maybe she has heard interesting tidbits that haven't reached me. "Some. The pro-Stalin protests in Georgia. And Bierut's death."

The Polish leader Bierut had been in Moscow for medical treatment when he heard about Khrushchev's demolition of the memory of Stalin at the secret session of the Twentieth Party Congress. Bierut read a copy of the speech and then promptly died of a heart attack. Polish Communist Party meetings turned into anti-Soviet protests that a visit from Khrushchev couldn't stop.

"Things are brewing here at home too," Furtseva says. "We have reports of people tearing down busts of Stalin or defacing his portraits and monuments. People are condemning him at Komsomol meetings. Stalin still has plenty of support, so this unrest is starting to split our own ranks. Foreign policy is your husband's department, not mine. He knows the details. I only know that subversive imperialist elements are using Khrushchev's critique of Stalin to stir up trouble and drive a wedge between communist countries. The Western imperialists want to destroy us one by one. If they succeed, we'll lose Poland, Hungary, and maybe even all that we gained after the war."

I push my glass away. My head is swimming. "I imagine Khrushchev is being pressured to soften his position on Stalin so that people stop questioning Soviet power."

"This is a very dangerous time, Vera Ilyanovna."

"Times of change always are."

"We need to know who our friends are. Khrushchev needs to know."

The kitchen is quiet. Furtseva is a protégée of Khrushchev, and it's possible what I say here will reach his ears.

"I assure you, we stand beside you and Khrushchev. My husband is devoted to him even if he doesn't make a ridiculous show of it like Shepilov does." Dmitri Shepilov is another of Khrushchev's protégés and has his eye on the top post at the Foreign Ministry if Khrushchev ever moves to take it away from Molotov. Nikolai also wants to be foreign minister, but his chances are slimmer. Like Furtseva, Shepilov has just been appointed a candidate to the Presidium, a more powerful position than Nikolai's at the Ministry. When Khrushchev needs someone to confirm what he's saying, Shepilov is known for jumping out of his chair and crying, "Just so, Nikita Sergeyevich!" It's revolting.

"Khrushchev's true friends need to be vigilant," Furtseva says. "Marshal Zhukov is one of us. And Leonid Brezhnev. We have to watch Khrushchev's back. Stalin's men are still very much among us, and they won't let him die so easily."

I'm proud to belong to any circle that includes Zhukov, the hero of the war. I don't know Brezhnev well enough to gauge him, but if he stands with Khrushchev's friends against the pro-Stalinists, I'm with him. This conversation with Furtseva may be a way to help repair my rift with Nikolai by boosting his profile in the Presidium. I assure her again that my husband and I stand ready to support Khrushchev any way we can in these troubling times.

Furtseva looks content and pours more vodka. "That's settled, then. I'm always happy to help a true friend, Vera Ilyanovna. Give me a little time and you should have access to any information you need in any archive in Moscow."

We return to the Kremlin together and part cordially in front of government staff, who now know that an alliance has been forged between us. I'm so pleased with myself that I consider putting a call through to Nikolai at the Foreign Ministry but decide to wait to tell him of developments when he comes home.

He arrives late, close to midnight, shedding his polished veneer the moment he comes in unbuttoning his jacket. At a glance, I know he's heard of my new relationship with Furtseva; survival in the government depends on everyone knowing the factions that rise and fall at every opportunity. I'm sitting up in bed sewing a hole in my stocking, and he circles to my side to sit by the basket. "So we're in Furtseva's camp now, are we?"

"Khrushchev's camp. The anti-Stalinists." I tell him about the tea at my mother's and what a clear alliance with Furtseva could do for our futures. It might not get Nikolai the Foreign Ministry right away, but it's best to plot strategy for the long term.

He nods and rubs his eyes. "Please tell me you didn't bring up Marya at that tea."

"Do you think it'd be better if one of our strongest allies doesn't know about her? Of course I brought up Marya. Furtseva should know what she's getting in us."

"Marya is a liability, an excuse for Furtseva to turn on us one day and question our loyalties."

"Then it's even more important to clear my sister's name."

"And now your mother knows what you're doing?" he says, accusingly. He loves my mother more than his own. "You don't mind giving her false hope?"

"Real hope. I've found out that Marya might've been a—"

He gestures to stop me and gets up for the door. I'm suddenly angry. Nikolai should care about what I've discovered. If he loves me, he must feel something for my sister, his sister-in-law. I call after him, "It couldn't hurt to choose hope, Kolya!" But he's already left, banging the bedroom door behind him.

Within days, Ivanov calls to tell me the KGB archives are open to me. I begin to spend as much time as I can in the central archives, assigning archivists to look for old intelligence files related to Marya, Henry Barrow, or his department of the British military government.

It's exhausting work, and I'd get nowhere without the archivist Burakova. She has worked here for twenty years and knows every dark corner of her collections. She proudly explains to me the intricacies of the archival system, and I endure this minutiae out of admiration for her expertise. We are soon working well in a rhythm several evenings a week, the only time I can spare from the Kremlin, where I've been gathering reports from East German leaders who are anxious about Khrushchev's criticism of Stalin and what it means for Soviet power. It's a relief to concentrate on something else.

Burakova brings an armful of files into the little room I'm using and places them carefully on the desk.

"How much more are there?" I ask, stretching my arms over my head. I'm drowning in files. I can hardly keep up.

"As you requested, these are the files related to intelligence gathered from British military government headquarters in Berlin from fall 1946 up to July 1947."

I nod, though I'm not happy with the broad parameters of the search. I could be here months looking for a hint, some chain of evidence from Marya to intelligence in our possession. If there are documents from Henry Barrow or his office somewhere in these stacks, and they link to Marya as the source, that would be proof that she told the truth to the MGB after her arrest. It would prove she was spying *on* Barrow, not *for* him.

But if I find nothing, I'll have to admit that Valentin Gusev may have been right. Marya had lied after her arrest, she'd never spied on Barrow, an act that would've shown her loyalty to us, not him, no matter how their relationship looked on the surface. I need to find something in this ocean of files. And I have to believe I'm not wasting my time.

I get up, stretching my legs, and take out a cigarette before I remember that Burakova has forbidden smoking in her archives. Frustrated, I go back to my desk. I should slog through all the files the archivist brings, but I'm not sure anymore if there's anything to find.

Unless . . .

I go into the hallway, calling for Burakova. "It's the wrong time frame," I tell her. "Maybe we're looking for documents filed under the wrong dates."

"We cross-reference documents in many ways besides dates, Vera Ilyanovna. The card system is very—"

"Yes, I'm sure, but maybe we'll move more efficiently if we search for intelligence with the same basic parameters but related to May 1948 through 1949."

I remind Burakova that this was the time we blockaded the city of Berlin. Barrow's work centered on contingency plans should the transportation routes be cut off to or from the city. In 1947 when he knew Marya, these were just scenarios. No one knew if the plans would ever be needed.

But they were. Almost a year after Marya's arrest, we closed off Berlin. This was in retaliation against the Western powers' attempt to wrest control of Germany using the capitalist means of the so-called Marshall Plan and a new western German currency. Our blockade dealt a heavy blow to their schemes, and they began to supply the city from the air in a strategy they called the Berlin Airlift.

At that moment, Barrow's scenarios became a reality, and extremely valuable intelligence for us. Even if it was gathered in

1947, maybe the information had been filed in the archives with other documents related to the Airlift a year later.

Burakova understands my explanation and gets to work. She even hails an assistant, who takes away the old records while Burakova wheels in a trolley and transfers new files to my desk. Energized again, I dig into the many documents related to those tense months in 1948 and 1949 when we all felt close to the new war with the West that none of us truly wanted but that Stalin had insisted was inevitable.

The pages begin to blur in my mind, and I nearly miss it, a scrawl of initials on the bottom of a typed page: HB.

I blink, look at it again, and I'm suddenly wide-awake. It's a document from the office of a General Halifax of British Headquarters, dated 1946. It outlines certain logistical needs should we close road and rail routes, cutting off the British Sector of Berlin from the British Zone of Germany in the west. I turn the page, the same initials, HB. There could certainly have been more than one man with those initials, but Henry Barrow worked in Halifax's office as an expert on logistics. It's enough for me to pick through the report and finally reach the end, where a hurried note added a few missing pieces of data. Signed, Capt. Henry Barrow.

I thump my fist on the desk in triumph. Finally—here is intelligence from Barrow in our possession. The question is: how did it get to us? I pore over the report closely to find the source of it. If Marya was an operative, she would've had a code name. After going through the report twice, I have to accept that no one had bothered to note down where we got it from. I toss it aside in disgust and continue picking through the file. But now I've hit a vein of gold, and a second report from Barrow is right there. I look through it, praying that whoever had sent it to the archive had been more thorough about where we got our intelligence.

At last, on a slip attached to the last page of the translation, I find a name.

Rheingold.

I sit back abruptly. I remember that code name and the agent behind it. But it's not Marya.

12
Marya

Berlin, 23 June 1947

Vera and an officer I'd never seen before were waiting for me at the perimeter of the Hirschfeld Barracks. It was after midnight. They sat on folding chairs outside the gate in the crisp white beam of a floodlight. It was strange to see my sister relaxed out in the open, her ankles crossed, a pile of spent cigarettes on the ground next to her. The officer passed her a bottle and she drank before passing it back. He leaned close to her and said something, and she burst out laughing. I didn't know if I'd ever seen her laugh like that. So free. Maybe the joke was on me. Tonight I'd stolen papers from Henry and delivered them, without knowing, to Felix Markow. Felix, of all people. That was Vera's joke all right.

When I was close enough to see his uniform, I saw that the officer was a colonel, rather young for the rank, another highflier like my sister.

"Ah, Masha, there you are. This is Nikolai Vasylyvich Koshkin, my colleague and friend—I hope I may call you that," Vera said. He nodded warmly. "He was kind enough to fill in for the political instructor at tonight's lecture," she said. "A pity you missed it. He spoke about the history of the Great Patriotic War. You would've appreciated it. I was telling him about your excellent war record."

I looked at her hard but kept my voice polite. "All I did was speak a little German."

"One of the most crucial skills of our time, as useful now as it was in the war," Koshkin said. "I hear you speak several languages?"

"Only German, English, a little French, and Polish."

"She has a gift," Vera said. "Her accent is impeccable, I hear. It's her ear for music. From our mother."

"We don't have enough personnel with your skills, Lieutenant. If you ever grow tired of working as an interpreter, come talk to me. I'd be happy to find you more rewarding work."

I had no idea what Koshkin meant by that. "What office do you work in, Colonel?"

"In Marshal Sokolovsky's office. My sphere isn't just Berlin, but all of Germany." He put on his cap. "I won't ask where you were so late after curfew," he said with a smile. "Officially, I don't approve. But then, the war did deplete our population. It's the duty of every Russian woman to repopulate the country." He said this turning to Vera. I saw the tiniest irritation in her face.

"My sister is very aware of all her duties," she said. "Thank you for waiting with me, Nikolai Vasylyvich."

Side by side, we watched him circle the perimeter to a dark car parked on the street. He rapped on the windshield, and a moment later, the engine started and the lights flashed on. After a last wave at us, he climbed into the back and was gone.

Vera and I passed the gate and entered the barracks. We went together down the silent hallways past open doors and empty rooms with no shades, the floodlights spilling onto bare floors. We'd been there a week and more women had come, but none moved into our hallway, not even the other officers. I began to guess why the rooms stayed empty. Vera didn't want to share a wall with anyone. Our room was at the very end of the hallway, on a corner, which meant we had two outer walls, thicker than the interior ones. In my cottage, Vera had said privacy was unnatural, unsoviet. But she made sure we had it here, a private room, a hallway all to ourselves, where no one could listen in and report our conversations.

In our room, I grabbed my night things, went to wash up, and returned to find her uncoiling her hair by the window. It had always been her one vanity, how fast and thick her honey-colored hair could grow. She began to brush it. "Nikolai is a very important man. If he's careful enough, he'll be in the politburo one day."

"You were flirting with him."

"It's to my advantage if he thinks that."

"How? He wants us to have Soviet babies. It's our duty as women."

"It is." She continued brushing, and her hair fell luxuriously over her shoulder.

"You're joking. I've never seen you with a man. I don't think you like men."

"I'm not like you, Masha. I don't need love."

"Everyone needs love."

"Romantic love, I mean. You're soft-hearted and always were. You can't imagine that there are people who are simply not interested."

"No sex, then?" I asked brutally. I was a disgraced woman for being with Henry when we weren't married. Mama would weep if she knew.

"Sex is just an itch to scratch now and then. Or a means to an end. You know that as well as I do."

I snatched the brush from her hand. "Do you want to know what sex with Henry is like?"

"Not particularly."

"It's like dissolving in champagne."

"Drowning, then? Doesn't sound very pleasant to me."

I was done playing this game. "I stole from him tonight, Vera. Don't tell me that was a great service to the Motherland. It was wrong."

"Everyone must make sacrifices for the greater good."

I threw her brush aside. "And you had to bring Felix into it, didn't you? To torment me."

"Believe it or not, I'm not interested in tormenting you."

"Then why did you do it? Why Felix?"

Vera bent stiffly to reach her brush on the floor and sat down to finish her hair. "Think about it, Masha. Why would I bring that particular German into this operation? Hmm? Don't tell me you're one of those people who pretends to forget what happened to them in the war."

I flung myself onto my bed and drew up my knees. Of course I hadn't forgotten, it was just that I didn't want to remember the details of Felix's last hours with my unit. It was his sixth day as my prisoner, and artillery was booming in the distance. The village buzzed all around us, the quiet days over, the war rushing in on us again. The refugees trickling in from farther west reported that the Germans were trying to retake the land they'd abandoned. Apparently, their Führer was livid about the German retreat and had ordered an about-face. Victory, or don't come back.

We scurried around preparing for a fresh attack. I was sorry to see our infantry march off, the motorized units roaring west, leaving so few of us in the village. We burned or packed up our papers and orders in case we had to move fast, either west or east. We weren't sure how it would go.

"What are you going to do with your German?" the major asked, gesturing at Felix. He'd been acting as my valet again, packing my few things into my rucksack. High over our heads, in the sky, was a whistling, and we all paused to listen, the detonation too far away to shake us. I was amazed at myself. I didn't tremble at the noise anymore. Felix was the same, watchful, ready to fight or flee. But he was my prisoner. I couldn't let him do either one.

"We could take him with us."

"Or send him to the rear," the major said. "Let them deal with him. We don't need an extra mouth to feed. Or we just shoot him."

"No! We can't be like them."

Felix must've sensed we were talking about him. He looked at me, and I said, "Come outside and pack your things." I picked up his personal effects, the ones I'd decided to give back to him, the photographs of his family, his lovely wife smiling into the camera. Another of her holding a wide-eyed toddler, his daughter Greta. He had a son, a few months old, but no photo of him yet. I'd seen the letter where his wife told him about the newborn. Felix had a life in Berlin I couldn't imagine.

Outside, the wind was beating the snow into crystals that stung my eyes. Blinking, I accompanied Felix to his igloo, where he tied up his eating utensils and a few other things into his blanket. A detonation rocked the ground, much closer, and we stumbled together. I wasn't sure if the ground had moved or if my fear had caught up with me.

"You all right?" Felix asked, his eyes concerned, the rest of his face muffled by his scarf, as mine was. He was shouting in the blowing wind and the increasing intensity of the guns.

"I'm fine."

"Got nothing to worry about. Those are our guns. We couldn't hit an elephant in a desert with those."

I appreciated him trying to help, but on my way to the front, I'd seen what his guns could do. "We'll be moving soon. You're coming with us. We won't hurt you. I won't let them." I made the decision right then, as I said the words.

He pulled the scarf from his mouth, his face unshaven and strafed with blowing snow. The warmth in his smile sent heat to my fingertips. "You're my good-luck charm, Fräulein Lieutenant. You—"

His gaze darted to the side as if spotting something behind me. He cried out just as I was pulled off my feet and then slammed into the snow. The crystals filled my nose and mouth, and I gasped at the pain of tiny, frozen cuts on my lips and face. I could barely breathe. Then I was flipped over, coughing, trying to blink the snow from my eyes. Loud cursing in German—two voices, Felix and . . . I didn't know who. I tried to get up and was pressed back into the snow, my pockets searched. Too late, I remembered my pistol. For the first time, I called him by his first name. "Felix!" I tried to roll over, hurt, offended he was doing this to me.

Another voice, a different German. "A woman. My very own hellcat."

"Leave her alone." That was Felix.

The other German grasped me by the hair, my fur hat gone, and yanked me to my feet. "She's our prisoner now."

Felix tried to get between us. "Kamarad, we'll be faster without her."

The soldier pulled me by the hair, and I stumbled, gasping in pain, behind him. "There's a group of us not a kilometer away."

"Where'd her gun go?" Felix asked.

"Here."

We were in the trees outside the village. No noise I made helped, no one could hear me. I struggled and kicked, my hair about to come loose from my scalp. And Felix? Felix was walking slightly behind us carrying my gun. I let out a shout of fury and tried to kick him. The man who held me shook me hard.

"Behave. We might be nice to you before we bury you in this fucking snow."

We'd talked about this, the women in my training course. If we were captured, what to do. Of course we would kill ourselves, and if possible, take as many Germans with us as we could. The theory had been clear but, now, how was I supposed to do it? I didn't have a convenient hand grenade in my pocket. And besides, I didn't want to die. I didn't want to be taken prisoner. What they did to women . . . I'd seen it. We all knew.

I went limp, forcing the German to shift how he held me, to hold me up by the arms, and in the small space he gave me, I pulled away just enough to plow, head-down, into his chest. It surprised him, this man I finally saw, identical to Felix, the same long coat white with ice, same dirty gray wool wrapped around his head. I saw only his nose and the crystalline blue of his eyes, wide with surprise and fury.

"Kamarad!" Felix called, and in the split second the man hesitated, I heard a sickening crack. The man dropped to the snow.

I reeled around. Felix held the gun by the barrel, heaving for breath. The man on the ground was only stunned; he began to move. Felix knelt and brought the grip down on him again. And again. Even as the blood splattered on the snow, I didn't understand what was happening. What Felix was doing, and why.

Finally, he dropped the gun in the snow. His face had gone still as if he weren't quite there. The man on the ground, the soldier, his comrade, didn't move. He was like the many men I'd seen on my way to my unit, sprawled and frozen in the roadways, in the fields, them and us. My stomach spasmed, and I had to swallow hard not to be sick.

"Felix."

He stayed kneeling beside his comrade, and I recognized the look on his face. It was just like when he was taken prisoner, the shock too deep to cope with. I knelt beside him and shook his arm. "Felix, come on. We have to go back."

He let me help him to his feet, and only then did he look directly at the man on the ground. Felix wavered, and I had to steady him by clutching his coat. "It's all right, Felix. It's all right."

He shook his head slowly. "God. God in heaven."

"Come." I got him to turn, and we limped, leaning on each other, back to the village.

We stayed awake all night, waiting for news, listening to the front, feeling it rumble under our feet and boom over our heads. The major allowed Felix to stay in our hut with us, in what little heat we had, as a reward for what he'd done for me. Even as the major had said this, he'd sounded puzzled, looking hard at Felix and then at me. I could hear him wondering, *Why did he kill his own man? Why did he become a traitor for you?* I asked myself the same things.

Morning came quietly, the village slowly waking up again, women fetching snow to melt, the old people coming out for air, the children scattering to see what they could find of the battle. The door of our hut opened suddenly, and at last, Captain Sergeyev from the communications point arrived in a blast of frozen wind, shaking in his thick coat like a bear. We scrambled to receive him. He was six days late, and we'd had no word he was coming today. The interrogation of Felix could finally start. Felix looked at me, his terror so fresh and obvious, I felt it in my chest.

"Not been any trouble, has he?" Sergeyev asked, pulling off his mittens. The major informed him what Felix had done, and we all trooped out to the body of the German in the snow, the officers admiring Felix's handiwork while Felix hung back, looking at the ground. After Sergeyev spoke to me, getting my testimony about the incident, he grinned and said, "If enough Germans brain each other, we'll win this by spring." He turned his attention to Felix.

All through the questioning, as I translated, Felix eyed me anxiously. This was the first time I experienced how dependent a prisoner was on me, his mouthpiece. He was thinking of me as someone who might plead for him and remind the captain to show mercy. He was a squealer again, speaking openly. Sergeyev made quick work of his questions, and then pulled on his fur hat.

Suddenly I realized—Felix was leaving now. He would be taken to the rear and processed and put in a camp for prisoners of war. He would go hungry or fall ill and die. Or he'd live and be sent east to work in a mine or a quarry. I couldn't see any of these things in his future. If he stayed a prisoner, he'd grow tired of living. He'd pine for freedom, that prize we'd come close to as we whispered together in the firelight. I couldn't send him to a life of humiliation, pain, or death. Not after what he'd done for me. These were the thoughts I had—my free thoughts—as Sergeyev searched for his mittens, and Felix looked from me to him and back again.

I told him in a whisper, "You'll be taken to the rear now."

"Are you coming too?"

He sounded like a boy, such impossible hope. He had to know it couldn't be. Sergeyev was talking to the major, who took cigarettes from his pocket. They lit up at the lamp and then stepped out of the hut. Felix and I were alone.

At the same moment, we grasped each other's hands and stumbled to the corner farthest from the door. "I'm not going," he said. He was almost hurting me, his fingers in mine. "You're my Glückspfennig. See?" He turned my palm over, pressed a dented coin into it, with a hole in the center. "My good-luck charm. We'll both get out of here without a scratch."

"There's nothing I can do."

"I want to stay here. I can work."

"It can't be done." I looked to the door. What could I do? "I can't help you escape or send you back to your lines."

"I don't want to go back. I want out, out of this damned war. I want to be free. Don't you?" He was mad with fright. I saw it in his eyes, and to see it was the sharpest pain I'd ever felt. "I'll do anything," he said. "Anything you want, my lucky pfennig, my dear Schwesterchen." It was the first time he'd called me little sister, what our soldiers called me. It made me flinch; he had no right. But then, I thought of Vera and had an idea. The tiniest chance.

He saw the change in my face, and he blazed with hope. "Marya?"

"There's something I can try. I don't know if it'll work—"

He pulled me close and kissed me. If the captain had come in at that moment, we would've both been shot. No man had ever kissed me before, and it was nothing like I'd imagined it, my tender girlish fantasies. The strength of his grip on my body, his hand on the back of my head, stunned me. I couldn't move. Everything in me sparked like it did when I heard the sirens or the roar of artillery. I wasn't scared or offended or angry. It was pure thrill.

But the shame soon rushed in. How could I do this while my people spilled their blood fighting his? How could I forget that my brother was out there somewhere, and Vera, and Moscow, my home, was still in danger? Disgusted with myself, I pushed Felix away, and we fell back from each other, breathing hard. I couldn't look at him. I scrambled to the door and out into the snow. The white light brought tears to my eyes. My last glimpse of Felix in the war was a washed-out figure in his long coat, his face turned toward me as they took him away.

After he was gone, I worked on the protocol of the interrogation, or at least, that's what I told the major. I made several false starts; I wasn't sure what I should do. My duty, of course. I tried, but the lucky pfennig was on the table next to my papers, and I found myself writing frantically to Vera. I wrote about how Wehrmacht soldier Felix Markow was taken away by Captain Sergeyev after six days with me in captivity. Markow, I wrote, has a burning hatred of the Nazis. He has a keen political sense. He's too intelligent to waste in a work crew or in a labor camp. Help him, I wrote. Is there better work for him, work he could do to defeat the fascists and support our side? He would do it to live, and out of his convictions, I assured her. He was ready to do anything. He'd even . . . I hesitated, then told the truth about what Felix had done for me. Captain Sergeyev had ordered us to keep the killing a secret in the village, but the major would include it in his confidential reports. The kiss, the warmth I still tasted on my lips—I could never let anyone else, certainly not Vera, know about that. It was the most shameful thing I'd ever done, and if I could have reversed time and made it not happen, I would have. But he had also saved my life. I had to try to save his.

I gave the note to a courier with instructions to find Vera wherever she was on the front.

As much as I tried, I never forgot Felix. No prisoner I ever saw after that was like him, but the ghost of him was there in how I treated them. Now and then, a prisoner seemed special, a little different. Maybe he was especially angry at the war, or his own side. Maybe his parents were in a Nazi camp because they were socialists. If this prisoner seemed alert, intelligent, impressionable,

I wrote a special note in the interrogation protocol that he might be a candidate for reeducation. I did this because of the response Vera had sent to my letter months after Felix was taken away. *Your German is an apt pupil. We request you send men to us at your discretion for special training.*

And I did.

VERA WAS FINISHED braiding her hair. She reclined on her bed and smiled at me. "Felix Markow is a reminder of the excellent intelligence work you did in the war. He is and has always been a tool or a weapon, nothing else. Think of him that way and you'll feel better about your new duties with Barrow."

"People aren't tools."

"Of course they are. What else are they good for?"

"Sometimes I think you try very hard not to be human."

"And I think you willfully misinterpret what I say. Being useful is a good thing, Masha. Markow could be dead under a sheet of ice in Siberia but he's here in Berlin, helping you in your duties. His usefulness saved his life as clearly as he saved yours."

"Did you threaten him to go along with this?"

She sighed and lit her good-night cigarette. "He doesn't need threats. He's ours to use as we see fit. Thanks to you."

"I'm not like you. I don't *use* people, Vera."

"Maybe we're more alike than you think."

I couldn't stand to breathe in her smoke and her smell any longer. I opened the door, then tipped my mattress, bedclothes and all, onto its side. I pulled it as well as I could out the door, heaving it back little by little, turning it in the hall until I got it through the doorway of the room two doors down. I didn't want to share even a wall with Vera. I let the mattress thump to the ground, then fetched the pillow and blanket that had slipped off.

Up on her elbow, Vera watched this calmly. "Good night, Masha. You did good work tonight."

I slammed her door and closed myself into the room I'd claimed. The walls were bare. There was no shade, no furniture, no light except the floodlight frosting the window. As I settled onto the mattress, a cold shiver ran through me. My new home was as lonely and bare as a prison cell.

13
Vera

Testimony for Chairman A. Cheptsov
Military Collegium of the Supreme Court of the USSR
Moscow, 28 February–3 June 1956

[RECORDING]

Rheingold, who delivered intelligence to us from Henry Barrow's office in Berlin, was the code name for one of our more talented and slippery German agents, Felix Markow. On the first page of his KGB file, there's a photograph of him at age twenty-three. I remember his face, its careful, controlled fury at the war perhaps, or at being captured and then recruited by Marya, who held him as a prisoner in early 1942 when she worked in military intelligence. I met him briefly in the war and had much to do with him in Berlin the summer Marya was arrested.

I browse his dossier to refresh my memory. He was born in his mother's native city of Koblenz, and as a boy was moved to Berlin, where he grew up in one of the city's socialist strongholds. His mother died when he was young. He married at nineteen, his wife several years older than him. At the time he was captured, he had two children.

Turning the page, I find his summary of his occupations before he began to work for us. Before the war, he'd been a professional vagabond, he claimed, starting apprenticeships in carpentry, ironwork, and other practical crafts only to break them off. He briefly attended university courses—unofficially, as he told it—favoring philosophy and history. He never attempted to study formally and he never attained a diploma or degree of any kind. This left him a man with a wide range of half-learned skills, an intellectual seeker without the discipline to finish what he started. His army service cured him of that. In the German Wehrmacht, he claimed he was competent and reliable but had no interest in dying for the Führer.

After his own account of his background, the file contains reports from his instructors about his training. This was an early phase of our efforts to recruit German prisoners of war, and so Markow received an eclectic and rushed education in the basics of codes and cyphers and other skills. His instructors were pleased with his abilities, especially his talent for memorizing facts quickly, but they were unsure of his loyalties. This was true of most of the Germans we recruited.

One instructor claimed he had an especially cordial relationship with Markow, who entrusted him with a message for Marya. The instructor agreed to send it to her wherever she was on the front, and Markow's note, which was, of course, never sent, is included in the file. It is faded and appears to have been scribbled in haste. I hold it under the lamp and decipher the odd German script.

My dear Glückspfennig, I'm still alive thanks to you. Take care of yourself. Good people need to live and put the world back together when this is all over. Maybe we'll see each other again in peace. Your Felix

Well, well. I sit back with a fresh cigarette, the note in my hand. He'd called her his dear lucky pfennig, a very sweet nickname. Endearing, but not necessarily unusual in her situation. In one of the letters she sent me during the war, Marya told me how some German prisoners had called her angel or sweetheart. They saw her, their interpreter, like wounded men see a pretty young nurse, as their link to mercy and hope. But "lucky" was an interesting thing for Markow to call her, considering the extreme act he performed for her when he was in her custody. When my sister was attacked by a German soldier, Markow killed him, his own comrade. This made him an even more interesting recruit to us than he would've otherwise been. I also have no doubt this made him all the more memorable—and perhaps trustworthy—to my sister.

With that history between them, the chance of Markow acquiring intelligence in Berlin from her British lover without her being involved was close to zero. Rheingold—Markow—must be the link between Marya and intelligence from Barrow's office in our possession. It can't possibly be coincidence. She must have been the source for the documents Markow gave us.

This proves she told Gusev the truth in her interrogation. She did spy on Barrow. She passed his secrets on to us, but not directly. She chose to use a German she knew from the war as a courier. But now the question is *why*? If she did this service for us, why was it a secret? Why didn't she give us the intelligence directly so that we knew the good she was doing? Why wait and tell us only *after* her arrest when she was too compromised for the MGB to believe her?

Your Felix. I have a feeling that endearment might matter after all. It troubles me deeply.

I return to the file. Markow's training ended in summer 1942, and he was released to make his way back to his own lines. This was a moment of great danger to him; many if not most turncoats gave themselves away and were shot by their own people. We received no word of him until half a year later from a contact in Ukraine. From there, we received reports about his army's movements and morale until the chaos of the last battles in 1945, when we lost contact.

We picked up his trail again in May 1945. As his army dissolved for good, he joined the soldiers who deserted their units and made their way back to their homes through the shattered remains of the Third Reich. Shortly after the German surrender, he surfaced in Berlin and found his family gone and his apartment occupied by Red Army personnel. Believing his family harmed, he seemed to have lost his composure. He would have been shot if an observant officer hadn't understood his complaints in broken Russian that he worked for us, had for years, and what did we do to his family? Markow was taken into custody and turned over to the local MGB, who quickly learned of the service he'd done for us in the war.

He then received additional, more thorough, training in skills that would serve him better in peacetime. He was such a good student that we released him once again to reunite with his wife and children. On the surface, he was a laborer working in reconstruction, but in secret, he performed much more valuable tasks for us. The file doesn't mention whether he continued to work for us for the money, out of idealism—or because we gave him no choice.

I close the file and get up to pry open a small panel of my window. The cool night air relieves the ache in my head. I've made progress, but I still need a clearer idea of my sister's motives. Even if Marya were conducting an espionage operation without our knowledge, it's still not quite enough to overturn her conviction. The circumstances of her arrest were too . . . incriminating.

The threesome—Barrow, Marya, Markow—turns in circles in my mind. In 1947, I knew nothing, not a hint, about Marya taking intelligence from Barrow and passing it to us with Markow's help. But I should've known. I should've guessed it. Markow had hinted he was working with her himself.

14
Marya

Berlin, 29 June 1947

At Henry's door, I knocked our secret code: knock-knock—pause—knock-knock-knock—pause—knock, and nearly collided with his roommate, Johnson. He had slick hair and a thin mustache and looked like a magician who should be pulling things out of a hat.

"Hallo, young M. Haven't seen you in ages." He lowered his voice. "Old Henry is in a *mood*, love. Cheer him up for me, will you? I have to live with him." Johnson shot an exasperated look at the ceiling, slipped around me, and went to knock on the door of the flat down the hall.

Henry was just closing his rolltop desk when I went into the sitting room. He turned the key but left it in the lock. I wanted him to take the key away, hide it from me so I wouldn't have to steal from him again. No one had trained me how to pick locks, and I wasn't interested in trying. Vera had instructed me to take tonight's papers to a drop-off in a park called Witzleben, and if there was a way to avoid it, I'd take it.

"I'm glad you're early, Mouse. Come here." Henry held out his arms and I was eager to fill them.

"What's wrong? Johnson said you're in a mood."

Henry gave me a long, searching look, and I could barely keep his gaze without trembling, or breaking down. If he'd noticed his papers were gone, if he suspected me already, all was lost.

"I wasn't sure you'd come," he said finally. "If that sister of yours would let you." He released me and selected a record from the shelf. "How about Charlie Parker, *Ornithology*, but only if you'll dance?"

I was too relieved to do more than nod. Jazz filled the room, and Henry gathered me up and spun me around. We molded our bodies to the beat, and everything was fine, just fine.

"Did you have any trouble getting here?" he asked.

I updated him on the things that were safe to tell him, that Vera was impossible, that I'd dragged my mattress into another room of our barracks and now slept in my little cell, cold and bare, the floodlights beaming at me all night. "I'm not sleeping well," I said.

"Me either. Sod it, let's run away together. We'll finally get some rest."

"I planned to rest here."

The music was over, and we moved together to the couch. Henry wrapped me in the crook of his arm, and I snuggled down, grateful to just be held. I drifted away, dozing to the rise and fall of Henry's breathing. The burden of what I was doing to him exhausted me. At work, I'd been making mistakes all week, sloppy translations, tasks I promised to do and forgot about. There'd been complaints about me, and I was too preoccupied to care.

I didn't know how long I'd been out when Henry's body shifted, and his heart sped up.

"Marya?"

He hardly ever called me that. I was his mouse, a nickname he gave me early on because of the squeaks I tended to let out when he did certain things to me in bed.

"Don't be annoyed at me," he said.

That woke me up. "I don't like conversations that start that way, Henry."

He smiled briefly around his cigarette. "I can't just sit on my hands all week doing nothing while you're over in your sector dealing with your sister. I was thinking, if there's no way to convince her to leave us alone, maybe we could . . . compel her."

"What do you mean?"

"I've been gathering information about her. Quietly. I know some chaps who do that sort of thing and owe me a favor or two. They're very discreet."

"Are you mad? Henry, if she finds out . . ." I imagined her fury, how fast she'd get me on a train home.

"They haven't found anything solid yet, nothing we can use against her. But she is a little odd, isn't she? Keeps strange hours, has almost no daily routine. We all have some sort of pattern to our days with work, our duties, but she doesn't. She vanishes now and then for an hour or two, or longer."

I listened in disbelief, trying to guess who he knew at SMAD or in the MGB who would be able to shadow my sister or build a profile of her movements. But it was true; she was odd. Even I wasn't sure what she did with her days, or her nights now that I'd moved into my own room.

"She doesn't have a Western boyfriend, if that's what you're hoping to find out. She's got her eye on one of our officers. Aside from that, she investigates political crimes for the courts. That's what she told me, anyway."

He nodded and took a thoughtful pull of his cigarette. I'd forgotten about his background, that he was a policeman. Of course he wouldn't just let things lie. But this was too risky for the both of us. If his people found out about the papers I'd stolen from him, everything would be over. And if Vera discovered his people were watching her, she would punish me, haul me out of Berlin and send me home. She'd make sure I never saw Henry again.

I took the cigarette from his lips, crushed it out, and then straddled his lap. "You're going to stop this, Henry. No spying on my sister."

He cupped my legs in his hands, his fingers moving under my skirt to the skin above my stockings, melting me slowly. "If we find something," he said, "some secret about her, we can—"

"No. It's too dangerous. Your people will find out about me. As for Vera . . . I don't know what she'd do to me. To us."

"I have to do something, Mouse."

"Don't take this risk." I kissed the strong, warm pulse at his neck. "I risk enough for the both of us."

"You shouldn't. It has to stop. Marya, darling . . ." His voice was hoarse; he was already giving in.

THE SOUND OF the shower behind the bathroom door got me moving. Henry would be five minutes, maybe ten, and as much as I wanted to join him, as hard as he'd tried to convince me with kisses, caresses, and words that made my face go hot, I had rolled away from him in bed, pretending to fall asleep. But I was listening as dresser drawers opened and closed, and then the bedroom door, and then the bathroom. I had very little time to betray him again.

Walking to his desk was like moving through tar. Slowly, I rolled up the lid, opened a random file, took out random sheets of paper. I looked behind me, the papers in my hand. Vera had scolded me about taking original reports last week, and that was exactly why I did it again, to show her I wasn't a marionette dancing while she pulled my strings.

The shower still ran, the bathroom door still closed. Henry was missing the moment to catch me, to stop all this. I put the papers in my purse and climbed back into bed, sniffling. A few minutes later, Henry came in smelling fresh, a knee on the mattress.

"Hey Mouse, are you crying?"

"No." I tossed the blanket over his head and while he disentangled himself, I fled to the bathroom. I came out dressed and found him in civilian clothes studying a map of Berlin on the kitchen table. "I'm seeing you home, and don't argue with me."

I looked at my watch. I was due at the Witzleben Park in half an hour. If I couldn't get to the drop-off, it wasn't my fault, this snag in Vera's operation. What difference would it make if I slipped the papers under her door instead of leaving them for Felix in the park? She'd get them one way or another. "I suppose it's all right to the sector border."

"Actually, I'm going with you all the way into Karlshorst."

"Henry, the patrols are getting more strict. If they see you—"

He began folding the map. "Marya, my love, why are you arguing with me?"

"You're being foolish."

"You're being stubborn."

We glared at each other, and then broke into smiles. We agreed he would escort me to the border of Karlshorst, but no farther. Our people had no qualms about arresting a Western officer prowling around our sector at night. I didn't want him getting too close to the secured perimeter I lived in now.

In the street, the air hung thick and heavy, not a breath of wind. Holding hands, we started toward the palace at the end of the boulevard, the route we used to take in winter when it grew dark early and he'd escorted me deep into the Soviet Sector for my safety. He'd stopped in spring when the days grew long and I made it home while it was still light.

"What's that?" he asked.

"What?"

On the corner at the foot of a streetlamp was a pile of rags. As we got closer, I saw it was a thin, patched coat on a child curled up on the pavement. Her cheek rested on her mittened hands. I knelt beside her, moved her collar gently from her face, and held my breath. Greta.

Henry stooped beside us and touched her back. He knew some German from his work, and I'd given him private lessons in the everyday German he didn't get in his army courses. Tenderly, he said, "Wake up, little one."

She jerked awake and lifted her cheek from the man's hat she'd used as a pillow. A few coins rattled inside. She hugged the hat to her chest and blinked up at us with fierce and sleepy warning. She was such a strange creature wearing a coat and mittens on a scorching summer night. It reminded me of what I was like after my father died. Anxious, as if it might suddenly rain on the clearest summer day or turn freezing cold, and it was wise to be ready.

"Your parents must be worried," Henry said. "Where do you live? We'll take you home."

To Felix's house. Henry and Felix in the same room; I couldn't tolerate it, that clash of worlds. "I'm sure she can get home alone, Henry." I turned away from his puzzled look and said to Greta, "Go on. Go home."

"You know her?" he asked.

"I've seen her once before. In the street." I waited for the girl to say something, to tell him more, but she stayed quiet. She removed her left mitten and handed it to me. I didn't know what I was supposed to do with it until I glimpsed stitching in a strange pattern across the red yarn. *Lynarstraße 12, Wedding.*

"That's progress, then," Henry said cheerfully. "What's your name, sweet?"

She peeled off her other mitten and held it out. There was a different message stitched in the yarn: *Greta Markow.*

"Pleased to meet you, Fräulein Greta." He shook her hand, and his smile was so tender, I knew he'd lost his heart already. "What are you doing out so late? Where are your parents?"

She dangled the other mitten in front of him as if jogging his memory.

"Wedding is the French Sector. That's about an hour away on foot. Did you come alone?"

She nodded.

"Why are you so far from home?"

Greta looked at me as if I knew what was going on. And then I did. If Vera had told Felix about my Sundays with Henry, the origin of the papers Greta picked up, then Felix could have sent her to intercept me. But why? If he wanted to talk to me, he could have met me himself at Witzleben Park.

"Let's go, then," Henry said as he reached for Greta's hand.

We took almost the same route northeast as I'd done when I dropped off the first bit of intelligence on the banks of the Berlin-Spandau Canal. Greta quickly tired out, and with an exaggerated groan, Henry lifted her onto his shoulders. She was soon fast asleep.

It was nearly dark when we reached a block of run-down houses on Lynarstraße. The lights were on; the Germans had to do their ironing or repairs at night with rationed electricity. One house was fully ablaze, the curtains and shutters open to the night air on each of the four stories. People were moving in the window spaces, their conversation buzzing all the way into the street. A boy leaned out a third-floor window, pointed at us, and cried, "Look, there she is!" The windows filled, women and children peering down at us.

The door was thrown open and a woman rushed out, stopping abruptly when she saw us. I didn't know her, I could've sworn I didn't, but my heart thrashed at the sight of her.

"Are you this girl's mother?" Henry asked. It was the first time I'd ever heard his policeman voice used in anything but jest.

"Yes, sir. What happened? Is she . . . ?"

Greta's mother. Felix's wife. I stepped closer to see her better in the light. She was so different. I couldn't believe this woman with her frizzed hair and milky pallor was the same lovely woman I'd seen in the photographs Felix had carried on the front. Her name was . . . Helene. That was it. He'd called her Leni.

Henry transferred Greta to Leni's arms and began to lecture her on the dangers of leaving her child to wander around Berlin, a city rampant with crime. As he talked, Leni said to one of the boys in the hallway, "Go see if you can find him." Then she carried Greta into the house and up the stairs. Henry wasn't done with his lecture. He began to follow her and paused only when he saw I wasn't coming.

Crossing the threshold of Felix's house seemed to be as monumental as any border I'd ever crossed. The past, the war, was colliding with my present in ways that felt like they were spinning out of my control. I didn't know what any of this meant. Did Felix want to see me? Was that why I was here, guided, in a way, by Greta? I wasn't sure I wanted to know what Felix had to say. Last week, with a street between us, we'd silently agreed to keep our distance. We should honor that.

I shook my head and followed Henry inside.

Everyone seemed awake, women and children in the halls and in the stairwells. I didn't like the atmosphere. As I climbed the stairs, I saw how the women looked at Henry. I saw the shift of a hip to get in his way, the brush of a skirt against his leg. If he noticed, he didn't say anything. The women gave me hostile stares. They must've thought I was a loose woman who'd got herself an Allied man for sugar and chocolates and now flaunted it in their home. Chin up, I pretended to ignore how they looked at me, though the back of my neck burned.

People were gawking at us from the other doors in the hallway. We guessed which one was Felix's; it was the only one that was open and empty. We stepped directly into a kind of sitting room, damp and full of rickety furniture. There was a sink, stove, and kitchen cupboards on one wall. The air smelled of cabbage and onions.

The bedroom door was open. Leni was tucking Greta into bed next to a boy of maybe five sleeping in only his undershorts. Greta was already in a nightgown, her eyes closed and body limp. A broken doll sat on the windowsill, one-legged, its hair so badly trimmed, I was sure one of the children had done it. The bed of the parents was also in the room, and the frames of the two beds nearly met. It reminded me so painfully of how I was raised, a spasm of pity touched my heart.

Leni waved for us to leave the room. "Where was she?"

"Begging in the street," Henry replied, "alone. In the British Sector, an hour away from here. A hundred things could happen to her at this time of night. Was it worth a pocketful of coins?"

"I didn't send her, sir."

"Who did? Where is her father?"

"A damn good question. I ask myself that every day."

From the street, there was a sudden shout, and Leni moved to the window, her back tense. I joined her and saw a crowd of young people spilling out of a house across the way and congregating, smoking, talking, some with bottles in their hands, in the debris of a vacant lot. There was laughter, but with tension in it, as if the party was about to turn rotten. I was so focused on it, I almost missed the blur of someone dashing down the sidewalk and vanishing out of my line of sight and through the street door below me. Pounding steps on the stairway, the apartment door thrown open.

He froze on the threshold. Felix, hair in his face, jacket open, breathing hard. He stared at Henry in confusion, and then at me. His expression melted into relief.

"Felix," Leni said with resignation, "you bastard. You swine. You listen to this man's lecture. You're the man of the house, aren't you?" She left the room, pushing past him. He had to step aside for her to go out, and moments later, a door slammed down the hall.

I hadn't been this close to him in five years. He seemed more faded than I remembered him, like the war was fresher for him, its way of draining the color out of people.

"Herr Markow," Henry said, "did you send your daughter to the British Sector at this time of night?"

Felix hung his hat on the hook. "May I go see Greta, sir? I was very worried." His voice . . . the same quiet intensity from the war. Back then, I'd thought if he spoke louder, he would shatter.

"Please answer my question," Henry said patiently.

"She was probably looking for me and lost her way. It's happened before." His face was set in a polite mask I'd seen in other Germans, neutrality when facing an ally, careful not to betray a thing.

"I don't want to see that girl anywhere in my sector again on her own. She should stay close to home."

"Yes, sir."

"How can she go to school if she's out at all hours? She goes to school, doesn't she?"

"Yes, sir. After the summer, she'll be in her second year."

Henry noticed the children's primer on the table and browsed the brittle pages. He set a packet of cigarettes beside it, an offering that warmed my heart. On the black market, cigarettes could buy anything, pencils and notebooks, a slate and chalk, and much more.

"Right," he said, "just don't let it happen again, Herr Markow. A daughter is . . ." I could see Henry struggling for the word, a glint in his eye that led, I knew, to Fern.

"Priceless?" I supplied him in German.

"Yes, that's right. Keep her close, Herr Markow. Good night."

Just as I was nodding my farewell, angry cries erupted in the street, and the scream of a woman. We all rushed to the window. There, down below, was a knot of young men in the vacant lot pushing each other. I couldn't tell if some were trying to stop a fight or get one going. At the curb, a young woman hugged a friend, who was crying.

"Stay here," Henry said to me, and made for the door.

"Henry!"

I followed him into the stairwell, but he was already at the street door, and gone. Back in the apartment, at the window, I watched him slow down as he crossed the street, reaching into his jacket, lighting a cigarette as he approached the crowd. I was terrified and yet fascinated; this was Henry the policeman, determined to keep the peace. He greeted the crowd in English loud enough for the people on the edges to stiffen or move away from him, an officer of the occupation forces. The young men who'd been ready for a brawl fell away from each other but in a bad-tempered way, offended at the interference. Henry began to talk softly to the crying girl, but he kept an eye on those men.

There was a movement beside me, and I remembered where I was—who I was with. I turned to find Felix gazing at me as if he couldn't believe I was there.

15
Marya

Without saying anything, we moved away from the window as if neither of us wanted Henry or the crowd to see us together. I didn't know what to say to Felix, how to start. I dug into my purse and held out his coin in my palm.

"My lucky pfennig," he said in surprise. "You still have it."

"It worked. We survived."

"I survived. You're living it up. Look at you, all grown up now."

"I wasn't a little girl, you know. I was eighteen." I tried to sound offended, but I was smiling despite myself. I followed him to his bedroom doorway, where he looked in on the sleeping children.

"Greta has grown so much," I whispered. "She was just a little thing in your photographs. Two or three?"

"She's not growing well. She'll be eight in a couple weeks and she's too small for her age. Peter too. He doesn't look five."

"Peter." I remembered Felix in the war mentioning the son he'd never met. "You got to see your boy after all."

"Sons were born to be cannon fodder. That's all we were good for." He splayed his fingers on Peter's fine hair. "If somebody tries to put him in uniform, I'll burn down the world first."

We closed the bedroom door and moved into the sitting room. "Did you send Greta to get me?" I asked.

"I wanted to have a drink with you. And say thank you."

"For what?"

"Treating me like a human being in the war." Felix rattled around in the cupboard, taking down two schnapps glasses. "I'd almost forgotten what that was like. I served with some rotten people. I don't use this word lightly, but I'd call them evil. Wasn't a lot of humanity on the front. Or the wrong kind." He poured.

"I remember shouting at you about the evil things your army did." I left the question unsaid, whether there was a difference between the crimes of his army and what he personally had done on the front.

He held the glass out to me, a tremor in his hand. "It was easy to get . . . lost out there. But I was lucky. In the middle of it all, I got six days to learn there was a way back. I thank you for that." He raised his glass. "To old enemies."

"To old enemies at peace."

We drained our glasses in one burning swallow, and I fell into a coughing fit that dissolved into laughter. Usually I could hold my drink better than this.

"Another?" Felix asked.

"I'd rather not go blind, thanks." I took the envelope with Henry's papers from my purse and set them on the table between the glasses. "I have to go. Maybe I can help Henry with the girls outside."

"Fräulein Lieutenant, wait. I didn't really call you here just for the drink. I have a proposal for you. How much has your sister told you about the operation?" He put his hand on the papers I'd brought.

I wanted to get back to Henry, but in Felix, I had someone else connected to Vera and what she was making me do. Felix was the only person I could talk to about it. I admitted how she had entrapped me, how the papers I was getting from Henry were supposed to help us in case the Westerners violated the peace we'd worked so hard to forge.

"When did she contact you about all this?" I asked. "She hasn't been in Berlin very long."

"She came to see me a few weeks ago."

"And told you about me and Henry?"

He nodded. "It's not an official MGB op. She gave my orders directly; she'd never do that if this was running through normal channels. She's freelancing, I'm sure of it. She wants the intel for her own purposes, and she wants herself kept out of it. She obviously doesn't want anything in this operation traced directly back to her."

"Why?"

"Who knows? Your security services are the most twisted, byzantine organizations on the planet. Everybody is ready to stab everybody else in the back. I bet Vera is padding her armor."

Vera had enemies. My skin bristled at the thought of bigger dangers, wider and darker consequences to the operation she'd got me involved in. "What exactly are you doing for us? Besides . . ." I gestured at the envelope.

"You really want to know?"

"I want to know what Vera knows. She barely tells me anything."

"I'm a bit of a jack-of-all-trades, but they've mostly got me recruiting informants, Germans who funnel information to Moscow.

Most of them don't know who they're working for. Your people tell me what they need, maybe a secretary in a certain Allied office, a rail conductor, an engineer at a power plant, and I go reel them in."

"How?" This was fascinating, an insight into Vera's world. I'd grown up knowing anybody could be an informant, but I'd never thought about how they became one.

"I have a gift for persuasion," Felix said rattling the schnapps bottle. "People tend to do what I ask them."

"Why?"

He seemed to think about this. "You know life is ironic. After they took me away from you in the war, they taught me how to do a few things, cloak-and-dagger stuff. After the war, I got to refine my skills, and strangely enough, I'm not bad at it. In fact, I'm not really good at anything else. The problem is, the Soviets own me. Or they think they do. Your sister certainly does."

"I asked her. She said she didn't force you to be a courier."

"No, but it went without saying I'd have some problems if I didn't do what she wanted." He glanced out the window. I could hear the murmur of the German girls reporting to Henry about something that made their voices rise with anger and hurt. "I know we're running out of time," Felix said, "so listen. I've been working on something special. Something for myself. If I play it right, it's going to buy my way out of everything. The MGB and your sister and Moscow. I'll be free of them. But I've run into a little problem and you're the only one who can help me solve it."

I put out my hand, warding away whatever he was about to say. "I'm involved in enough right now. Whatever you're doing, I don't want any part of it."

"Just hear me out."

"It won't change my mind. Believe me, I sympathize with you

wanting to break away from the MGB and my sister, but I have my own problems."

"If you help me, you'll be helping yourself. We want the same thing, right? To get your sister to leave us alone."

I couldn't deny it.

"There's a certain document I have a chance to get from the Americans," he said. "It's dynamite waiting to blow. But I can't get it without exposing myself. That's where you come in."

"You want me to talk to an American?"

"I already did. I need you to meet her next week. Briefly. Take the document from her and hand over an envelope. That's it. A two-man operation, one to do the trade, one to watch your back. Easy."

An American woman? I was intrigued, but I also doubted things were as simple as Felix was making them out to be. "Who is this American?"

He rummaged behind the curtain under the sink and returned with a small photograph of a studious-looking woman with big curls in her hair. "An emigree named Irina Petrova. She's been in America since she was two. She's a real Yankee now and works at their Dahlem HQ."

"Why would she give you an important American document?"

"She has some interesting hobbies, and I had the chance to photograph them. I don't judge people. You can't account for tastes. But I can safely say if the US Mil Gov or her poor mother in New York sees what she's been up to, Irina will be in some deep, deep water."

I understood now. "You're blackmailing her."

"She walked into it herself. I saw an opportunity, and I'm taking it."

"What information is worth blackmailing an American for?"

"A list. A list of Soviet personnel working in secret for the Amis. When I have that, I can demand anything from Moscow. Your people will fall over themselves to get it. They'll pay a fortune and thank me afterward. But I need you to do the trade."

"Why me?"

"You're my lucky pfennig."

I shook my head and started for the door.

"Wait, Marya. In case Irina's people are on to her, they'll expect a man to show up, not a woman. It's just a precaution."

"Send your wife."

"She wouldn't do it even if I asked."

"You think I will?"

"What do you want? Money? I could pay you after I sell the list. I'm going to offer it to your sister and let her negotiate with Moscow."

That was why he wanted me involved. Because of Vera. To entangle her in all this. Make it personal.

"She'll never go along with it."

"She'll do it because she's ambitious. I saw it two seconds after meeting her in the war. She'll get it done, and I'll be free."

"It was good to see you, Felix, but you've gone completely mad. It'll never work. And even if you pulled it off, my sister would crush you."

"Maybe she'd try, if things went wrong. But I'm hard to kill."

"I wouldn't be able to protect you from her."

"I'm not asking for your protection. I'm asking you to meet me here one week from today at 13:00 hours. That's all. The rest will be easy."

"Good night, Felix."

He slipped around me and turned his back to the door, blocking my way. "Marya, I'm asking you again. Nicely."

"I said, no."

"I need your help. There's no other way."

"I am helping you. I'm being sure your mad scheme doesn't get off the ground."

"Scared of crossing your sister, are you?"

My face blazed under the skin. "I'm not scared of her."

"You've been scared of her half your life. In the war, you told me a few things she did to you."

"I did?" I'd forgotten. Honestly. I searched my memory of those six days he was with me, looking for the moments when I'd told him about Vera. Vaguely, I remembered the firelight, our conversations ranging far beyond political philosophy, the roots of revolutions and freedom, circling back to personal things. Ourselves, our families. He'd told me about his, but I'd forgotten I'd told him about mine.

"Remember how she could erase you from her life whenever she wanted? Pretend you didn't exist? How she was always testing you? And now she's got you spying on your boyfriend. The war changed us all, but I don't believe for a minute you're doing that voluntarily. She put you up to it, didn't she?"

"Open the door, Felix."

"Maybe you resent her. You don't want her to make her career with that list. But think about it. If you help her get it, she'll forget about the little operation with the Englishman. That's nothing compared to this. And you'll be doing your country a great service by handing over a bunch of traitors to the Motherland. Vera will love it. She'll free you too."

"I grew up with her. It's very dangerous to try and predict how she thinks and what she'll do."

Felix was leaning back against the door gazing at me from under heavy eyelids. "It's still no? Final answer?"

"Final answer. Now, open the door or I'll call for Henry. Or your wife."

A long sigh, and he began rubbing his forehead at a small scar, some deep pain he tried to massage away. "Let me make some assumptions, here. Seeing as you're an official of Soviet military government, I'm assuming—correct me if I'm wrong—that it would be upsetting to your people if they knew you had an intimate relationship with a member of the Western Allies. Is that right? The question is: do you want to do your country a service by helping me, or do you want the MGB to think the Englishman has turned you into a foreign spy?"

I stepped closer to him. But I couldn't touch him. I couldn't wrench him away from the door. "Felix, don't do this to me."

"Believe me, I don't want to. Help me, and I won't."

I shook my head.

"I have proof," he said, "of the Soviet lieutenant with the British captain."

"Liar."

"I'd never lie to you. Marya, just do as I ask. Please. It'll work."

"What proof? You have photographs? Of me and Henry?"

At the kitchen niche, he took a tin off the shelf and came back with several photos. Me and Henry holding hands on the boulevard, me and Henry kissing at the gate of his house, me and Henry on the balcony. It was sickening, how many times Felix had violated our happiness with this—I tossed the photos onto the table—this surveillance.

"You took these for my sister?"

"For me. In case I needed to show you I'm serious."

"Are there more?"

"Yes. And the negatives. You'll get them after I have the list.

Marya, listen to me. I'm not interested in exposing you. I don't want to get you into trouble. But I need your help. Do this little favor for me. For old times' sake."

"The answer is still no."

"Then I have no choice but to give what I have to the MGB. Not even Sister Vera will save you then."

I saw the possibility of an investigation outside of Vera's influence. If Felix informed on me, I would lose everything, and Vera would have no power to stop it, even if she wanted to. She might be swallowed up in the ripples of punishment expanding around me, a wave that could reach our family in Moscow, ruining their lives too.

"You're bluffing."

"And your Captain Henry Barrow: What will he do when he figures out what you've been taking from him? Should we invite him to come back in here? Look around a bit?" The papers I'd stolen from him were in the envelope on the table.

I dumped the photos of us into the sink and lit them with the matches on the shelf. Henry and me kissing, Henry and me holding hands on the boulevard, the flames eating away at us. I'd done the same to his portrait and his letters because of Vera. Slowly, the world was forcing me to burn away everything I had of him.

"I'm sorry, but this is how it has to be," Felix said. He stood beside me at the sink. "If I had a choice, I'd do it another way."

"I treated you well in the war and you didn't learn a thing from it."

"That man I killed for you, remember him? I knew him. He was a bastard but he was always keen on finding missing comrades. I'd loaded enough guilt on myself up to then in the war, but that was something else. He'd come to find me and I bashed in his brains. For you. Now all I'm asking in return is that you spend five seconds exchanging papers with an American. In the whole scheme of things, it's harmless. I'm not asking you to commit treason. Marya, look at me."

I wiped the smoke out of my eyes. I recognized the need in Felix's face, and something else from the war that still made my blood rush. I didn't know what it was, why it was still there in him or me, or what I had to do to make it go away.

16

Vera

Testimony for Chairman A. Cheptsov
Military Collegium of the Supreme Court of the USSR
Moscow, 28 February–3 June 1956

[RECORDING]

I met Rheingold shortly after the unsatisfactory meeting with Henry Barrow at the dance hall in the Soviet Sector. Barrow had given nothing away about his true identity and his intentions with Marya, and I wasn't about to leave things at that. I decided to continue surveillance on him, but with a new informant, someone we owned completely and who had the skills and experience to help me find evidence that Barrow was or was not a British agent.

I'd consulted the list of local MGB operatives, and when Felix Markow's name came up, I looked no further. He was perfect, considering the history he shared with my sister. At the time, I didn't know about the note he'd written her in the war—that *your Felix*.

However, each had saved the life of the other, giving me a certain leverage when dealing with Markow. I assumed once I explained that I was working to protect her, Markow would do what I required and keep his mouth shut. This was not an MGB assignment but a personal one.

Markow's Berlin file had noted the address of an MGB safehouse near the Berlin-Spandau Canal where he could be reached. In the heat wave that gripped the city in those days, I traveled into the French Sector battling the thick air, mosquitoes, and odors of the people crushed onto the trains with me. It was almost a relief to reach Markow's ramshackle safehouse with the bar on the ground floor, the hallway stinking of cheap alcohol. I was wearing civilian clothes and had to introduce myself quietly to the woman at the reception. She fetched the landlord, a bald little man in a sweat-stained shirt. According to the file, he'd been an excellent agent for us since before the war. I asked him if Felix Markow was in.

"Pardon me," he said, "but you look a lot like another woman who's been coming by for Herr Markow. She's smaller and younger and—"

My sister. Who else could it be? Back then, I had no idea Marya and Markow were working together to funnel intelligence to us. As far as I knew, they last saw each other in the war. I was naturally curious to know why she'd come to see him, and set her photograph on the reception desk.

"This woman?"

"Yes, that's her."

"How often have you seen her here?"

The man made a full report. Apparently, Marya had first come to the safehouse in January, accompanied by Herr Markow. From there, she showed up perhaps once a week, usually on Saturday afternoons or evenings. This relationship, whatever it was, unsettled me. If the landlord was telling the truth, these meetings had been going on months before I arrived in Berlin.

Upstairs, he knocked on Markow's door, making some excuse about needing to check the radiator though it was blisteringly hot that day. I heard three locks turn on the other side of the door before Markow opened it. He was in shirtsleeves and suspenders, a cigarette dangling from his mouth. He looked like a man of experience around my age—I was twenty-nine in Berlin—with the weight of the war in his eyes. The vulnerability in his face made him handsome in his way. It was just the thing to appeal to the soft heart of my sister.

"Do you remember me?" I asked.

His face was neutral but his eyes couldn't hide the rebellious spark I'd seen in him in the war. "How could I ever forget you, comrade? Welcome to my humble lodgings."

He had the decency to fetch his jacket while I stayed near the door. The room was small, shabby, unremarkable, the air close. I didn't intend to stay long.

"My sister has come to see you," I said. "Why?"

"Landlord's been gossiping about me again."

"Is it true?"

"Gossip is never true if it's about me."

The locks on his door were impressive, of thick steel that gleamed like new. They would be difficult to cut through. Easier to take down the whole door. I turned the first lock with a snap, bolting us in together. Markow moved out of my way as I went to the window. It had no glass and looked out upon an unsavory yard.

"Herr Markow, I was told my sister comes here every Saturday, which surprises me. The landlord has no reason to lie about this except in his eagerness to be helpful."

"God protect us from helpful people."

"Indeed. Why does she come to see you?"

Markow was standing in front of a chest of drawers. He leaned against it, lighting a cigarette clutched far too tightly for a man trying to look unafraid.

"We just talk. Reminisce about the war. Cry into our cups. It's harmless."

"Every Saturday."

"She doesn't come every Saturday. The landlord and me don't get along. He likes to stir up trouble for me. Is that why you came? He called you in?"

I stepped past him to the door and turned the second bolt. It slid into place with a firm, satisfying thud.

"I came to give you a job."

"I'm always happy to be of service to my Soviet friends."

"You talk with Marya," I said. "You reminisce. Nothing else?"

"No, that's about it."

"Then why are you nervous?"

"You're an intimidating woman."

This made me smile. Hardly anyone admitted such an obvious thing to my face. It was refreshing.

"What exactly do you reminisce about," I asked, opening the wardrobe. At the foot of it, near a torn pair of malodorous shoes, were three unlabeled bottles of something I had no doubt had been brewed in a bathtub.

"The war, like I said."

"Yes, I understand you performed a great service for my sister back then. I'm sure she holds a special place in her heart for the man who committed murder to save her life. What a hero you must be to her."

"It's not like that," Markow said, looking uneasy.

"Then what is it like?"

He shook his head. His reticence was unfortunate. He wasn't willing to cooperate when his life would be so much easier if he did. I returned to the door and slid the third and final bolt into place.

"The only way out now is the window, Herr Markow."

"It's my room."

"It's our safehouse. Do you believe I'd be punished for anything I might do to you here?"

"You wouldn't throw me out the window, would you?"

"No, but I know some ways to get you to jump."

He thought about this, smoking in meditative silence while looking at the window space. "We do talk about the war. She asked about what happened to me after I was taken away from her."

"What did she want to know?"

He rubbed a scar on his forehead and said, "my training. She was curious what your people taught me how to do. So I told her. How to search a room without the owner knowing it. How to pick small locks. Where a man might hide a wireless. How to photograph documents. Codes, cyphers."

"Why did she want to know all this?"

"Got the impression she saw that stuff in American films and wanted to know how accurate it was. Do spies really do that? That kind of thing."

It was hard to believe Marya came to Markow to chat about tradecraft and American films. I went to the bed, its crumpled sheets tugging at my innate sense of order and tidiness. And decency. I'd seen Marya with the Englishman, but I wondered how strong a pull this German was for her after everything they'd done for each other. Perhaps Markow was downplaying the meaning of her visits? Shielding her reputation?

I asked him for a cigarette, and after it was lit, leaned against the dresser beside him, my tone reasonable. "Herr Markow, I came here because I believe Marya might be in a bit of trouble. You seem just the man to help her."

He tensed. "Of course. What is it?"

"Has she mentioned an Englishman to you, an officer named Henry Barrow who lives on the Schloßstrasse in the British Sector? No? She's been amusing herself with him for a while, and I'm afraid he might be setting a trap for her that she's not willing to see. I haven't found any evidence that he's an operative, but I can't shake the suspicion there's something not right about him. If he's weaving a web around my sister, I need to know about it. Do we understand each other?"

There was something satisfyingly fierce in the way he crushed out his cigarette against the wallpaper. He would've been happy if it was Henry Barrow's eye.

"I'll get on it."

"Be discreet. Don't let her know what you're doing. I want regular reports."

I opened the three bolts on the door and left feeling pleased with myself. Only now, years later, do I know what a fool I was. So focused on the task at hand—investigating Barrow—that I neglected to notice what Markow had been telling me about Marya.

In her MGB interrogation, she insisted—for a while anyway—that she was spying on Barrow. In our archives, I found good intelligence from Barrow's office. Markow, our agent and a man Marya knew from the war, delivered the documents to us. He must have got them from her. If all of that is true, Marya had been acting as a field agent in Berlin, actively spying on Barrow with the help of Markow, a man who certainly knew his tradecraft. Why she would do all this is still a mystery. I wonder if she had envied my work as an operative in the war and quietly tried out such work in Berlin, measuring herself against me.

17

Marya

Berlin, 6 July 1947

The train rattled to a stop and I climbed off the S-bahn at Wedding Station. From there, I plunged into the gray and mottled streets of this working-class district, as Felix had called it when he'd talked about it in the war. This was the Berlin he'd grown up in, concrete and stone, the confusing tumble of shops on the ground floor of the buildings all along the block. The signs claimed they'd once sold brooms, soaps, coffee, shoes, cigars. Now the doorways were boarded-up or blocked with rubbish. In one, a pair of boys were playing with a dented canteen and bits of wire. In another, a woman slept with her knees up, her hair in her face.

Until this morning, I swore to myself that Felix had been bluffing about exposing Henry and me to the MGB if I refused to meet the American Irina Petrova. I'd intended to go to Henry as usual, but I was too anxious. Maybe Felix wasn't bluffing. Deep in my memory, I could still hear the pounding of fists on a door, the secret police demanding my papa's arrest. If helping Felix eased that fear inside me, I'd do it.

At Felix's building, as shabby and scarred by poverty and war as the others on the street, I held open the door for a teenage boy hefting a bicycle on his shoulder. He looked exhausted and ignored me as he carried it up the stairs. I followed, and on the first floor I knocked on Felix's door. Hearing a muffled answer, I went in.

Midday light drenched the room. The dining table had been pushed to the window, and Felix's wife, Leni, sat on top of it, Greta in her lap. The poor girl leaned toward the fresh air of the window space, her body shaking with deep, guttural coughs.

Leni's face reminded me of my mother's, gray lips, dull eyes. In the war, Felix had said he'd met his wife when she worked in a store that sold gramophones and radios. It was her parents' store, and she was serious about her job, discussing the technical features of each machine, advising him while he followed her around, amazed such a lovely woman lit up when talking about decibels or radio frequencies. After my time in the ruins of Berlin, I could guess what had happened to her family's store.

"Was there soup?" Leni asked.

"Pardon?"

"Outside the door. Did the neighbor leave the soup?"

"I didn't see any."

Another fit of coughing from Greta. Leni held her tightly so she wouldn't topple out of the window. There were dishes stacked in the little kitchen, washing bundled up on the couch. The room smelled of decay and neglect. I was embarrassed to be there, to see how the housework had grown around Leni's ears.

"Where's Herr Markow?"

"Damned if I care. Not like there's anything needs done around here. Not like I didn't spend the last two days trying to get penicillin that wasn't watered down to nothing." Greta gasped, another coughing fit, and Leni held her. "What do you want with my husband?"

I wasn't used to Germans talking to me in that tone, but I didn't want to aggravate the situation. I let it pass. "He asked me to come today. We have some business."

"Business." She sounded bitter and amused. "He's always doing business, isn't he?"

I noticed there wasn't a gramophone or even a radio in the apartment. "What happened to your family's business? The gramophone store?"

Leni looked surprised, then turned away and rested her cheek in Greta's hair. "Felix keeps a room over a bar near here. He can drown himself in schnapps whenever he wants. Look for him there."

I assumed she meant the bar Greta had fled to after she took the papers I'd left at the drop-off point at the canal. I turned to leave, was on the way to the door, and without knowing why, I veered to the kitchen. In a basket were a few moist-looking potatoes, a carrot, a browning onion, some wilted dandelions. Before I knew what I was doing, I took a pot from behind the curtain under the sink, filled it with water, and set it on the portable stove plugged into the wall. I wasn't sure the Germans had power just then—we tended to allow it at night to conserve coal—but when I turned the knob and held my hand near the burner, I felt it slowly heating. I got to work on the soup, thinking of things I hadn't thought of in years, the rationing of food to be cooked, as my mother had rationed, how many potatoes for a hearty yet sensible soup, an onion, the carrot. I kept the potato peels, more calories if Felix's family was desperate enough.

The door to the flat opened and slammed closed, and the little boy lumbered in, the second child, Peter. His knee pants, not to mention his knees, were filthy. He'd managed to smear something dark, hopefully mud, on his shirt. His hair stood up stiffly with grime. He ignored me and waddled to the table.

"Mama, I'm hungry."

Leni shouted, "What did you do to your clothes? Have you been playing in filth? Do you think you're a little prince with clothes to spare? Go change."

"But I'm hungry."

"There's no food for filthy boys."

Peter looked at me, and what an easy mark I was. He had such a fine-featured little face, too thin for a child. "I didn't do anything."

"Don't look to her for sympathy," Leni snapped. "She's a Russian."

Peter broke into tears and scuttled into the bedroom. I went back to the soup. I couldn't feel the wood of the spoon in my hand as I stirred. Leni was passing down her hatred of me—of my people—to her children. That was how it started. That was how it held, deep in people's hearts and minds, for generations. She had no right to hate us, to believe the Nazi propaganda, or condemn all of us for the terrible actions of my army when we finally invaded Germany. Did she believe our men's cruelty and violence—as wrong as it was, very wrong—had happened because *we* were the barbarians? Did she know what her men did to us in my country? Did Felix ever tell her? We should've been better than the Germans. We shouldn't have abused the people we defeated. But it wasn't us she should hate; it was war and what it does to us all. That was what she should teach her children.

"What's this?" Peter was back in the room, changed into slightly cleaner clothes. He was snooping in my bag and pulled out the book I'd brought along, the book of fairy tales my parents had given to me when I was little. I wanted to show it to Henry tonight. He should know more about me—real things: my culture, our stories and symbols and sense of beauty. Still shaken by Leni's hatred, I wanted her children to know these things too. I left the kitchen, wiping my hands on a towel.

"This is my favorite, oldest book," I said to Peter. "My parents gave it to me when I started school."

Peter ran his hand gently over the cover. The colors glowed on the rose-lined arabesques and the mythical creatures—a winged horse, a dove with the head of a woman, a dragon flying through the sky near a church. I turned the pages, lingering on my favorite story, Vasilisa the Beautiful. She held a stick in her hand, and on the end was a skull whose eyes glowed and lit her way through the forest. Behind her back, among the black trees, more skulls gleamed on their posts. These evil lamps surrounded a wooden cottage whose windows beamed a strangely inviting light. The house stood on a pair of chicken legs. "Baba Yaga the witch lives there," I said in an ominous tone. "Vasilisa went to her seeking a light that would never go out." Peter shuddered with delight, and even Greta strained to see the book from her mother's lap.

The soup was bubbling, and I went to tend to it. Greta was fighting her brother for the right to turn the next page of my book. I saw Leni looking too, but sideways, as if she couldn't bear to be caught peeking. I decided to let them borrow the book so they'd have time to see that my people didn't only hurt and destroy, we made things of beauty to feed the soul. We all had to start healing somehow.

I ladled out the soup, and once the children were eating, I went to the door. Leni rushed to intercept me, her hand on the latch. "He doesn't live here anymore," she said. "I threw him out."

I didn't know what to say to that.

"When he first came home from the war," she said, "he used to toss and turn at night. Sometimes he'd cry out in his sleep. *Marya*. That's what he said. He wouldn't tell me who that was."

He'd done that? Called to me in his dreams?

"The minute I saw you last week, I knew," she said. "There you were. *Marya*. After you left, I asked him what you were to him and he just looked at me." She shook her head. "Didn't even have the decency to answer. And then you come in here today—"

"It's not what you think. We were just—." What? What were we in the war, Felix and me? He'd killed a man for me. I still wasn't sure what that meant.

"You're blushing down to your toes; do you think I don't see it? Does that Englishman from last week know what's in your head?" Leni opened the door to the quiet hallway. "Don't come here again," she said. "Fräulein."

I FOLLOWED THE Nordufer west, moving fast to outrun my pounding heart. When I saw Henry tonight, I'd tell him about the war, that I knew Felix, how knowing him had changed something in me, not that I was sure what it was. I hoped I could explain it right. It was a muddle in my head, memories, feelings I couldn't define. If he loved me, Henry would understand as I understood what he'd told me about his wife and daughter. I was keeping enough secrets from him. Felix didn't have to be one of them.

At the bar where I'd first seen Felix, I recognized the large window space, shuttered in the early afternoon, and the awning over the door. A bald man was using a long pole to open the shutter. "No rooms free," he said as he hooked the shutter into place.

"Is Felix Markow here?"

The man planted his pole upright next to him like a spear. He looked me over, and his eyebrows rose. I didn't like his look at all, his sudden wet smile. "Bad luck. I think he's out, Fräulein."

I looked at my watch and peered into the dark of the bar on the other side of the first open shutter. I wanted to get this over with, do the trade with Irina Petrova in the American Sector and get to the British Sector before Henry started to worry.

The owner leaned his pole against the wall. "You want to wait in his room, Fräulein? I'm sure he wouldn't mind, pretty girl like you."

I couldn't believe he was offering that. Maybe Felix had warned him a woman of my description might come asking for him today. He was arrogant if he allowed me to be in his room alone when he had something I wanted. Maybe his photographs of Henry and me weren't there, but this was the chance to search for them. I had to try.

I followed the landlord into the narrow foyer, waited as he took the key from its hook, and followed him up the stairs. He turned the key in the lock and left it there.

I pushed open the door, and went in. The curtains were half closed and there were several tears in the fabric so that ragged bits of light penetrated the room. The bed dominated the space, messy, the blankets kicked to one side. On the other, where Felix slept in the heat, I assumed, was only the bare-sheeted mattress. There was a low chest of drawers Felix appeared to use as a desk; a chair sat close to it, and on the top were pens and pencils and the faint traces of black lettering on the wood. Mold discolored the ceiling at the corners and crept down the wall that faced the window. The flat he'd shared with Leni was poor, but this room was desolate.

I dived into the search for the photos, beginning with the place I didn't want to touch at all—his bed. I was cautious, old reflexes from the war; you never knew what the enemy might hide in an innocent place, waiting to blast your hand off. I pressed the surface of the mattress, looking for resistance inside the flocking, a sign of an envelope stuffed inside. When there was nothing, I did the same for the pillow, the blanket, and moved on to the frame. I was kneeling at the footboard, feeling the space between the frame and the mattress, when the door opened behind me.

"So it is you, my lucky pfennig," Felix said, sticking a bent cigarette between his lips. "Landlord said he did me a favor, let a pretty girl into my bedroom." He sat on the bed with a low grunt and finally got his cigarette lit. He reeked of schnapps and his eyes were glassy. "Don't let me interrupt. You were searching for something down there?"

I climbed to my feet, the unpleasant sensation of dirt and crumbs sticking to my knees. "It's the middle of the day on a Sunday, you stink of schnapps, and I'm supposed to follow you to the American Sector?"

"If I want to hear that tone of voice, I'll go home to my wife."

"You should. Greta has been coughing for days. Your wife had to look for penicillin."

A flicker of anxiety on his face, wiped away quickly. He leaned against the headboard and crossed his shoes on the mattress. "They're better off without me. Leni tells me that all the time." His voice shifted, bitter and husky like hers. "We were doing just fine before you came back from the war."

"I doubt she means it."

"She means every damn word she says, and I don't need marital advice from you, Marya."

I rounded away from him to the wardrobe and threw open the doors. A few shirts, none of them fresh, and trousers on the shelf. I gave up subtlety and pulled the things out of the closet and onto the floor. I fetched the chair and climbed on it so I could reach the back of the top wardrobe shelf. I found a broken belt, a ratty hat with the lining torn, an extra sheet. No photos.

"They're not here if you're looking for what I think you're looking for," he said.

I climbed down from the chair and started on the chest of drawers. The top held papers, all of them blank, bits of office debris, a ruler, random papers like ticket stubs. In the others, underthings, junk, and on the bottom, books. I flapped the covers. "Where are the photos?"

"Maybe in one of those drawers after all. They could have false bottoms. Spies do that sort of thing, you know."

I pulled out the drawers, all the way, dumped the contents onto the floor and banged my fist on the bottoms. I destroyed one drawer and bent another. No false compartments.

"Did you look under the bed?" Felix asked.

I snatched the pillow from behind his head and walloped him with it. It felt so good, I did it again and again. He fell onto his side, laughing at every blow, his hand up to ward me away. "Truce! I'm sorry."

"No, you're not." I was trying hard not to laugh too, not to let the sound of Felix's laughter pull me where I didn't want to go. When the moment passed, I scooted to the foot of the bed, patting down my hair while he searched the sheets for the cigarette I'd knocked out of his mouth. He'd listen to me now. I could feel it.

"We don't have to go to the American Sector," I said. "There must be another way to free yourself from the MGB."

"The other way involves a bullet, so no thanks. Don't worry, Marya. We can do this. Relax. Yours is the easiest part."

"My blackmailer is telling me to relax."

"I'm sorry about all that. I just need your help that much. I need your luck."

"I have no idea what I'm doing. I was in military intelligence but I wasn't an operative. I don't know what spies do. Do you plan to teach me before we go?"

"Give you a trench coat and dark glasses, you mean?" he said, laughing. "Don't bother. Just be yourself. You'll be fine."

"What if something goes wrong?"

"It won't."

"I'm here because you threatened me, Felix. I can't trust you."

"You might want to rethink that. You trust your boyfriend, don't you? Your hunk of English meat."

I didn't like him talking about Henry that way. "What's he got to do with it?"

"Keeps confidential papers lying around at home, does he? Compared to those, my photos aren't important at all. Photos you can't find because I take care to secure confidential materials. And yet"—he spread his arms—"Mr. Barrow's secret plans are right there out in the open waiting for you to spirit away. Ever wondered why?"

I knew what Felix was trying to do and lashed back. "Your wife said you call out my name in your sleep. Why do you do that?"

He gave a forlorn smile. "There goes our truce."

"Don't try to shove a wedge between me and Henry. Do it again and you can go to the American Sector by yourself."

Felix looked impressed. "You're a lioness for your man. All right. You asked so I'll answer your question. I used to have these dreams after the war. Nightmares. About a lot of things. One of them was you in a blizzard, the snow blowing all around and the wind just blasting . . . pulling you away. I couldn't reach you. You got farther and farther away and I couldn't stop it."

I felt the familiar cold of the front, crawling up my bare arms. His dream wasn't far from the truth except that he had stopped the other German from pulling me away. I didn't understand why he dreamed it differently, as if it wasn't a fellow soldier he'd been up against but a force of nature he couldn't fight.

"I try not to think about that," I said. "I remember talking by the fire. And your igloo."

"Good old igloo. Still almost froze to death but it was cozy."

"You sang 'Thoughts Are Free,' remember?"

"I did?"

"We were being philosophical. We talked about freedom and what it meant, what it really meant, not just for you as a prisoner and me as your guard. It was ... bigger. It had to do with our countries, the whole world."

He was gazing at me, a familiar light in his eyes. "I remember."

"At home, in school, and in the youth league, we were taught to serve something greater than ourselves, and I believed that. I still do. The war gave us a chance to prove it. My sister would say there is no higher honor than serving the country. But after talking to you, I started to ... remember things. Things that made me wonder how free our country had been even before your army invaded."

"Bolsheviks," he said, "and Nazis. Looked like cousins to me."

"Maybe it seemed that way because of Stalin," I said, not daring to condemn the entire system I had grown up with and still lived under. "Many of us in the army started talking freely in the war. We could never do that at home. We talked about fundamental things that had to be changed when peace came. We'd fought and bled and so many of us died. We deserved more freedom, didn't we? We thought Stalin would give it to us."

"Why are you waiting for someone to give you freedom?"

I looked at him, not sure what I'd been saying exactly. But he understood. We both knew what it was like to live in a country that controlled and threatened its people, tried to dictate how we lived our lives. Felix understood things about me and my world that Henry never would. A wave of sadness rose up inside me, and before Felix could notice it, I got up quickly and went to the door.

WE TRAVELED SOUTH to the American Sector together, and not together. When we walked, Felix was slightly too fast—on purpose, I thought—and I had to skip to catch up with him. Even then, we kept a large enough gap between us that when we passed through the crowds of a black market, people flowed around us. On the streetcar, I sat and he stood several seats behind, bending to watch out the window. Since I wasn't sure where we were going, I watched him, twisting in my seat to see if he was getting ready to leave at the next stop. The man behind me was so irritated that he turned to follow my gaze and then back to me, frowning. I knew he thought I was a man-hungry German woman who'd spotted an opportunity. I raised my brows at him, daring him to say something, and he looked down at his folded newspaper.

The streetcar slowed and Felix made his way through the crowded car to the rear door. I stood quickly and shifted with the people shoving forward or backward, trying to secure an empty seat or position themselves to leave. Felix was one of the first to hop off the car. Through the window, I saw him lighting a cigarette, watching as the people pushed to get on at the same time as I tried to get off. I finally squeezed myself through the doorway and stumbled to the street. Felix led the way again, smoking, a hand in his pocket. We passed lanterns where the national colors of the Americans hung, houses decorated with their flag. I remembered—they were still celebrating their national holiday of independence. I didn't consider it as important a revolution as ours, but I revered the idea of rebellion against tyranny. I trotted to catch up with Felix and wondered if he'd chosen this weekend of celebrations in the American Sector to symbolize what he thought would be his own act of rebellion against us, his day of independence.

We left the busy streets for quiet neighborhoods of refined houses and flowering green yards that reminded me of my beloved Karlshorst. In the distance, there was the noise of a crowd. Shouting, cheering, applause, the echo of two men talking from what sounded like loudspeakers.

Felix's pace slowed. We were close to the rendezvous, and my heart sped up. We stopped next to a house on a deserted street. Felix reached into his pocket and then opened his palm. He held a little red paper flower. "I'm going to pin this to your dress, all right?"

"Why?"

"It's how Irina Petrova will recognize you. Other people will have all the American colors, red, white and blue."

"No one is going to ask why I'm wearing Soviet red?"

"It's just plain old red." He carefully pinned the flower, and I held my breath at the pressure of his fingers at my chest.

"I don't like this."

"It'll be over before you know it." He took a thick envelope out of his pocket. "Give this to Irina. At five after three, you need to be at the refreshments table closest to the wooden shelter where the loudspeakers are. Just ask for a cup of water. Irina will do the rest. Once you have the list, just walk. Stroll away drinking your water. I'll find you. Got it?"

I looked at my watch. Half an hour. I was thirsty already. The sun was high, and I wished I'd brought my scarf and sunglasses. I was going to walk into this totally exposed.

"What if I'm caught?"

"Everything is going to be fine. You know what to do."

"You still plan to go to my sister?"

"I did this morning. She's very interested, and don't worry, I didn't mention you."

"You think she won't figure it out?" I shoved the envelope into my purse. I hated not knowing what was in it, what I was about to walk into. "If she pays for the list and you're free, what are you going to do?"

"I'll leave most of the money with my family and go away."

"Where?"

"The sea. I want to spend my life lounging on a sand dune on the North Sea, the wind in my hair. Maybe I'll buy a fishing boat." He was grinning, but I wasn't sure he was joking. "Now, let's do this. At the end of that street"—he pointed between the houses—"is a patch of ground the Amis use as a sports field. We'll go in separately. Watch the game a bit but keep track of the time. Don't look for me. I'll be watching your back. Clear?"

THE SPORTS FIELD was just as Felix said it would be, a wide space for the baseball game, little flags and markings on the ground to signal the boundaries. In a wooden booth, two Americans spoke heatedly into microphones, commenting on the game. A refreshments table was nearby. As I passed it, I looked for Irina Petrova among the women, but I didn't see anyone who looked like her photo. I squeezed around shoulders and hats until I could see the game from the sidelines. I had fifteen more minutes.

Most of the spectators were other Americans, but there were many Germans. There was a kind of tutorial going on between the bases of the diamond, one German in every position where an American stood. The soldier in charge of the young Germans—all teenage boys, as far as I could tell—instructed them with gusto. The German boys, ragged and thin but also tough and eager, streaked across the field to loud cheers from the crowd.

I was struck by how the sport and the sunshine lifted up the Germans around me. They responded to the ease and generosity of spirit the Americans treated them with. This didn't happen much in our sector. We were also a warmhearted people, but the Americans hadn't seen their land invaded, their towns and cities destroyed, and their families broken as we had. Many of us had suffered too much in the war to be this friendly to the people who had devastated us.

I looked at my watch. Time.

I weaved through the crowd to the refreshment table, the envelope tucked under my arm. I hoped to see Irina Petrova serving the water, but it was a GI who looked barely out of school. He offered me a cup and a big grin. I thanked him, and as I turned, I collided with a woman, spilling the water on her dress. We both fell back gasping.

"Hey, watch where you're goin'." Her American accent was so strong and odd, I could barely understand her. Irina Petrova. She looked just like she did in the photograph Felix had showed me. The same dark-framed glasses that made her look studious, the same big curls in her hair. It was as if she'd purposefully made herself up to resemble the photograph for my benefit. She gave me a sharp look, snatched the envelope from my hand, and used it to dab at the water stain on her blouse.

In English, I said, "Careful, that's from—"

"Here, hold this." She shoved a rolled-up magazine into my hand and then took the handkerchief offered her by the soldier to dry herself. I felt a tug behind me, and I lost my grip on the magazine. The thief was gone before I could turn, the crowd shielding him until I saw, cutting between people—Felix.

Turning back to Irina Petrova, I saw her rushing off into the crowd in the opposite direction.

I stood confused, my hands empty. This wasn't how I thought

it would go. Felix had said I was to walk, and he would find me. But he'd already taken the magazine where Irina Petrova had obviously hidden the list.

I didn't know what to do now. Walk, I supposed. I took another cup of water, drank it down, and wandered through the spectators until I was at the edge of the street. No Felix. I looked more closely at the many men in civilian clothes in the crowd, but he wasn't there. He was gone. I could feel it. He'd gone with the list and left me here with nothing. I didn't even have the photographs he'd promised me.

I tore the paper flower from my dress, flung it to the ground, and went to find a streetcar that would take me north.

18
Vera

Testimony for Chairman A. Cheptsov
Military Collegium of the Supreme Court of the USSR
Moscow, 28 February–3 June 1956

[RECORDING]

On Red Square, Nikolai and I mingle in the crowd of Central Committee members and foreign envoys watching the May Day parade. It's a fine, clear day, a day to wear hats with brims and no coats. We're on a raised platform and have a good view of our forces, the infantry and the men of the navy marching in perfect step, and then the artillery roaring past. There are cameras everywhere, so we are sure to look happy despite the strain my sister's case has put on our marriage. But my smile is genuine when the small children dash across the square, skipping and waving bouquets of white flowers. They rush up to the high balcony of the Lenin–Stalin Mausoleum, where they present their bouquets to the Presidium members and ministers. Khrushchev grins like a grandfather; he's very fond of children. From where Nikolai and I stand, we have a perfect view of the balcony and the leadership, and can assess who is standing closer to whom, who is smiling too hard, who is looking grim when we should all be bursting with pride and cheer on this lovely day.

In my ear, Nikolai says, "Nikita Sergeyevich is in a fine mood; I'll wager he'll raise ten toasts at the banquet."

"Fifteen," I say. With a nod, my husband and I shake hands. This is the most harmonious we've been in weeks. Neither of us have spoken about Marya's case since the night Furtseva came to tea at my mother's.

After the parade, we head to the luncheon, members of the Presidium with Khrushchev at the head table, other officials and foreign guests spread around the hall. Khrushchev greets me and Nikolai warmly and invites us for a summer afternoon with his family in his new villa in the Lenin Hills. Cheered by this public recognition witnessed by at least a dozen people who matter, I tuck into the appetizers, careful with the salads, caviar, blinis, and my favorite—fried smelt with lemon; I'm only one woman with one stomach and the luncheon has barely begun. After we take our seats, Nikolai smiles and squeezes my hand under the table. He really is looking trim and splendid in his light summer suit, very much the urbane man I married. On this glorious day, I'm willing to put aside our differences and remember how proud I am to have him by my side.

Over the course of the meal, Khrushchev presents toast after toast until even I lose count. We're warmed by the good cheer, the sparkling crystal all around us, the wine and champagne. Our senses are dulled; we're late to observe the trouble brewing. Glass in hand, Khrushchev rises from his chair once again, red-faced and bullish, a new venom in his eye. "Some of you," he says, "would toast

Stalin. An old habit, all that loathsome adulation." He turns his glare to the men of the Presidium seated around him. "Never mind his brutality, his abuse of power. Some people at this very table are still hypnotized by him. The cult of Stalin. And some of us refuse to be blinded anymore!" He continues his tirade, the rest of us mesmerized, though the powerful men in Khrushchev's line of fire are getting nervous. Malenkov and Kaganovich clap halfheartedly. Molotov, who is still foreign minister—barely—has been turning colors throughout the speech and is now gray; I fear for his heart. I catch Furtseva's eye; she's looking rosy and good-humored and obediently nods or claps at the proper time.

At one point, Khrushchev turns to the question of why he gave his secret speech. Why critique Stalin now? "I am an old man," he says, "and might depart at any moment. Before he leaves this world, every man has to give an account of what he has done and how he did it."

This is not a moment to clap, but my heart is full. Yes—we must have the courage to confront how we have lived our lives while we are still living, for only then do we have the chance to change.

Late in the feast, I spot an old colleague at another table and go to greet him while Nikolai drifts toward a heated discussion between two Hungarians. I monitor this clash myself, drawn as we all are at the Kremlin to any disagreement that threatens to erupt. One of the Hungarians gestures violently, turns his back, and stalks toward Khrushchev's table. His countryman follows at his heels and the argument commences again, louder than before. Suddenly, they throw themselves at each other. Those of us nearby are too shocked to do anything but stare as the men crash into the table, knocking over chairs as they wrestle to the ground.

This is high entertainment. We crowd in, our chitchat forgotten, all of us wholly focused on the brawl. My husband is speaking sternly to them in Hungarian. By his attitude, I can see he's telling them to stop this nonsense. He picks up two glasses and pours wine on those fighting dogs, to the delight and horror of the guests crowding around. The damp Hungarians climb to their feet, but neither looks embarrassed or ashamed. One smooths his hair and pushes his way out of the crowd, the other curses his back and leaves in the opposite direction.

"Wine diplomacy?" I say to Nikolai as he sets the glasses back on the table. "What were they arguing about?"

"What's everyone arguing about these days?"

We turn to Khrushchev. The Hungarian episode hasn't spoiled his mood; he's chatting to a small crowd, telling one of his famous jokes. The guests laugh and the mood in the room shifts again as if Stalin's ghost isn't floating among the chandeliers.

The waiters are cleaning the floor around our table, righting chairs, sweeping aside the fallen cutlery, a broken coffee cup, scraps of paper. It's then that I notice my purse is missing. I'd hung it on the back of the chair during the meal, and it was one of the chairs the Hungarians had knocked over. I think of my embroidered coin purse and my cigarette case from Berlin, if they're being swept up in someone's dustpan. I leave Nikolai to look around the table just as a waiter picks up the purse from the floor. When I say it's mine, he hands it to me, and I inspect it. Everything is there.

Before I can register where it comes from, I sense a change in the crowd around me, a new note of alarm that makes me turn, looking for its source. I find it in the waiter who had given me back my purse. He is speaking quietly to Dmitri Shepilov, my husband's rival for the Foreign Ministry. The waiter is handing him what looks like a soggy piece of paper. They turn to stare at me.

His antenna up, Nikolai gets to them before I do. Shepilov shows him the paper, a kind of card, I see now, with a photograph

I barely glimpse before Shepilov tilts it away. Nikolai can see it, and he glances at me. I don't know if I've ever seen my husband's anger balled so tightly in his dark eyes. But his voice is smooth, a diplomat bringing down the temperature of the room before it gets too warm again.

"I'm sure this can be explained away quickly," he says, gesturing for me to come closer.

Shepilov raises his voice and brandishes the card in the air. "This is very strange, Vera Ilyanovna. Very strange indeed. I'd like to hear your explanation."

He's loud enough for what I am now certain is the second act of a piece of theater started by the Hungarians. The audience gathers once more in loose groups, openly eager to see this next entertainment. Nursing a wine at the table, Furtseva watches me and gives away nothing on her face. I notice Molotov, still technically my husband's boss, hovering in the background, his color returned since he is not the one being attacked for once.

Still in his actor's voice, Shepilov says, "Do you recognize this paper?"

I do, though I've never seen it before. It's an employment card in English and German, issued by the British military government in Berlin to a woman named Ingrid Stetter. The photograph is clearly Marya.

The missing British paper from her KGB file.

"What is this doing here?" I ask calmly. Showing my anger will only reflect badly on me.

"We're asking you that. The woman in the photograph, who obviously worked for the British, looks very much like you." Shepilov peers at the card closely. "It was issued nine years ago in Berlin. You were in Berlin then, weren't you?"

The room is quieting, a vacuum freezing around me. Shepilov doesn't have to raise his voice anymore.

"My wife's sister was also in Berlin at that time," Nikolai says in an offhand way.

"And so were you, Nikolai Vasylyvich." Shepilov's tone drips with the implications of a link between the British card and my husband. It's an obvious attack on his rival for the Foreign Ministry, an attempt to muddy Nikolai's reputation.

Nikolai's smile takes on a razor edge. "You're correct, Dmitri Trofimovich, I had the honor to serve in Berlin with our military government and lay the foundation for the German Democratic Republic, our socialist friend and ally today. I fail to see what any of this has to do with that card. Perhaps you have questions about my wife's past service to the state? We'd be glad to answer them." I understand his strategy. With so many spectators around us, Nikolai wishes to be seen as the protector of his wife, a morally high position should Shepilov continue to root around in the filth of accusations and conspiracy theories. I appreciate Nikolai's willingness to defend me, but Marya is my sister and this is my fight.

"I can speak for myself, thank you, Kolya." I turn to the crowd and spot Khrushchev pushing his way through, looking curious. "Ah, Nikita Sergeyevich," I say, "my friends and emissaries from abroad, I'm glad you're all here to witness this farce."

Shepilov says, "You deny that photograph on a British card is you or your sister?"

"It's my sister."

"A convicted traitor and spy, if I recall," Molotov says, apropos of nothing as he works some grit out from under a fingernail. He has joined the theater troupe, I see, though he and Shepilov aren't friends.

"I believe I heard about that case," Shepilov says, as if on cue, "and here's the evidence to prove Vera Ilyanovna's sister was a traitor."

"And how," I say, "did this so-called evidence so conveniently land on the floor of this hall? With all of you here to see it? Are we supposed to start believing in coincidences?"

"It must have been in your purse," Shepilov says. "When the fighting started, it was dislodged from your purse and fell to the floor."

"Nothing of mine fell to the floor."

"We don't know that. The floor has been cleaned."

"I can assure you I've never seen this card before. It wasn't in my possession. Maybe the Hungarians dropped it in their fight? If I were to guess, I'd say they were fighting over a woman."

There is a slight shift in the crowd's mood, the faint sounds of laughter.

Shepilov says, "Don't try to change the subject. This is serious evidence of treason and espionage. We ask you again, what are you doing with this card?"

"It's in your hand, Dmitri Trofimovich, not mine. I've never held it. But I do think I know where it came from. I've been examining my sister's file, and I was informed by the investigator in her case that such a card existed. It was missing and now it's found. I'm very relieved to finally have it." I put out my hand. Shepilov hesitates.

"Why were you reading your traitorous sister's file?"

"Because I believe she might be innocent."

"With this evidence? It sounds like you're trying to erase the taint from your family, even by stealing evidence from a file. Shameful!"

I doubt he realizes it, but he's just handed me my counterargument. To show they can't get at me so easily, I take my time lighting a cigarette. Interestingly, Khrushchev is observing all this, but his gaze isn't fixed on me but on Shepilov, as if his protégé is being tested. Maybe Khrushchev knew about this theater? I catch Furtseva's eye; still, she gives away nothing. Furious but controlled, my husband is trying to read the room as I am, most of his attention on Khrushchev. Many people do the same, old habits from when Stalin's moods ruled our world.

I recall my days as a prosecutor and my voice changes its pitch to reach the audience, calm, firm, factual. I tell the room the juiciest of details, my sister's affair with an Englishman in Berlin—a crime under Stalin, but why? How could love be a crime? Wasn't this just another of the excesses of Stalin that Khrushchev so aptly laid out for us in his historic speech?

I turn to him, his focus on me now that I've mentioned him, and I gesture at the whole room as I continue to speak: "Is this not the moment in history when we return to Leninist principles in our hearts? When we examine what appears to be weakness, to look at our mistakes, analyze them, correct them? Are we not in a new age when we speak the truth, when we have the courage to give an account of what we've done?"

I snatch the card from Shepilov and brandish it in the air: "Nikita Sergeyevich has led the way. Do we dare to follow him? To act? His example inspired me to face my fears about my family and seek the truth about my sister. I don't know if this card is authentic or counterfeit, or who brought it here. But it's obvious someone is trying to embarrass and humiliate me or the people closest to me. But no! I thank this shadowy friend. I thank him for giving me the chance to show, in this new age of openness, that there's no need for secrecy anymore. I am not afraid, comrades. We should not be afraid of the truth anymore!"

Nikolai and Furtseva clap first, and it spreads rapidly through the crowd. I press the British paper to my heart and nod at Khrushchev with gratitude. His eyes are glistening from wine or the light I've just shined upon him.

"Courage," he says, breaking into a grin. He bellows at the room, "Vera Ilyanovna's got more in her eyelash than some of you in your whole bodies. She's an example to us all." He raises his glass for what must be his fifteenth toast. "To courage!"

19
Marya

Berlin, 6 July 1947

I stepped onto Henry's street, and it worked its magic on me. The boulevard, the fine houses, they swept away my anger at Felix and my shame at being a part of his blackmailing plot. It didn't matter now. It was done.

Opposite Henry's house, I left the central path for the street and glanced up at his balcony. In uniform and cap, Henry was at the railing staring down at me, not waving or smiling. He just drank from his glass and looked at me like I was a stranger in the street.

A car honked, and I scrambled out of the way. The front door was ajar. The foyer smelled of something freshly baked and fruity, one of Frau Koch's desserts. On the stairway, I looked up. Henry was waiting at the landing, his drink still in his hand and his face . . . closed. Cold. Shivering, I climbed the steps, the clack of my shoes loud in my ears.

When I reached the landing, Henry stood sentry in his doorway. Close up, his eyes were cracked and heavy and full of hurt. I knew what it meant. Of course I did. I stopped in front of him, and a flicker of something passed his face—horror, I thought, at the possibility that I would make a scene in the hallway where his neighbors would hear. I would not embarrass him in his own home. It was the least I could do.

Without a word, I passed him and stopped short in his sitting room. The tables were at the walls, the chairs pushed to the side. The cleared space on the floor was covered by papers, a grid in neat stacks. There was room to step between them if I was careful, but I didn't try.

"You're not curious?" he asked. "What all this is?"

Henry smelled so clean, so *him*. I closed my eyes and breathed him in and tried not to break down.

"Well, then, if you don't have the guts to say it, I'll help you along. Last week, I was working here at my desk"—the rolltop was open and empty—"and I noticed a funny thing. A report was missing. All right. I assumed I'd left it in the office. I searched for it there. Nothing. I quietly asked my colleagues. Nothing. The report was definitely missing. How could that be? What happened to it?"

For a moment, I wanted to say, *Did you ask Johnson?* Maybe his roommate took the papers. It was a possibility. Why did Henry seem to be blaming me? Because I was Russian? The English hated us. We all knew that. I pressed my fist to my mouth. I wasn't thinking straight. It was like someone else had taken over inside my head.

Henry bent down a little, looked me straight in the eye. "I'm only human," he said. "Maybe I overlooked something. I just needed to search my desk more carefully. So I did. And found a second report missing. Can you believe that? One could be an oversight. But two missing reports? They aren't in my office. My colleagues don't have them. So I laid out all my papers." He waved his arm at the room. "Each individual report. Each page. I know what files I have and what's in every single one of them. I know each file like my own hand. Two reports are missing. I've never mislaid a document, never in my whole bloody life. So where are they?"

The first tear slid down my face. I was afraid to move and wipe it away.

"Where are they?" he asked again, very calmly.

I took a gasping breath and tried to tell him, and what came out was, "I don't know."

"Stop crying."

I put my face in my hands.

"Stop crying, Marya, you won't get me that way." I heard him stalking over the papers, over his perfect grid, destroying the order he'd made. "Do you know what you've done? What this means?"

I nodded.

"What do you have to say?"

I gathered up all the air I had inside me. "I'm sorry. I'm so sorry."

"That makes it all right, then." He threw himself onto the sofa and lit a cigarette, the flame shaking. "I have to know: did you intend to do this all along? From the very beginning?"

"No. No, Henry, it was my sister. She threatened me. She said—"

"Even if that's true, *you say no*. You're a good woman. I thought you were. A good woman stands up for what's decent. If someone asked me to steal from you, I'd refuse. I'd go to jail first."

"She wanted to send me away. We could not see us, you and me, anymore . . ." My English grammar had collapsed. I couldn't think.

"If your sister really pressured you to do this, why didn't you tell me? I told you I'd help you."

I ordered the words in my mind. I was back to translating as if I'd never absorbed his language into my heart. "If I drew a line on the floor and on one side is your country and I'm on the other, which would you choose?"

"She got you that easily?"

"It's a real question, Henry. I'm not a Western woman. I'm not here to find a husband. I'm a Soviet officer. I have responsibilities to my country."

He looked surprised. "So you're a fan of Stalin after all?"

"No. That isn't the same as working for my country."

"How is that not the same? Moscow controls you."

"As London controls you."

He poured himself a new drink. "That's definitely not the same."

"There is a difference between being loyal to your country and people and loyal to your government, yes, I know that. It is the basis of revolutions. But I had to choose between my country and you. That is different. You're my heart, my happiness. But I won't give up everything I am for you. I can't turn my back on my country for you."

"I never asked you to."

"What do you think emigration is?"

His glass clinked as he set it down hard on the cabinet. "So your sister fed you a sodding lot of nonsense about your duty as an officer, and I'm assuming there was a lot about the war, some threats mixed in—and in the end, you betrayed me willingly."

"I didn't want to. I had no choice."

"You did have a choice. You just said." He kicked some of his papers aside. "There was a line on the bloody floor."

"You never answered my question. Me or your country? Which would you choose, Henry?"

"You, the spy? It's no contest. You, the woman I thought I knew for eight months? Nothing in the world more important to me than her. I was willing to give up almost everything for her. But since she doesn't exist, I'm saved the trouble." He went back to his glass. "I'm going to have to tell my people about those reports. I'll be investigated, there might be a court-martial. I might go to prison. At the very least, I'll be sent home with a dishonorable discharge and a kick in the backside. It's the end of my career, Marya. The end of a lot of things." He took a deep drink.

"Henry, my love—"

"I think you should go, Comrade Lieutenant. Don't come back."

I had trouble standing, needed the wall to support myself. He was throwing me out? Just like that? How could he after everything he'd said? What he'd promised me? "You said you would stand by me, Henry."

He almost laughed, a strangling sound. "That was before I knew you'd been spying on me."

"'Whatever comes, I'll stand by you.' That's what you said. 'Whatever happens'—"

"Oh, for fuck sake." He swept the papers up in his arms and flung them at me. "You want secrets? Take them. Take everything, but get out." Papers were fluttering around the room as he tossed them again. One sent a burning slice into the hand I held up to protect myself. I fled into the hall and out the door, stumbled into a man on the stairway. "Oi!" he cried. It was Johnson. I pushed past him and ran.

AFTER DARK, VERA was waiting for me outside the barracks. I saw her from the end of the street and she saw me. She wasn't smoking, which didn't strike me as strange, though it should have. My sister clung to the few habits she had. But now, frosted on the edge of the nearest floodlight, she was different. At attention, in her way, shoulders back, fists clenched. By the time I could see her face, I felt her tension in my own jaw.

I walked past her and through the gate, ignoring the guard. Vera followed, and as the double doors of the barracks loomed before me, I couldn't stand the thought of going in, of going to our private hallway, alone with her. I veered off into the dried grass and walked along the dark, blind row of barracks windows. I didn't know where I was going. I was inside the perimeter. There was nowhere to go but in circles.

"Marya."

"Go away." I hated how girlish I sounded. I even kicked a stone in the grass, I was so childish, as if there were no other way I could be angry at her. With her, I was always eight years old.

"Tell me what happened."

"You don't already know? You know everything, don't you?"

We'd come to a dark strip where the floodlights didn't reach. I didn't know if we could be seen from the windows or heard from the other side of the fence. I didn't care.

"Listen to me, Masha. You have every right to be angry. But you must set it aside and think calmly, or all is lost. Markow has stolen something very valuable from the Americans, and I need you to get it for me."

"You'll get it if you pay for it, didn't Felix tell you that this morning? What you won't be getting is anything else from Henry. He knows. He threw me out, he was—"

"So you do know about the list." She gestured, a shadowy movement in the dark. "I must have it, and I need it done quietly, no fuss. What Markow wants as payment is ridiculous, impossible. It can't be done, and I'm not in the mood to bargain. I can get it from you the easy way, or from him the hard way. Which would you like it to be?"

Her callousness stunned me. I'd told her Henry had snuffed out my happiness, the only joy in my life, and she was completely unmoved. I didn't mean a thing to her. I was a tool in her plans.

"I suppose you're aiming for another promotion," I said. "I know how ambitious you are, Vera. You want to go far. You'll be in the Kremlin one day. The people on that list get to die to add to your power."

"You don't understand—"

"I'm your sister. I understand you better than anyone else in the world, even Mama. She doesn't know what you are now. What a reunion we've had, Vera. How proud Mama would be to see us like this."

"Stop overreacting. Will you get the list for me or not?"

There was no talking to her. I tore myself away to the perimeter fence and banged my palm into one of the slats. It barely shook, planted solidly by the German workers. I moved on to the next, slapping and pressing the wood, yanking at chicken wire, all along the perimeter. There'd be a space where the women of the barracks had cut away a door to the world. There were always people who found a secret way to free themselves. If no one had done it here yet, I would.

"Masha." Vera caught my arm. I shook her off and went to the next strip of fencing.

"The mission with Henry has failed," I said. "Send me home now. I don't care anymore."

"Not yet. You might still be useful."

"This is my *life*, Vera."

"And there's no greater use for it than to serve your land and people. Or have you been corrupted by the West? Do you only care about yourself and people you love and no one else?"

"I thought I could be loyal to my country and selfish with Henry but look at me now. It wasn't a real choice after all, was it?"

"The only choice is them or us. This is about how to live, Masha."

Them or us. It split my head, this *them or us*. But what did Vera know about that? She believed in all the things that divided us, not the things we all share as people. It was a convenient way to think. Being cruel was so much easier. Starting wars. Controlling people like I'd let her control me all my life.

For the first time, my discussions with Felix, my experiences in the war, my life in Berlin, sharpened to one simple truth. "I want to be free to choose how I live, Vera."

"Free to do what? Count coins? Use this or that cosmetic? Buy this or that car? Have you become so small-minded? The Westerners talk so much about freedom because they can't see their own chains."

"We can't see ours either." I moved down the fence. "I do see them. I have for a long time, but I never said anything."

"Because you're a sensible, intelligent woman. Most of the time. Just because you've hit an obstacle in the mission and your flimsy heart has been punctured doesn't mean you should call everything into question. You've done well in your life and will continue to do so, with guidance."

"Not from you."

She grasped my arm again, hard this time, and pulled me into another dark strip just out of sight of the floodlights. I struggled, but she was stronger.

"You need me now more than ever, Masha. Let's talk about Henry Barrow. For the sake of argument, let's assume he's the honest, upright man he appears to be. He realizes his Russian girlfriend has been taking confidential information from him. What does he do? Runs to his superiors and pours out his heart about you, of course. If he threw you out today, he'll go crawling to British intelligence tomorrow. What do you think happens next?"

I was sick thinking about it. "He'll be in terrible trouble. Because of me. Because of you."

"You need to worry less about him and more about yourself. The British have good noses for this sort of thing. They'll be very interested in you and what you might do for them. They'll handle it subtly. They won't throw Barrow out of Berlin or out of his job. They'll keep him in place as bait to lure you into their sphere. If Barrow comes back to you with kisses and oaths of love, you'll know what's behind it."

Her grip was hurting me. "He wouldn't do that."

"You'd be amazed what people do to save their own skins. When it happens, go along with it. Give nothing away. That's an advantage we can use."

"I can't do this anymore. I can't live like this. Doing one thing and thinking and feeling another."

"Don't be stupid. It's the only way to survive."

"Your way. Not mine."

Her grip eased. "Masha, trust me on this and do as I say. Anything else will lead to catastrophe."

It already had. In one stroke, Vera had taken my deepest wish—that Henry would come to his senses and see that I loved him and forgive me—and twisted it into another game between us and them. Today, he'd discovered he couldn't trust my love. Now, I feared I couldn't trust his.

"You've ruined everything, Vera. Send me home now. I want to go home."

"Oh, grow up. Do you think this is a game? Everything we're doing is deadly serious. There's no going home to Mother to get out of it. We're in it. You were in it long before I came to Berlin. Or do you think it was coincidence that Henry Barrow left confidential documents at home? Outdated ones, at that? The ones you brought are nearly a year old. Does he strike you as a sloppy man when it comes to his work?"

Felix had warned me about the same thing. "He wouldn't. He said . . ." I was shaking, cold and hot. Henry had been so angry with me, and it wasn't an act. My betrayal had shattered him. It had real consequences for him. If Vera was trying to soften it, to make me think that what I'd done to him was a lesser crime because he'd lured me to it, it wouldn't work. "I don't believe you. This is what you do, Vera. You take what I love and twist it. You always have, my whole life."

"Really? That's what you think? Stupid girl, open your eyes, I'm trying to help you. I've been trying to help you since I came to Berlin, and it's true whether you believe it or not. And now I need your help. I need that American list."

"After what you've done to me, you have the nerve to ask for my help? If you need the list, fine. Get it yourself."

"I can't just—" Her voice dropped to barely a whisper, her face so close to mine, I felt the heat from her skin and her fast, ragged breaths. "My name is on it."

I let out the same strangled laugh Henry had earlier. "Right, Vera. You're an agent for the Americans. You."

She half turned away from me. I could see her dark profile. "Yes. Me."

Suddenly I was so tired, I swayed where I stood. This was what she truly thought of me. *Stupid girl*, she'd said. She wanted that list and would tell any lie to get it. I was supposed to believe Vera— who had never stepped outside the party lines in her life—would work for dollars and hot dogs. She truly thought I was that gullible, that easy to manipulate. And maybe I was. Up to now.

"Did an American spy come knocking on your door, then? And what do you do for them anyway? Meet in some dark alley to pass them our secrets? Do they pay you in green money?"

She flashed a look of utter fury at me, but her voice was calm. "I was recruited while on Rudenko's staff at the International Military Tribunal in Nuremberg. I spent a year in the American Zone; contacting them was easy. Since then, I've become something of a window into our world for them. I tell them about the hidden structure within the military government, secret departments, our personnel, our assumptions, hopes, way of thinking, taboos. They are interested in who and what we are under the surface. This is not about cracking a certain code or passing them a certain document. It's about them building a complete picture of the adversary."

"The adversary. Us."

"Stalin's government. The country Stalin has created. The country that sends the secret police to arrest a good and loyal comrade like our father years after he died." Her voice had risen, and she wrestled to control it again. "We are from a country of heartless laws where there is no justice. A country of gulags. A country of scared people. That is what we are, Marya. I'm working to change it. I don't love the Americans, but they're our best chance for reform."

"That all sounds very nice but I don't believe a word you say anymore, Vera. Maybe someday you'll know what a horrible woman you are. Maybe you know it already and you don't care. I don't care anymore either."

I began trudging over the grass toward the doors.

"Masha, *please*—"

The tone of her voice—I'd never heard it before. Soft, and something else beneath. Almost desperate.

We stared at each other. I could feel the heat of her struggle with herself. She was ashamed of her burst of real warmth. That *Masha, please*. To her, sentiment showed weakness. It was too much like me.

When she finally spoke again, she raised her chin, back to her old commanding tone. "I'm giving you one week to get that list to me with no questions. I'm doing this for you. I know you don't want the German to get hurt, so I'm willing to keep him out of it as long as I get that list. You have no idea what a risk I'm taking. But if I don't get it, and someone else does . . ."

"What? What would you do to me?"

"Whatever is necessary to save my mission."

I'm doing this for you. Vera lied to herself as much as she lied to me.

20

Vera

Testimony for Chairman A. Cheptsov

Military Collegium of the Supreme Court of the USSR

Moscow, 28 February–3 June 1956

[RECORDING]

On my husband's arm, I leave the May Day luncheon in good spirits. We're silent in the car home, in the elevator, in the apartment as we open the windows to air out the rooms. I take the armchair next to the bookcase and put my feet up on the ottoman. From there, I watch my husband putter around, hanging up his jacket, taking off his tie. I try to steady my hands as I bring the cigarette to my lips. Now that the immediate danger of the intrigue has passed, I feel sick to my stomach.

After finishing his little errands, my husband turns on the radio—loud—and stretches out on the couch.

"I'm going to kill him," he says beneath the music.

"Who?"

"Shepilov. Molotov is about to lose the Foreign Ministry. It'll go to Shepilov or me, and Shepilov wanted to make sure it isn't me by humiliating you. He planned the whole thing."

"I'm afraid he's going to get the Foreign Ministry no matter what, Kolya. He's a Presidium candidate and you're not. Maybe what happened today was planned by you."

"Are you mad?" Nikolai sits up. "If you think I'd do something like that to you. . . ." He's slipped out of his usual moderate tone and struggles to reclaim it. "I'm not the one who reopened Marya's case. I'm not the one who's been running between the Lubyanka, the court, and the archives digging up dirt from the past. I didn't want anyone to know what we have in the family. You know what that could do to us if it all comes out. Why would I put you on the spot in front of Khrushchev and the whole world?"

"Maybe because the main danger to us was the secrecy, not the case itself. So . . ." I light another cigarette and sink back into my chair. "I've defused the danger by airing out the secret. If all of Moscow knows about it, how can it hurt us?"

"Vera, what is wrong with you? Pull yourself together and think about who your real enemies are, because it's not me. I'm your closest ally. Have you forgotten that? What we are? What I've done for you?"

I haven't forgotten. Nikolai's words finally crack through the protective shell I built around myself at the luncheon. I'm ashamed of what I said to him just now, and I reach for his hands. "I'm sorry, Kolya. I don't know what I was thinking. Of course it was Shepilov. Who knows how long he's known about Marya. He could've stolen the card from her file years ago waiting for a moment to use it."

"We'll make sure he regrets it. In our own time."

I kiss him to seal the bargain, then sit back, the British card in my hand. In the photo, Marya is pale as a spirit, wearing a very English tweed jacket. It could still be a counterfeit manufactured to convict her, but I don't think it is. State security wouldn't have gone to the trouble. Pity the card has been touched by so many fingers. I might have found prints, a clue as to who precisely handled the thing between the KGB file and the Kremlin luncheon.

"Do you remember the German Felix Markow? From Berlin?"

"I'd rather not."

"I'm the same, but if you think about it, he helped make us what we are today. Operation Sentinel. American spies in our ranks. Markow's private little covert action. I've found an unexpected link between Markow and Marya, and I'm worried it could lead to Sentinel."

My husband massages his forehead. "Everything about Sentinel is classified. For good reason. Leave it."

"It's too late for that. I've found intelligence from the Englishman Henry Barrow—my sister's lover—in our archives. Delivered to us by Rheingold—Felix Markow. Marya acquired the intel, Markow delivered it. I have strong reason to believe Markow was teaching her the tricks of his trade. She's not a traitor, but maybe she was a spy after all. For us. Trained by Markow, the origin of Operation Sentinel. Is that a coincidence? Maybe . . . but I don't believe in those."

"You triumphed today, Vera, but don't let it go to your head. You're not invincible, you know. If you take this much further, you might find that out sooner than you'd like."

He goes into the bedroom to change, and I'm finally alone with my thoughts, where I'd rather be after such a turbulent day. I've been deep enough in Marya's case, in my own memories of Berlin 1947, that it's easy to follow the thread in my mind back to the beginning of Operation Sentinel, 6 July 1947.

IT WAS A scheduled meeting at Treptower Park, where Markow was to update me on what he'd found out observing Henry Barrow on my behalf. As arranged, I waited for him at eleven in the morning near the photo booth where mostly couples and some mothers with children lined up to have their pictures taken for three marks. After a few minutes, I spotted Markow strolling in my direction drinking what looked like cola out of a glass bottle. He had a second one, already open, and he held it out to me.

"Peace offering."

"I can't stand the stuff."

"It's liquid and it's cold. You going to refuse a little refreshment on this warm day?"

The bottle was surprisingly cold to the touch as if he'd lifted it from a pile of ice only minutes ago. Instead of asking him where he got it, I pressed the bottle to my cheek, grateful for a chance to cool my nerves.

"Shall we walk, Herr Markow?"

We did, weaving around the line at the photo booth and continuing into the park. The war had left much of it barren, and every blade of grass grew, I knew, on bloody ground. Platoons of men, Germans and our own, were at work removing earth from a large area of the park that would one day be the biggest Soviet memorial in Berlin, far grander than the one we'd put up rather hastily, though beautifully done, in the Tiergarten. As we passed the lines of sweating Germans bent over their shovels, Markow looked hard at each of them as if searching for someone he knew. He relaxed somewhat when we were past the construction site and in the open park.

"Well?" I said. "You've found something on the Englishman?"

"Not yet." From his bottle, he took the kind of drink men do when they need courage, deep, long, swallowed whole. "But it's still your lucky day," he said. "This afternoon, I'm going to get my hands on something you're really going to want, and I'm offering you the first opportunity to buy it."

I'd known he was the right man for the job. "You did find something on Barrow after all?"

"No, this is much more interesting."

"Herr Markow, I hired you to find—"

"It's an American list," he interrupted, his mouth obscured by the lip of his bottle. "A list of Soviet personnel right here in Germany in the pay of the United States."

We stopped walking. I confess it took several moments for what he'd said to sink in. Markow looked over his shoulder as he'd been doing all along. The couple walking closest to us were ignoring us completely, the man an American soldier singing in operatic style in Italian, the girl snuggled against his shoulder and looking up at him in adoration. We waited until they were gone.

"Are you playing a joke on me?" I asked quietly.

"I'm dead serious. I can hand the list over to you as soon as you have the payment."

"As *our agent*, it's *your duty* to give us that kind of intelligence."

"For free? Sorry, I have plans for my future, and I need the funds."

I knew Markow to be a valuable agent, but I would've been a fool to trust him when it came to something like this. He was scared; that was clear. As we continued our walk, he noticed every soldier who came anywhere near us, and the origin of his uniform, as I did, falling silent when it was an American, though each one who passed us was young with a girl on his hip. They weren't interested in us.

"Why are you so nervous?" I asked Markow.

"Plan to steal top-secret information from the Amis and see how relaxed you are."

"You said this afternoon. You don't have it yet?"

"I will."

"How? How are you getting this? Who are you getting it from?"

"If I told you that, you'd do it yourself and I'm out of the deal. You'll just have to trust me."

I was still wary, of course. Intelligence like this was too good to be true. "If the list is genuine," I said as we crossed the meadow again, "how much do you think we'll pay you for it?"

"Fifty thousand US dollars."

I laughed. "Would you like us to give you the British crown jewels on top of that?"

"The list is worth it."

He was right, but I didn't want to give that away. If I could get my hands on a genuine list of Soviet traitors, it would be a coup. It'd cement my reputation for years. Money was nothing compared to that.

"I have to consult with my side about payment. I'm not authorized to promise more at the moment."

Markow looked unhappy but nodded. We were almost back at the line of people at the photo booth.

"And I do need to know who's giving you that list, Herr Markow. I don't want you writing down random Russian names and running off with a fortune."

"I wouldn't do that to you," he said, grinning.

"I want to know your source or I won't go forward with this."

Markow looked exasperated, but in the end he said, "It's somebody inside US Mil Gov. I'm not telling you more until I get the list. Tonight, when I have it, I'll get a message to you with more information. The fewer people who know about this before it happens, the better. Afterward, I'll tell you whatever you want to know." As irritating as it was, I had no choice but to accept these conditions.

That night, I was called out of the barracks to pick up an envelope addressed to me that had been left at the guard post. The guard insisted he'd only closed his eyes a few moments, and when he opened them, the envelope was on the little table beside him. Inside was a slip of paper written in code: *Mission accomplished. Source: Irina Petrova, US Mil Gov.* I stuck the note into my pocket as if it meant nothing, but I returned to the barracks buzzing with Markow's triumph. He'd done it. Until then, I hadn't quite believed he would. The list would soon be in my hands, and I could begin hunting down the traitors one by one.

However, I found myself in a dilemma. If I told my MGB superiors about the list right away, they might refuse to negotiate with Markow and proceed immediately to more robust tactics. At the time, I knew Marya had been going to see him for what I'd thought were mainly sentimental reasons. I had no idea about her spying on Barrow. I worried about what the MGB would think if they dissected Markow's life and found out she'd been seeing him in a Western sector in secret. As far as I knew, she had nothing to do with the list, but my colleagues might not see it that way.

I also hesitated to go to my superiors in the MGB because one of them could be a traitor on the list. I couldn't risk exposing my hand. I didn't have the money to pay Markow myself, or the personnel who could search for the list quietly without alerting my superiors or running off with the list themselves. Any way I looked at it, I couldn't handle the case alone, as much as I wanted to.

I sought the help of only one person, someone outside the MGB whom I could trust—Nikolai Koshkin. At that time, he was a war comrade and friend working in Marshal Sokolovsky's office. We'd reacquainted ourselves in Berlin, and I found him just as quick, discerning, intelligent, and discreet as he'd been in the war when our paths had crossed in Moscow, and later in Nuremberg. I was glad to have an excuse to work with him.

He agreed that Markow's list was too delicate a matter to leave to the local MGB. We considered our options, and the risk of alerting Moscow about the list. If the deal fell through and we didn't get it, the consequences for us would be severe. Moscow tolerated no failure. Under no circumstances could the names of those traitors get into someone else's hands. We needed authority and resources that would allow us to act as we saw fit to fulfill the mission. In the end, Nikolai tapped his contacts in Moscow, and from there, I was given authorization to pursue the matter quietly.

In the following days, Markow was cautious, not appearing at the safehouse or at his family's apartment. We left word with his landlord that we were interested in negotiating payment as quickly as possible. We also tried to locate Irina Petrova, but the Americans must have smelled something wrong with her. By the time we knew where to find her, she'd been pulled out of Berlin and sent back to her home in New York.

Petrova. I wonder if Ivanov can help me find her? After all, she is American, and he is the KGB deputy chief for North America. He might even be able to get me over the Atlantic quickly and quietly, so I can have a little chat with her about Markow's list without relying on local agents. Maybe she'll tell me if he worked alone when he acquired the list. In Berlin, I hadn't known he and Marya were working together to get information from Barrow. But since they were, what about the American list? Was my sister also a part of one of the biggest missions Markow and I were ever involved in?

21

Marya

Vera was knocking on the door of my miserable little room at the barracks. I knew it was her. I knew her step, the way she breathed, her silence. How she could wait. The door didn't have a lock; she could've come in. But she waited and I waited, curled up on my mattress, my thumb plugging the bottle I'd been drinking out of, nestling it under me, warming it like a baby.

"Marya, pull yourself together. You have things to do."

A spasm hit me, a sick feeling I choked down by biting on the neck of the bottle. Henry was gone. He was gone from my life. If I'd had the energy, if I'd slept at all the past few days, or drunk less, I would've got up and flung open the door and raged at her.

"I gave you one week," she said from the hallway, "and you've wasted half of it feeling sorry for yourself. If you're not too drunk to look at a calendar or a clock, I suggest you get moving. Are you coming to breakfast?"

I couldn't think of food. My stomach was twisted up. Behind the door, Vera let out a long sigh as if she were the one suffering, and she marched away. Tap-tap-tap. I hated how the soles of her shoes rang on the floor. It did my head in.

When she was good and gone, I struggled to sit up. The bottle sloshed beside me, and I set it carefully on the floor. On my feet, I groped for my uniform and my bath things and opened the door. In the hallway, on the wall directly opposite, hung a calendar. The thirteenth was circled several times in black. The sixth, seventh, eighth, and ninth were crossed out. There was a star on the tenth. Today. I didn't care what day it was and I certainly didn't care about getting that American list for Vera. Let her pay Felix and be done with it. I tore the calendar off the wall, tossed it on the floor, and went into the bathroom.

I spent as little time as possible fixing myself up while not looking at myself in the mirror. Henry was gone. I had almost nothing left of him except the bracelet he'd given me. I had one of his letters, the only one I'd saved. It was hidden from Vera, rolled up in the handle of my hairbrush. I'd burned his portrait at my cottage. Only Felix had photographs of us now.

I went back into my room, pulling my uniform dress over my head and flinging it onto the mattress. I dragged a civilian dress out of my bag and put that on. I slipped on my sandals, grabbed my purse and papers, and went into the hallway. I found Vera in the main corridor pretending to examine the rotation for kitchen duties on the wall, her hands clasped so tightly behind her back, I was surprised her fingers didn't break. Her eyes were haggard, as if she hadn't been sleeping either.

"Ah, she lives."

"Tell my superiors I'm assigned somewhere else today." I didn't wait for Vera to agree. I knew she'd do it. I left the barracks for the train station.

AT THE BAR where Felix kept his room, I found the landlord and a few shady-looking men unloading a truck. Empty crates were stacked at the curb. When I asked if Felix was in, he gave me his wet smile.

"Hasn't been here in days."

I didn't like that. Not at all. "You'll let me into his room again, won't you? I'm worried about him."

"He said you're allowed, Fräulein. You and no one else." He led me up the stairs, unlocked the door, and we both stared into the room.

The contents of Felix's wardrobe and drawers were scattered on the floor. I'd done that when I was there last time looking for the photographs. But now the mattress and pillow were slit open, and the chair rails pried up from the walls and scattered like broken tracks on the floor. The wardrobe doors hung off their hinges, the curtains ripped from the window. The pages of his books were torn away and strewn across the room. The bindings lay abandoned in a heap.

"When did this happen?" I asked the landlord.

"No idea. Didn't hear a thing." He rubbed the dome of his skull and backed into the hallway.

Someone had been searching for the list: my sister or the Americans or some other enemy of Felix. I picked at the debris looking for a hint of who'd done this, or what happened. Sheltered under an overturned drawer I found a white box with a pink ribbon. It was torn open, brown papers tossed around it, some still containing perfect little chocolates. I tried to refill the box as best I could and tied it with a bow. There was no card or tag, but if Felix had managed to get such a precious thing, I had no doubt it was for Greta. I remembered him saying something about her turning eight years old soon. I tucked the box in my purse. Maybe he'd gone home for her birthday and hadn't wanted to take this half-ruined gift.

Nothing in the room gave me a clue about who had searched it so violently, or if they'd found what they wanted. If they hadn't, they might look for Felix at his wife's home. She'd told me never to come back, but this was urgent.

I retraced my steps along the canal and turned up Lynarstraße. In front of his house, I sighed with relief. Felix was up on a ladder, driving a nail into the plaster under the first-floor window. A silver garland hung from the nail and dangled to the ground.

"Almost done, Peti." He climbed off the ladder and gave the hammer to his son. When Felix turned, he finally noticed me, and anxiety flared in his face.

I stalked up to him and pushed him so that he stumbled over a broken brick on the pavement. "That's for leaving me at that game."

Felix burst out laughing. That's how harmless he thought I was. "Your room over the bar has been searched, did you know that?" I said. "I was worried about you." I pushed him again, and he held out his arms, making shushing sounds and glancing at the window over our heads. Greta was there, and then Leni appeared beside her, staring down at me coldly.

"We'll talk later, all right? Tomorrow." Felix moved the stepladder to the other side of the door, climbed up, and fixed the end of the garland to the nail already driven into the wall. He called to Greta, "Birthday decorations all done." She beamed at him from the sill.

"I'm not coming back tomorrow," I said as he climbed down. "I did my part. I want what you promised me." I took the box of chocolates from my purse and gave it to Peter, who seemed to know they were for his sister. He placed it carefully in the toolbox.

"It's all right," Felix said. "Everything's fine."

This close, I saw the cracks in his eyes and smelled the drink on him. "No, it's not. My sister wants me to get the list from you. She's trying to undermine your deal."

He didn't look surprised. "Things are a little complicated. I really need you to stay out of it."

"What about my photographs?"

"I burned them. Negatives too."

Just one. I'd wanted just one picture of Henry to remember him by, and I couldn't even have that.

"Hey, hey Marya, don't cry in the street, people'll think I'm being mean to you. Come on." Felix put his arm around me and walked me to the curb a few houses down. I wasn't crying, not really, it was only the pressure behind my eyes. Felix was looking at me as if deciding whether to tell me something I wouldn't like.

"If you tell me I'm better off without him, I'll rip your heart out."

"I wasn't going to say that." He pulled a paper out of his pocket, folded in quarters, and I snatched at it. A photo, Henry and me outside the gate to his house. He was half-turned, opening the gate for me. My face was in full view; I was smiling at something that had caught my attention in the street. I looked like another woman from back when things were simpler and I was happy.

"It's not a good angle if you want to weep over his pretty face," Felix said.

I didn't ask him why he'd kept that one photo. I could guess. I threw my arms around him and drew back quickly before he had to decide whether to hug me back. "Thank you."

"We'll talk more tomorrow. Now, get out of here before my wife kills me on our daughter's birthday."

As he turned to go, a black car roared down the street and squealed to a stop beside him. The two doors facing him opened, men in suits piled out, scooped him up, and threw him into the car. Doors closed, and the car roared to life again. It passed me in a hot gust of wind and exhaust, so close that I fell back against the curb. Through the back window, I saw only the hats of the men who'd taken him.

It happened that fast. Seconds.

From the upstairs window of their house, Leni was leaning out, clutching the sill, her eyes wide with disbelief. Greta was beside her, her cheek pressed against her arm. On the doorstep, Peter woke up from his shock. "Papa!" He tore off down the street, screaming and flailing his arms.

The terror of a five-year-old ripped at my heart. I ran after him and caught him from behind. "No!" He kicked the air, squirmed out of my arms, and I had to stumble after him and grab him again.

"Peter, stop. You can't catch them."

"Yes, I can! Papa!"

I wrestled him home, pinned to my body, as he scratched and tried to bite me. Leni met me at the street door, fell to her knees, and took him tightly into her arms. Greta's eyes were filled with tears, and it was worse than Peter's rage, this silent girl's confusion and fright.

"What happened?" I asked Leni. "Who was that?"

Her son in her arms, she looked up at me with her usual look of anger and accusation. "You're telling me they weren't Russians?"

"No." But I wasn't sure. If it was my people, if it was Vera, she'd wanted me to see him taken. It was her warning. The same thing could happen to me.

Leni was still clutching her children. "You led them here. You did this to him." She lifted Peter, who hung from her like dead weight, and carried him into the house. I followed, Greta silent like a ghost beside me as we went up the stairs. When I offered to take her hand, she shook her head violently. She was looking at me as if what happened to her father were my fault.

Leni installed the children on the sofa, and then came at me with her fists up. I backed into the kitchen, talking as firmly as I could. "Frau Markow, I didn't know this would happen. I didn't lead them here."

"Liar."

"Are you going to the police?"

It stopped her. It seemed she hadn't thought of what to do next. The Germans had no jurisdiction over occupation forces, if someone from the old Allies had taken Felix. But something had to be done. We couldn't act as if nothing had happened. At the very least, the French could be informed. It was their sector.

Leni dropped her fists. "I'll call the police, all right. I'll tell them the Russians did it. I'll tell them about you."

"The Germans don't have the authority to do anything about me and you know it. I'll try to find out if my people did this. But there are other possibilities. I think Felix had a lot of enemies."

Leni went to the shelf and came back holding my fairy-tales book. I'd forgotten I'd left it there for the children. "Take it. We don't want you here. We don't need your help. Just go." She thumped it against my chest, a sharp ache in my ribs.

"I'll find out what I can, Frau Markow. I swear I will. I can ask"— *Henry to help us*, I was going to say, then remembered. He wouldn't want to see me. Anyway, it was Vera who would have answers. I was sure of it.

The children sat pale and silent on the sofa. I considered going to them, saying some encouraging word. But at a look from Leni, I silently turned and left.

When I got back to the barracks, I waited for my sister, pacing our private hallway until the sun went down. She didn't come. No one had seen her. Vera had vanished too.

22

Vera

Testimony for Chairman A. Cheptsov
Military Collegium of the Supreme Court of the USSR
Moscow, 28 February–3 June 1956

[RECORDING]

This is my second time in New York, and as the airplane banks over the harbor and the Statue of Liberty, I acknowledge the vibrant energy of the American way of life and the many perks it brings—to people with money. But out my window, deep between the skyscrapers, I also see the grime and despair of the people left behind, who have little or nothing of the city's glamor. It is for those people, the working people and the weak, that we must correct the errors of our system. A humane communism can still change the world.

I leave the airport and wait for the driver Ivanov arranged for the rest of this trip, the familiar city noise throbbing in my ears.

Moscow can be loud, full of bulldozers and building cranes, but I've rarely experienced the din of New York's streets with its many cars and buses, engines and horns. Our squares are often full of people, and motor vehicles are rare. This place feels and smells as if it is made for the mechanical inhabitants, and the humans are forced to endure them. It sets my teeth on edge, and I'm glad for the driver, a man in a crumpled suit who calls my name while chewing his disgusting gum. He escorts me to the peaceful backseat of the car and pulls away from the curb, honking as warning or for the joy of it. I assume he's KGB and chat with him about harmless things.

Before heading to the meeting with Irina Petrova, I perform a few tasks that justify my diplomatic passport. Throughout the day, I have several enlightening meetings with certain non-governmental organizations and officials at the United Nations.

Afterward, the driver brings me to the New Yorker Hotel, where Ivanov has booked me a room. I step into the shade of the heavy marquis, charmed by the gaudy grandeur all around me. I much prefer the simplicity of my dacha, but there is something to be said for marble and shining brass in small doses.

We're to meet on the terrace floor overlooking the lobby. Petrova is already there, lounging on a sofa near a potted palm, her sandaled foot bobbing to the rhythm of the music whose origin I can't see. I recognize her from the photograph I acquired from the KGB, and sit beside her, greeting her as if we're strangers who happen to share a space. I'm excited to begin this meeting, hopeful it will fill in the gaps in my knowledge about Operation Sentinel.

After ordering a martini from a passing waiter, I turn to Petrova, who says the code. "I'd have a Sea Breeze if I were you. The perfect cocktail for summer."

"I have never had one, thank you. I think I will try it next."

This exchange is difficult for me to do without sighing. I have never liked these silly coded phrases. But now we're both certain who we are sharing the sofa with. I look around. Along the ornate railing are other palm trees, other sofas. In one, a man reads a newspaper, his face hidden. Very traditional. In another, two men who I take to be FBI are pretending to be businessmen negotiating over their cigars. I'm sure they'll be keenly listening to us over the music. It doesn't matter. I have no secrets, or else I wouldn't have agreed to hold this conversation in an open lobby as Petrova suggested.

If she cares about the surveillance, she doesn't bother to show it, a sign that she told American agencies about me as soon as Ivanov began the negotiations for this meeting. She had insisted she hasn't worked for American intelligence since she was in Berlin, and then sent to prison for the "misunderstanding," as she called it, around Markow's list. She agreed to speak with me only after we consented to pay her a certain amount. She is American, after all.

Petrova is a garish woman with a false face caked with cosmetics as if she doesn't trust her own beauty. She works at her parents' greengrocers in Brooklyn, the only work she got after her release from federal prison. I explain to her that I am seeking justice for a woman who went to prison just like Petrova, after being entangled with the German Felix Markow in Berlin. I set Markow's photograph on the sofa between us, and she flushes at the sight of him.

"I remember him. He used to chat with a German secretary at US Mil Gov. They went to school together, or something. He'd pick her up for drinks and I bet she blabbed about everybody at HQ while he got her drunk. Who knows what else he did to get her to talk? She wasn't much of a catch even for the American boys, and he was pretty handsome, the jerk."

Petrova gives me a significant look. I assure her that I, too, thought Markow capable of any low acts to get the information he wanted.

"Well," she says, "the German girl must've tipped him off I was born in Russia. He tried to charm me, but I brushed him off. I thought that was the end of it. But then about a month after, I get an envelope. Anonymous. Full of photos."

"Did these photographs catch you at an intimate moment?"

Looking irritated, Petrova leans closer, her voice low. "I don't know how that guy got the photos, but he had them. A couple days later, he showed up outside my house. Said he'd give me the rest of the pictures if I could get him a list of Soviets working for us."

"How did he know you had access to that kind of information?"

"He'd been watching me all right. And that blabbermouth probably did the rest."

Without saying it aloud, I assume that blabbermouth, as Petrova calls the German secretary, was one of the informants Markow had recruited for our networks.

"How did you acquire the list?" I ask.

Quietly, Petrova explains there was no actual list, not at first. Each agent had an alphanumeric code recorded upon a card, which had its own code. The code of that card was recorded on a second card, which contained the actual contact information for the agent. The second card was stored in a separate location.

In order for Petrova to make a master list of agents, she had to gain access to both card files. In her routine work, she had access to the first, but not to the second. She succeeded in gaining access via a subterfuge that formed the basis of her prosecution and prison sentence later. She refuses to go into more detail.

"Why," I ask her, "did you take such a large risk? What did you do that would have worse consequences than getting caught by the Americans?"

"I said no comment about what I did."

Petrova is on her third cocktail and is starting to look mean. I imagine her in the shrill neon of a back alley, willing to go with anyone anywhere as long as it isn't home, where she would have to face some painful reality I can see only as a sad crease in her eye.

"And so there was an exchange of some sort?" I ask. "You gave Markow the list and he gave you the compromising photos?"

"No, he sent a woman to do his dirty work for him."

I raise my finger to order another drink before urging Petrova to describe the woman. My mouth is dry and grows drier as she insists she doesn't remember. They met for only a few moments. After some urging, Petrova remembers the woman was young, petite, and had light-brown hair. Her German was almost perfect except for a tiny accent. Definitely Russian.

From the side pocket of my purse, I take out one of the few artifacts of my sister's life in the Gulag, something one of my contacts acquired from Siberia four years ago. A Gulag photographer had captured my sister in a portrait that was to be smuggled out to our mother but never was. Marya is wearing a dark dress with a geometric pattern on the shoulders, her hair pinned up in such a way that only I know just how thin it's become. Her eyebrows are strange, too dark for her face; she had to draw them in. Her eyes are exhausted, begging. *Help me. Get me out.*

"That was her, all right." Petrova says, subdued. She blinks at me. "Quite a resemblance, there. You related?"

"My sister."

"He got to her too, huh?"

Her question makes me uncomfortable and I choose not to answer. "She did the trade on Markow's behalf? Are you sure?"

"Yes."

"And the list?"

"I said, it was a trade. The photos for the list."

"She had the list? Not Markow?" I'm tingling with excitement. I have to be sure.

"Yes," Petrova says. "He told me to give it to a girl wearing a red paper flower and she was the only one."

"Did you speak with her?"

"Not really. It was just the trade. It was the only time I ever saw her."

I thank her for her time. After she leaves, I sit back with a cigarette, puzzling over this new information. We'd paid Petrova enough to get the truth out of her, but on the other hand, she is a traitor who has served years in prison for giving away American secrets. One can never trust what a traitor has to say. Maybe she told me what she thought I wanted to hear. All she's done is confirm Marya from the photo.

But if Petrova spoke the truth, it changes everything. Marya was directly involved with Markow's attempt to sell us the list of Soviet traitors, a central role in what came to be Operation Sentinel. Back then, I had no idea Marya was a part of it, and she had said nothing herself, not even after her arrest. Why? Why the secrecy when she was working for something we wanted? She wasn't out to split the money with Markow; she didn't care about money. So what was she doing, acting as an operative so deeply in the background? What did she get out of it?

"Mrs. Koshkina?"

The men who'd been smoking their cigars nearby cross the short distance, their shoes squealing on the floor. They wear identical suits and their hair shines. One is older, one younger, and surprisingly, it is the younger who seems to be in charge.

"Why don't you come with us quietly," he says, flashing a card too fast for me to read.

I cross my legs and exhale a gust of smoke. It's very hard not to laugh at these earnest men with their twanging accents. I catch the eye of the man on the other side of the potted plant, who has lowered his newspaper. He's so obviously Russian with his sad Slavic eyes, I almost shake my head in despair. Well. I smile up at the young FBI man.

"Where would you like to take me, sir?"

"We understand you booked a room here. We could go there for a little talk. We won't take much of your time."

"I am very flattered, sir. At my age, I don't often get such attention. But I'm afraid I have no interest in male company at the moment."

"We don't want to make a scene, ma'am."

"Then why are you making one?"

The two men advance on me. The Russian behind the potted plant leaps to his feet. This is becoming comical, and slightly embarrassing. I snap at him in Russian—*I'm fine*—and the language seems to shock the FBI men into a moment of hesitation. In English, I say, "All right, we will have our little conversation, gentlemen."

I lead them to the bank of elevators. The Russian stares at us, and just as the door closes, I see him dash toward the stairs.

23
Marya

Berlin, 12 July 1947

The rain fell lightly, darkening the pavements with little gray spots, freshening the air on Henry's street. For a while, I watched his balcony from the boulevard. The French doors were closed, the curtains drawn. He'd decapitated the flowers. Only the brown stems stuck up out of the box on the railing. I held my scarf in my hand and let the rain cool my head. For the first time, I was here on a Saturday. Henry would be home—or he wouldn't be— and either way, I had to knock on his door if I wanted his help.

The landlady Frau Koch met me in the foyer. "He's not here, Fräulein." Her tone was cool, reflecting Henry's feelings for me, I was sure of it.

"Was he sent home? Back to England?" Maybe he'd confessed to his people about me and the missing papers, and their judgment had been swift.

"He's on duty, as far as I know."

This threw me into confusion, a whole new set of maybes. Maybe he hadn't told his people about me at all. Maybe he had, and Vera was right, his people were keeping him in Berlin as bait for me, a Russian girl they could manipulate and recruit. But then, she'd said he would come to me with kisses and apologies. He hadn't. It was me trying to get to him. I'd had no luck quietly asking my people about the disappearance of Felix, and I still didn't know where Vera was. Henry used to be a military policeman; even if he hated me now, he might help me with Felix's case out of professional pride.

The rain grew heavier, cool and sharp, sweeping into the foyer. Frau Koch held open the door while she frowned at the moisture pooling on the tiles. She wanted me to leave, but if I did, maybe he would come home just after and I will have missed him. I considered leaving a note, but that wouldn't do any good; it wouldn't help Felix now. The landlady would tell Henry I'd been there, and so I said, "If he comes, please tell him I've gone to his work." In the stand next to the mailboxes, I noticed my umbrella. I'd left it here . . . how long ago? It seemed an artifact from another age. I lifted it sadly and stepped out into the rain.

By the time I reached Lancaster House, a large white building curving along Fehrbellinerplatz, it was raining miserably. Maybe that was why British HQ felt so deserted. Even the small barriers and checkpoints seemed empty until a sentry stuck his head out of his booth. "What the blazes are you doing wandering around in the rain. Are you lost?"

"I came to see Captain Henry Barrow. He works here."

"He might, but I can't let in every girl who wants to meet a chap. Let's see your papers."

I couldn't very well show him my military card. "I forgot them at home."

"That won't do. You'll have to clear off and come back when you have them, Fräulein."

A puddle of rain was pooling around my sandals and my hair hung heavy on my shoulders. I could only imagine what I looked like to him, a bedraggled foreign girl looking to cause trouble for one of his countrymen on a rainy day. "Please sir, I must see him urgently."

Until now, the sentry had stayed in his shelter, only his face peering out. Now he sighed with irritation and stepped out, the rain sliding from his cap and pattering his tunic. "Look, miss, if you don't clear off, I'm going to have to arrest you. And neither of us want that, do we? Not in this rain. Just go home."

"If you arrest me, will you take me inside?"

He wagged a finger at me. "Not getting in that easy. If I arrest you, I'll keep you here until the Germans come for you." He straightened suddenly, and I followed his gaze to a car that was rolling up to the barrier. The driver climbed out and waved at me.

"Fine weather, what?" It was Henry's roommate, Johnson. "Glad I caught you, young M. I was just home with the landlady and she told me you'd scooted off. Here to see old Henry? He'll be over the moon. Get in."

The sentry protested. "She doesn't have any papers, sir."

"I'll vouch for her. Write that down in your book. Captain Archibald P. Johnson. Got it? Right. Off we go, love."

I took the hand he offered me and climbed into his car. "How is Henry?"

"He hasn't been his usual sweet-tempered self lately, I'm afraid. How are *you*?"

"Terrible."

Johnson gave my hand a sympathetic pat, then parked and rushed around the car to open my door, brandishing my umbrella.

Inside the entryway of Lancaster House, I dripped onto the floor and stepped carefully over the rain-slick tiles. Johnson talked all the way to the staircase and escorted me to a corridor on the second floor.

"I'm going to have to leave you here, love. It's like this." Johnson smoothed his mustache nervously. "Henry hasn't been in the best mood, and well, if he sees I brought you in, he might burn everything in my room."

"He would never. He's a peaceful man."

"You're a good girl. His office is the last door on the left. Good luck. It's been an honor playing cupid." He trotted off, leaving me alone in the corridor.

I tried to smooth my hair and dress, but it was hopeless. Henry would have to see me like this. I squelched down the hallway to the last door on the left and gave it a hesitant knock.

"Sod off. I'm working."

"Henry. It's me."

He didn't say anything for the longest time. I opened the door, slipped inside, and closed myself in before he could stop me. He didn't even try. He was at his desk, a pencil in one hand, a cigarette in the other. His papers were stacked neatly, but the ashtray overflowed onto the desktop. There was a plush chair at the wall that held a blanket thrown across the arm. A shirt was balled up in the wastebasket, and a pen cap lay on the floor next to his left shoe. But I couldn't keep looking at everything in the room that wasn't his face.

He'd shaved, he'd brushed his hair, and it still didn't prepare me for the shock. His color was bad, as if he hadn't slept, eaten, or left this room in the six days since we'd last seen each other. His eyes filled my heart, the fatigue and grief there for all to see.

"Henry—"

"Please, sit down." His politeness cut deeper than a show of anger could ever do. "What are you doing here?"

"I wanted to see you again."

"Well, you've seen me." He plucked a paper from the stack and settled in to read.

"I'm sorry to disturb your work." I tapped a file and he flinched as if I'd touched him in a tender spot. "I'm sorry about how things have happened, and what I've done. Maybe you still think it was all an act on my part, that I'm only a filthy spy. But I'm not, I swear I'm not. I wasn't acting when we were together."

"I don't want to hear it."

I grasped the cold wooden arms of my chair. "All right. I won't waste your time with sentiment. You used to be in the military police. Do you still have contacts there, and with police in the other sectors?"

He looked up from his papers warily. "Yes, why?"

"I'm here to ask you, a policeman, for help. Three days ago, Felix Markow—Greta's father, remember?—he was taken away in a black car by men in suits. It was broad daylight in front of his house. I couldn't stop them. I couldn't tell who the men were, from what country. Felix has enemies. He took something from the Americans, and maybe they have him. Is there a way for you to find out?"

"Unbelievable. You didn't come here to see me at all. You came to help Markow."

"I came for both things."

"Why? What's it got to do with you?"

"He knew about us. He told me he had proof, photographs, and I had to help him with one of his plans or he would tell my people."

A flash of angry surprise on Henry's face. "He was blackmailing you?"

"Yes."

"And you let him?"

"What do you mean? I had to go along with it. I had to protect us—"

"You could've come to me." Henry took a long drag of his cigarette and sat back in his chair, gazing at me coldly through the smoke.

"I should've told you, yes, but I didn't want anything to spoil what we had."

"To spoil your mission."

"No. Henry, I meant—"

"You kept me in blessed ignorance, eh? You kept a lot of things from me, didn't you?"

"I'm sorry."

"Let's not start that again. Your sister is an MGB officer. She could have taken care of Markow, right? You could've used her to get him out of the way of your mission." He mashed his cigarette in the full tray. "Such as it was. But you didn't do that."

"She would have overreacted. If she knew he'd threatened me—"

"She might have had him kidnapped in broad daylight in a Western sector and taken away for good?"

I touched my arms, the goose bumps.

"So we're back to my original question," he said. "Why are you helping your German blackmailer now that it looks like he's getting what's coming to him?"

I'd lose nothing by telling him the truth. Nothing I hadn't already lost. Still, something constricted inside me when I started to talk. "I knew him. I suppose you guessed that already. It was in the war. On the front, I was an interpreter like I am now, but . . . in an intelligence unit."

"Ah. Really." He flicked his lighter, lit a fresh cigarette.

"It wasn't what you think. I was involved in interrogating German prisoners of war. Felix was special, my very first prisoner. We had him in custody much longer than usual, almost a week. We had time to talk. About important things. Not just the war. About our lives. The world. We seemed to understand each other and . . ." The old shame rushed through me, but I forced myself to tell the truth, what no one should ever know. "It was early in the war, but I'd seen what his people had done to us and our land. We were in the middle of fighting, defending Moscow. I didn't want to like him. But I did."

Henry let out a noise as if he'd just heard the punch line to a bad joke. I tried not to let it throw me off. The truth. He'd wanted to hear it, and he deserved it.

"We were right there on the front, and when the fighting got closer, a German soldier attacked me. And then Felix—"

"Escaped?"

"Killed him. He killed one of his own soldiers."

Henry lowered the cigarette he'd just raised to his lips. "Why?"

"To save me."

His expression shifted from confusion to wonder. "Bloody hell. What did you two . . . ?"

I didn't know how to get him to understand something I couldn't sort out myself. "The army was so strange, for us women especially. I was eighteen. What did I know about men? We were to feel patriotic and hate the enemy. Otherwise, we weren't to feel anything at all. But how was I supposed to do that? The war made me feel things . . . sharper and faster. *More*, not less. When Felix came, he was . . . He was like someone I'd always known. You were like that too, Henry. It was easy with you."

He rested his elbow on the desk, his forehead in his hand.

"What Felix did for me was treason. Murder. If he hadn't done it, I wouldn't be here now, do you understand? Do you know what the Germans would've done to me if I'd been captured? Felix wanted to live; we both did. He helped me, and I helped him. Maybe it was . . . affection, I don't know. Or a debt to pay. Or both. But it's nothing like how I feel about you. He's not you." My head pounded, the little muscles aching in my neck and all of me cold in my damp clothing. Henry wouldn't look at me. I wasn't explaining this well at all. "Henry, I can't abandon him. I don't expect you to understand it. I only ask you to help me find him. Help me and I'll go and never come back if that's what you want."

One long stretch of silence, disturbed only by Henry's shallow breaths. Then he fished a notebook from under a stack of papers, found a pencil gnawed thin near the tip. "Tell me what happened to him. Exactly what you witnessed."

This was easy compared to what I'd just confessed to him. I told him the details and answered his questions, asked in a factual tone. He was fleeing behind his old profession and I was grateful. The policeman in him steadied me too. In the end, we were almost speaking easily. The honesty felt good, but I knew I'd waited too long. Like he'd said, I should've come to him from the beginning. I watched his hand move across the page, and how his head bobbed as he listened, and the tilt of it, like a boy studying. I was going to miss him.

"The car had no tags, no national colors, nothing at all to identify it?"

"Nothing I could see. It happened so fast."

He picked up the telephone and asked for a line to someone named Courtois at French headquarters. Henry replaced the receiver and as he waited for the connection, he looked over what he'd written. After a minute or two, the phone rang.

"Thanks, I'll hold." He cupped his hand over the receiver, looked at his papers again, and said, "Marya, will you marry me?"

I answered before his words had sunk in. "Yes."

We stared at each other in astonishment across the desk.

A voice, tinny and far away, spoke in the telephone, and Henry said, "Courtois, how are you, old man? Good. Good. I have a query about a case you might have on your desk. The name is Felix Markow . . ."

I stopped listening. I was in a fever, hot with joy and surprise, and a moment later, cold with terror. I hadn't known what I was saying—but then, yes, yes, I had. Joy burst through me again. Henry beamed back at me as he spoke to his colleague with new vigor. His smile—it was like life returning to the earth. I was impatient for him to finish. I had to tell him—what? That this was wonderful and yet, impossible. Stalin had said—

Stalin again!

He was behind the law forbidding us to marry foreigners. This was a precaution—I heard Vera explain in my head—to prevent foolish Soviet citizens from harboring foreign spies in their beds.

What nonsense. All of it. I couldn't stand for it anymore.

"There's no trace of him, not even from the German side?" Henry asked into the phone. After listening a few moments, he said, "If anything comes in, let me know. Yes, I will, you too. *Merci, au revoir.*"

He hung up the phone and we were both out of our chairs and in each other's arms, laughing, spinning around his office, knocking into the furniture.

"How do we do it?" I asked, when I had my breath back.

"I'll arrange it. Come home."

"Home?"

"My house. Monday at dusk."

"Not Sunday?"

"Tomorrow is too soon and next Sunday too long. You'll change your mind."

"I most certainly will not. But the marriage—" He was kissing me along my cheek and over the bridge of my nose. It tickled, and I laughed. "It will be illegal."

"I know a German registrar who owes me. He'll see to it. We're really going to do this?"

What would Vera say? She would accuse me of loving what was foreign more than I loved my own land and people. But she was wrong. Love didn't close a door here if it opened one there. Love was big and held the world. This wasn't true for many people, the ones with small hearts. Unfortunately, those were often the very people who made and enforced the laws. They wanted us to believe the world was made up of us and them, two armies that could never join for long, always ready to go from ally to enemy. I didn't believe that. I believed in the generosity and openness of people who followed their own hearts. Felix had sung *Our thoughts are free*, the only way to free ourselves.

"Yes, we're doing this, Henry."

"Even if I can't find Markow? The French are leaving it to the Germans until there's some indication an ally was involved. There isn't yet. The Germans have almost nothing to go on. I'll ring the Americans next. Though to be honest, that kind of snatch and grab; no offense, but the mode of operation seems very . . . Russian. It's happened before, in our sector too. They sweep in, pick up a German, and he's never seen again."

"I know."

We were back to Vera. I touched Henry's cheek and wondered

if she had also gone to a man she trusted for help, if she was capable of trust at all. The only man I'd heard her call friend in Berlin was Nikolai Koshkin.

I hugged Henry tightly, worried about what would happen when I returned to my sector. If I wasn't careful, I would lose everything I'd just won back.

24
Marya

Berlin, 13 July 1947

The next day, the day before my wedding, I finally caught someone at Nikolai Koshkin's office willing to help me find him. I was still hoping he knew where Vera was, and even if he didn't, I was ready to use their flirtation to my advantage if I could. For my sister's sake, he might do me the favor of looking into Felix's disappearance quietly.

Koshkin's aide was a young black-haired man with a Jewish name and a romantic nature. He flirted with me in a good-hearted way and asked me out to a film. I had to play the old game of acting both shy and firm. "I'm a proper girl," I said, "and don't have time for such things. Is the colonel at home?"

He pretended to be hurt, but I knew he was like so many men, secretly pleased that I refused him. It showed I wasn't a tramp. "He's hosting a reception tonight. He won't like being disturbed."

"I do appreciate your help," I said sweetly.

He rang the colonel's home. A voice on the line, and the aide said, "Yes, it's the office. Got a Lieutenant Nikonova wanting to see the colonel urgently. What should I do with her? Yes, I'll wait." He gave me a bored look that made me smile, then he was all business again. "Yes, all right." He replaced the receiver. "He's sending a car for you."

Koshkin lived in a villa in a neighborhood of lovely hedges and gardens gated off from the rest of the world. It looked like some of the higher officers were already enjoying their version of the isolation order from Moscow that had sent me to the barracks. At the villa, the reception was already under way. The windows blazed with light, and from behind the high hedges came the buzz of conversation and the melody of a string quartet. I hadn't dressed for the occasion; at the very least, I should've been wearing a war medal. The maid waited for me on the doorstep, an older German woman who led me inside and into what looked like a library. Books lined the walls in glassed-in cabinets, and I couldn't help taking a few moments to admire them and think of Vera hoarding our papa's books for herself. At the end of the room, the glass doors were open, and people scattered on the lawn around lanterns of red and gold paper. I didn't see Vera anywhere. At a glance, I was the only woman in uniform. The rest seemed to be wives of officers, proudly wearing the baubles and gowns their husbands had liberated from the Germans. I felt very plain, and suddenly worried about how I was going to dress at my wedding tomorrow.

"Comrade Lieutenant, delighted to see you again." Nikolai Koshkin greeted me looking slim and elegant in dress uniform. He was the perfect image of a Soviet officer, the kind they liked to show in the propaganda. I had no doubt he spoke several languages, played piano concertos, and was popular with the Westerners he came in contact with. Vera would find his polish and self-possession attractive and useful. "I imagine you're here to see your sister," he said.

"She's here? She hasn't been back to the barracks in days."

"I've been honored to have her as my guest." He fixed his pleasant gaze on me, and something about it strangled any questions about why Vera slept here, or if she slept alone.

"I'm glad she's all right. I've been worried."

"She works too hard," he said, leading me by the elbow to the refreshments table. "And to be honest, she was having trouble sleeping at the barracks because of the strain between you. Sisters," he said, shaking his head. "I have two. They're oil and water one minute, soul mates the next." Without asking, he fixed me a plate of caviar on crackers and handed me a glass of champagne. I didn't know what to think about his . . . arrangement with Vera. He was chivalrous? Predatory? A fool to be used by her?

On the lawn, a cluster of guests broke up, and I finally saw her. Vera—in an evening gown of pale silk that hung from her shoulders and clung to her waist. A jewel sparkled at her throat. I'd never seen her so beautifully dressed. It made her move differently, more relaxed and elegant. Cigarette between her fingers, she was speaking to a general, her face bright and smiling. Her gaze slid to the other guests nearby, watching, as if she were the hostess of the party. I hardly knew her like this. She was a stranger.

My hands were full, the champagne, the caviar, so Koshkin gestured to her on my behalf. Vera noticed instantly, and her face grew still. Instead of coming to us, she went to speak to the quartet, the musicians on their feet for her. They changed places, three of them sitting again, the violinist still standing. He readied his bow and began a melancholy song. The guests quieted or were shushed.

Vera positioned herself near the willow tree and began to sing. Her fist at her heart, she sang of the Cossack lying by the green willow, the black raven waiting for him to die. She sang of him asking the raven to fly home to his family, to tell his bride he'd married another. He'd found a new bride, a bullet by the wide field beyond the river. The song never failed to bring a tear to my eye, and hearing my sister sing it made me shiver.

She had our mother's talent for musicality, her perfect ear for tone and melody. But the emotion flowing out of Vera through her voice—I'd never seen her like that before. She sang as if she knew everything. She knew I was marrying tomorrow. She knew death flew over us all like the raven. She was warning me. If I wasn't careful, I'd become the bride whose love would never come home.

When she was done, applause and shouts of approval erupted from around the garden. She bowed her head, her hand to her heart. Koshkin congratulated her with a few words in her ear, and they approached me together. He poured her a drink and then retreated to the party.

The two of us walked near the hedge. "I sang that for you," Vera said.

"I know."

"How did you like it?"

"It was beautiful. Where is Felix?"

She laughed and drank her champagne. "You're so obvious. You can't say his name without bleating like a lamb."

"Did you have him kidnapped?"

"Why should I?"

"To get back at me."

"Masha, I know this will come as a shock, but the affairs of the world aren't always about you. Things do in fact happen that have no connection to you whatsoever."

"You brought him into all this because of me. Because I knew him. And now you've snatched him away like you took away everything else that I had."

Sighing, Vera set her glass on the tray of a passing servant. "A word of advice. You'll never move forward in this life until you let go of all the little wounds you've collected in that soppy heart of yours." She poked me in the chest, and I slapped her hand away.

"If you have Felix," I said, "and he doesn't survive, I'll never forgive you. Never."

"Just as you'll never forgive me for hiding Nastya the cat when we were girls." She counted off on her fingers. "For being better at school. For letting the boys tease you at Komsomol meetings. For going to war first." She gestured. "And so on. Marya, you're a grown woman, intelligent and talented. You have a promising future ahead of you if you learn to bury this imaginary feud you have with me. It's all in your mind. Do you remember what I told you the day we met in Berlin? The true thing that allowed us to win the war?"

I remembered, but I wasn't about to let her lead me by the nose through her argument.

"Unity," she said. "Together, we're strong, you and I. We're not enemies. We're sisters. That means something to me, more than you know. Does it mean anything at all to you? Because all I see is that everything and everyone around you matters more than I ever did." She turned abruptly and glided over the terrace into Koshkin's house.

25
Vera

Testimony for Chairman A. Cheptsov
Military Collegium of the Supreme Court of the USSR
Moscow, 28 February–3 June 1956

[RECORDING]

vanov has been generous; he's booked me a suite on the thirtieth floor, and that is the only reason I and the two American agents can maintain some level of personal space. The older one positions himself near the door as if afraid I'll bolt. The younger, the boss of this get-together, leans against the side table and crosses his arms. I can safely assume this room is bugged, and I don't mind. Nothing I say here would be any more secret than my conversation with Petrova in the lobby. She was so forthcoming, I'm certain she was coached by these charming men I'm forced to host.

"Coffee, gentlemen?" I ask, picking up the phone. "I've had a very long day."

"No room service, please," says the young one, but I've already reached the concierge and order a carafe of coffee with cream and three cups in case the gentlemen change their minds. I find the menu to the restaurant in a drawer and settle into the armchair to read it. I haven't eaten decently all day, and I'm feeling the restless dissatisfaction of hunger. I don't want it to affect my judgment or how I deal with these men. I hope the coffee comes quickly.

The young American says his name is Mr. Brown, and I cover my mouth with my hand. I shouldn't laugh. Maybe it's not an alias and he really was born with such a plain name. The man guarding the door has graying hair, and I begin to think of him as Mr. Gray. Brown's hands are interesting; the yellowing stains between his fingers show a nicotine habit as bad as mine, and his fingernails are trimmed or bitten to the quick. Taking pity on him, I fetch my cigarettes and offer him one. He accepts with annoyance, lighting mine before his. He instantly relaxes in the smoke.

"Sorry to barge in on you, Mrs. Koshkina, but we're a little puzzled. We can't figure out why a Soviet official came all this way to talk to Miss Petrova about the incident in Berlin nine years ago. It's old news, isn't it?"

"May I ask if you've heard of what is now being called Premier Khrushchev's Secret Speech?"

"Might've heard something about it," Brown admits, smiling at, I'm sure, how public this secret speech has become. Before I left Moscow, Ivanov told me the Americans have a copy of it, passed to them by Israeli intelligence, who got ahold of one of the copies circulating in Poland. Sometimes espionage is a lovely example of international cooperation.

"If you've had a chance to see the speech," I say, "then you will know about the changes happening in the USSR. We are entering a new age in which we heal from the excesses of Stalin and move on to a more open and just society. We hope this will be an age of reform, and that is good news for the world."

"What's that got to do with you being here?" Brown asks.

"I assure you, I'm not here on behalf of the Soviet government. My conversation with Miss Petrova was a private matter. The new spirit in my country has allowed me to start investigating the case of my younger sister, who was convicted of treason nine years ago for acts she committed in Berlin."

I show him Marya's photo. "As you surely know," I say, "many people in Stalin's era were convicted on false charges or for acts that should not have been crimes. My sister's case is complex, and it has led me here to Miss Petrova, who was kind enough to give me another hint about my sister's activities nine years ago. Since you were listening so keenly downstairs in the lobby, I assume you're well aware of the confidential list Petrova gave to the German who was blackmailing her?"

Brown exchanges a glance with Gray. I believe they're both taken aback by how talkative I am. Honesty is a weapon in their profession; they see it so rarely, and it puzzles them.

"We tried to acquire the list," I say, "but we never got it. The German disappeared. Kidnapped, apparently. Not by us. We assumed it was your side."

I don't mention that as far as we knew, the list was gone along with Markow. At the time, Nikolai and I tried to track him down under orders directly from Moscow, whose patience was running out quickly. We were certain our failure to get the list would lead to a purge that could hit anyone anywhere.

I'm sure Brown was briefed about the case before he came here and knows all this already. But he says nothing, merely smokes his cigarette and lets me talk. I wonder if he thinks I'm not aware of what I'm telling him, if he assumes that since I'm a woman, I talk too much. Why not oblige him? There's something relaxing about thinking aloud with silent men in the room and what I take to be a man or two next door listening in with their headsets. It's almost like a performance. I shouldn't disappoint.

"Petrova said the German didn't have the list, my sister did. But Marya didn't give it to us. Markow claimed he had it, and we assumed he did. But now I'm not so sure. There's no evidence it was ever in his possession. So what happened to it? If he had it, your side must have got it back after you kidnapped him."

Brown finally rouses himself and says, "Or your sister had it, and she gave it to somebody else."

I look up at him sharply just as the phone rings. We allow the shrill sound to carry on before Brown eyes me and I pick up the receiver, expecting someone at the embassy. Instead, after the connections, I hear a rasping breath that I know instantly even before he speaks. My husband's anger flows across Europe and through the transatlantic lines.

"What are you doing, Vera? *What?* You said you had party business in Leningrad. What are you doing in *New York?*"

"How nice to hear from you, Kolya. We're having a fruitful discussion about my sister. There are new developments—"

"Have you lost your mind? Get on a plane and come home."

"I'm leaving tomorrow."

"Tonight."

"That is not for you to decide, my dearest."

The line clicks off. An operator's voice breaks in, timid, says the other party has ended the call. I ease the phone back into its cradle, my hand shaking. Sometimes a lie is necessary to smooth the path before us, the reason I lied to my husband about where I was going. Otherwise, he would have blocked the trip. I'm ashamed of this ruse, but what choice did I have? I'd told him I would pursue Marya's case wherever it takes me.

"If you're in some kind of trouble, ma'am," Brown says, "we'd be happy to help."

"That is very generous of you, sir, but that was my husband Nikolai Koshkin, who I'm sure you know is the deputy foreign minister. He's concerned about a diplomatic incident."

"We're just having a friendly conversation."

"Of course. But I fear my husband is somewhat irritated. I believe it's best if you leave."

Gray opens the door, and a bellboy is on the other side with a tray and the coffee, his hand raised to knock. Down the hall, a man straightens up from the wall. I recognize him as the Russian from the terrace, back here after reporting to the KGB, I assume. I shake hands with the Americans in the hallway under the Russian's watchful eye. After they leave, he approaches me and I snap at him, "I'm not in the mood. I'll report later."

I lock myself in my room and throw myself into the armchair. All along, I've said I would follow this case where it leads me, and it's led me to my sister in possession of a list of Soviet double agents she'd helped Markow get from Petrova. We never got the list. As Brown so aptly said, *she could have given it to someone else.*

Henry Barrow. It had to be him.

But why? If she was spying on him, why would she provide him with such a valuable piece of intelligence? Was she playing both sides? It would be treason. I'd known this investigation might lead me back to her guilt, but it's hard to stomach. I drink down my coffee and cream and it brews in my gut. I must keep following the known facts before I derail myself with such speculations about Marya.

Fact: On Saturday, 12 July 1947, I received a call from the Charité Hospital in Berlin to say an unnamed man answering to the description I had sent out to hospitals in our sector had been dumped on their doorstep. The doctor showed Nikolai and me into a private room. A curtain was drawn over the window, and I had to get close to the man sleeping in the bed, see past his swollen face and black eye before I knew it was him. Felix Markow.

The doctor informed us Markow had been pushed out of a car at the ambulance driveway, and the car had sped off. No one knew who'd driven it. Markow had three broken ribs, at least a dozen contusions on his body, four broken fingers, a likely concussion, two missing teeth, as well as superficial injuries on his face. The doctor was livid. "Someone has beaten this man senseless," he said.

We had no doubt the Americans had done it. They had a reputation for a kind of easy brutality, a preference for solving problems with violence. When he was no longer of use, Markow was dumped back in our sector, an arrogant move to show us that our agent was neutralized and worthless.

We assumed Markow had cracked under the pressure. He'd talked, and the Americans knew where the list was, or had it back already. All we had was this broken man.

But I had to be sure. He was wearing his own clothes, smeared with blood and grime. It was distasteful to search him, but I did my duty, finding nothing in his pockets, along hems or in any place where he might have hidden the list, or maybe a part of it, on his person. Seeing his shoes under the bed, I knelt to check them. He shifted under his blanket and groaned.

"Marya," he said thickly.

I leaned over him. "Yes, Felix, I'm here," I said as Marya would say it.

"Go," he said. "Take it away. Take it to . . ." And then Markow descended back into sleep. At the time, I thought he was dreaming, and his words were a jumble that made no sense.

In my hotel room high over the streets of New York, I turn off the lamp and go to the window. Night has fallen and the city is ablaze with lights, each one like the burning fire of truth. I'm very afraid. I'm on the edge of proving what I never wanted: my sister's guilt. I'm not sure how to proceed. All along, I've said I'm after the truth, and it has taken me to Markow again and again. If Marya had collaborated with him to get intelligence from Barrow, if Markow had trained her, if she'd helped him acquire the list from Petrova, then his words in that hospital in Berlin have a new meaning. If he had truly been asking Marya to go with the list, take it away . . . take it to *me*, then something had happened to stop her from doing what was, after all, her duty as a Soviet officer. But if he'd wanted her to take it to someone other than me, and she'd done it, then she was a traitor. If she was playing a double game and the list ended up with Henry Barrow, she was a traitor. I need to know once and for all if he received the actual, physical list from Marya. After nine years, maybe he is ready to tell me the truth.

I drop back into the armchair, pick up the phone, and demand an external line to the British embassy.

26
Marya

Berlin, 14 July 1947

On my wedding day, I dragged myself out of bed and went straight to the medical officer. My blood pressure was high but I didn't have a fever, which surprised me. My body felt hot to the touch and the blood pulsed in my head.

"Rest and stay out of the sun," she said, signing the form that excused me from duty that day. Following her advice was easy; I spent most of the morning stretched out on my bed worried about everything. How to get out of the barracks without being seen. Whether I'd make it to the British Sector for my wedding. Maybe Henry had regrets and hoped I wouldn't come. Maybe he couldn't find a registrar to marry us. Worst of all, I was alone. A bride shouldn't be alone on her wedding day. How could I marry without my mother? My sisters? All the people who'd known me throughout my life?

At midday, I dressed in the same clothes I would wear for a normal visit to Henry. I had nothing special except my grandmother's cross in my purse, and Henry's bracelet, warm gold on my wrist. I had no makeup and didn't want any. I didn't need to paint myself for him. I concentrated on my hair, twisting and pinning it so that I looked like a country maid in the city for the first time. Henry would like that. Before I left my room, I suddenly remembered Felix's pfennig, and dug for it in my purse. He needed good luck even more than I did, and I clutched the coin in my palm for the both of us.

One last time, I checked Vera's room. Nothing had changed. I considered leaving her a note, but what for? I sat on her bed awhile, my hand on the blanket. It was wrong to marry without her; it wouldn't be real. It would somehow prove her right, that everything mattered to me more than she did. But it wasn't true. It was just . . . she'd twisted my happiness, the things I loved, too many times. I didn't know how to forgive her for that. She clearly blamed me for the tension between us instead of looking at herself.

I tied my scarf over my hair, put on my sunglasses, and went outside to the perimeter fence. Anyone looking out of the windows could see me, so I strolled the fence, looking for the most secluded part opposite a blind wall of the barracks. I found a small concrete building where something mechanical hummed and grumbled inside. Generators of some kind, I guessed. The grass was gone near a particular part of the fence, leaving a patch of dried dirt. Just there, I pressed at the fence, testing the wire. A wooden plank moved, and when I unhooked a loop of wire around a second plank, it swung away to reveal a hole in the fence big enough for me to get through. This was what I'd been looking for the night I argued with Vera: a way out. Someone else in the barracks had made her own escape to freedom without the sentries seeing. I squatted and shimmied through, protecting my dress from the dirt.

Traveling west, I endured the dusty streets and crowded S-bahn carriages and the odors of unwashed bodies. The Berliners were grouchier in this weather than usual. If they talked at all, they complained about the rations, the mosquitoes, the sanitation, whether the water from the public tap was safe to drink. I was relieved to reach Henry's street, the quiet peace of his world.

Henry was waiting for me at the top of the stairs, splendid in his uniform, the shoulder strap gleaming and smooth across his heart. He came down to hug me in the foyer, smelling wonderful, from his soap to his shaving cream to whatever it was that made him smell like a fresh breeze. Music from a radio echoed in the hall, an orchestra. It wasn't right. I should've had live music at my wedding, and clapping and singing and drinks and delicacies all night long with all the people who loved me.

"You look beautiful," he said.

"I don't have a proper dress. I look how I always do."

"That's what I meant." He touched my face. "Are you all right?"

Today was folly, it was dangerous. We both knew it. "Not really," I said. He hugged me again, tighter and longer, and then led me up to his rooms.

In the sitting room, white bunting waved in the breeze of the fan. A white cloth was on the table, and a bottle of champagne on the sideboard next to little sandwiches and pastries. Henry's beloved Billie Holiday was singing from his record player. I guessed she'd been soothing his nerves all day. Frau Koch fretted with the glasses and the decorations until Henry told her to stop. She was a guest now, a witness to the ceremony. I was surprised Johnson wasn't there. He could hardly miss preparations for a wedding in his own flat. Henry said he'd been called away to Minden and had no idea what we were doing today.

A German in a brown suit rose from behind the dining table.

This was the registrar, and the tools of his trade were spread out in front of him: the seal and ink, a leather folder and book, a blotter and placemat, a heavy inkwell with a silver pen. Someone thoughtful had placed a small vase of flowers in the middle of these painfully official items. The registrar shook my hand. "Could I see your papers, please?" I took them out of my purse, translated copies of my identification papers. They weren't notarized, one of the many irregularities of the ceremony. He didn't seem to care. He opened his leather folder and began to fill out a form.

I quickly drank down a glass of port, then retired to the bathroom to splash cold water on my face and run it over my wrists. I felt a little faint.

A knock on the door. "Ready, Mouse?"

My stomach clenched, and I bent over the sink. Was this normal? This terror? Did all brides feel like this? I straightened up, pinched my cheeks to get some color back into them, and opened the door.

HENRY AND I stood at his dining table, transformed into the altar of a civil ceremony, the registrar on the other side, presiding. I barely listened to what he said, a lecture about love and responsibility. I didn't need a city official to tell me about that. I needed Henry's hand, a little moist and far too warm, in mine. He was gazing down at me with a twinkle in his eye. He wasn't listening to the registrar either. We knew what the other was thinking. Won't he ever shut up? He finally did while Henry and I fumbled with the wedding rings he'd bought on the black market. Our hands were shaking, and I was glad when both of us managed to exchange rings without dropping them.

The kiss that sealed our vows was quick and strange; we were both smiling too hard for it to come off well. Henry wanted to pour the champagne but had to postpone it when the registrar called us over to sign the papers. What name was I supposed to use? We hadn't discussed it, and I considered keeping my own name, my right under the laws of my country. At the last moment I signed as Marya Barrow. I assumed I'd never use this name in my normal life, so I considered it a gift to Henry, a sign that I was his in heart and name, even if we still had no future that I could see.

"Well done, Mrs. Barrow," Henry said, handing me a champagne.

"I'm not your mother, Henry."

"Thank God for that. But she's a good sort. You'll love her."

As we all raised our glasses, I knew he thought I'd changed my mind about emigrating. We had a hard conversation ahead of us.

The registrar doubled as photographer, and we posed for our wedding portrait. I had to stand on a low stool so Henry's head wouldn't be cut off in the shot. "I think I'm an inch or two taller than I was this morning," he joked. The party broke up quickly. Frau Koch shook our hands and kissed our cheeks and went back up to her attic flat. The registrar packed up his traveling registry office into a large satchel. Left on the table was a book, the *Familienstammbuch*. It contained our marriage certificate, he explained. All important family papers gathered over the years belonged in the book: the birth certificates of our children, their baptisms, and God forbid, deaths in the family. I wondered if Henry had arranged for us to get this very German symbol of who we were supposed to be, the roots of a new family.

We said our goodbyes to the registrar, and we were finally alone. I threw myself into my husband's arms, but it was too hot to stay that way for long while dressed. We shed our clothes and danced skin to skin, drunk and laughing, to the music in our heads.

"I can't believe we just did that," he said.

"I know. Is it real?"

"It's real."

As we kissed, he clutched my hair, the small of my back. I kneaded his skin and muscles until my fingers ached. I could barely breathe through our kisses. He was proving something to me, and I to him. *You are mine. Mine, and no one else's.* "Carpet?" he asked. "Sofa? Bed?"

I laughed. "I get a choice now that we're married?"

"Only the best for my wife. The armchair is pretty comfortable." He guided me in an awkward tap dance toward it. "Or the kitchen?"

"You mean the table?" I asked, scandalized. "Or the floor?"

"The counter would be a rather tight fit."

I smacked him lightly on the shoulder, and he roared in mock pain, lifted me up, and made the choice himself.

AT DAWN, I roused myself from the carpet as slowly as I could so that my head wouldn't shatter. The light was wrong, gentle through the white sheers, and I remembered I wasn't in the barracks. For the first time, I'd stayed a whole night with Henry until morning. I'd planned to do it, but it still felt odd, like I'd overslept an alarm on an important day. I rolled over to him, still a little drunk and giggling. I didn't remember how many bottles we'd emptied last night or what had been in them. He lay on his side, wrung out, his hair darker where he sweated at his temple. He looked like a boy exhausted after playing rough. My husband. I couldn't quite get used to that. I was his wife. I splayed my hand, the ring new and snug on my finger.

I dressed quietly. I wanted to turn on the radio to get the date, to be sure it was Tuesday the fifteenth, my first full day of married life. And what did that mean, anyway? What would be different now? Uneasy, I knelt beside Henry and caressed his hair.

"Wake up, my husband."

He snorted awake, a splotch of red where his cheek had lain on the carpet. He reached for me and I allowed a kiss, sloppy and hungover, before pulling back. "It's already morning. I have to go now."

He sat up and rubbed his head tenderly, then groped for the nearest bottle. He turned it upside down and nothing came out. "Go? Where?"

"Home. To Karlshorst."

"I'm a little slow right now, Mouse. Did you forget something in the barracks? Something you want to take with you?"

It was just as I'd feared. He assumed I was going with him to the West. I sat on the sofa and he leaned against my knee. To soften the blow, I lay a gentle hand on his hair. "I'm not going to England, Henry. We talked about this."

He slid his head back to look at me. "That's a cruel joke, my love."

I had to explain it all to him again, patiently, as if he were a child. "If I emigrate, I would be considered a traitor, an enemy of the people. They would take it out on my family. My mother is nearly blind, I told you. She can barely work anymore. My little sister, Nina, might be expelled from university and never get a good job." I thought of Vera but didn't mention her. "My actions would be a black mark against them, and they're poor enough as it is. The only way I could emigrate is if my people thought I was dead."

With a grunt, Henry pulled himself onto the sofa beside me. "That could be arranged."

"Don't be ridiculous." I got up, and he grasped my hand.

"Then why did we do all this? For the laughs?"

"Because we love each other."

"We don't need the rings for that. Marriage means we're staying together."

"It can't be done."

"Because you won't let us." He let go of me and threw himself back against the cushions. "How do you see us going on, then? In the future?"

"As we have been. I want things to stay the same."

"They aren't the same, can't you see that?"

"Nothing has changed in my world, Henry." I went to the table. "In my world, my family will suffer for my crime."

"What crime?"

"In my country, emigration is a crime. Marrying you is a crime." I held up the *Familienstammbuch*. "This is evidence they could use against me. You must understand."

"You married me. You made a decision for *us*. Maybe there's something we could do for your family. We'll try. But you have to think about us now. If we can't live together in Berlin, then we get out. Take the chance, Marya. We have a future together if you let it happen."

"In England. That's easy for you; it's your home. I don't see you considering life in the Soviet Union."

"I did, actually. You'd be amazed at all the things I considered the past few days. If you don't want to live in England, there's Canada. You'd love the weather. Just like home." He tried to smile, and it did help a little to ease the tension. "Listen to me now, Mrs. Barrow," he said, taking me into his arms. "Wherever we end up living, we'll have a place in the country. I promise you that. We'll have a cottage. We can build one just like yours in Karlshorst."

"You can build a whole house?"

"I'm very handy."

I squirmed in his arms. "I don't know."

"We'll have cats. Boy and girl. They'll have kittens."

"Now you're bribing me." But I was smiling, imagining a fat little cat of my own, a mewing family of little ones nestled in a crate by the cottage window.

"What would you do?" I asked. "Go back to policing?"

"Why not? The local bobby, strolling his beat. The worst crimes would be stolen bicycles and broken milk bottles on the doorstep. I'd be home every night for tea."

"You'd be bored."

He squeezed me. "Never. Not for a moment."

"What would I do? I planned to study languages and translate great literature."

This stumped him for a moment. "Then you'll do it. We'll sort it out. And maybe we'll have children."

"I hope so, but I'd still have to work."

"Then you'll work."

"Good."

"Right." His tone was final and triumphant.

"Wait. Henry." It was so hard to decide. He wanted me to live for myself no matter what the consequences were to other people. It was a selfish way to live, as Vera would say. Selfishness, the greed for our own desires, was the vice my whole society was set up to fight, or so we were told. I didn't believe any of this as firmly as Vera did. After all, my husband was my selfish desire, mine alone. But I did believe in the ability to live according to a greater spirit, not just for myself, but for the good of all. This civic spirit had taken me to war, and it lived in my bones. I couldn't just think of my own happiness. Leaving with Henry might be good for me, but devastating for everyone I left behind.

I rested my head on his chest and listened to his heart. "I'm scared."

"It'd be odd if you weren't. But it'll come out all right in the end."

I wanted to believe him. I tried. I tried to imagine vanishing from my life. Giving up my family, the work that I loved, my status as an officer. And though I wanted to deny it, Felix was a factor too. If I left Berlin suddenly, I might never know what happened to him. "Henry, I don't think I can decide this until I find Felix. Please understand."

His body tensed. "Your husband is supposed to understand his wife going after another chap on her first day of marriage?"

"It's not just about him. I swore to his wife I'd find out what happened. "

"A conspiracy of wives, is it?"

"Henry."

Under his breath, he called Felix a choice name, then said, "I haven't been able to trace him, the car, or the men who took him. I didn't expect we would. The French have their ears open but no mandate to dig much. I don't either, without tearing Markow's life apart. For your sake, I don't want people looking too closely at it. The Germans are convinced the Russians took him."

"Did you talk to the Americans?"

"The Yanks insist they don't have him. What about your sister?"

"She didn't say anything. Except that she thinks I don't love her."

"I imagine an MGB officer is hard to love."

"She twists everything around. It's like she can't help it. She keeps trying to convince me you're a spy."

He separated himself from me and picked his shirt up from the floor. "What else does she say? I have cloven hooves and a forked tail?"

"Henry." I stopped him buttoning his shirt. "You aren't, are you?"

"Aren't what? The devil?" I wasn't smiling, and he kissed me quickly. "Sorry, Mouse. No"—he raised his hand as if giving an oath—"I am not a filthy spy. Do I have to swear an oath on a Bible?"

"It's all right. I believe you."

He held me close for a long moment, our hearts beating fast. It seemed a bad sign to argue this much on our first day of marriage.

"If you have to go find Markow," he said, "I can't stop you. But when you come back, I'll have everything ready. I'll put every military policeman in our sector on a quiet alert. Cross the border anywhere, approach any one of my men, and they'll know what to do. We'll fly away from all this. We can do it. But you have to come back to me."

27

Vera

Testimony for Chairman A. Cheptsov

Military Collegium of the Supreme Court of the USSR

Moscow, 28 February–3 June 1956

[RECORDING]

Overnight I receive three phone calls from our embassy, and I'm glad for the distraction of speaking to someone who claims to be concerned about my well-being. I haven't slept in my hotel room high over New York. How can I, when a voice whispers about my sister's treason in my ear? I assume the KGB man is dozing on his feet down the hall, still guarding my door, but I don't open it to see. I keep it locked even when dawn strikes the city and a warm glow spreads across my window. At six, the phone rings again.

"Mrs. Koshkina?"—a British accent. "We have a representative on his way to you. Mr. Johnson should be there in an hour."

A man named Johnson, not Barrow. Sighing, I thank her for the news and the time to tidy myself. My limbs feel heavy as I shower and change clothes, and I spend a long soothing session brushing my hair. I'm drinking the cold remains of last night's coffee when the phone rings again. It's the concierge informing me I have a visitor who would like to know if he may come up. How thoughtful.

Finally, I unlock the door and peer into the hallway. The KGB man is gone; a new man now lounges by the vase. He straightens when he sees me. In English, I inform him I have a visitor coming, and at that moment, he comes. Dapper in a light suit, carrying his hat. He has a thin mustache and a ready smile I don't altogether trust.

"Mrs. Koshkina?"

"Mr. Johnson, I presume."

His smile widens, and he glances at the man by the vase, who is watching us with open hostility. Inside the room, Mr. Archibald Johnson, as he introduces himself, goes straight to the window, admiring the view, then asks if he may sit. He's very polished, but fatigue rims his eyes.

"I've just come up from the embassy in Washington," he says. "When we got wind you wanted to talk to old Henry, I jumped up and made sure I'd handle the negotiations. We were flatmates in Berlin when . . . when everything happened."

"Negotiations? Mr. Barrow will only see me under certain conditions?"

"Not exactly. I had a chat with him last night—he's in London— and he refused outright to see you or even telephone."

It's only to be expected, but my disappointment doubles my fatigue. Henry Barrow has the answer to my sister's story, I'm sure of it. Her ultimate guilt or innocence depends on if she gave him the American list or not.

"Then what is there to negotiate, Mr. Johnson?"

"I think I can change his mind, but I need to understand what you're after. We can speak frankly?"

"Please. I'm too tired for anything else."

"He doesn't like or trust you. He thinks you're up to something, something that'll be bad for Marya in the end."

"Worse than the Gulag, he means? I'm trying to help her. I explained that to your ambassador on the phone last night."

"Henry doesn't buy it. Now I'm paraphrasing him, but he wants to know why you suddenly care about what happened to her."

"I always cared. Always. If he doesn't know that—"

I press my lips together, breathe away my anger. The sun is climbing and I gaze out at the towers of New York, calmed by the wide view of the city. It reminds me of my apartment and the view of Moscow that soothes me when I'm at home. I'm drawn to horizons; I want to see farther, and in seeing, to understand.

The opportunity to talk to someone who knew Barrow well is too valuable to pass up. Leaning against the window, I tell Johnson what I've discovered about my sister, the full truth as I've been able to uncover it. He listens stunned, I think, at my frankness.

"I don't believe a word of it," he says. "I saw that girl many times. She was sweet and friendly and not a deceitful bone in her body. She was no spy."

"When she was interrogated after her arrest, she claimed she was spying on Barrow. That was the only reason for their relationship on her end."

"Rubbish. She was in love with him. Not even a blind man would've missed that."

Johnson was confirming what I had witnessed in Berlin, my sister with Barrow. In many ways I was blind back then, but not to what was happening in Marya's heart. She loved him. She did. But how to reconcile that with her own remarks in her interrogation? And her relationship with Markow? And her actions?

"How did Barrow feel about her? Was he leading her on?"

"God, no. He was lost. When it came to her, he was the most exasperating chap I knew. He wouldn't even look at another girl. When they had a falling-out, well, let's just say he was a hard man to live with. They were both trapped if you ask me."

Trapped. An interesting way to put it. It opened up the possibility that Barrow might've been more of a victim in the events in Berlin than I'd thought. If he was in love with my sister, could someone else have used that fact to entrap him?

"Was Barrow involved with British intelligence in Berlin?" I ask Johnson, watching him closely. At the moment, I have no way to confirm anything he's told me, not even his identity. He never did say exactly what work he does at his embassy, if he truly works there at all.

If he is an agent, he's very good. He gives nothing away when he answers my question. "Intelligence wasn't really my department, but I can tell you this. Henry despised those chaps. Can't imagine him taking orders from them." Johnson rises, offers his hand. "I'll ring him again. See if I can change his mind about talking to you."

"I appreciate that, but why are you so interested in helping me, Mr. Johnson?"

"I owe it to old Henry. What that girl's arrest did to his life . . ." Johnson shakes his head, then puts on his hat. "If there's a chance of helping her, I'm convinced he'll talk to you. I just have to get through his thick skull. I'll call you with news."

"I'm willing to meet him in London. Anywhere. Tell him that. And give him this."

I hand him the Gulag portrait of Marya. Whatever polished

mask this Englishman has worn slides away for an instant, long enough for me to see the pity for the way my sister is now.

"When Henry sees this," Johnson says, "he might—"

"Put a bullet through my heart? I know that, Mr. Johnson. If they truly loved each other, then what happened in Berlin was a tragedy that hangs over us all."

Johnson pockets the photograph, promises to get it to Henry quickly via diplomatic post, and leaves. Only then do I order up breakfast and eat my fill of eggs and bacon, enjoying it as I imagine one enjoys a last meal.

In the afternoon, Johnson telephones with the message I've been waiting for: *Tomorrow, noon, the Soviet War Memorial in the Tiergarten, West Berlin.*

28
Marya

Berlin, 15 July 1947

We're going to fly away, I thought as I reached the back perimeter of my barracks. My first time in an airplane ever. Henry and I were going to glide west across Germany, high over the Soviet Zone, too high for the sentries and patrols to get me, and then land in the West, the British Zone. A new life.

I didn't know if I could really do it. But that didn't stop me from dreaming as I looked for the hole in the green fence. My stomach whirled at the possibility. I was changing altitudes already.

The sun was higher and the air sizzled; I longed to wash, change into my uniform, and drink liters of tea in the canteen. The doctor had given me only a day of rest and I had to go back on duty. But if my sister had returned to the barracks, I was going to confront her first. She knew where Felix was. I could feel it.

Near the hole in the fence, a young officer was leaning against the planks. I didn't recognize him until he flicked aside his cigarette and took off his cap to wipe the sweat from his dark hair. It was the aide from Koshkin's office. "So you decided to finally show up. Looks like you've been having a fine time. Gone all night and wandering in midmorning. Where have you been?"

"None of your business. Does Colonel Koshkin want to see me?" I didn't mention my sister, but I had no doubt this had something to do with her.

"Of course he does, or do you think I'm here to run after you? Wouldn't go see a film with me, but you're ready and willing with other fellows, I see."

I slid my hands behind my back and wrestled my wedding ring off my finger. "What is this all about?"

He waved his hand at me to follow him, and we walked the perimeter all the way around to the gate, him complaining about how Russian girls changed when they got to Berlin. They all became tramps and teases, not like the good girls at home. I could've said exactly the same about the boys, but I kept quiet. I was too anxious about what Koshkin wanted.

The sentry gave us a smirk as we passed onto the grounds. Inside the building, Koshkin's aide stopped in the corridor, looking around with interest and smiling at the women who stared at him, and then at me. "Well," he said to me, "going to change into your uniform, or do you always go on duty in a crumpled dress?"

I closed myself into the bathroom, the wedding slipping further away, part of a dream world. The white tile, the stiffness of my summer uniform, the smell of women. That was real. I stared hard at my ring to bring last night back to me. That was real too. I was Henry's wife. I tucked the ring into my pocket, my hands shaking as badly as they had at the ceremony.

As I followed Koshkin's aide out to his car, I had the feeling I should've never left Henry. I'd missed my chance to fly. "Where are we going? To SMAD? I could walk there, you know."

"Don't complain about getting a ride. We'll be there in a minute." He said nothing else as we drove, but I kept a close watch on his hand resting on his leg and too near mine for comfort. I barely saw the houses sliding by outside the window. I was still hungover and anxious too, and the pounding in my head was getting worse.

The car came to an abrupt stop in front of a large building in the Bauhaus style that I recognized as one of our administrative buildings where we dealt with war reparations. Originally, it had been a German hospital, beautifully designed, with sprawling grounds and many outbuildings. I followed Koshkin's aide along the path to the doors, and we paused in the shade cast by the stone canopy. The doors opened, and a pair of women in civilian clothes emerged digging out their cigarettes. They quickly got out of our way, and I felt them staring after us as we entered the building.

The corridor was shockingly cold compared to the heat outside. The people we passed either pretended not to see us or gaped openly at me. I knew that look. No innocent person was escorted like this. I must've been accused of something, and therefore guilty of a crime. My throat felt rubbed raw, and when I coughed, I flinched at the echo in the hall.

We went down a stairway, and the air grew cooler, and stale, as if the windows were never opened. At the bottom of the stairs, Koshkin's aide opened a door. There was a rush of pressure in my ears and a swirl of changing air, the faint scent of disinfectant.

"I'm off, then," said Koshkin's aide. "Good luck." He went back to the stairs, the door slamming behind him.

A yellow light illuminated the corridor. At the end of it was a table next to another set of doors. I hadn't noticed the sentry there. By a low lamp, he was reading a book. He turned it facedown on the table. "You're the interpreter?"

My heartbeat slowed a little. Maybe Koshkin only wanted me for a job. "Yes. Nikonova." I showed him my card.

The guard consulted a ledger on his table. "Wait here a moment." As he slipped through the door, I glimpsed another hallway where daylight glowed from what must have been windows near the ceiling. I didn't like any of this, the lack of signs or other information, the hollow silence. I pressed my hand against my breast pocket and felt Henry's ring. This was real. Soon I'd leave this building and go out into the fresh air and sun again.

A few minutes later, I heard two sets of footsteps, and when the door opened, there was Nikolai Koshkin, the guard behind him.

"Excellent, you've finally arrived," said Koshkin. "We need your expertise." There was a taut air to him, a jerkiness in his movements as if his nerves were raw.

I allowed him to lead me down a long corridor dotted with closed doors. Small windows ran along the walls near the ceiling but they were covered in rusted grates which let in tiny swirls of light. I didn't understand how my skills as an interpreter would be needed in a place like this. It was just a basement.

"What is this place?"

"A temporary detention center. This way." We turned a corner and passed through another set of unmarked doors. The air grew cooler still and the smells stronger. More disinfectant, so acidic, I tasted it when I breathed. There were doors here too, all along the corridor. From behind one, a sudden muffled cry of a man in agony. I stumbled and bit my tongue. Koshkin's cheek twitched.

"Is my sister here?"

"Yes," he sighed, "she is."

"What has she done?"

He turned his sad brown eyes onto me. "What do you think she's done?"

I didn't know what to say. I didn't know how much he knew about Felix. Or maybe this was about me. Maybe Vera was under suspicion because of the mission she'd given me—her freelancing, as Felix had called it. Or because she'd neglected to report my relationship with Henry. Maybe she hadn't been in a love affair with Koshkin at all. Maybe he'd trapped her. But I couldn't believe she'd let herself be snared by her passions. I wasn't sure she had any.

An interior corridor, not connected to the outside world. Electric light came from dusty bulbs strung near the ceiling. Behind one of the doors, someone coughed words I couldn't understand. There was a sharp answer and the unmistakable sound of something hard striking something soft. I gasped and looked at Koshkin. Unmoved, he continued to the last door in the corridor. He opened it and murmured to someone on the other side.

Vera came out, closing the door behind her. She was in uniform, though the top buttons of her collar were undone, an unheard-of violation of the dress code while on duty. Her face was bright with sweat and her eyes wide as if she were forcing herself to stay awake and alert. She blinked at me in disbelief, and then turned to Koshkin. "I told you not to call her. I can get the rest of the names from him myself."

"It's taking too long. We need this done."

Vera blocked the door. "Marya, listen to me. Go. Go to your duties. We'll talk later."

The door was made of iron. It had whined and echoed when it closed. "Felix is in there, isn't he?"

"I said, go."

"Isn't he?"

Koshkin raised his voice. "Enough." He turned to me. "Markow asked to see you, and we're granting him this on the condition that he gives us the rest of the names on the list."

"She's useless at this kind of thing," Vera said, which we both knew was a lie. She was obviously trying to convince Koshkin to send me away. Her hands shook violently as she lit her cigarette. "She'll coddle him and get nothing."

"Let your sister pass. I don't want to order you."

Vera tore herself away, stalking up the corridor, Koshkin rounding on her, talking sweetly. He put a hand on her waist and she pushed it away. Disgusted, I opened the door to Felix's cell and closed myself in.

IT WAS SMALL and contained almost nothing. No bed or bunk, no toilet, no pail, no sink, no table. There were two chairs side by side near the door. I assumed Koshkin would sit in one, Vera in the other.

Felix had to stand. This was an old interrogation technique. He was in the far corner, slumped as if the wall was the only thing keeping him upright. His suspenders had been taken away. He was holding up his trousers so they wouldn't fall to his ankles.

I had no tears, seeing him like this. My fury and horror burned them away before they could come. He was so thin in the same stained undershirt he'd worn when they'd taken him away five days ago. It was smeared with blood. His eyes, nose, and lips were bruised and swollen and crusted with blood. His beard had grown in thinly along chin and cheeks, reminding me of how he'd been in the war. No, that wasn't true. Even as my prisoner, he'd never looked this battered and torn. No one, no human being, deserved to be treated in such a way that he was like this, beaten and at the end of his powers, holding up his trousers at his own interrogation.

I was through with this place, this world I'd been serving. When

I left this building, I was going back to Henry, and we would leave Berlin today. We would fly away. I was done with my country. I couldn't stand it anymore.

Felix watched me, no change in his face, no hope or disappointment, sadness or anger. I recognized this from prisoners in the war. He was preserving the last drop of his energy. He was waiting for the next threat he would have to deflect. Maybe he was so far gone, he didn't recognize me. It looked like he could only see out of one eye.

"God, Felix. They can't do this to you. They can't."

His face showed a hint of amusement. "Seems they have." The words came out thickly as if pushed around a clot in his mouth.

"Come. Sit down."

I brought a chair to him at the wall. He cast an anxious glance at the door, then lowered himself, groaning. "Food?"

"I'm sorry, I didn't know to bring any." I searched my pockets, discovered a forgotten rum toffee from Henry. I picked off the paper and held it out to Felix in my palm. His left hand, filthy and stained with blood, reached for it. His right was bound with a blood-flecked bandage. His mouth opened slowly and only a little, and with great difficulty, he shoved the toffee between his teeth. His shoulders sank and he closed his eyes.

I brought the second chair next to him. "Why don't you just tell them all the names on the list? Or where you hid it?"

He shook his head.

"If you don't, they'll kill you." Not they. Vera. The rage in me spread like a poison in my body. I was horrified at this creature who was my sister. "Did she order it? Your kidnapping?"

The muscles were moving slightly in his mouth. "Paper?"

I gave him the wrapper. Gingerly, he spat the smooth disc of toffee onto the paper, smearing it with blood. He folded it one-handed on his leg and slipped it into his pocket. With every move, he flinched and groaned. "It was the Russians all right. I figure Vera ordered it, or Koshkin. They're quite the couple. Made for each other."

"Is any of this worth it, Felix? Give them the list. It's your only chance. "

"I've seen it." He tapped a black-tipped finger below his working eye. "I'm a dead man no matter what I do."

"I'll talk to them. To Vera. I'm not going to let her kill you."

"Did you hear me? I'm dead already. She won't let me live. I know too much. Once she has all the names, I'm no use to her anymore and that's it for me. So quit"—he swallowed, gurgling, and had to catch his breath—"wasting time. I won't get out of this. You won't save me this time. Didn't deserve it in the war, don't now."

"This isn't about what you deserve. What do any of us deserve?" I was afraid to touch him, that I might hurt him. I put my hand on his bare wrist, and he shifted uncomfortably, leaning closer. There were so many things I wanted to tell him, and no time. "I got married yesterday."

Surprise passed over his face, then a faint and painful smile. "Congratulations. He's a lucky bastard."

"The bastard, as you call him, tried to find you. I told him about us. In the war. I told him—" Embarrassment stopped me from admitting the thoughts and feelings of a teenage girl long ago.

Felix cradled my cheek in his good hand. "It's all right."

"No, it's not."

"I want you to do something for me."

It sounded like the start of a final wish, and I snapped at him. "Stop being stubborn. Tell me where the list is. Give me the names. Something. They'll let you live."

"They threatened my family, Marya. My wife. My *kids*. You think they're the kind of people who are going to let me walk out of here? They're not like you. Don't do their dirty work for them. Once you start, they'll never let you stop." He gasped at some sudden pain. When he could breathe easier again, he said, "I'm going to give your sister the rest of the names. Most of them. Tell her I'll do it if she leaves my family alone. And then I need you to go to Leni. Listen. Tell her she was right about me. And I love her even if I didn't always show it."

I tried to shake my head and he stopped me.

"Marya. I need you to do this."

"No."

"Tell Greta if she ever decides to talk again, I'll hear her. Wherever I am. Tell her that."

"I won't."

"Yes, you will. And Peter. Tell him not to grow up angry. It's hard. I know."

He pressed his lips to my cheek three slow times. "For my wife and children." Then one light kiss on my lips. "For the bride. I wish you all the happiness in the world, if there's any left."

"You're giving up. Why?"

"I know when I'm beat. Now, get out of here. I'm sorry for bringing you into this. Don't go after your sister, just get out. Get far away from here."

"Henry wants me to emigrate to the West."

"Then go."

But he still hadn't let go of me. For a long time, we stayed in an awkward hug. His breathing got easier, more regular. I let him sleep, a warm and heavy weight leaning against me. It was some comfort for him if I couldn't do anything else.

He jerked awake suddenly. "Did I ask you about the book? Did Leni give it back?"

"Book?" I thought he was speaking from a dream.

"Your pretty one. The fairy tales."

"Yes, I took it back."

"Good old Leni." His eye closed, his battered face relaxing. "Get it as far away as you can."

"Why?"

"Just do it, Marya. Better yet, burn it."

"If I wanted that, I could've left it with your wife."

"I wanted you to see it first."

"I know every page by heart."

"Not anymore. I put in one of my own."

I sat back. My book with its illuminated pages, the intricate patterns, the otherworldly creatures. And then I imagined a page of his, a single column of names.

"Felix, you hid the list in my book?"

"There are twenty names on it. Most of those people will get a bullet in the back of the neck. Moscow will be very happy with Vera after that. Very sure of her loyalty."

"That was the price you were willing to pay for your freedom. You knew that when you took the list to begin with."

"The situation changed the moment I saw those names, and stop arguing with me, dammit."

It was the pain talking, his fatigue and fear. I pressed his lucky coin into his hand and held it there. "I'll go get the book and come back as soon as I can. Don't aggravate Vera and Koshkin."

"Aggravating them is the only fun I have left in this life." He nudged my ear, the strands of hair that had come loose. "Please, Marya. Destroy the list. Let me save you one more time."

He wasn't making sense. If he was giving Vera most of the names anyway, why would the physical list be a danger to me? I wasn't on it. I wasn't a traitor. All at once, in his sad and battered face, I saw the truth. The one name that Vera couldn't let anyone see. My sister was on the other side of the door. My sister. Over a week ago, she'd told me her name was on the list, and I'd thought it was a lie to distract and manipulate me. I'd been so sure. But if it was true, it made her an enemy of the people. A traitor. And I would be a traitor's sister, under suspicion. I lived with her; I wouldn't be spared. The MGB would never believe I didn't know what she was.

"Not her." I was shaking my head. "Not her."

"Be shocked later. You need to get out of here. Come on."

We helped each other to our feet, clumsy, leaning against each other. I hugged him fiercely to hear his heartbeat one more time. "I'm so sorry, Felix. She told me, and I didn't believe her."

"You're better than her, Marya. You're free. You hear me? Get out of here and live."

29
Marya

I closed his cell door behind me. In the corridor, Vera straightened from where she'd been leaning against the wall, dropping her cigarette onto a little pile smoldering on the floor. In the yellow light, she looked ill. But proud too, her chin up, her gaze hard and steady again. Felix had once mentioned her having armor, and I saw it then, something embedded into her skin. Underneath it—who was she? I had no idea what moved her, what she hoped for, worked for, and why. She was betraying our country. She was undermining everything she'd claimed to believe in. Maybe she believed in nothing at all.

"Well?" she said, very controlled. Her gaze slid to my uniform, and I noticed the bloodstains. They choked me. I couldn't say anything. It was hard to think when the world was turned inside out.

The sister I thought I knew didn't exist. If I answered her, who was I talking to?

Koshkin emerged from the shadows where she'd banished him, I assumed. He didn't go near her or try to touch her again. I wondered how much he knew about her. Maybe his name was also on the list. Two lovers united by treason. Could that ever be a basis for love?

"Did he give you names?" he demanded.

"He'll tell you everything now," I said, surprisingly calm, "if you leave his family alone." I couldn't look at Vera. "He's sworn to cooperate fully."

I didn't wait to be dismissed, just marched right down the corridor and through the doors, turning blindly, looking for the high windows with the iron grates, a way to the outside world. I found a German sign, Ausgang, over another set of doors. It soothed me to translate the word literally in my head. Ausgang—the way out.

Vera caught up with me as I was about to push the handle. She grasped it and held it closed. "That night outside the barracks, I tried to tell you what would happen to the German if I didn't get the list. I tried and you didn't listen."

"You're a spy, Vera. For them."

"I'll explain it all to you soon. After this is over. Did he tell you where the list is?"

I pushed her. "You're killing him. You're killing him to save yourself." I lashed out at her again, and she deflected my hands, knocking them aside and then slapping me hard.

"Calm down."

She'd never hit me before. Never. I held my cheek, tears stinging my eyes. "Do you even know what you are?"

"I'm doing what is necessary. You can still save him. Tell me where the list is, and I'll see that he lives. He'll be sent to Russia, it's the very minimum punishment for men like him. But he won't die in that cell."

"You're lying. He doesn't want me to negotiate for his life anyway. He's not afraid to die. He's less afraid than you are."

She grasped my arm and twisted it, a spike of pain that surprised me as much as the slap. Even as girls when she was mean to me, it was never this, never with her hands. It was always the heart and the mind she twisted, bludgeoned, sliced. "Where is it?"

"You'll throw me in a cell too? You'll have me tortured too? You'd do it to his wife? His children?"

"That was only a threat. Everything else, everything that's happening to Markow, what could happen to the both of us if this all goes badly—I gave you fair warning. If you'd listened to me—"

"You can't bully and lie to me and then expect me to trust you."

Abruptly, she let me go. "Marya, if you don't cooperate, his death is on you."

"Murderer. Traitor," I hissed.

"Get out, then. Let him die. I gave you the chance."

I turned to the door and she grasped me from behind and whispered in my ear. "If he told you where the list is, destroy it. For our family's sake. And for yourself. This isn't just about me. I warned you. We're all in this."

I yanked free and slammed the doors behind me.

I HITCHED A ride back to the barracks and went straight to the communal library, empty at that time of day. The sun streamed through the windows and the air hung heavy in the stuffy heat. From the shelf, I removed three copies of *The Young Guard* and breathed out when I saw my fairy-tales book tucked behind them.

I'd hidden it to keep Vera from taking one of the last beautiful things I had.

Back in my room, the sun shone brightly on the floor. I regretted I had no shade. Outside my window, all the way to the perimeter fence, there was no one, but the feeling of being watched was intense. I knelt on my mattress with the book, my back to the door, angry at what Felix had done to one of my most precious things. The illustrations were so beautiful, reaching to the heart of our old traditions, our patterns and stories. When I rattled the book, nothing fell out. I assumed Felix had glued the list over a page. Yet no page was thicker than the others, as I saw when I examined the book from the sides. But then, I noticed one page about two thirds through that didn't lie as straight as it should, as if it had been cut at a slightly wrong angle.

I looked more closely. Felix had trimmed a page out of the book and pasted a single typescript sheet onto the remaining strip still attached to the book's spine. The list. Twenty names in the English alphabet. As I ran my finger down the page, I looked for ones I recognized. Just below an Ivanov, Leonid, I saw Koshkin, Nikolai Vasylyvich. For a moment I was amazed, a colonel at SMAD, an American spy. Shaking my head, I continued to read and stopped at the thirteenth name. Nikonova, Vera Ilyanovna.

I climbed to my feet, hugging the book, pacing and brooding. Why did she do it? Why? She was the model officer. She was devotion and duty itself. She knew her history of the Communist Party. She quoted Lenin and worked for the good of our whole society. She lived the stark and simple life of the old communists, the direct opposite of the American way. What did they have that she wanted? Baseball, dollars, cola? She didn't care about those things. Not that I knew what she cared about anymore.

I got down on the floor, the book open in front of me. My own movements were strange to me, remote. At one point, the sewing scissors were in my hands and I was cutting the list out of the book with wildly jagged edges. Then I began to pack, though not much. I didn't care about things, and besides, the MGB shouldn't think I'd fled to the West, though I assumed Vera would guess. The faces of my mother and Nina floated into the room, and I pinched myself until they left and I could carry on. I packed the letters from my family, my medals, a change of clothing. At the last minute, I noticed the blood on my tunic, Felix's blood, and changed into a fresh uniform.

In the doorway, a tremor passed through me. After a few moments, I was steady enough to close the door behind me forever. The barracks were quiet. I passed no one in the hallways or in the library, where I replaced my fairy-tales book on the shelf. Two cooks worked in the kitchen, where I nicked a bottle of vodka. Outside, the paths shimmered in the heat. The sentry looked up drowsily from his chair but stayed in his box and said nothing. In the glaring sunlight, my eyes teared up, and I wiped them over and over on my sleeve on the way to my old cottage.

I wanted to see it one more time, the red slats and the blue shutters and the windows all around. Weeds were cracking the path to the door. Abandoned things decayed that quickly. A note was fading on the door: NO ENTRY BY ORDER OF SMAD. I tried the door anyway. Locked. I circled round the garden gate to the back.

Nothing had changed. There was a slight wind, a rustling of overgrown grass. A fly circled my head and was gone. Under my dear magnolia tree, I took a drink of vodka. Then I found a rusting spade where one of my housemates had left it near a flower bed and jabbed it at the dried ground at the foot of the tree. When the hole was deep enough to swallow up my hand and wrist, I set the spade aside.

After another drink, I took the list of traitors out of my pocket and smoothed it out. Then I began to tear it into small pieces. I sprinkled the scraps into the hole and thought of Leni Markow as I took out my box of matches. I thought of Greta and Peter, who, like me, would lose their father too soon when they'd been the lucky ones; their papa had come home from the war. But there was another war now, and he wouldn't survive it.

The flame blossomed and took hold of the first scrap of paper, a quick inferno that sealed the fate Felix had chosen, with my sister's help. And mine. I hadn't seen what she really was, the revolt inside her, but she'd seen it in me, with Henry. With how I lived. Everything. To be at war with your society is a deep and lonely conflict. Our father had known it, and so did she. All along, she'd understood what I was going through and she hadn't said a thing.

I let the smoke sting my eyes, the ash swirling in my lungs and burning my throat. When the flame was gone, I jabbed a stick at the ashes, stirred them into the earth, and then covered over the spot.

I CROSSED INTO the French Sector in the afternoon sun. I was disoriented, the vodka bottle in my fist. I was aware of only certain things: bright colors, children, the rare motor vehicle on the street. This would likely be the last time I'd take this route, that I'd do something as odd and unnatural as cross from one national sector of Berlin to another. Silly, invisible borders.

At Felix's house, one of the neighbors stiffened at the sight of me in my uniform. I spoke in my native accent, why not? No use pretending anymore. When I asked if the Markow family was in, she pointed to the door at the end of the corridor that led to the yard.

Leni was kneeling at a low wooden box that appeared to be a vegetable garden planted in a half-sunny, half-shady patch of the yard. Greta and Peter were squatting on the concrete, playing with tin soldiers. When I snuck up on them, so deep in their game, I recognized soldiers of the era they were born into, in the uniform their father had worn, the now-forbidden Wehrmacht. The children shouldn't have these things anymore. Even toys were political. It angered me to see these tin soldiers and made me sad too. None of us had asked to be born where and when we were.

Finally, the children noticed me. They seemed confused, recognizing my face but not the woman in the uniform. I grasped them quickly and kissed them on the heads. They twisted away and ran to the ruins at the edge of the yard before I could tell them my kisses were from their father.

I walked toward Leni at the vegetable patch. Her hair hung in her face in strands where it had slipped out of the pins. As difficult as her marriage had looked from the outside, this was a woman who had loved her husband. She bore his loss like an extension of the war when the women waited and didn't know if their men would ever come back. In a way, Felix, the man she'd known, never had.

I knelt beside her. Neither of us said anything at first. The sky was very blue, a spot of color over the drab buildings that enclosed the yard.

"Frau Markow, I'm so sorry." I began to cry, a short and violent attack, and I soon reined it in. I didn't say that Felix was as good as dead, that we were killing him, my people, my sister, at that very moment. I didn't tell her that I was the one who had sealed his fate, or that his stubbornness in that cell, his silence about what he knew, was giving my sister and me a chance to live. I didn't care anymore what his crimes and flaws had been. I saw only his sacrifice. He'd given me the gift of freedom, what he'd longed for himself, and I would never again be ashamed of him and our friendship.

30
Vera

Testimony for Chairman A. Cheptsov
Military Collegium of the Supreme Court of the USSR
Moscow, 28 February–3 June 1956

[RECORDING]

My husband is the guiding hand in these last moments of my investigation. I can feel his presence in the man watching my hotel room in New York, the two men who materialize in line behind me at the airport, and two others who catch my eye on the plane on my way to the bathroom. Even if they are KGB men instead of errand boys from the diplomatic pool, they are being held at bay when, under normal circumstances, they could stop me traveling from one Western country to another.

After seventeen hours in transit, it is a relief to hear the doors of the DC-6 slam open and feel the gust of warm air at Tempelhof. Berlin at last. Seeing it from the air had been strange, the reality outside my window jumbled up with the ruins I remember and the images from old films. It will be different from the ground, I think. More real. I pack up my things and prepare to disembark, nervous to see how the city has aged. I don't want to be reminded of how long it has taken me to come back and finish what was begun nine years ago.

At the top of the gangway, I pause in the heat that bakes the tarmac. Numerous planes are parked all around, and people are boarding, or disembarking, and men scurry around loading luggage or refueling. A stream of people are heading toward the terminal. In all of this bustle, I look for Nikolai and am surprised he isn't here. Maybe he's on his way. I've made no secret of where I'm going; I told our embassy I would return to Moscow as soon as my meeting with Henry Barrow is over. That I will have a lot to answer for goes without saying. Uncovering the truth has a cost, and I'm prepared to pay it.

My only regret is that my family will pay just as much, if not more. If I discover today that Henry Barrow was a spy all along who lured Marya into giving him the American list of Soviet agents—if Marya was truly guilty of treason—then my investigation will have done nothing but reopen a wound I should've left alone. I've given my mother hope she should've never had. I don't know how many more years she'll care to live with her sorrow. And Nina, she's become anxious about her fiancé, her wedding, her future, all because of me reopening Marya's case. And, of course, there's Nikolai. The last thing I wanted to do was push him away or ruin his chances to continue the work he does for our country. The innocence of my sister hangs on much more than I considered when I began down this road. Now that I'm close to the truth, I'm not sure I want to know it.

Inside the terminal, I buy a bouquet of flowers, then step out into the street. After being so deeply mired in Marya's case, I'm immediately comfortable hearing German at the taxi stand and seeing it on the signs. As arranged, Archibald Johnson is waiting for me, looking slightly disheveled from what I imagine was a long day and night of traveling from America to London to Germany. He's waving his hat from the tread of a black sedan. The British will be escorting me to the meeting with Barrow in what is still the British Sector of the city. I gesture to the Russians who have been shadowing me since New York, and they break for their car idling a few lengths away. Two other men with the square jaws and shoulders of Americans are watching us from a vehicle just behind Johnson's. What a happy international family we are as this motorcade takes to the streets.

During the ride, I try to focus on new aspects of the city, the things that would delight my sister. Young trees have been planted, a sign of healing that Marya would love. When she was here, the streets were bald of anything green and wholesome. Women are strolling in new clothing, the young men at work, everyone busy, everyone building. And shop windows—full of sausages, butter, lard, everything that is fat and good. I believe that Marya, with her generous heart, would be glad to see all this too.

The motorcade rolls past the shattered remains of a church. Johnson informs me that the Germans will never repair it, that it will stay as it is to remind them of their past, and what they have done. It's a powerful gesture, and I wonder how long it will last. I don't believe we humans are made to remember our worst actions for too long. We are apt to pave them over in our minds and hearts. It's happening already in Moscow, I know, in the struggle for Stalin's legacy. Very soon, people will refuse to remember the truth, and I fear our wounds will never heal.

The motorcade turns onto the boulevard that I knew as the

Charlottenburger Chaussee but what is now called the Straße des 17. Juni to commemorate the revolt of the people in the German Democratic Republic several years ago, which we helped pacify—with violence. The Tiergarten is all around us now, green with fresh trees. The motorcade does a U-turn at the Brandenburg Gate, as gray and pockmarked as I remembered it, and we pull up to the Soviet War Memorial.

I get out of the car, carrying the flowers to the granite steps. Henry Barrow chose this as our meeting place, a Soviet patch within the British Sector, the closest we can come to ground that belongs, in a way, to both of us. He is already there, a civilian in a brown jacket too loose for him. I don't suppose the years since the events in Berlin has dimmed his hatred of me, and I'm right. His gaze over-flows with it. He's aged, as we all have. He has the sheen of bitterness and suspicion that comes with the hard experiences of life. I'm sorry to see him like this. He wouldn't believe me if I told him, and so I say nothing. Our conversation must wait for a few more moments.

I speak to the soldier on guard duty, who takes one step to the side, a sign that I may pass. As I climb the steps, my war wound stings my leg for the first time in years. I set my bouquet next to the wreaths and blossoms that are already there, and murmur a thanks to our brothers and sisters, the war dead, who sacrificed their lives so that the world may live without tyranny. For their sakes, and ours, the rest of us must remember never again to place our hopes and futures in the hands of one man.

Barrow has joined me on the step. He takes off his hat and speaks not to me, but to the wreaths.

"Marya was here," he says, "the first time I ever saw her. She was tidying up the flowers. She'd brought a little hand broom to sweep up all the dead ones. I'd only been in Berlin a few months; I was practically a tourist, snapping photographs. I thought she was ordered to work here, but she said it was her idea. She wanted to do it for the people who died. She let me take her picture."

He stops as if it's hard for him to go on. We hear the traffic from the boulevard behind us, a cough from one of the men from the motorcade. They are spread out in national groups, observing, smoking, listening. Even Johnson, who hasn't spoken to Barrow since I came, hangs in the background, hands in his pockets, watching us.

"I should've walked on," Barrow says. "If I'd known what would happen to her, I would've left her alone."

He's holding her photograph, but not the one he claims to have taken of her here. It's from the Gulag, Marya as a prisoner enduring Siberia and trying hard not to show what it's done to her. It's the photograph I'd given Johnson, who must have passed it on to Barrow before this meeting, as I wanted.

"None of us can see the future, Mr. Barrow. It's hard enough to see the past."

"I hear you've been trying. What's your verdict, then? I'm told you've gone through a whole investigation, reopened her case as you call it. You've found what? This woman, your own sister, had the cold heart of a spy?"

He thrusts the photograph at me, and I recoil inwardly at the pain in my sister's eyes. I feel attacked and must retaliate.

"And what about you? Long ago here in Berlin, I told you I assumed you were an agent of British intelligence. My sister was in love, and what were you? You were older, more experienced. You knew exactly what you were doing to her."

He's shaking his head angrily. "I loved her."

"I'm sure you did, after a while. She was easy to love. But it takes a ruthless kind of heart to love a woman and still lure her into betraying her country. That's what happened, isn't it? You blinded her so completely that she wanted to please you. She brought you the kind of intelligence any agent would kill for: a list of Soviet personnel who reported to the Americans. The British and Americans are allies, but you play your little games against each other in the shadows, don't you? That list was a coup. Were you paid a bonus for getting it? Were you promoted?"

"I never cared about any list. As soon as you showed up in Berlin, I tried to get Marya to leave with me. But she wouldn't go. I should've tied her up and dragged her away. Maybe she would've hated me for it, but it would've saved her from everything that happened later. It would've saved her from you."

"What a coincidence—I was trying to save her from you." I put up my hands, a peace offering. "Please, Mr. Barrow. I didn't meet you here to go over old grievances. Let's agree that we both loved Marya in our ways and move on. I assume Mr. Johnson told you about my investigation into my sister's true activities in Berlin. I believe you were aware that she took documents from you and passed them to us?"

"That wasn't her. It was you. You made her do it. You threatened to tell your people about us if she didn't spy for you."

I remember how we sisters were in Berlin. It shouldn't surprise me that she would blame me for something she might consider a low act, betraying the man she loved.

"I assure you, I knew about your relationship back then, but I had no idea she was spying on you until recently."

"Bollocks."

"Call it what you like, but the real key to Marya's actions was a German named Felix Markow. Did she ever mention him?"

"I met the poor bastard."

"It sounds like you have some sympathy for him." I'm genuinely surprised. "He was one of our agents, did you know that?"

"I know Marya loved him, and he didn't deserve it. Looks like she had a habit of loving people who don't deserve her." He walks to the end of the steps and stands with his back to me for a few moments. I can see him breathing deeply and leave him to calm himself. I'm grateful for the chance to do the same and look up at the great statue that rises over the monument, a vigilant Red Army soldier with his rifle over his shoulder. This memorial is our ground, and it gives me strength.

"I'm not here to fight with you," I say. "I've been trying to understand my sister, and believe it or not, I would like you to understand too. My investigation has revealed that she was working closely with Felix Markow. She took documents from you and delivered them to him. They ended up with us, and that seems to prove she was spying for our side, not yours. The problem is the American list. She helped Markow get it, and I need to know what she did with it. After Markow's death the list never surfaced. I have a witness who insists Marya had it in her hands. Please set aside your anger at me and tell the truth. Did she give it to you?"

Barrow has been pacing on the step, and he turns to me with a bitter smile. "All this talk of an investigation, and you have it all wrong. She wasn't playing Russian spy with that German, and she wasn't helping him out of the goodness of her heart. He was blackmailing her."

I was preparing my follow-up question in my head, but his answer threw me off course. "Blackmail?"

"Your thorough and honest investigation didn't turn that up? Hard to believe."

"I didn't know. Felix Markow was blackmailing Marya? Are you sure? Was there proof?"

He slips her Gulag photo into his pocket, draws out another, larger photograph that he unfolds twice. It shows Marya and Barrow outside of his former house in Charlottenburg. The two of them are young and happy to see each other. Their relationship is unmistakable. On the back, written in German, are their names and the date 22 June 1947.

Rheingold. That snake. That miserable turncoat. Felix Markow had been watching them as I asked him to, but if this photograph was his, then he'd taken advantage of Marya behind my back.

"I must borrow this," I say urgently. "A handwriting analyst can compare it with a sample of Markow's writing—"

"Don't bother. It's his. He gave it to Marya in exchange for following his orders. It was either that or he'd tell your lot what she was doing with me. All along she was scared of being arrested, deported, thrown in prison, because of me. So she went along with Markow. And with you, for the very same reasons. She wasn't just protecting herself, you know. She told me our relationship was a danger to everybody connected to her. Even you."

I tear myself away from him and gaze up at the statue again. Ah, Marya. If this is true, if Markow had been blackmailing her, forcing her to do what she did—learn spy craft, take documents from Barrow, and ultimately, the list from Irina Petrova—then the structure I've been building for months, the argument that she was loyal to us because her espionage work benefited us, was for nothing. If she was forced to do it, her actions weren't out of loyalty to the country but to save her own neck. And mine too.

There's a sheen in my sight, a heat haze all around me. Markow, the dark intelligence steering my sister to her ultimate doom. Her relationship with Barrow had been a love affair, and what of it? It didn't make her a Western spy. My sister's deeper struggles in Berlin, her misery, could only happen in the system we lived in, which forced her to twist her heart for political reasons. Markow knew how to take advantage of that, and of my sister's nature. So what did he mean when Nikolai and I found him wounded in the hospital and he said that Marya should take the list somewhere? Had he arranged to sell it to the British with Marya forced to help? If so, she *was* guilty of passing Soviet secrets to the West.

Barrow comes up beside me. "Looking a little pale, Vera. The truth choking you?"

"Did Marya give you the American list?"

"What if she did?"

I step closer to him. "Because that, combined with everything you've just told me, would mean she is guilty of espionage for a foreign government. She would be a traitor, an enemy of the people. Guilty, do you understand?"

"Your laws made guilty people out of the innocent. You think you had nothing to do with that? You're a lawyer, aren't you?"

"Did she give you the list or not?"

"No. Satisfied?"

I don't know if I can believe him, as much as I want to. He would shield her, try to make her look as innocent as he claims he was.

"For the love you seem to have for my sister, tell me the truth: When you conducted your affair with her, were you an agent of British intelligence?"

"If I say yes, what difference does it make now?"

I launch myself at him, my body no longer mine, my fingers in claws and a guttural wail emitting from my throat, a sound that isn't me, that I don't know, that I've never heard from myself. I find none of his flesh, though that's what I want. He has grasped my arms and thrown them aside, and then a man pins me from behind, shouting my name.

"Vera, stop it!"

Nikolai, my husband. His voice cuts through my fury. How can he be here? How? I turn in his arms, and I see the horror in his face—at me, his wife, who has lost her temper and her dignity at our memorial, the place where our dead heroes are supposed to be at peace. Around us, the men of the motorcade have charged in, unsure what happens next, the Americans, the Russians, the British looking incensed.

Barrow stands over me, he seems to blot out the statue of our soldier, the very sky of Berlin. "Well, Vera," he says. "Here you are. You say you're looking for the truth. You're all grand and philosophical about it. I'll tell you this: You were never interested in the truth back then and you aren't now. You're a lying, selfish, manipulative bitch. This has nothing to do with the truth, and it's not even about Marya. It's about you. You and your guilt. I hope it rots you from the inside. I hope you take it to your grave."

He walks away to a chorus of voices. In Russian: "Stop him, he has attacked a Soviet national!" American English: "Give the Brits a hand, cover them." The British Johnson: "Get in the car, Henry, for God's sake." Barrow seems not to hear as he strides up the street, his back to them all, lighting a cigarette.

31

Marya

Berlin, 15 July 1947

After I left Felix's family, I didn't see the point of trying to pretend I was all right. He was dead or dying while Vera watched or gave him the death blow herself. My sister, the traitor, double agent, and murderer. And what did that make me? Could I erase it all by walking away?

Near the canal, I passed a pair of gendarmes, who turned to stare at me. They called to me in French but I didn't understand. I was abandoning my family, my country, my work, my language, my past. I couldn't understand anything anymore. The French followed at a respectful distance as I stepped onto the wooden bridge, grasping the railing as I walked. The whole structure was swaying beneath me, and when I looked down at the water shimmering below, I was almost sick.

"Do you need help, mademoiselle?"

The gendarme looked concerned, and I appreciated it. I thanked him in one language or another; I wasn't sure what came out of my mouth. Did it matter? A few more steps, and I'd be free. At the end of the bridge, behind the heat haze, was the British Sector. A British soldier would see my uniform. He'd see my misery and would speak to me, and I would say I wanted asylum. I want to be free. My husband is waiting for me.

Another drink from the vodka bottle and I got moving again, one foot in front of the other. How hard could it be to leave behind everything I ever knew? German pedestrians pressed themselves to the railing to let me pass—me, a Soviet officer, a bottle in my fist, dragging myself across the bridge. I must've been quite a sight to them. If I'd been a man, they would've been more obvious about their hatred, but I was a woman, and they looked at me curiously before moving on.

At the end of the bridge, I turned and waved goodbye to the gendarmes. I didn't know them, but I would miss them anyway. One raised his hand in return. Goodbye.

I spun around and crossed into the British Sector, marching at speed because I was free, though I didn't feel free. I could go wherever I wanted, couldn't I? I'd go to our memorial in the Tiergarten where I first met my husband.

I knelt on the steps and paid my respects to our dead and our victory and the girl I used to be. I cried and prayed for Yuri and the other souls of the dead, though I didn't know how to pray. I'd never learned the words. Then I busied myself picking up the wilted and rotting flowers, sweeping them into a tidy pile out of sight. I straightened the ribbons of a wreath. I'd done this with Henry the day we met, ages ago. This was the last time.

I stood to attention. Saluted. Goodbye.

From there, it didn't matter where I went. My bottle was nearly empty. I shuffled, stumbled, wandered. To the Germans around me, I was a laughingstock, I was sure of it, the drunken Russian soldier. How many of us had they seen and suffered? I deserved their disdain. I was abandoning my past—everything I was—to live my own selfish life. Forever, there would be a shadow over me; I would be tied forever to my cowardice. I was running away from my world because it didn't suit me. Was the act any less despicable because I was doing it for love?

I found a streetcar and boarded it. No one asked for the fare. I rested my feet and watched the city pass, its ruins, crumbled boulevards, blackened scars. *Auf wiedersehen.* An empty sentiment. I would never see it again, this city where I'd been happy.

"Excuse me, miss. You understand English?"

Soldiers, a pair of them, one twisted in the seat in front of me, the other standing in the narrow aisle. Both wore an armband with the letters MP. There were Germans in the rear of the car, watching. The car wasn't moving. I didn't recognize the buildings outside, but I knew from the military policemen's uniforms and their accents that I was still in the British Sector.

"Yes, I understand." My words were slurred, my pronunciation bad. I sat up straighter. This was a matter of professional pride. I repeated more clearly, "I speak English, sir."

"Do you know where you are?" The policeman glanced at the bottle I still clutched in my lap.

"Yes, sir. The British Sector of Berlin."

The despair on my face must have told him I was not there as a tourist, or to shop in a Western store. "Do you want to stay?" he asked.

For me, this was the true border. Not those ridiculous sector lines, the signposts and guards. It was this: a statement before witnesses of my intention to seek asylum in the West. A permanent crossing, one life to another.

Their uniforms, the music of their words, gave me strength. They were Henry's men, messengers from a new world. I slipped his wedding band from my pocket, transferred the warm gold onto my finger.

"I want to stay. Please take me to Captain Henry Barrow. He's waiting for me."

The policeman raised his hand, a signal to the driver who got the streetcar moving again. The other policeman murmured that he would like my name, and other particulars, and as I told him, he noted it all down in the notebook on his thigh. I pinched the skin between my thumb and index finger to stay alert. My relief was making me sleepy. I'd done it. I was in their hands. My fate was uncertain, but I'd crossed this first border. There would be others. Berlin was an island surrounded by the Soviet Zone. With a chill, I wondered how Henry's people would get me out safely. He'd said we would fly.

The streetcar stopped, and many people got off, including us, the policemen helping me down the steps. I stumbled, unable to hold myself with much dignity, though I tried. Strangely, at that moment, I was aware that I represented my country and people. This was an escape, a request for asylum. I wanted to show the world and myself that it was a brave thing and not the desperate act of a grieving woman.

One policeman waited on the curb with me while another disappeared into a building, then came out minutes later. "The car is coming," he said. "Cigarette?"

I shook my head and we waited, the policemen tensely silent until the car drew up beside us. During the ride, I dozed, was gently shaken awake, helped out of the car. They were escorting me to a building I recognized but couldn't place at first. Its many windows looked down on me blankly, without warmth.

Inside, I was led into a quiet corridor. A robust woman in tweeds stopped us with a smile. "Well, there you are. Marya, is it?"

Her familiarity surprised me, but maybe Henry's people were less formal than he'd let on. Maybe British HQ—I remembered where I was now—would be a friendly place. She introduced herself as Miss Gains. "We'll get you situated until Mr. Johnson arrives," she said briskly.

Johnson? The fog in my mind stirred, tried to clear, but it was stubborn.

"You look all in," she said. "Are you hungry? We'll get you some supper. If you could wait in here."

She brought me to a room with a table, two chairs, a lamp. "Where is Captain Barrow?" I asked.

"He's on his way, don't you worry. I'll have the girl bring in some refreshment."

She closed me in alone. The room had plain white walls and the feel of an interrogation room. I tried the door. It opened easily into the corridor. I closed myself in again and looked around. There was a small calendar on the wall that seemed an advertisement for an automobile manufacturer. There was no photograph of the British king or prime minister, as there would be of Stalin or Lenin in our rooms. This place seemed free of beady-eyed leaders and politics.

A silent young woman brought in a tray that contained an astonishing amount of food and drink. A carafe was full of orange juice, such a delicacy, I guzzled it down. The food was a puzzling selection of mush of different colors, as if Henry's people feared for my digestion. I ate though I felt no hunger at all. I was reverting to a childhood mode in days of uncertainty. One eats when one doesn't know what tomorrow will bring.

As I was finishing, there was a knock on the door, our secret knock. I dropped my fork and cried, "Henry!" He came in smiling, and I rushed to him, grabbing his tunic in my fists. "How could you take so long? Where were you?"

"I'm sorry." He encircled me in his arms. "I didn't mean to make you wait. But you're here. You're finally here."

I pulled back, confused that I wasn't happier now that he was there. My fears weren't dulled by drink and fatigue anymore. I felt the sharp edge of panic. "You're glad I'm here?"

He kissed me deeply, and it helped a little to take the edge off my doubts. He held my face, his expression shifting, mirroring my own wretchedness. "Markow?"

I nodded and hugged him tightly. The cracks in my composure, the bulwark that had been holding me up, crumbled. Henry was my husband and my support, and I could shift some of my burden to him. I didn't have to be strong alone. I didn't have to be courageous or cowardly—I wasn't sure what I was—on my own. "When are we going?"

"Tomorrow. Less suspicious to cross the border in the morning."

"We're going by land?" We'd have to cross our borders twice, once to get into the Soviet Zone outside of Berlin, once as we left it to enter the British Zone. "I thought we were flying."

"We're seeing about arrangements, but we need to be ready to go by car as well."

I couldn't quite believe it was going to happen. "You're really coming with me?"

"I'm coming with you." He gestured at the bag he'd tossed to the floor. "I won't leave your side until you're safe in our zone." I began to protest, and he said, "Once you're settled, I'll have to go back to England to get the visa paperwork running on that end. But it won't be long and I'll come back to Germany to fetch you."

I imagined myself alone in some camp for displaced persons in the British Zone. That was what I would be. Displaced. A woman without a country. "How long will it be?"

"A few weeks, maybe a little longer—"

"You don't know?"

"Things will go faster for you than others. Don't worry." He gave a small laugh. "All right, worrying is the sensible thing to do right now. But let me do most of it from now on. You've done your part. The hardest part. You're here." His good cheer faded, and he took a packet of cigarettes out of his pocket. "Did you say goodbye to your sister?"

"How could I? She would know what I was planning to do." Maybe she did, had read it somehow in my face. I imagined Vera waiting at the border for me, and shuddered. "We should fly, Henry."

"They're working on it." He couldn't seem to get his match lit. The heads kept breaking off, three until the flame took. His hands were trembling, and I caught his anxiety.

"Who is working on it? Mr. Johnson? It's a common enough name. I don't know him." I drew a breath. "Do I?"

Henry held the flaming match to his cigarette, and let it burn until he winced, shaking it out. "Right. I think you should sit down, Mouse."

"No."

He flung the match at the floor, yanked the cigarette out of his mouth and threw it down too. He was buying time; I could see him thinking. I knew him, my husband. I watched him suffer.

"Marya, I'm sorry things had to be this way."

I curled my hands over the back of the chair, the cold creeping up my spine. "Sorry? About what?"

"I don't really know where to start."

"At the beginning, usually," I said cautiously.

He looked down at his hands. I couldn't stand his shuffling and hesitation, and I shouted, "Tell me the truth!"

"I am!" he roared back. As he paced, he rubbed the back of his neck as if he were recovering from some fresh and violent collision. "After we met last year . . . at the Memorial—"

"I remember where we met."

He glared at me. "And the Reichstag, when we—"

"You're backing into it, Henry. I know language. Language is my profession and now just say it."

He bit down on his lip, then said, "I did my duty. I reported to our intelligence chaps that a Russian officer had made contact with me."

"Made contact with you." I couldn't believe that's what he called it. If that's the way he'd thought of it while I was falling in love.

"Johnson was assigned to monitor things. He doesn't really live in the flat; it was just temporary while he—" He stopped.

"Henry . . ."

He swiped up the cigarette he'd dropped and turned it in his hands. "I couldn't rely on my own judgment when it came to you. Lovely girl. Intelligent. Sweet. A SMAD officer. And your sister in the MGB."

"You knew about that? Before I told you, you knew?"

"Our side did a background check on you, and Vera came up."

"I'm sure that made me a very interesting woman to you."

"To them. I didn't care. But I had to tell them about you. How was I supposed to keep you secret and call myself an officer of my government? Johnson warned me from the start. She looks sweet, but watch out. Wily Russian seductress and all of that. I insisted: No, no, she's . . . you're . . . not like that. You're real and honest."

I moved closer and was now in front of him, forcing him to look down at me. I could see on his jaw where he'd shaved badly, the fine red slash. "Vera said you left your papers out for me to steal."

"I hated that part. Bloody entrapment."

"So it was all a test? An act? When you saw those papers were gone, you pretended to be angry at me for doing something you *wanted* me to do?"

"I didn't *want* you to do it, and I wasn't pretending. After so long, I'd thought you weren't going to take the bait. So when you did, I lost my temper."

"You're worse than me." I pressed my hands flat on his chest. "You were talking to spies long before I ever did. But when I told you the truth, you had the nerve to be angry at *me*?"

"I was angry at *myself*. The one thing I can't stand is a hypocrite."

"Hypocrite." I pushed him, and he allowed himself to stumble back. "I proved you wrong when I took those papers. That's why you were so angry. Hypocrite!" I pushed him again. This time, he held his ground.

"We deserve each other then, don't we?"

"I loved you."

"You don't anymore? It's gone? Just like that?"

"Bastard." I tried to pull away. I'd leave the room, the building, the sector. I'd changed my mind. I wanted to go home.

"Marya." He was holding my arms.

"Let me go. I'm going home."

"We're talking this out."

"There's nothing to say. You . . ." My mind was in confusion. I had to reach for the English out of an American film. "You set me up!"

"And you stole from me. Are we even now? Are you going to stop acting like you're the only victim here?"

"You don't love me. You never did."

"If that was true, I would've never married you."

"That was part of your plot."

He released me to go to his bag. He slapped the book the registrar gave us, the book of our family, onto the table with a bang that rattled my heart. "That's real."

"How do I know?"

"Because I'm telling you it is. I was talking to Johnson just now, before I came in. I showed him this and he nearly had my head off. I wasn't supposed to marry you. He used words like 'compromised' and 'jeopardized,' and he can go to hell. I'd marry you all over again. I was thinking we should, in a church in Blackburn so my family can be there. They're going to love you." He was nearly shouting in the end. My ears were ringing.

He was making excuses for himself, and plans, more plans for me. He wanted me to give in and go back to being his blind little mouse. I pulled at the wedding band on my finger, and Henry reached for me. "Marya, no—"

"Stay away from me." My finger was swollen and the ring only came off after a painful twist. "They warned me about you. Vera. And Felix too. I should've listened. I should've seen it myself. For a man who claims he's not a spy, you were very good at trapping me, Henry. What was supposed to happen after the trap sprung? What did British intelligence want with me? I'm just an interpreter."

He didn't say anything, and it infuriated me. "Tell me!"

"You have access to confidential documents and—"

"I was supposed to bring them to you? Spread them around on the bed before we made love?"

"I wouldn't have taken anything from you. I wouldn't have gone through with it."

"You went this far."

"They told me play along or they'd send me home. That was the choice they gave me. I did what I did to stay with you. For as long as I could."

If he was telling the truth, Henry had been trapped too. It had never occurred to me that his country could be as ruthless in its way as mine, twisting good people into acting badly.

"Marya. Mouse, I'm sorry about everything." He was rubbing his eyes, as exhausted as I was. "Is there any way to salvage this?"

I lowered myself into a chair. My energy had gone. "I don't think so."

He picked up the book of our family and then set it back down as gently as he would a record in his collection. He was standing over me, wanting to say something. It hung in the air. But then he went to his bag on the floor and lifted it over his shoulder. "I'll find someone to see you safely back to your sector."

I thought of Vera, Felix. Mama, Nina. My work, my status. I'd said goodbye to that life. It seemed impossible to go back and pretend nothing had changed. "I asked the British for asylum, and you're turning me away?"

"You said you wanted to go home."

"I don't know where that is anymore."

Henry perched on the table and lowered his bag to the floor. "If you want, you can stay and go through the normal process for asylum. You'll have to spend a bit more time in a displaced-persons camp, but with your language skills, I'm sure you'll get a visa and a good job."

But I'd be alone. Alone in a strange country. I couldn't imagine it. "Are you staying in Berlin?"

"I had to badger a few people for permission to leave on short notice. I don't think I can go back on it now. I don't really want to. I'm done here."

I looked down at the ring in my hand. "So you'll be in England, and I'll be there too at some point."

"Seems a waste, both of us being there alone. It's a funny kind of marriage."

I surprised myself by laughing a little, though there were tears in my eyes. Leaving him would be easy. The door was there. It wasn't locked and Henry wouldn't try to stop me again. I could walk out. But I couldn't even get up from my chair. "We can't just forget this all happened, Henry. What we did to each other."

"No, but we don't have to let them win, the people who put us in this situation."

It was true that if the world hadn't been the way it was, we would've been left alone to be who we were and love who we chose. Slowly, I leaned against him and felt my tension begin to melt away. Henry hesitated, then put his arm around me. "Believe it or not," he said, "we're probably not the worst married couple in the world. With some people, you wonder why they stay together."

"Why do they stay together?"

"Stupidity."

It felt good to lean against him. Steady and secure. "We are very stupid people, Henry."

"Yes, we are."

A series of polite knocks on the door, and Johnson, the intelligence man, looked in on us. "Hello, young M. Delighted to see you again. All sorted, are we?"

Henry and I stood up together. He looked wretched, as terrible as I felt. We were one in our misery again. Of course I was going with him. I couldn't give up on us so quickly. Maybe the true strength of a marriage was to hold out even when we were unhappy. I didn't know how much more we could take. We were sorely tested and it was unfair. We just wanted to be left alone.

32

Marya

Berlin, 16 July 1947

The next morning, on the way to the border, I pressed my face to the car window and wondered at the scenery. I had never been this far west in my life and kept asking Henry if we were still in Berlin. The blocks of gray houses and ruins were behind us, and there were fields now, and garden sheds among rows of vegetable patches, and houses glimpsed through the green boughs of a wood.

Over his shoulder, the driver said, "Border up ahead, sir."

Our hands found each other. Henry's was uncommonly cold. "You're ready?"

I had identification papers the British had made for me with a new photograph. I was now a German employee of the military government named Ingrid Stetter. I couldn't understand Russian, and under no circumstances was I to speak it. "No matter what happens," Henry said, his face close to mine, "you can't give yourself away."

I didn't like this, my new life of freedom beginning with lies and forced silence. Instinctively, I dug into my purse for Felix's lucky coin, and then remembered I'd given it back to him. All I had was Henry's hand, and I grasped it tighter to steady myself. Maybe my luck was running out, as it had for Felix. I wanted the car to go faster, to get the border behind us before it was too late.

"We'll be through before you know it." Henry said it cheerfully, but the muscle in his neck was strained as he stared out the windshield. The car rolled to a stop on the British side of the border. Henry chatted with the guard while the passes were shown and questions asked. "How's the other side look?"

The guard frowned toward the wooden guard post not far away—the Soviet Zone. "They've been beefing up their manpower since that incident with the brigadier in May. Very particular about papers. You'll have a delay, if you ask me."

"We're not particular about papers?" Henry asked, taking back ours.

The guard saluted. "Good luck, sir. We'll watch your back."

The frontier of my life lay ahead of me, the first checkpoint in the Soviet Zone. There was a control booth, and two guards at a red-and-white barrier, lowered to block our way. They watched us come. There was, I supposed, a soldier with a field glass who'd warned the others of incoming traffic. They were my soldiers, my people, and as our car drew closer and finally pulled over at their orders, my blood froze.

The guard gestured at our driver, glanced into the backseat at us, then took our passes. He pored over them with another guard, a heated discussion, though I couldn't hear what they were saying.

One looked at his watch, then over at the control booth. Then he approached us again.

"Please exit the car."

The car seemed a safe place to me, the road an exposure I couldn't bear. There were a few bushes on one side, and a meadow that led to a forest. Henry climbed out of the car and spoke softly to the driver. They lit up cigarettes. One of the guards returned and asked for our identification. At that point, I left the car myself, standing close to Henry, presenting my new papers with shaking hands. The guard looked closely from the photograph to me. "Deutsch?" he asked.

"Yes," Henry said, "she's an employee of the British military government."

The guard looked at him as if there were a delay in understanding what Henry had said. Then the guard took my papers with him to his comrades, who were gathered in the control booth. Two other guards still manned the barrier and stared at us with complete neutrality.

It was a warm and muggy morning, but a breeze chilled the sweat on my skin. Henry and the driver chain-smoked near the car while I leaned against it trying not to shiver. "Why is it taking so long?"

"I don't know." Henry took off his cap and rubbed the damp from his hairline. "Can you make out what they're saying?"

I couldn't read lips. One guard was on the telephone, and as he held the receiver to his ear, he stared at us out the window of the control booth.

"I think they suspect something," I said softly.

Henry followed my gaze, then dropped his cigarette and crushed it out. "Steady, Mouse. They won't do anything to us. We're still on our side, and my people can see us."

I wasn't sure this would help us. I breathed out to be certain that I could breathe at all. The palpitations of my heart scared me. Finally, one of the guards returned to us, holding our papers without giving them back. He began to ask us questions, precisely where we were going, the nature of our visit to the Soviet Zone.

"We're only passing through," Henry said. I was amazed at how well he controlled his voice, firm and polite. "At this rate we won't reach Minden in time, but we've got to try. We've got a meeting at ten."

The guard shuffled the papers and looked up at me. "You are secretary?"

I wasn't sure if I should answer, if I could without giving my accent away. In slow, careful English, I said, "I am an interpreter."

The guard didn't know this word. I tried it in German, and he still didn't understand. Henry tried to help, explaining that when others spoke German, I spoke in English to help everyone understand.

"Ah," the guard said and used the correct term in Russian. I almost nodded, and only caught myself at the last moment. It was the hardest thing to pretend not to understand my own language. There were a million tiny ways to give myself away.

Up until now, we'd been the only car on the road. The sound of another engine grew behind us, and we all turned to watch the new vehicle roll closer. Oh, I knew what was coming. Knew the black civilian car, no markings. I knew what that meant. I moved closer to Henry, but I couldn't take his hand. He'd told me not to. I was only supposed to be his German interpreter.

The guards approached the new car and spoke quietly to the driver. My throat tight, I whispered to Henry. "They're all speaking Russian."

At the guard's direction, the car pulled in next to ours. The back door opened, and I knew all was lost. I recognized her regulation shoes, her skirt, her tunic. Vera.

She glanced at me and then spoke briefly to the guard, showing her card. He left her, and only then did she approach us, her face lighting up not at me, but at Henry. She spoke in English.

"They are so thorough, our armies." She offered her hand. "Pleased to see you, Captain."

Henry hesitated before taking her hand. "Maybe you know how to get things moving faster," he said carefully. "We've been delayed too long."

"I have no influence. We all live under same rules." Vera turned to me. I saw the shattered fatigue at the edge of her eyes. I saw many other things, a reflection of what had been done to Felix, a tiny light that told me his fate. From deep inside me rose a thin stream of bile.

"I am told you are German interpreter," she said to me.

I didn't answer. There was no need to play her games anymore.

"I could use someone like you," Vera said, taking out a cigarette, which Henry lit, watchful and silent. "You should work for me, Fräulein."

"I'm happy where I am."

"No one is happy here"—she waved around us—"a border in what is it?" She looked to Henry. "Is it called limbo?"

"I call it Berlin."

"It is not natural to live on a border. One must be one side or the other." She was looking at me again. "The other side is Soviet Zone. Is that where you want to go? I will take you there, and much safer."

Henry moved closer but didn't touch me. "Sounds like you're trying to poach my employee."

"Poach." She beamed at him. "I do not know this word. Do you know it, Fräulein?"

Stop, I thought. *Stop this theater*. It was unbearable. "It's like stealing."

"I do not steal people," she said, and the bile rose in me again.

Quietly, I said, "You don't have to do this, Vera. Let me go."

The guards were still at their posts, watching us, looking puzzled, I was sure, at the resemblance between me, a German according to my papers, and Vera, an MGB officer.

"Come," Vera said, "let us walk in the field while we wait. I shall borrow her," she informed Henry, "not . . . poach." She laughed at her new word.

"Stay where I can see you." As attuned to his body as I was, I could feel the tension wafting from him. I felt sorry for him. There was nothing he could do, and he was twisted up inside, trying to find a way out.

We didn't go far, just to the field by the side of the road. We were out of earshot of the guards and Henry, but everyone could see us. In all my life, I'd never felt so exposed. I knelt to pluck a flower from the grass.

"You will stop being silly," Vera said, "and come back with me."

"I'm never going back."

She stooped next to me. "You've had your little rebellion, Marya. I've seen it coming. It's natural. You're young." She said it as if I were a baby at twenty-four and she a wise old woman of twenty-nine. "The minute you left yesterday, I knew you'd run away. But it's over now. Come back quietly and no one will know what you've done. You'll take up your duties as before. All will be well."

"Listen to me, Vera. I'm going with Henry to the West. I love him."

"You love the idea of spreading your wings, a taste of freedom. Do you think I don't understand that? That I don't feel it too?"

"You're so trapped in your own web, you can't stand to see me escape it. I won't be like you, playing both sides and telling myself it's freedom. It's not. Felix knew it. He chose his own way."

"He chose his fate, that's true. But really, don't waste your time with him. He was only a German turncoat."

Her disdain was worse than if she'd hated him. At least hate gave power to the thing. She discarded Felix like he was nothing, hardly human. "He didn't expose you. He was protecting us and you knew it and you still let him die. What's happened to you? I used to look up to you. You were the strong one. Principled. But you're as corrupt as the rest of them. Working for the Americans doesn't make you a better woman." I crushed the flower in my hand and tossed it away.

Calmly, Vera inhaled her cigarette, her gaze on the guards, who hung back out of deference to an MGB officer. Then she glanced at Henry, his fists in his pockets, watching us. "Did you tell him about me?"

"What difference would it make if I had?"

"Don't be stupid. Does he know?"

I shook my head, and she let out a long breath.

"Then our options are open. My offer still stands. Say goodbye to him with finality, please. We don't need a lovesick Englishman on our hands. Come back with me, and there will be no consequences. If you continue to refuse—"

"You'll lock me in a cell, starve me, beat me—"

"Don't be so dramatic. I'm trying to save you."

"You're trying to save yourself."

Vera grabbed my arm and pulled our heads together. "If I let you go, you're automatically a foreign spy, a traitor to the people. You know what happens to those. Now, think of Mother and Nina. What happens to them? Have you given a thought to what this would do to their lives?"

"You can protect them."

"If my position remains strong. If you flee now, with me here able to stop you, you'll be digging my grave as well as your own. It's too late to slip away."

"You didn't have to come here. You should've left me alone. Why can't you leave me alone?"

"There are bigger things in this world than your man and your precious idea of freedom. What have I told you all this time? A woman's duty is not to her selfish desires—"

"It's to her people. I know, I know. Well, I have served, and I'll live my own life from now on."

"Do you think I cooperate with the Americans because I love apple pie? Or money? I don't care about any of that. They are the most powerful ally in the fight to free our country of the regime that twists the law into a weapon against us. Bolsheviks. Stalinists," she hissed, "the people who wanted to arrest our father when he'd given everything of himself to serve them and the Revolution. They've twisted what he fought for, our ideals. Instead of freeing us, the Bolsheviks control, jail, and silence us."

"Like you did to Felix."

"His sacrifice allows us to carry on trying to reform our country from within. To earn freedom for all of us, not just for yourself." She poked me in the chest. "It's your fight too. You have it in you, I know it now. Join me."

"What do you mean?"

"Why do you think I thought up that ridiculous little mission with your Englishman? It was a test. I wanted to see what you could do. If you had the guts. If you have what it takes to change our country. It's easy to rebel like a child and run away. It's harder to stay and fight."

I looked to Henry, still vigilant. He took a step toward us, and I shook my head.

"Why didn't you tell me what you've been doing, Vera? I would've understood."

"I didn't know that. I hadn't seen you in years. For all I knew, you would've turned me in."

"Never."

"I had to test you."

"You should've talked to me instead of bullying me. If I'd known what you were doing, I might've helped."

"Help me now. Fight for our freedom, for what Papa believed in. You believe it too, I know that now. I can handle the guards over there. I'll give them some reason why you're here posing as a German. We can do this. I'll teach you what has to be done. It's a hard life, but we can do some good. I can't do it alone."

She was handing me a way home, one I could live with. To resist from within, to protect our family and Vera's own mission. I felt the pull of it, this new kind of service. I didn't wholly trust her after what she'd done to me and Felix, but she was my sister, and she needed me. She was fighting Stalin, an almost inconceivable task, like fighting the sun. I was still the girl who'd gone to war, but I had never truly considered fighting at home, rising up against the injustices we all saw and tried to ignore. I'd never given a thought to what would happen when Stalin was gone. I only hoped we would be led by people who opened us all to the world. Not just in the propaganda, but truly, in our hearts. And when we succeeded, I could go to Henry freely, as it should be.

"I want to go home," I said.

Vera let out a breath. "I knew it. I knew you were a soldier."

"And I want to go with him."

"I understand. The sacrifice is great, but you'll learn to live with it."

"Vera, I don't know how I can leave him. I promised—"

"I'll help you. You can live with this loss. And when we free our country, you can go back to him."

"I have to. I'm his wife."

Vera gripped my arm. "You married him?"

It seemed like years ago. It shook me to remember that this was only the second full day of married life. "In secret with a German registrar. I signed the papers."

Vera's face broke apart one slow detail at a time, the slump of her muscles, her mouth, fissures of pain deepening in her eyes. I'd only seen her like this once before, one of my earliest memories. After our father died, her grief had broken her apart like this. She had reassembled herself behind the marble composure I'd come to rely on.

She hugged me tightly and kissed my face, leaving her tears on my cheeks. "I failed you, Masha. I failed, and I'm so sorry. It won't work."

"Why?"

"You're compromised, don't you see? Even if you come back with me and tried to live as you were, you can't. He'll think he's responsible for you. He won't let you go, and he'll endanger us all."

"He would never endanger me."

"Masha, there's nothing to be done. If you leave like this, I'm through, and Mother and Nina. If you stay and he makes a fuss, it's just the same. Our people will know you tried to run away with him, your Western husband, and they'll send you to prison for that. They'll get me too. Because I didn't stop your affair—your marriage—when I had the chance." She let go of me and stared at nothing. I'd never seen her look so helpless, with no plan, as if she was beaten. It was impossible for Vera to be beaten.

Henry stepped off the street and onto the grass. "What's happening?"

I looked at Vera, and the question in her eyes was the same one I was asking myself. *Does he love you enough to wait?*

I had to find out, as much as it tore everything inside me. "I must go back, Henry."

"No. We talked about this. You said—"

I tried to explain without breaking down. "We must be patient. One day, I hope it will be soon, when the world changes, we'll be allowed to be together. I'll come to you when I can do it freely without endangering everyone else I love."

He turned to Vera. "What have you been saying to her?" His gaze returned to me. "Marya, what are you talking about?"

Maybe he never truly understood what danger we were in. His country wasn't like ours. For that, I was grateful. "The cost of leaving is too high. I thought I could do it, but . . . Henry, I can't abandon everyone. And I can do good work if I stay. I know what I can do now. When I go back, don't tell anyone about me. Keep the secret. For me. You must be patient and wait."

He went to Vera, who had stepped away from us, a hand over her eyes. "If you have a speck of decency in you, if you have any love for your sister, you won't do this to her."

"I love her very much, Captain. But if she leaves, she sacrifices the people left behind and even a part of herself. She sacrifices a great deal more . . ." I saw her considering what she might tell him, a hint of her work for the Americans, but she shook her head. "Perhaps you will understand if you read Anna Akhmatova's poems."

Henry was beside himself. "What? *Poems?*"

I knew the poem Vera was referring to, and she was right. I couldn't abandon Russia for England when my country needed me. I couldn't be an apostate for a green island.

Vera was looking at me. "She understands. It is her wish to stay. Will you respect that, Captain?"

"Marya, you can't go. You're my wife."

"Always. I'll come back when I can. I swear it." I couldn't hug or kiss him in front of the guards, who were beginning to grow restless and move closer, despite the caution they'd showed at the MGB trim on Vera's uniform. I held out my arms to keep Henry away and nearly broke at the look on his face. "Please, understand. You can't speak of me to anyone. Your silence will protect us."

"No." His face set, firm, full of stubborn devotion. "No, I won't let you go like this."

Vera returned to the driver of her car.

"Please, Henry," I said. The Russian driver glanced at me and then went to the guards. "Do as I ask. It's the only way we'll survive."

He grasped my arm. "Come on, quick—"

"Henry, no—"

Vera and two guards advanced on us. The deepest sadness in her voice, she said, "Marya, I'm afraid you're under arrest."

The guards were upon me before I knew what was happening, ripping me from Henry's grasp. I struggled against them, and my sister who was doing this to me. Vera, my big sister, was doing this to me.

Henry let out a cry and lunged for me, but more guards rushed in between us, and then his driver, holding him back. The men dragged me as I stomped and thrashed and fought to the car. They threw me inside, the moment when freedom was ripped away. It happened so quickly. A heartbeat and freedom was gone.

Vera climbed in beside me, speaking in my ear. "Be still, Masha. Listen. Tell them what I'm about to tell you and nothing else. Then be silent, no matter what happens. We'll only get through this together."

She held her finger to her lips.

33

Vera

Testimony for Chairman A. Cheptsov
Military Collegium of the Supreme Court of the USSR
Moscow, 28 February–3 June 1956

[RECORDING]

've come to the end of this investigation into my sister's actions that last summer in Berlin, when she was free. It is strange to watch the reels turn as I talk, knowing this is my final recording. I realize another advantage to this way of preserving my testimony about Marya; I'm not tempted to rewind and replay the entire story as I might be tempted to turn back to the beginning of a written account. Without realizing it, I've revealed as much about myself as I have about my sister, and much of it isn't flattering. But I'll leave it. The search for the truth is the seeker's journey to take, and the answer is only the last shining stone in a long and crooked path.

My own guilt has a good deal to do with my errors of judgment in this investigation. Barrow was right about that. In 1947, I had done what I thought I had to do, what was right according to my training, our laws, my duty. In the end, I arrested my own sister in the act of fleeing to the West, which the court interpreted as proof that she was their spy, being slipped out of Berlin for their own reasons, or at her request. I can barely describe how painful that moment was. It was the hardest thing I've ever had to do. For a long time afterward, I thought: What have I done? Marya had clearly broken our laws. A simple case, really. And yet, she was my sister. How could I face myself, knowing how many years she would pay for her actions? How could I choose my duty over the natural loyalties of family? How could I face our mother and sister?

It was wrong of me to stop Marya. I say that openly now. She was convicted as a spy but I don't believe this was ever about espionage. This was always about a desperate woman trying to break free. The British identity card with her photograph wasn't evidence of espionage, it was proof that we couldn't let Marya follow her heart without subterfuge. She wasn't the only one. We know how many of our people fled Berlin and Germany and other former theaters of war, who left everything behind that they ever knew because we couldn't let them be. Let them live.

I do not know how dangerous these words are now, if the slow thaw in our country since Khrushchev opened the wounds of our past allows me to speak this freely, to say these truths and stand by them. Since returning from Berlin last week, I have had to endure a good deal of uncomfortable questioning from the usual circles. My husband, Nikolai, my Kolya, has exhausted himself doing what he's always done, working tirelessly to protect and defend me. He's a good man, better than I deserve, and his loyalty shames me because I had been foolish enough to doubt it. It was one of my many misjudgments in this investigation. I will take whatever punishment comes: demotion, the desertion of my friends, and worse, whatever it might be. It can't be worse than what my sister has endured because we didn't trust each other and I couldn't leave her to be the woman she truly was.

I'm still guilty of that. Since the start of this investigation, my actions have been typical of the secret police, breaking the suspect down so I can rebuild her into the person I require. I needed Marya to be completely innocent, and for that, I needed to explain away her actions from the affair all the way to the border of Berlin. If I could've proven her a spy for our side, acting out of loyalty and zeal, I might have made it easier to pardon her. But it wouldn't have been the truth. The truth was much simpler. We were wrong, and she was right.

Comrade, I hope that the case I've laid out for you here shows what service Marya did for us in secret, with no reward, even if she was compelled to do it by Felix Markow. For her errors, her years in prison are punishment enough. For her service to a country struggling to face its own mistakes—she deserves her freedom at last.

[END RECORDING]

DECISION

On 3 September 1956, the Military Collegium of
the Supreme Court of the USSR reexamined the
case of Marya Ilyanovna Nikonova and came to
the following conclusion:

The verdict of guilty handed down by the
Military Collegium on 13 August 1947 is upheld.
However, in light of new information about the
important work done by Nikonova for the state, and
upon the recommendation of Procurator-General R.
Rudenko, the appeal for a reduced sentence and
immediate release has been granted.

Chairman, Military Collegium
Cheptsov

34
Marya

Siberia, 1956

Autumn is here, and we prisoners look anxiously at the sky and at the few straggly trees within the zone, searching for signs of change. The clouds are like smoke drifting over our heads, and the bark of the trees reminds me of my skin, dry and cracked from the wind. I imagine I smell the snow that will fall in a matter of weeks. We'll have to endure another cold, dark season or die trying.

I've stared at the sky too long and don't notice the guard standing the regulation distance away from me. He's grinning. "It's your lucky day."

This would normally mean a new work assignment indoors, but the weather is fine after days of rain that left the camp drowning in mud. My boots make a sucking sound as I follow the guard to the administrative building. I'm afraid to go in and muddy the floors until I see that the straw they put down is slick and filthy already. A group of prisoners are in the hallway with buckets and mops.

The guard waves me into an office, where an official I've never seen before asks my name and makes me sign papers I have no time to read. He says nothing as these papers are stamped, and I am given one, and a notice of transport by train. A train! I haven't been transported in years and then it was usually by truck as if I were a sack of wheat. I'm sad I'll be leaving my friends here and sent to a different camp, but it has happened to me several times over the years. After a while, one camp is like another.

But something odd is happening. The official speaks, repeating an address in Peredelkino outside Moscow, where I'm to report for my rehabilitation papers. I feel a shift in my chest as if my heart is waking up from a deep, long sleep. "Rehabilitation?"

The official laughs. "You're going home, don't you know?"

Home? Was it a joke?

He steers me into another office, where an official is calculating my wages for nine years of captivity. He counts the rubles in front of me and chuckles when his colleague informs him how stupid I am. "You think we give out money as a joke?" he says, the rubles in an envelope, an amount I can't remember. It won't penetrate my head. Two hundred? Three? Almost nothing for nine years of my life.

Clutching the envelope, I ask, "What do I do now?"

"Go for disinfection unless you want to take the lice with you."

I leave my papers and money with the elder of my barracks, whom I trust, and go for disinfection. My head is full of fog, and I'm trembling all over. There must be a mistake. I have six more years left of my sentence, don't I? Or maybe it's a trick? I've heard of such things, a prisoner is promised her freedom, and when she gets her papers, she discovers the cruelty of the system we live in. She's not allowed to go home after all but must live in permanent exile the rest of her life, far from her family and everyone she loves. I rush back to the barracks elder, asking for the papers, and examine them closely. It's true, I'm to go to Peredelkino. Why there? I don't know anyone there.

The elder gives me a dress a comrade has donated, knowing I have nothing decent of my own. I can't go home in the rags of a prisoner, she says. Another comrade trades shoes with me; hers are in better condition. Another gives me a scarf for my hair. As she knots it under my chin, I begin to cry. Am I going home, or into exile? Am I free? Why aren't I happy? Isn't this what I want?

Several women are waiting for transfer, and we climb together onto the truck and lay down on the wooden bed like fish in a tin. The journey is long, with many stops because of the mud, and my whole body trembles, the sky passing endlessly over my head. Nine years. Nine years, and in a few hours I'll be free. I'm sick to my stomach and can barely breathe. There's something new in me— hope—and it's eating away at me from the inside. I'm afraid I'll die of it before we reach the station.

The train journey makes me ill. It's one thing to live nine years in various camps, and quite another to see the country rush by my window in a week. The people scare me a little. They're farmers and workers, they have chickens and goats and many children. It seems to me that people are moving faster and talking louder than they did when I was imprisoned. I wonder if this is a good sign, if we're done whispering and can speak openly and honestly to one another at last.

During the journey, my thoughts rush around in my head. Where will I go? How will I live? What work will I do? I've been freed from prison, but who will hire me? I won't be allowed to go to university, that old dream. I'm still a Paragraph 58er. I'll always carry the taint of my years as a traitor. And Henry, the plans we made—they're long gone, more dreams from my youth. I don't indulge in the fantasy of him waiting for me, waiting nine years for his wife. It's too painful to consider how horrible that would be for him. I hope he's moved on in life, and I wish him happiness. I refuse to be a burden to my mother and Nina, if they would have me at all. I've had no word from them in all these years, and I'm anxious to know if they're all right. Surely, Mama is still alive; she has to be. Hopefully she hasn't lost her sight completely and still has fingers supple enough to play her oboe. Nina is all grown and maybe she's a doctor or a scientist. Maybe she doesn't hate me for bringing trouble and sorrow to the family. Though I wouldn't blame her if she does. So where can I go? Where is home?

This is happening too fast, freedom like a river they've thrown me into. I'll drown, sink like my father in the Moskva. I don't know how to live anymore.

WHEN I CLIMB off the train at Peredelkino, no one is there to meet me. I walk the streets, not understanding how the town works, how anything can be found or done in this strange new world where there is no one to tell me what to do or where to go and when. I stop at a birch tree and press my hand to the white bark, and am feeling a little better when an old woman hobbles up to me. "You're from Siberia, poor child. I can see it." She takes my arm and leads me with her slow and unsteady steps to the address I was given at the camp.

It's a lovely dacha. Bushes grow fat in the front garden, and the shutters are red, a piece carved from each in the shape of a leaf. I don't know the big and rosy woman who answers the door, but she bursts into tears, dabbing her apron at her eyes. "Marya Ilyanovna, you're finally here! Vera Ilyanovna will be so glad!" She grasps my hands and leads me inside.

It's the home of my dreams, a Russian version of my cottage in Karlshorst, all of wood, with carpets, and an ornate oven, and so many things of beauty and comfort that I stand in the center of the room afraid to touch them, or breathe, or blink. If I'm not careful, it will all disappear and I'll wake in the Gulag again.

The housekeeper helps me bathe and dress in fresh clothes, and then I eat a thick stew, running my fingers over the silky fringe of the white tablecloth. A pain in my stomach warns me I'm not ready for such rich food. I'm not ready for any of this. The housekeeper has informed me this is my sister Vera's dacha, and she is coming. Vera is coming, and part of me wants to arm myself with a knife or a candlestick, and part of me wants to crawl under the table and hold my breath and wait for her to blow by like a cold wind, without noticing me. I used to do that when I was little and we played hiding games. It never worked. She always found me. She was the one who was good at hiding.

As I wait for my sister, I wander the dacha looking at the patterns on the carpets and listening to the birds chirp and sing outside the open windows. On a table is a faded photograph of our father near a candle burned to a stub. "Papa." I pick it up, kiss the glass, and see that it is already smudged as if someone else has kissed it today before me. Near the piano, I spot more photos, one of Yuri in uniform, his quiet resolve to fight the Germans when all he wanted to do was build his machines. I kiss him too. Next to Yuri's photo is one of me from early in the war. I was eighteen, a proud officer and still a girl in my heart. That was the girl Felix had loved. He'd loved me as I'd loved him, as a dear friend devoted to freedom, and he carried me in his heart until the end. What an honor to touch someone so deeply, especially when we'd been trained to hate.

I hear voices in the hallway and I replace the photograph, then turn to meet the great personage I'm sure my sister has become.

Vera halts in the doorway. Her face lights up and then crumbles just as quickly. I don't smile or go to her or say a word. She hardly seems real to me. She's like the dacha, another thing out of my dreams. If I close my eyes, she'll disappear.

In her, I look for the transformation that I've gone through the past nine years. But she's the same; a sharp, intelligent face, proud, guarded. She's wearing a suit with matching jacket and skirt, a brooch in the shape of a glittering bird. Her earrings glitter too, and her hair is precisely styled. If anything, she seems stronger than before, at the height of her power and status.

"Masha." She approaches me slowly as if I might be a threat to her. "You're finally here."

I don't know what to say to that. It's not as if we agreed to meet and I'm responsible for the nine-year delay. To her credit, she doesn't try to hug or kiss me, but takes refuge in her cigarette case, a cheap thing with a broken map of Berlin on the lid. I watch the flame as it touches her cigarette, the familiar and elegant movement of her hands. "Well, you're free now," she says. "The worst is over."

What does she know about it? What the years have been for me? My old anger sparks deep down. I thought it had died years ago.

"What do you want to do with yourself?" Vera asks.

I try to decipher this odd question. What do I want? When was the last time anyone asked me that? I try to think and see only thick white fog where my desires used to be. "I'm too old to start anything new."

"You're thirty-three. You have much life ahead of you. Didn't you think about this in Siberia?"

"Other prisoners, they had people to go back to. Homes. A family. Hopes. I had none. Nothing. In nine years, you never sent me so much as a package. Or a letter. I needed news, sentiments, a hint of life in the outside world. I got nothing from you, Vera. Nothing."

"I know. I—" She wrings her hands. "I wanted to help you earlier but I couldn't. Please understand."

Abruptly she goes into another room, where I hear her telling the housekeeper to run an errand in the village. After the woman leaves, Vera sits with me on the couch, grasping her skirt at the knees. "All these years, you were never far from my thoughts, Masha. Never. But I had to be careful and wait for the right moment to plead your case. Thanks to Khrushchev, that moment finally arrived. You were clearly guilty under the laws of the time, so I had to reconstruct a version of events that was intricate enough to question not just your actions in Berlin but the laws that condemned them. To free you"—she reaches for her cigarette in the ashtray—"I lied to the court." She's shaken, I can see, by what she's done. I'm amazed that despite everything, she still seems to respect the law. "I told the court it was your idea to take the papers from the Englishman, using the German as a courier. I claimed he'd been training you in spy craft. I originally thought I could make you into a good little Soviet spy doing secret work for us, for no reward. You said it yourself in your interrogation."

"You told me to say that. In the car, when you arrested me, you told me to deny I was in love with Henry. You told me—" The shame of what I said to the MGB floods back to me. In their interrogations, I said what Vera had instructed me to say because I hadn't known what else to do.

"You did the right thing," she says, touching my wrist tentatively. I draw it away, and she folds her hand on her lap. "I knew one day I could free you if we planted the idea that you were working for us, not the West."

"You could've just let me go with Henry."

"No, Masha. Once you showed up at that border with *your husband*—"

I flinch at the angry edge in her voice.

"There was no other option. Arresting you was *terrible*, I know that, but it was the only way I could prove how loyal I was to the regime. I was willing to arrest my own sister. That saved me, and our family. If I'd let you go, the MGB would've torn my life apart to find out if I shared your guilt. What I've been doing for the Americans would've come out, and we'd all be lost. You would still be in prison, I'd be dead. Mother and Nina . . . exiled. Imprisoned. Disgraced."

She touches the brooch on her jacket, and it seems to calm her. "I weathered the scrutiny after your arrest, but it was a close thing, Masha. If Nikolai hadn't taken my side, I wouldn't be here. I decided to wait for the right time to free you. I needed to do it from a position of strength. And I admit, I was scared to face it all. I'm not proud of who I was in Berlin. What I did to you. Markow. Barrow. The men on the American list who were sacrificed to save the rest of us." She glances away. "But we survived. Our family survived. You're home at last. And I've been able to continue my work to quietly reform the country. There's still work to be done. Stalin isn't as dead as we'd like to believe."

So her double game is still on. Half of herself for the Soviets, half for the Americans, after all these years. I look at her more closely for signs she's splitting apart, as I would have, but there are only the tiniest wrinkles around her eyes. I don't envy her this life and wonder how long she can endure it before it breaks her. She's very strong, my sister.

"You still hate me," she says. "I can understand that. I deserve it."

She has no idea. On the border of Berlin, when the guards pushed me into her car and she climbed in beside me, I was too shocked to feel anything but panic. Only later, as a prisoner in the Lubyanka, did I feel the hate sharpen inside of me. But I never betrayed her secret. I couldn't do that to my own sister, no matter what she'd done to me. For years, I wrestled with this, the twisted way Vera showed her love. How could she love me and do the things she did? Was it a streak of evil? Was it a sickness inside of her? Was she not, in the end, capable of real love? As the years went on and I endured the Gulag without a word from her or my family, the edges of my hatred faded into a dull ache. "I did hate you for a long time," I say.

"When did that change?"

"Just now when you came through the door."

She thinks I'm trying to be witty and laughs a little. I can hate the idea of her, I can hate what she's done to me and Henry and especially Felix. But when she's here in front of me, I see Mama and Papa and Yuri and Nina and myself in her. She's my sister and I could never truly hate her. I don't have it in me. I still don't know if that's a weakness, or one of the few strengths I have left.

I hear the sound of footsteps in the hall, then through the door bursts a young woman of exceptional brightness, as if she's landed on Earth from a star. I stand up, trembling. "Nina?"

My little sister, a woman now. She throws herself on me, and we both land on the sofa. To my shame, I don't notice our mother until I wipe my eyes and see her on her knees beside the couch. Her eyes are unfocused, her face turned to the light coming through the window. I slide to my knees and take her dry hands and lay them on my cheeks. "Mama, I'm here." I dissolve then; both of us do.

The rest of the day we cry and talk and hug one another while Vera watches at a distance, smoking her cigarettes. I let the chatter wash over me, nine years of news filling me up. Nina's announcement that she's getting married next month brings me more joy than I've felt in years. From the Gulag to a wedding! I try not to think about my own wedding, and there are more tears, for Henry, wherever he is. At one point, Nikolai Koshkin arrives in a fine

Russian shirt and breeches. He's my brother-in-law now, distinguished and bursting with self-importance. He was on the American list too, a spy like my sister, but he's done much to shield Vera from scandal and protect my family. So I greet him as a sister-in-law should, kissing his cheeks, suppressing the ache of grief for what he helped do to Felix.

THERE'S A ROOM for me in the dacha, for me alone. I don't like that; I'm not used to sleeping alone anymore, and I'm afraid of what terrors will come to me as I lay awake. Deep in the night, when my family retires, Vera comes in with a large antique box. She sets it heavily on my bed as if the weight is hard for her to bear. For one long moment, she holds her hand to the lid, her head bowed. She is struggling with something inside her, and I take a step closer to see it. My sister is fighting back tears, and it astonishes me. I don't want to know what's in that box, what has the power to move Vera to tears. She wipes her face and surprises me again by wrapping her arms around me. She is fleshier than I am and smells of smoke, and our barracks room in Berlin, and our childhood. I'm not used to being hugged anymore and don't know where to put my arms, but I try, and we stay that way, embracing each other for a long while. It feels like she's holding me together, setting my feet firmly back in this world again.

"Welcome back, Masha," she says, and she laughs a little. "Look at me. Weeping like an old woman."

"There's nothing wrong with a good cry."

She gestures at a stack of handkerchiefs on the bedside table. "You might be needing those. We'll talk more tomorrow. Good night."

After she leaves, I listen to the house, wait for it to grow quiet. Then, heart trembling, I ease open the lid of the box.

Letters. Dozens. Hundreds. Numbered and arranged in tidy rows stacked one upon another. The letters smell old but not musty. They smell of the varnish used on the box, and of something else, something wonderful swirling deep in my memory. I run my fingers over the envelopes, not knowing which to take. The first? The last? I dread both.

There's a small velvet pouch tucked into a corner of the box. I open it first, and gasp in wonder. My gold bracelet, the one Henry gave me, confiscated at my arrest. I thought it was gone forever, stolen by a guard or locked away in a dark room at the Lubyanka where the precious things of prisoners are hoarded or forgotten. When I put it on, it dangles huge on my wrist. Next, shaking the pouch into my palm, I catch a gold ring—my wedding band. My sight clouds, and I blink a long time to clear it, to see that the ring is mine, this precious thing Henry had given me. I try it on, and it slides loosely on my finger until I find some thread in a drawer and wind it around the gold. Now it fits snugly again. I'll never take it off.

Armed with my bracelet and ring, I feel strong enough to read the letters. I start at the beginning. Letter number one. Like all the letters, it has already been opened. It's dated 9 August 1947, days before I was convicted of treason nine years ago.

My dearest Marya, my wife . . .

I read all night. Every single letter, some of them twice. Henry had no use for censors. He wrote all his thoughts, all he was doing to free me. He cursed my people and my sister. He swore he would come to find me, in disguise. He swore to God he would commit murder if necessary. As he grew calmer, as he realized the difficulties of my situation, he wrote letters of encouragement. We would succeed, we would be together, it was only a matter of time and negotiation. He had allies, contacts. I was only to keep the faith and stay alive.

As the years passed, he wrote of his life in London. His time in the army had ended badly; he'd barely avoided a court-martial. Later he worked for an insurance company. It was dull work and gave him time to harass his government to help me. His moods shifted with every letter—anger to despair, determination to resignation, grief to an ashen loneliness. Four years after my arrest, he confessed he'd met a woman, a nurse named Tess.

I break off reading. Though I think I have no more tears, I throw myself onto my bed and storm and thrash and stop my mouth with the blanket. There's no hope, none left in this world.

But I can't leave things at that. I sit up, wipe my face, and reach for the box again. It's uncharitable of me to blame him for his loneliness. I try to convince myself I'm happy for him as I continue to the next letter.

The nurse disappeared after six months. The following year, there was a Lucy, who vanished after three months, and a Betsy who lasted a year. He confessed all of this to me in anguish, as violations of his marriage vows, done because he despaired, he missed me, he couldn't stand my silence—*my* silence! I throw myself back onto the bed and bury my face. Henry is human, a man with a body, and a generous soul that he has to share. And yet—*my* silence has driven him to other women? In Siberia, I'd missed him as I'd miss an arm that Vera had lopped off, a fundamental wound that would never heal. I wished him well, and a good life, and that he'd forget me so he wouldn't be sad. I couldn't have endured my life in prison if I'd thought he was angry at me for leaving him. I can barely stand it now.

I drag myself back to the box. The letters from the past weeks show a renewed hope. They are to be delivered, he said, by diplomatic pouch. There are no other women. Always, he addresses me as *Marya, my dear wife.* I tuck away the last letter and curl up on the bed beside the box, the grief inside me flooding out. We can never get back the time we've lost. Nine years, a chasm in our lives we can't possibly cross. As much as I long to meet him on the other side, it's too late. I'm certain we're too different now, and there's no going back to how we were.

IN THE MORNING, once Nina goes back to Moscow to work and my mother joins the housekeeper in the garden, I'm alone again with Vera. Her face is as red and fatigued as mine. She knows what I've been through all night.

"He's a very devoted man," she says with a trace of irritation.

I have no words for what I'm feeling. Just drained, as if I've lived nine years in one night.

"I was in Berlin a couple of months ago," she says. "There are two Berlins now, East and West. It's possible to go between them with the proper papers and connections, and some goodwill. There isn't much of that, to be honest, but many things are possible."

I touch my hair, thin and mousy. "Did you see him?"

"Oh yes. If he was a lesser man, he would've put a bullet through my heart. He's as devoted to his grudges as he is to you." She smiles faintly. "Do you want to go back? If you do, I'll get word to him. He'll be waiting for you."

A rush of terror, and I leave the table and wring my hands. "I can't. I . . . I've forgotten how to speak German and English."

"Nothing you knew well is ever truly forgotten. With practice, everything will come again."

"No. No, Vera." I don't say: *He'll be there.* I don't say: *Look at me, look in the mirror. He won't know me. He won't want me.*

"You've suffered long enough, Masha. You're free." She shows me papers, an exit visa. "Go see him in Berlin. Afterward, you can go to London with him if you want. If you don't, come back here. Everything is arranged. The chance is there, if you choose to take it."

I'm pressing my knuckles to my cheeks. I can't dare to hope. She'll snatch it away from me, won't she? Or is she different now? Can a woman like my sister ever change?

Vera leans close and kisses my head as if I'm the little girl she used to hold in her arms. "Thank you for what you've done for me all these years. I can never repay you." She straightens abruptly and reaches for her cigarettes. "And don't be silly, Masha. Of course you want to go. You always did."

FIVE WEEKS LATER, I arrive in East Berlin by train, and meet an East German official who takes me into a little room at the Friedrichstraße station. He speaks Russian as he stamps my papers and asks me easy questions, my name, where I am from. He doesn't ask why I'm entering West Berlin, and I understand that Vera or her husband has arranged for this interview to be a formality. Before I leave, the official slips me an envelope of money, also from Vera, I assume. I look closely at these new deutschemarks, the currency of the western part of the city and country. Mindful of pickpockets, I clutch my purse under my arm as I leave the station, passing the border from east to west.

It's late October, and on the street, I recognize the warm, golden light that I used to enjoy in Berlin this time of year. But everything else around me—it's all new. The rubble is mostly gone, and I find myself on a wide and busy street full of buses and cars and bicycles and people, many with healthy faces, wearing clothes that look fashionable to me. Cars whiz past, their shapes and designs strange and new and something from the future. For the first time, I begin to wonder what it means that it's 1956. Stalin is dead and his will isn't law anymore. How much can change in nine years? In my country, and this one? In me? Too much, I fear. Too much for Henry. Of all the people who pass, none have red hair, none have

Henry's eyes, or walk like him, or look at me like he used to. He isn't here.

Clutching my suitcase, I stand at the curb so disappointed I want to collapse where I am even if it means being trodden by the passersby or clipped by a bus. I was to meet him by the book-shop, which is right behind me. I'm in the right place, and he isn't here. He has probably seen me and despaired. Or he's searching the crowded streets for the woman he married. I imagine his gaze passing through me and over me and moving on, searching for a woman who doesn't exist anymore.

I begin to walk without knowing where I'm going. I remember the Tiergarten is west if I walk long enough. The noise of the city has given me a headache, and I long for green and open spaces. But I don't have the energy to go far. After buying a drink from a ven-dor, I find a bench in a little park of scrub bushes and young trees. As I'm drinking, a thin man in a long brown coat sits on the other end of the bench and sets something between us. Out the corner of my eye, a splash of color—it's a bouquet of flowers tied with red ribbon. Several of the stems are bent or broken. The man hasn't been careful; he's been squeezing them too tightly.

He's too thin to be Henry, who will always be strong as an oak. Besides, this man is rude for not asking if the place beside me is free. Maybe I'm waiting for a friend or a lover. And then, sadly, I realize I don't look like the kind of woman who has either one.

"Marya?" His voice is timid, full of hope and fear. "Mouse, it's me."

My heart beats like it hasn't in years. I can't look at him. I don't want to see how much he's changed. So thin now. Why? Didn't Tess–Lucy–Betsy feed him at all? Was it some shared sentiment with me, who went hungry in the camps? He was thirty-one when I knew him, and now he's forty, different worlds in a person's life. Maybe he's gone gray, but I don't have the strength to find out. I look at the trampled ground between my shoes. I can't breathe. I know what's going to happen. He's going to see how worn and faded I am. He's going to leave because there's so little left of me. But then, he presses his warm hand onto mine. Terror and delight ripple across my skin. I've forgotten his touch, but my body remembers.

Finally, I dare to look at him. Joy, simple and vast, floods back as if it had never left us. The years vanish, and we reach for each other, and just like that, we have changed the world.

Acknowledgments

First on my thank-you list is always my wonderful agent, Laetitia Rutherford, along with the team at Watson, Little Ltd. in London. There's nothing like having a brilliant and supportive editorial agent in my corner. A huge thanks to my editor, Liz Stein, at William Morrow. She probably got a few gray hairs as she helped me iron out the twists in this very twisty book. To my copy editor, Rachelle Mandik, a big thanks for her sharp eye on the final text. For answering all my questions, big and small, about Russia and Russian culture, a massive thanks to Olesya Salnikova Gilmore and her mom in Moscow. The pandemic made writing this book even more of a lonely pursuit than it usually is, so a special thank-you to all the friends who kept me sane and encouraged in the process, especially Heather Chavez, Sara Ackerman, Amanda Carter, the FB group Debut 2020, the HFChitChat group on Twitter, and so many others. Finally, thank you to my family for all the love and support, and for only complaining a little when I buy more books than I could ever read.